O TIME IN YOUR FLIGHT

BOOKS BY HUBERT EVANS

Novels

The New Front Line
Mist on the River
O Time In Your Flight

Poetry

Whittlings
Endings

Junior Novels

Derry of Totem Creek
Derry, Airedale of the Frontier
Derry's Partner
Mountain Dog

Biography

North to the Unknown

Short Fiction

The Silent Call

O Time In Your Flight

A Novel
by Hubert Evans

Illustrated by

Robert Jack

Harbour Publishing
1979

FIRST PRINTING: OCTOBER 1979
SECOND PRINTING: NOVEMBER 1979
TYPESETTING: PULP PRESS, VANCOUVER

O TIME IN YOUR FLIGHT
COPYRIGHT © CANADA 1979 HUBERT EVANS

ILLUSTRATIONS COPYRIGHT © CANADA 1979
HARBOUR PUBLISHING

ISBN 0-920080-44-8

HARBOUR PUBLISHING
BOX 119 MADEIRA PARK
B.C.   V0N 2H0

JACKET BY FRANK LEWIS

PUBLISHED WITH ASSISTANCE FROM THE CANADA COUNCIL

PRINTED AND BOUND IN CANADA

CHAPTER ONE

All On A Summer's Day

Gilbert was being allowed to go to the station with his father but Chester had to stay home, their father said one was enough. So there Chester stood at the top of the veranda steps beside their mother, his face all screwed up and tugging at his thumb stall. Their father said goodbye to their mother, adjusted his panama and took up his valise and walking-stick.

"I'll write on Sunday," he told her. "I should know by then how matters stand."

The sidewalk along that end of Blair Street was only two planks wide so Gilbert walked ahead, remembering to toe out and to keep his shoulders squared. There were two ways to the station. The long way was to turn right at the gate, right at the school corner, along the cross street to the pop factory corner, then along the Avenue past Mrs. Devon's front room store. The short way was to turn left at the gate, go along Blair to the tracks, then behind the water tank, the piles of ties, and the freight shed and come out at the horse trough at the back of the station. The collegiate was across the tracks from the station but on the river side of the Avenue. In bad weather this was the way their father took to and from school and it was the way he took this morning.

The coal-oil wagon stood in front of old Mr. Wallace's house and Mr. Mullin, the coal-oil man, was filling a can from a tap on one of the barrels.

"We're in for another scorcher, Mr. Egan," he said, half turning but keeping an eye on the funnel.

"Seems so, Mr. Mullin."

Mr. Mullin's straw dummy hat was pushed back over his tightly curled black hair and his bib overalls had patches on both knees. He belonged to their church and helped Doctor Scanlon pass the collection plate, he in his black coat in one aisle and Doctor Scanlon, mutton-chop whiskers, claw hammer and striped pants, in the other. On special Sundays when more people came, Mr. Mullin stood with Grandpa Williamson at the door, extending the right hand of fellowship and showing strangers to pews.

From the cinder path leading down to the tracks Gilbert saw Mrs. Lamont's sunbonnet bobbing among the berry bushes at the side of their house but Nick was nowhere in sight. A sparrow was taking a bath in the drip from the water tank and one of the piles of ties was gone, the three-cornered one he and Tommy Dempster usually sat on when they came after school to watch the shunting engine or waited for the through freight to go thundering past. The blackboard on the platform said the eastbound was on time so they went straight in. His father set down his valise, hooked his walking-stick over his arm and took out his purse. The telegraph was ticking but Mr. Greer took no notice. Ruby Greer sat across the aisle from Gilbert all last year and she was so bossy he would not have been surprised to see her in there behind the counter trying to run things. Every chance she got she stayed after four to clean blackboards and a person would think she was the teacher instead of Miss Burwell.

They were out on the platform when the Waldy Hardware wagon pulled up with Mr. Waldy driving. He handed the reins to his delivery man, hopped out and ran his hand along the flank of the horse, then down over its shoulder. Mr. Waldy knew a great deal about horses and the men who could beat him in a horse trade were few and far between, Grandpa Williamson said. He would never use a check rein or dock a horse's tail which men in *Black Beauty* did to be in style. A horse with part of its tail cut off is tormented by flies and when their mother read out that part of the story, Chester clenched his fists and said what a person who did this needed was a good hard punch on the nose.

Although Mr. Waldy smoked cigars and their father was against the use of tobacco in all its forms, the two were friends and curled together. Their father bought his stovepipes, nails and things from Waldy Hardware even though Mr. Waldy went to the Presbyterian church and the town's other hardware was owned by a Methodist. When their father came from the rink Friday evenings, his overcoat smelled of tobacco. Gilbert liked the smell. His father's smell was mostly the perfume of Ed Pinaud mustache wax, except when they were camping and his father did not wax his mustache.

The wagon drove off and Mr. Waldy came over. He wore a summer vest, a tiny curling stone on his watch chain exactly like the one on their father's.

"Ah, Egan, seems we'll be travelling together. Taking the laddie with you?"

"Not this time."

Gilbert wished more people would speak to his father man-to-man like this, instead of putting on the Mister as if his father was different, a minister or something.

"She'll be a hot one in the city," Mr. Waldy said. "Luckily I'm going only for the day."

Gilbert would have given just about anything to have his father say that. Last summer and the summer before, right after school closed, they camped at good old Sparrow Lake for two whole months but yesterday when he asked how soon, how many days, his father told him it was high time he realized money does not grow on bushes. What sort of answer was that?

While Mr. Waldy was inside buying his ticket, Gilbert was given a little talking to. He was to do exactly as his mother said and not to argue, to remember to keep the woodbox filled, not to as much as set foot outside the yard without her permission. "Is that clear?"

"Yes Poppa."

"Then govern yourself accordingly."

His father gave Gilbert's behind a tap with his walking-stick. It was a very light tap, the nearest he could come to a fatherly pat on the shoulder.

As Mr. Waldy came from the waiting room, a livery stable cab drove up and two people got out, a woman in a frilly white dress and a fellow wearing ice-cream pants and one of those striped jackets *The Boy's Own Annual* pictures show English fellows wearing when they play cricket—a junior in one of the banks, Mr. Waldy said he was. The train was whistling for the bridge when Mr. Greer hauled out the baggage truck and wheeled it to the far end of the platform. On it were a square trunk, a smaller round-topped leather one, some mail bags and a telescope suitcase held together by shawl straps. Mr. Greer had taken off his eye shade and wore his stationmaster cap.

"Bear in mind what we talked about. You will be the man of the house."

"Yes Poppa."

"Off you go now." His father gave his behind a parting pat with the walking-stick and went to join Mr. Waldy at the edge of the platform.

The engine was one of the big three-wheelers which Tommy Dempster said were used only on the main line. Gilbert thought of going along the platform for a closer look at it but stayed and watched his father and Mr. Waldy go up the steps and into the car.

When his father found a seat at the window, Gilbert made ɪ shy, waving motion without raising his arm but his father did ɪot notice, or if he had, he did not wave back. At the very last when the conductor was calling all aboard, the bank fellow and the woman put their arms around one another and kissed, right there in front of everybody. They should have been ashamed. They kept on doing it until the train began to move and he had to run for the steps.

Gilbert remained on the platform until the last car passed the water tank. Heat waves danced above the rails. He untied the tapes of his blouse and went around to the horse trough to get a drink. The iron cup was fastened by a length of chain and as he reached for it, a brakie got there ahead of him .

: horse trough :

"After me you come first, bub." The brakie spat his chaw of tobacco into the dust, filled the cup at the spout and took a good long swig. Downtown there were notices of a five dollar fine for anyone caught spitting. The father of a boy at school who had to pay the five dollars wrote to the paper wanting to know if this was a free country or wasn't it? The boy's father was a moulder and when they poured brass the stink was awful the boy said, so no wonder his father chewed tobacco, he pretty near had to and what was he supposed to do, swallow the juice?

The brakie finished drinking, filled the cup and handed it across to Gilbert, then took out his plug, bit off a fresh chew, pretended to offer the plug to Gilbert, winked and returned the plug to the breast pocket of his overalls. They were railroaders', striped, not like Mr. Mullin's.

Gilbert took his time drinking. The brakie went along the siding between two strings of box cars in the direction of the water tank. Gilbert would have taken that way home had he been sure Nick Lamont was not still on the warpath. Nick and Chester were in the same boat when it came to staying mad, they could stay mad for days and Gilbert often wished he could be like them. Nobody could say they were softies.

"You remind me of some tramp puppy," his mother once told him. "A person gives you a kick and five minutes later you're back wagging your tail."

He pushed up the sleeves of his blouse and dabbled his hands in the trough. Ripples cast winking discs of sunlight on its moss-covered sides and bottom. He bent over, his chin touching the water, imagining how it would feel to be a minnow among the cool green tendrils, like the little perch he had watched swimming between the wild rice stalks at Sparrow Lake. Oh well. . . .

He shook the drops from his hands, tied the tapes of his blouse and started for home. The Avenue had houses on one side only because its opposite side sloped steeply to the river. Across the river, upstream from the dam, two fellows were launching a canoe at the canoe clubhouse. Downstream from the dam both sides of the river were lined with buildings, most of them stone, some with slate roofs. As usual, the square-towered English church had its flag up. Aunt Trixie said this was because most of the people who went there came straight from England. She said those who hadn't were descendants of Family Compact families that had gone to seed since Obediah Williamson's time. The English church Union Jack was a good sized one but it was faded. The one on the Royal Consort Hotel was even larger and was not at all faded. The Royal Consort began putting its flag up when the news came that the Boers were out to make more trouble for good Queen Victoria.

Mrs. Devon's front room store was beside a large horse chestnut tree and he stopped in its shade to have a look in the window, not that he had a copper to spend. All day suckers one cent, bulls-eyes six for a cent, butterscotch and peppermints four for a cent, Long Tom popcorn bags one cent each, fizz drink powder, any flavor, one cent, licorice whips one cent, licorice plugs made to look like chewing tobacco two cents each. Licorice plugs were just the thing. One recess after a spitting match, Ernie Yates took his seat with a trickle of what Miss Burwell took to be tobacco juice on his chin.

She lit right into him, made him wipe it off, go to the drinking water pail and take a good long swallow from the dipper. The joke was on her but she never caught on.

The school yard on the boys' side seemed smaller with nobody in it and the grey stone building had a shut away look with all its window blinds down. The girls' side, smack on the corner of Blair and the cross street, was separated from the boys' side by a high, close-boarded fence and was just as gravelly. It too had a play-shed and an eight-hole backhouse, but no pee trough. It smelled of lime.

Chester was over by the lilac bushes in the side yard trying to roll his hoop and making a poor fist of it. Their mother was in the summer kitchen ironing. Gilbert plunked himself down on the top step and began taking off his shoes and stockings. The stockings were ones Grandmother Egan knit and sent him at Christmas and in hot weather they were scratchy.

"Mr. Waldy was at the station. I guess they will sit together. The train was on time."

"I heard it pull out." She did not ask what kept him.

"How long will Poppa be gone, how many days, do you think?"

"Now let's not get onto that again. You heard him. He said it depends."

"On what? I like to know."

"On how many examination papers they want him to mark, I suppose."

Gilbert picked up one of his round garters, made it into a catapult between his fingers and snapped it at a fly. He knew there was no use piling on the questions. She would not say "I've heard enough of your gab", which was what he sometimes got from his father. Her quick, direct look told you enough was enough, and if you were talking simply to hear yourself talk or were making up a story, she saw right through you.

Gilbert collected his shoes, stockings and round garters and followed his mother into the kitchen. She set the used iron on the stove, changed the handle to the next one and tested its heat by wetting a finger tip with her tongue and lightly touching its face. The kitchen was like an oven and he wondered why she did not use the charcoal iron their father had Mr. Waldy send away for. It was the clear rig for hot weather. All you had to do was set fire to the charcoal inside, close the damper, and there you were. The iron even had a little chimney. His father, being a science teacher, was all for the latest inventions. As well as the iron, he bought her a three-wheel egg beater and an apple peeling machine. She went on beating eggs with a fork but she liked the peeling machine.

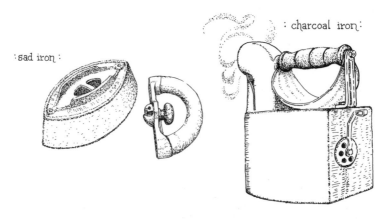

: sad iron :

: charcoal iron :

Dinner that noon suited Gilbert just fine, but it would not have suited his father. It was salmon sandwiches, two kinds of pickles and the last of yesterday's fig pie. Fig pie was one of his father's favorites but he was not much for pickles. He wanted his meat, mashed potatoes and gravy even on the hottest days. This noon, Gilbert, Chester and their mother ate on the front porch picnic style, screened from the sun by the virginia creeper and morning glory vines. Their father was not much for sitting around and eating picnic style.

"I prefer to get my feet under a table," he said, and at the lake the first thing he did after the tents were pitched and the stove in place was to set up the table in the dining tent.

Chester was cranky during the meal, probably because of the heat but more likely because his nose was still out of joint over not being allowed to go to the station. When Chester was cranky or tired, he went back to his habit of sucking his thumb and twisting a curl of his hair, so as soon as he cleaned up his plate, their mother took him upstairs and lay down with him. Gilbert carried the dishes to the kitchen, then went to the backyard and stretched out on the barrel stave hammock in the shade of the pie cherry tree.

Gilbert Egan was not one of your whiners or complainers and he was not one of those who set out to rule the roost. But if he had the say of it, they all would be at good old Sparrow Lake this very day. He closed his eyes and covered them with the crook of his arm. The story came, a mix-up of words and pictures. *Dinner is over, Chester and I on our bed playing tiddly-winks, Momma on hers in the curtained off part of the sleeping tent. A cool breeze, tent walls rolled up, my job after breakfast. When I do this I pretend I am high up on the mast reefing sail which is what English boys in Tommy's* Boy's Own Annual *have to do when they run away to sea. You need a cruel stepfather to run away to sea or the next best thing is to have the carriage upset and your father and mother get killed. Poppa comes from the tent in his bathing suit, striped, short sleeves and legs like ours. Momma comes out in hers, puffed sleeves, skirt, bloomers, long stockings. Poppa first in. Yips, does a few breast strokes, bobs up and down, makes waves but does not go ahead much. Stands up, blows water from his mustache. Makes me think of* Water Babies' *seal picture. He is against the dog paddle, holds up my chin, says kick, kick like a frog. He likes to splash people, not Momma, she tells him, "don't you dare." When Aunt Trixie came he splashed her and she squealed "Oh Richard stop," but it was easy to see she liked it. After our swim one slice each of bread, butter and brown sugar. Some days tea for them not coffee, our church paper, the* Christian Guardian, *says coffee contains the dread drug caffeine. Before supper I unreef walls, make sure sod cloth tucked in, rope shrinks when wet, stretches when dry, a good thing to know. Supper, no Bible reading like at Grandpa Williamson's, ours at breakfast while our porridge cools, cornmeal in summer, oatmeal heats the blood. No reading at bedtime like at home. No train whistles, no wagons going past, only sometimes an owl or loon, no people downstairs talking. If you drew a line from Sparrow Lake to the north pole, nobody except a few Indians and Eskimos who can do what they like, nobody getting after them and telling them what they must do. After Chester goes to sleep or stays quiet on his side of the bed, I make up stories on nights when she does not read to us but only hears our prayers. I can be a boy on a backwoods farm like my father was when there were wild turkeys and bears to watch out for. Best of all I can be him working to be an engineer living with Indians and running rapids away up north on those rivers he and Mr. Dubois talk about when you could buy a birchbark canoe for five dollars and. . . .*

The sound of hammering came from Mr. Dempster's smokehouse on the other side of the back fence. Gilbert opened his eyes and sat up. He was remembering the day last summer he learned why his father was just a teacher instead of the engineer he set out to be. It was the day they paddled across to sharpen the axe on Mr. Dubois' grindstone. The day was hot and turning the handle was hard work. Time after time his father would tell him to stop turning, wipe the water from the axe with the heel of his palm, say "still too much cheek, keep turning." He pressed so hard that Gilbert had to use both hands. After a while, Mr. Dubois came along on his way to the well. He set down the two water pails, took the yoke from his shoulders, nudged Gilbert to step aside and turned until the axe was sharpened. Then the two men squatted on their heels in the shade of the stable and had another talk about up north and how it was before the railway was finished. After it was, every stump along the tracks clear out to Vancouver had an engineer sitting on it twiddling his thumbs, their father told Mr. Dubois. Which was why their father ended up a collegiate teacher, carrying a walking-stick, waxing his mustache and staying dressed up instead of wearing working clothes like ordinary men. If their father had got to be an engineer, it would be like Sparrow Lake all year. On top of this they could have had mostly Indians for friends.

: barrel stave hammock :

CHAPTER TWO

Grandpa's Hello Girls and Others

The three days since his father went to Toronto could have been the same day for all the difference they made to Gilbert. It was not simply the waiting to go camping which made them the same. It was the sort of days they were. The flat feeling they gave was the feeling a person has when he forgets to turn the page of a story he is reading and reads the same part over again. Or another way of thinking about it was to imagine the days are spokes of a wagon wheel, all exactly the same, the wheel turning sometimes fast sometimes slow, but staying the same place, not going anywhere.

Lying awake these hot nights with not so much as his part of the sheet over him and keeping as far from Chester as he could without falling out of bed, Gilbert wondered about this difference between days. Some, the in-between days, you forgot about as soon as they were over, others you probably would remember as long as you lived. Lying in the dark with the barking of some dog or the far whistle of a train the only sounds, he thought back to things which happened while they lived across the river in the double house where Chester was born. His first memory, his very first, was a smell memory of carpet and a heavy sweet smell which he later knew was lilies of the valley. The room was not dark but it was not bright either, sort of shadowy. He must have been sitting on the floor because all he saw of the people in the room were their feet. A large shiny black boot was beside him on his right but he did not remember what was beside him on his left. A long time later when he told his mother all this she said he must have heard them talk about her sister Gracie's funeral but that he could not possibly remember it because at the time she still had him in dresses and he could barely toddle. "You and your imagination! Next thing you'll be telling us of things you remember that happened before you were born." She said Gracie died while Grandpa Williamson and the others lived in the red brick house on the river bank between the Church of England and the upper bridge, and that he was only two when the Williamsons moved to Balaclava Road. But she could not make him believe he was not at the funeral.

She and Gracie were Grandpa Williamson's hello girls and they were just about the first in Canada. Their mother kept Gracie's picture in a plush frame on her dresser. Gracie had curls all over her head. In the picture she wore a dark dress with puffed sleeves and had queer shaped buttons right up to her chin. She had happy eyes and when Gilbert stood in front of her picture she seemed to smile at him. If she had not been taken with the galloping consumption, Mr. Waldy might have talked her into marrying him, Aunt Trixie said. And he just might have. Mr. Waldy was just about the greatest talker that ever came down the pike. He did not talk simply to hear himself talk, which was what their father sometimes said Gilbert did. Mr. Waldy talked people into buying things, such as the charcoal iron and the three-wheel egg beater. The story was that in the days before he owned the hardware store, he drove around the country selling his Waldy Magic Healer Good for Man and Beast, and with it he sold lightning rods to the farmers. One farm lady—Scotch, Grandpa Williamson said she was—told Mr. Waldy it was not the lightning, it was the thunder she was afraid of. Mr. Waldy told her she was in luck because he had just one set of thunder rods left in the wagon. The lady thanked him and bought the rods right off. On top of that, Mr. Waldy sold her a set of lightning rods, just in case. Mr. Waldy for your uncle—cigar smoke, high-steppers and all! Imagine it!

Some nights, lying there in the dark, now and then fanning himself with his part of the sheet, Gilbert wished they still lived in the double house across the river. Its yard had spruce trees back and front which made it the next best thing to living in a forest. Some Saturdays while they lived in the double house he and his father spent the whole day together out in the country or up the river collecting specimens for the collegiate science class. His father showed him the five kinds of oak trees, white and black ash, hickory, basswood, small trees named ironwood and leatherwood, whose bark could be twisted and used as rope, a trick backwoods people learned from the Indians. One Saturday his father collected sea shell fossils from a cliff near the lime kiln. The shells lived there when the land was under water. They made you wonder.

He thought of that Saturday with the blacksnake and how he felt toward his father then. His father had gone a little farther along the river bank, leaving him to rest in the shade of a large spruce where they had eaten lunch. The tips of its lower branches rested on the ground making what he pretended was his wigwam. He crawled in and when his eyes got used to the dimness, he saw a toad crouched on the carpet of fallen needles across from him. He expected the toad to hop away, but it kept staring at something on the far side of the wigwam. That something was the largest snake head he had ever seen. The toad shifted its front legs. It was trying to get away but those unblinking eyes held it. The snake came closer, inch by inch, not wriggling like an ordinary snake but with its body straight as if it had rows of tiny feet along its belly. The toad sank lower, waiting for the snake to grab it. He wanted to run away but the snake's eyes were on him too. Suddenly he felt numb all over. He screamed and stumbled out into the sunlight. His father came running. They looked inside but the snake and the toad had gone. His father told him not to be afraid and put his arms around him. Now that he was older, his father did not do this any more.

Gilbert Egan was not one of your momma's boys who hang around their mother's apron strings and for the reason they do not have the gumption to do things by themselves. Chester had been like that but he was growing out of it. And a good thing too or he would have a hard time when he started kindergarten in September, the Foxy Foster gang and all the rest of it. If you did not have pluck and were not made of good stuff, woe betide you at Blair Street School.

The afternoon after their father went to mark examination papers to see if people passed, Gilbert and Chester had fun leap-frogging over each other on the shady strip of lawn between their house and the empty house next door. Then they had swigs at the outside tap and were sitting on the front steps cooling off when Mr. Wallace came along. Mr. Wallace was not for John A. which their father was. He was not for Mr. Laurier which Grandpa Williamson was. And from what Gilbert could make out he was nowhere in between. If their father had the rights of it.

"My certes, the man's no better than a socialist!" Gilbert heard his father tell their mother one time after he and Mr. Wallace had it hot and heavy over how the country should be run.

Mr. Wallace lived a few doors along the street toward the Lamonts. When he farmed at the Settlement he mostly farmed sheep. His sheep won prizes at fairs all over Ontario, and quite a few at the big fair in Chicago, which must have given the Yankees something to think about, especially the blow-hard ones. After their father could not be an engineer on account of the C.P.R. being finished too soon so that he had to be a teacher at the

Settlement school, he boarded with Mr. Wallace and Mr. Wallace's sister. When you got right down to it, the two were friends. Mr. Wallace kept an eye on the Egan house while they went camping and their father helped Mr. Wallace with his storm windows, spring and fall. Mr. Wallace told their father which farmer sold the best stovewood and their father shovelled Mr. Wallace's walk after a bad storm. Their Aunt Boo said it was a pity Mr. Wallace was "alone in the world" which was all she knew when Mr. Wallace had Bruce. Mr. Wallace said Bruce was part bird dog but did not say what other parts.

That afternoon when Gilbert and Chester saw Mr. Wallace coming, they moseyed out to the front fence, just in case. Sure enough, Mr. Wallace gave each of them a Scotch peppermint. Mr. Wallace was not so much a believer when it came to church, but he was a believer in peppermints for keeping away colds and sore throats. He also believed in Dutch Drops, Waldy Magic Healer and in keeping a potato in his hip pocket for the rheumatism. Their father called this gullible, which was what he said about socialists. Mr. Wallace was a great believer in fish. He called them "fush" and said they and oatmeal porridge were what made the Scotch so wise.

Chester asked where Bruce was and Mr. Wallace said Bruce was in his kennel licking his wounds.

"Bruce gets into fights as do a pair of laddies hereabouts."

"Well Nick always starts it. All I do is stick up for myself."

Mr. Wallace's square white beard went up and down as he sucked on his peppermint. He said Gilbert was a chip off the old block, whatever that meant.

On another of those flat, stand-still days, their father in Toronto and not so much as a peep about camping at Sparrow Lake, their mother said it woud be better for all concerned if Gilbert and Chester were separated for the time being. She said she did not mind how much rumpus they raised but there was to be no squabbling, not in her house.

"It's all his fault," Chester said. "He keeps pecking at me."

Their mother said she could well believe it but that Chester should not fly off the handle so easily. She told Gilbert to change his blouse, put on his shoes and stockings and trot on downtown to see if his grandfather had any small jobs which would keep him

occupied for the rest of the afternoon. He was to start for home
when the six o'clock whistle blew and there was to be no dawdling.

Gilbert lost no time in getting started. As he closed the gate
behind him, he saw Nick turning in at Mr. Wallace's. He hollered,
just for the fun of it. "Aw go pull the chain." Nick hollered back.

Instead of following the Avenue past the pop factory then down
the hill, Gilbert took the path angling across the slope behind Ernie
Yates' house and the gas works and came out at the upper bridge
where River Street started. Mr. Dempster's fish wagon stood in
front of the Royal Consort so Gilbert crossed the street to say hello
to old Nell. She had her nose bag on and when he patted her she
partly turned to see who it was. The look in her soft eyes showed
she recognized him and she went on munching her oats. She must
have eaten most of them because between munches she tossed her
head to get what were left in the bottom of the bag. She wore one of
those straw dummy hats with holes for her ears which men who
take good care of their horses use on the hottest days. The fish
wagon was a democrat with a box built on it. The box was blue with
a sloping lid and with a salmon painted on each side. The salmon
were almost as long as the box. Drips from melted ice made tiny
puddles in the dust, a sign that Mr. Dempster had been in the Royal
Consort for quite a while doing whatever it was he was doing in
there.

Gilbert gave Nell a goodbye pat and recrossed the street. Most of
the windows on all three floors of the knitting mill were open and
the hum of the machines was something like the sound from Mr.
Dubois' bee hives. Some days when he passed he heard singing as
well as the humming. Two of the mill girls were in the choir. They
had nice voices, though they never stood to sing a solo while Mr.
Mullin and Doctor Scanlon passed the collection plate. The woman
who sang the solos was supposed to be a trained singer. She always
held a large sheet of music in front of her. Aunt Trixie said she did
this to show the congregation she could read the notes. Her voice
went up and down in a way which made Gilbert feel he was sitting
in a canoe with someone rocking it. Aunt Trixie said the woman
sounded like a dying duck in a thunderstorm, which was not a kind
thing to say, least of all when it came from Aunt Trixie who could
not keep a tune to save her soul. The front wall of the axe factory
came right to the sidewalk but the forge was not going so he kept
walking. There was not much doing at the grist mill either, no
teams in the yard. In winter on market days there often was a line-

up of sleighs and farmers standing around in coonskin coats waiting for their grain to be ground. The foundry between the grist mill and the Chinese laundry was behind a high board fence with barb wire on top and notices tacked on the fence—Burdock Blood Bitters, Minstrel Show at Opera House Coming Soon, auction sales, Niagara Falls Excursion, Where Will You Spend Eternity, No Spitting—all stuff like that.

The telephone office was three doors before the Main Street end of the downtown bridge. The job Gilbert's grandfather usually had for him was slitting used envelopes for making notes or doing sums on. His grandfather was never short of envelopes, for as well as being the telephone company's local and district manager, he sold fire insurance, took care of the church money and kept accounts for his brother Abel's cartage business. Most of the envelopes were about fire insurance, which proved to Gilbert that people were not against fire insurance as many were against life insurance in the days when his father was a hard up young man and tried his hand at selling it so he could be an engineer. Time after time his father was told that buying life insurance was a sign the person did not trust God, for if God wanted you to be taken, you would be taken and all the life insurance in the world could not save you. One woman even told him he was on the side of the devil and slammed her door in his face.

one cent stamp

Grandpa Williamson was out and Aunt Trixie was too busy at the switchboard for Gilbert to question her, so he ducked under the counter and examined the envelopes scattered on the roll-top desk without touching them, reading the postmarks and looking for any with stamps upside down. Tommy said that anyone who stood the Queen on her head was against the mother country and on the side of the Boers. Except for a one-center which had the Queen's head tilted a little, all the stamps had been put on properly. A George Washington had a corner torn off, but what the Yankees did to their stamps was up to them. They could put them on crossways, upside down or inside out for all he cared.

He sat in the bentwood arm chair at the desk and watched his aunt and the other hello girl perched on their high stools at the switchboad. The stools had glass telephone pole insulators instead of casters. This was to protect the hello girls from electricity during thunderstorms. His mother said when she and Gracie were hello girls blue flames flickered along the wires and the little brass flaps on the switchboard flew open in batches. She said that ever since then lightning frightened her and she did not care who knew it. At home during a thunderstorm, and at Sparrow Lake too, where the lightning was even worse, she put on her rubbers and bathing cap and had him and Chester sit on the bed beside her. At home she came and sat on his and Chester's bed because her and their father's bed was brass and brass attracted electricity.

"I believe in taking reasonable precautions, Frances," their father told her, "but aren't you carrying things a bit too far?"

"Laugh at me all you like," she said and kept on doing it.

If a thunderstorm came right this minute, he wondered what Aunt Trixie and the other girl would do. Would they hop down from their stools and clear out or would they be like brave captains who stay with the ship?

Quick footsteps made him turn. A man with a violin case under his arm was at the counter. Aunt Trixie came. The man asked some questions which she answered straight off. "Trixie may be a bit of a flibbertigibbet but she has a head on her shoulders," he remembered hearing his mother say. The man wore a loose fitting velvet jacket, a floppy bow tie, and every so often one of his arms made a swift, jerky motion. When his questions were answered, he lifted his hat, gave Aunt Trixie a stiff little bow and left.

"Was that Professor Vance?" Gilbert asked.

"Sure was. You know about him?"

"Sort of."

"What does that mean—sort of?"

"One of the boys at school knows him but I never saw him before. How soon will Grandpa be back?"

"Not till late, I expect. He hired a livery rig and drove out the Settlement road. Some mix-up over a party line. He'd have taken you. Too bad your folks don't put in the phone." She gathered a fold of her skirt, hopped onto the stool, adjusted the ear things and gave her pompadour a pat. "Tell your mother it's Epworth League night, I might drop around later with Mr. Pickering."

Several calls came in on Aunt Trixie's part of the switchboard, right after one another, and for one she had to reach down and turn a crank. Gilbert thought he might as well mosey on home but the window beyond the switchboard was up, so he leaned over the sill to have a look at the river. The water at the foot of the wall was six or eight feet deep but so clear he saw several fish, suckers most likely. He let go a gob of spit on the off chance a fish would rise to it but none did. Mr. Waldy said that long ago, even before he was born, this part of the river had trout, real trout in it. There were still a few black bass but mostly there were only carp, catfish and suckers, none of them fit to eat, Mr. Dempster said. One of the boys at school said there were mullets and that they were good eating but Mr. Dempster said mullet was a fancy name people who ate suckers used to settle their stomachs. He said, any self-respecting cat would turn up its nose at suckers.

Most of the suckers lay head first to the current, a few in backwaters behind boulders lay the other way around and one in an eddy at the base of the wall lay crossways. If you were a fish you would have to know a great deal about backwaters, currents, eddies and so on, which was what Tom the water baby had to learn.

The steeple of the Presbyterian Church beside the little park at the far end of the bridge was taller than those of the two other Presbyterian Churches or the Methodist one. The Methodist one was taller than the Baptist one, which was taller than the Catholic one. The English church had only its flag and the Salvation Army had no church at all, only a hall. A dray rumbled across the bridge but from the window he could not be sure it was an Abel Williamson Cartage one. It stopped at the park trough for the team to have a drink. Stores under the opera house facing the park had their awnings down. He had never been in the opera house and for the reason that his father was a strict Methodist and was as much against going to the theatre as he was against card playing and dancing. But his mother said next time *Uncle Tom's Cabin* came, she might take him and Chester so they could see what slaves were up against.

The boy at school who knew about Professor Vance said the professor played in the opera house orchestra and that when he fiddled his arm did not jerk. The boy's cousin lived above a store on Main Street and when he saw the professor going past, he snaked up and walked close behind and a little to one side. The trick was to be there when the professor's arm jerked, and his cane hit your legs. When this happened the professor begged your pardon and gave you five cents. The cousin said the trick worked every time.

Before starting for home, Gilbert waited until Aunt Trixie wasn't busy and asked her what made the professor's arm jerk like that. She said it was because of a disease he had.

"Is it catching?"

"It is for people who don't behave themselves."

"Where did he catch it?"

"In Paris, France. What did he expect?"

"How do you mean?"

"Paris, France, of all places!" Aunt Trixie sniffed. "Let's change the subject."

CHAPTER THREE

Another Blair Street Week

The feeling his father's letter gave Gilbert was not his morning after Christmas morning feeling, and it was not his flat, let-down Monday morning feeling when he was faced with another five days of old Burwell. Then you had the following Saturday and part of Sunday to look forward to. And although on mornings after Christmas mornings, the anticipation was over for another year, you had your presents and were sure of a school-free week. But with their father staying in Toronto for at least another ten days, perhaps longer, Gilbert gave up hope of so much as setting eyes on Sparrow Lake this summer. When their mother read them the letter, Chester said what those examination people needed was a good hard punch on the nose. The way Gilbert saw it they were only part of the trouble. If their father had wanted, really deep down wanted, to take the family camping wouldn't you think he would have done so? It was not like him to let some man in Toronto, or anyone else, twist him around their little finger.

"The summer's only beginning, so just you two possess your souls in patience," their mother told them. "Why not make the best of things?" She allowed them to go around in their bathing suits and play with the lawn sprinkler any time they felt like it. And, partly to keep them occupied and partly because she was dead against flies, she started what she called her swat-the-fly campaign. Probably because some of the neighbors skimped on lime for their backhouses, or used wood ashes which did not do the trick, Blair Street had more than its share of flies. One thing you could say for Mr. Dempster, he was not careless about flies so there were very few of those big beady-eyed ones buzzing around. The bad ones were the house flies and their mother paid them a copper for every twenty-five of them he and Chester swatted anywhere in the house. A folded copy of the town paper, or part of the *Mail and Empire,* made the best swatters, the *Christian Guardian* and *Canadian Magazine* were too heavy. Besides copies of these must be kept. Once when Gilbert was two flies short of his twenty-five and while his mother was taking Chester upstairs for his noon rest, Gilbert held the screen door open just long enough for two flies to get in. He killed them the moment they settled and tried to make himself believe this really wasn't cheating, that the two would have come in sooner or later.

Before their mother handed over the copper she made a big thing of counting the flies one by one, though whether she was all that particular or was making a game of it was hard to tell.

Always after she read to them, their mother followed them upstairs and heard Chester say his now-I-lay-me, the two of them in their nightshirts, kneeling at the side of the bed, with heads bowed, hands flat together and fingers pointed upward. Since his last birthday when he turned nine, Gilbert was allowed to make up his prayer and to say it to himself which was a good thing because the part of the now-I-lay-me—"if I should die before I wake, I pray the Lord my soul to take", was not the best thing to go to sleep on. Instead he asked God to make him a good boy, to bless his Momma and Poppa and his little brother and anyone else he felt like blessing. He never once prayed against anyone, not Nick or even old Burwell, though she was one of those the Bible says sitteth in the seat of the scornful. Their mother did not kiss them, she was not one of those who go in for kissing. She usually wished them good-night then went back downstairs. But with their father away she got into the habit of sitting on the edge of their bed and talking with them for awhile. It was then that Gilbert got her to tell them more about where their family came from—his great-great-grand-father Obediah and the man on her mother's side who was the first Methodist lay preacher in Muddy York, got mixed up in the revolution against the Family Compact and had to make himself scarce for awhile. One evening she went across the hall to her room and came back with a photograph of Obediah's tombstone, with her in a frilly dress and a hat with feathers. The stone was not quite four feet high and she stood behind it with her gloved hands resting on its rounded top.

"This was taken in a small graveyard back of Hamilton mountain the year your father and I were married." The stone was splotched with moss so she read out what it said:

"Obediah Williamson
A Native of Long Island
State of New York
March 26, 1856
Age 86 years."

"Your great-great-grandfather seems to have been something of a poet. Listen to this:
'Afflictions sore for years I bore
Physicians were in vain.
At last God please to give me ease
and free me from my pain.''
She smiled. "They say one of his afflications was his wife. She was the daughter of a Pennsylvania Dutchman named Hess, who came to Upper Canada in seventeen-seventy, and settled nearby. They say she was a scold."

"Tell us some more, Momma. Please." Gilbert said.

"Some other night." A moth was beating its wings against the window screen. "Off to sleep now, both of you. No more talking." She blew out the lamp and left.

:table lamp:

But at other bedtimes that week, sometimes of her own accord but more often at Gilbert's urging, she filled spaces in what he already knew of their family history. She could not say what part of England the Williamsons came from, or how many generations of them lived in Massachusetts before farming on Long Island. Shortly after the American colonists won their independence Obediah, sixteen, struck out for Canada. Only two years older than Tommy Dempster! Gilbert thought.

"Obediah was not a United Empire Loyalist though certain of his descendants make out that he was. Years later, he took no part in the war of eighteen-twelve. 'I refuse to fight against my cousins south of the border,' he told the British, and made no bones about it. Which made him something of a rebel I suppose. Yet his oldest

son, Michael, became a justice of the peace during the time the
Family Compact ruled the roost. Michael was known as squire
among his neighbors which probably meant no more than that he
could read and write, which was more than some of them could. I
dimly remember Michael as a very old man when Gracie and I and
the others were children on the farm. He slept sitting at a table with
his head on a pillow because of his asthma. On fine days he walked
along the split rail fences and in the wood lot with a basket over his
arm, selecting hardwood chips for the smokehouse. We thought
him very important in his long black coat, stovepipe hat and shawl.
His first-born son, also named Michael, left for the California
goldfields some years before I was born. He was never heard from
again and I somehow got the notion he was the family's black
sheep. Your Great-Uncle Ben worked the farm after the old squire
died, but we moved down into Hamilton when your grandfather
became express agent there.''

"How did Obediah get here?'' Gilbert asked.

"I know when Hess came, he travelled for weeks, with all his
belongings on the backs of his horses. The forest was so dense that
he had to use narrow saddle boxes to get his horses between the
trees, or so the story goes. I guess Obediah did the same.''

If only that could have been me! Gilbert said to himself. Or if I
could have been Obediah, not much older than Tommy, only seven
years older than I am right now, this very minute, travelling north
through the woods, nobody getting after me, telling me what to do,
camping week after week, making friends with the Indians! Lying
there in the dark with Chester asleep beside him, Gilbert pictured
Hess and then, later, Obediah in coonskin caps, moccasins, fringed
buckskin shirts, hawk-eyed, trusty muskets under their arms, two
young fellows of his very own family, his very own flesh and blood,
living the life they wanted to live. Even Mr. Dubois wasn't in it with
them, though Mr. Dubois and Sparrow Lake would do for a
starter.

That same week, for the first time since school closed, Nick
Lamont came down off his high horse and yoo-hooed in front of
the house. Gilbert would have run out but his mother was serving
supper and would not let him leave the table.

Hearing Nick yoo-hoo for him from the sidewalk made Gilbert
think back to how things used to be between them. All the year they

were in kindergarten and until they were part way through First Reader, they were the best of friends. More often than not they walked to and from school together. Saturdays and after four they played together in one another's yards, or in the overgrown lot across the street. The day they discovered the mysterious open well back of the empty house they swore one another to keep mum—cross your heart, spit and hope to die—because if they blabbed their parents would forbid them to go there. They were such good friends that Gilbert got Nick invited to the Methodist Junior and Intermediate Sunday School picnic and Nick promised to take Gilbert to his church the next time there was an underwater baptism. Then at Easter, right out of a blue sky, at the very time they planned to build a Swiss Family Robinson tree house in the Lamont Snow apple tree, Nick up and turned against him. Those big boys in the principal's room belonging to the Foxy Foster gang were to blame for it. One thing sure, if Tommy had been going to the school instead of to the Catholic school it probably would not have started because Tommy would have stood up to them. Tommy's father had been in the British navy and had taught Tommy to box, "handle his dukes", he called it. Tommy showed Gilbert how to hit straight from the shoulder and to keep his head up. Nick's way was to lower his head and keep his arms swinging like a windmill, which was why he always got the worst of it.

The trouble was the big boys at school. It started with a game they made up at recess time in the corner of the yard beyond the play-shed after marble time was over. With a long plank and a heavy wooden box from the pop factory they made a teeter-totter. Two of them would catch a small boy and hold him on the low end of the plank until the biggest boy jumped on its high end from the top of the board fence. Up you went end over end. They did not so much as lift a hand to catch you as you fell. They let you hit the ground. If tears came to your eyes they called you cry-baby but if you took it as a joke they said you were good stuff and gave you a pat on the back. He and Nick were the only two who never cried. The principal never came out to the play yard or looked down from his windows to see what was going on down there so what could you do? If you tattled to him the big boys would make it worse for you. Gilbert took his bumps and laughed with them but Nick went them one better. He stumped them to do it three times in a row. His elbows and both knees were skinned but he only screwed up his face and walked away.

The very next day at morning recess one of the big boys—his name was Lloyd, and Foxy Foster was supposed to be his uncle—cornered Gilbert and told him everybody was saying Nick Lamont was the toughest and that he could knock the stuffing out of Gilbert Egan with one hand tied behind his back. What Gilbert should have done was tell Lloyd to pull the chain but at the time he did not know another big boy was telling Nick the very opposite. Gilbert did not want to be taken for a sissy so when Lloyd asked if he was scared of Nick Lamont, Gilbert answered, "no such thing." He had nothing against Nick, all he wanted was to stick up for himself.

Lloyd said, "Good for you, that's what I like to hear, now you're talking like a man."

Every week or so, to get them fighting, the big boys made them toe a line scratched in the dirt, and dared them to step over it. Nick was the one who always took the dare. With them egging him on, Nick came at you, his chin down so low that all he was able to see of you were your feet, his arms whirling like a chicken with its head cut off. Lloyd, who called himself Gilbert's second, kept telling him to punch, not back away. As if you could back away with all of them in a ring around you. The day before summer holidays, Nick landed a stinging punch on the side of Gilbert's head and this was the only time Gilbert got really mad. He got in an upper cut which made Nick's nose bleed so badly that the big boys stopped the fight.

That week for a change Gilbert and Chester had their Saturday night baths in the summer kitchen, their mother said the house was quite warm enough, thank you, without firing up the wood stove. She heated their bath water in the clothes boiler on the three-burner Blue Flame. In May when their father had Waldy Hardware deliver it for her birthday, she said she was not sure she trusted it, that burning coal-oil in lamps was one thing and burning it in a stove was something else again, but by now she had got used to it. The Blue Flame had a mica window in each of its burners which made it easy to see if a wick was turned too high or needed trimming. Gilbert and Chester squatted back-to-back in the large wooden wash tube while she scrubbed their necks and made sure their ears were clean. For cleaning ears she used a fold of wash-cloth over her pointing finger. Her hands were small and slender and the tip of her finger poked in so far that Gilbert "ouched" and asked why she didn't use a gimlet and be done with it?

"If you don't stop squirming, I just may have to," she said.

In cold weather when they had their baths in the real kitchen they had to be careful not to splash but in the summer kitchen splashing did not much matter, the weekly wash was usually done there. After they dried their private parts and she dried the rest of them, they put on clean flannelette nightdresses but instead of lighting the livingroom lamp and reading them the next chapter of *The Old Curiosity Shop,* she took them up to her room and let them curl up on her bed while she sat in her rocker beside the open window. Gilbert felt pretty sure what was coming. And sure enough she asked which poems they would like to hear tonight. "Chester has first choice."

"The doll got its arm trotten off, Momma." Chester always said "trotten".

"I once had a dear little doll, dears;
    The prettiest doll in the world;
Her cheeks were so pink and so white, dears,
    And her hair was so beautifully curled.
But I lost my dear little doll, dears,
    As I played on the heath one day;
Though I searched for more than a week, dears,
    I never could find where she lay.

"Then I found my dear little doll, dears,
    As I played on the heath one day;
Folks say she is terribly changed, dears,
    For her paint is all washed away.
And her arm trodden off by the cows, dears,
    And her hair not the least bit curled;
But for old sakes' sake she is still, dears,
    The prettiest doll in the world."

"What was her name, Momma, do you think?" Chester asked.

"Daisy," Gilbert told him, just for the fun of it.

"No such of a thing!"

Daisy was the doll their Great-Aunt Boo gave Chester one Christmas. Gilbert told him only girls played with dolls and kept at him until one day he held Daisy, by her feet, out their bedroom window and dropped her to the side door steps. Her head was smashed to smithereens. Chester tattled and Gilbert got the blame for it.

Gilbert's first choice was the one about Lasca, the girl who saved the cowboy's life when the cattle stampeded. Lasca was trampled to death by the thundering herd. Like as not she was an Indian girl. The cowboy could never forget her:

"...and I wonder why I do not care
for the things that are like the things that were.
Does half of my heart lie buried there
with Lasca down by the Rio Grande?"

Their mother recited just right, Gilbert thought; not like old Burwell made you do, your voice bobbing up and down for what she called expression; not like the minister when he led in the Lord's Prayer; not like their father at before-breakfast-bible-reading, and making it sound strict. When their mother recited or read to them you could almost see it happening before your very eyes. Aunt Trixie had heard older people say that when Frankie Williamson recited at church socials or at some concert or other, everybody clapped for more. And if she gave them a sad piece, tears came to people's eyes. "Backward, turn backward O time, in your flight, make me a child again just for tonight!" was one of her sad pieces. Not that she went in for sad pieces. When she recited from *Hiawatha* you felt you were right there on the shores of Gitchee Gumee, birchbark canoes, wigwams and all. She made *The Wreck of the Hesperus, The Inchcape Rock,* and the one about Mary bringing the cattle home across the sands of Dee, sound as exciting as *Robinson Crusoe.* One of her sad pieces made Gracie seem as real as though she was standing there in the shadows of the room. It went:

"Break, break, break
On thy cold gray stones, O sea!
And I would that my tongue could utter
The thoughts that arise in me.
The stately ships go on
To their haven under the hill;
But O for the touch of a vanish'd hand,
And the sound of a voice that is still!"

Listening, he wondered if she too was thinking of Gracie. He liked to think she was. But with their mother it was hard to tell. She kept her feelings to herself.

CHAPTER FOUR

Kinfolk

That Sunday Gilbert and Chester did not have to be dressed for church when they came to the breakfast table which they most certainly had to be when their father was home. When their father was home it was Gilbert's job to shine his and Chester's boots the night before. This was as much the rule as not having sugar on their porridge during Self Denial Week because children in foreign lands were going hungry and it somehow made them feel better if you did without.

For some reason their mother had got tired of eating porridge and after their father left for Toronto, she stopped making it and served Force instead. Chester was the one who got her to try it. Force was advertised in the *Christian Guardian* and though Chester could not read what it said he liked the funny pictures of Jim Dumps and Sunny Jim. Jim Dumps looked gloomy and Sunny Jim was smiling all over his face. The thing was, they were the same man before and after they ate Force for breakfast. Mrs. Devon did not have Force but D.V. Schiller Grocery sold it, so their mother had a box come with her weekly order. Gilbert and Chester liked it providing they did not have to go easy on the brown sugar, but their mother kept to her one slice of dry toast.

When their father was home, getting ready for Sunday morning church was not what you could call a happy-go-lucky affair. Things had to be done in a certain order and right on the dot, upstairs as well as down—beds made, closets tidied, chamber-pots emptied into the grey enamel slop bucket in time for their father to dump it down the backhouse when he went there to do his number two; downstairs, the dining table set for dinner, potatoes peeled, second vegetable prepared, cold roast ready to carve, brown gravy in its saucepan ready to heat, that day's pie (apple, raisin, fig, mincemeat, chocolate, or lemon) on the sideboard to be cut into six equal pieces, stove dampers closed, side and back screen doors hooked in summer, storm doors latched in winter, collections handed out from the Lord's Tenth box, and the family ready to set out as the bell of the town hall clock struck a quarter to eleven.

But this Sunday things went a lot easier and it was not as though you were having to catch a train. At first Chester did not see why he could not wear his running shoes instead of his laced boots, and Gilbert objected to the blouse she had for him on the grounds that she must have used a girl's pattern when she made it because it had puffed sleeves.

"Nothing of the sort," she told him, "it's the way you slump. If you don't get over your slouching you'll soon be wearing shoulder braces. Remember what your father told you."

Before leaving the house their mother made sure all the blinds on windows facing the street were raised or lowered to exactly the same level, which on sunny days such as this was two-thirds up. "I was taught that helter-skelter blinds are signs of an untidy house," Gilbert had heard her say. "I don't take much stock in that. But there you are." He took this as proof that the man in the Bible knew what he was talking about when he wrote that if you bring up a child in the way it should go, when it grows up it will not depart from it.

From the school corner where the sidewalk widened, they went three abreast which suited Gilbert just fine because it allowed him to practise his Indian walking without his mother noticing, even though he was pretty sure she would not get after him. When the four of them walked to church and he toed in ever so little he got a rap on his boot heel with the walking-stick as a reminder to "walk properly."

They had crossed the Avenue and were starting down the Crescent when a buggy stopped at one of the houses across the road and Dr. Kirkland hopped out. As he reached for his bag he saw them and raised his hat. It was something like a christy-stiff but higher and square on top. He had been the Williamson family doctor for ever so long. He had the name of being a joker. Last winter when their mother had a hard time getting over the "la grippe" and he came to see her, the first thing he said to her was: "Mouth taste like the bottom of a bird cage Frankie?" Gilbert thought that was a good one. He tried it on boys at school and everybody laughed. But one dinner time when Chester got pecky over what was on his plate, and Gilbert asked him if he had a taste in his mouth like the bottom of a bird cage, their father said, "Any more of such talk and I will send you from the table."

Although the Methodist Church was only a few blocks along Market Street from the foot of Crescent hill, its bell and the still smaller ones of the Baptist and English Churches were practically drowned out by the bells of the two Presbyterian Churches across the river, most of all by the Angus Dryden chimes of the one with the tallest steeple. The chimes were in memory of Mr. Dryden's only granddaughter who was drowned up the river when the canoe she was in upset. Aunt Trixie said that her friend who wrote for the town paper told her the chimes were brought over from the mother country and cost a lot of money. Mr. Dryden owned the tannery, the axe factory, the flour mill, the gas works, the power house beside the dam, where electricity was made, and was said to have his fingers in quite a few other pies. Up until last year he was headman of the collegiate school board. Ernie Yates told it around that his father, who worked in the tannery, said Mr. Dryden was so tight he would skin a flea for its hide and tallow. But Doctor Scanlon who was principal for years and years said the collegiate was fortunate to have Mr. Dryden on its board. Gilbert remembered hearing his father agree with Mr. Wallace that Mr. Dryden was hard-headed, but saying he was a man whose word was as good as his bond, which was more than could be said of a certain party the staff might be having dealings with in the not too distant future.

As they went up the church steps Grandpa Williamson was extending the right hand of fellowship to some lady, so they went on in and sat down. The Williamson pew reached all the way from the right aisle to the left aisle. It was the longest family pew in the church and though its right end had the Egan name on it, it was called the Williamson pew. This was because Grandpa Williamson paid for all of it years before a young teacher from the backwoods of Huron county came along. It was under the gallery and second from the back. A person might wonder why, with Grandpa Williamson being a church steward and a member of the Quarterly Official Board, it was not at the front with the Scanlon, Mullin and D.V. Schiller pews. The reason was to allow Grandpa to come in without disturbing people while the *Praise God From Whom All Blessings Flow* was being sung and to be first at the door to have a word with people as they left.

Aunt Trixie, Aunt Eunice and Aunt Boo were already seated. Aunt Kate was not with them which was a pretty sure sign that her husband who sold machinery for one of the foundries was home off the road. He was an out-and-out Presbyterian. Gilbert was first into the pew so he sat beside Aunt Boo. The top of her bonnet was not much higher than the back of the pew. She wore those black lace gloves with no ends to the fingers and was fanning herself with one of the palm leaf fans. Her veil kept moving up and down as if she was either sucking on it or mumbling to herself.

Miss Kellog came from a door to one side of the organ pipes, sat at the bench, pulled out a few stops and began playing soft music. The organ stood in a sort of pointed cave above which "O Worship the Lord in the Beauty of Holiness' was painted in big fancy letters on a banner which reached from wall to wall. The music and the words sort of went together and Gilbert began feeling quiet inside himself. He liked Miss Kellog. She had been his Sunday School teacher when he was in Infant Class. She went around giving music lessons the same as Professor Vance did, only on the piano. Ruby Greer took from her. He wondered if Miss Kellog and the professor were friends and if they ever played music together.

Next the choir came in; not much of a one because of the holidays, no trained soloist, only the two mill girls and a few other regulars. After they settled themselves, Reverend Allister came out. He parted the tails of his Prince Albert and sat in the big chair behind the pulpit with his head bowed. The music stopped. He stood behind the pulpit and raised his arms. The organ came on for all it was worth with the *Praise God From Whom All Blessings Flow*. The congregation stood. Everybody sang.

After the short prayer, the first hymn, the Bible reading, the long prayer and the second hymn, Mr. D.V. Schiller left his pew and came to the platform to read the announcements. He did not look as if he belonged up there but he did not look like a grocery man either. His hair was slicked down and parted in the middle, he wore a wing collar and a row of pencils showed from the top pocket of his vest. Once when he spoke to the Intermediate Sunday School on the subject of Home Missions, he used the text "Seeth thou a man diligent in his business he shall stand before kings," which was all right supposing this was what you wanted. His main announcement this morning was for the Ladies' Aid garden party to which members were asked to bring cake and sandwiches. The way he said it sounded like "sangwiches." Gilbert liked the sound. It made him feel hungry. The other way sounded as if they had sand in them.

The sermon was about Saint Paul. Not about the shipwreck or when he was bitten by a poisonous snake when he put more sticks on the campfire, nothing exciting like that. It was about when he went around preaching to people who did not believe. Gilbert had no way of knowing what his mother was thinking but one morning at table after Bible reading she told their father that if Paul walked in she would give him a piece of her mind over what he said against women. One thing about Reverend Allister, he did not go in for long sermons. The minister before sometimes got himself so worked up that he went on and on—firstly, secondly, thirdly, lastly, finally, in conclusion, until even grownups fidgeted and once Grandpa Williamson dozed off.

Aunt Boo pushed up her veil. Compared with outside, the church felt cool but the air had a shut-in feeling to it, not dusty and smelling of damp plaster like the Sunday School rooms downstairs, but somehow different from ordinary air. Yes, and the sunlight from the stained glass windows on the market square side was not the same as outside sunlight, you could not imagine birds sitting around singing in it or it making the waves of Sparrow Lake sparkle as they most likely were doing this very minute. Gilbert had discovered a good while ago that if he sat up straight and made his face look as though he was paying attention, he could make his father believe he was listening to the sermon and at the same time be thinking of something else. This is what he often did in school and unless old Burwell popped a question at him he could fool her every time. There she was up at the front teaching a lesson for all she was worth while the real Gilbert Egan was miles away doing whatever he felt like doing, and the boy across the aisle from Ruby Greer, sitting with his hands behind his back in the position of attention had nothing whatever to do with him. Aunt Boo's fan was sending little puffs of air against his cheek and without turning his head he saw she held her fan in a funny way, fluttering it back and forth under her chin instead of waving it as ordinary people do. *How old was she anyway? Was she older than Grandpa or was she younger? She must be younger because Grandpa was the first-born next to the brother who went to the California goldfields and was never heard of again. She must have been small for a twelve-year-old when her body stopped growing. What did it? Was it a germ or something? You would think that when her body stopped growing the rest of her would too. But except for her size, she's the same as a grownup. What if all of a sudden when I am twelve I stop growing? Gilbert Egan the midget. Like the one at the fall fair Tommy paid ten cents to see. Step right up, ladies and gentlement, see Gilbert Egan*

*the midget. There I'd be in a claw-hammer coat, a plug-hat, smoking
a cigar, riding my trick bicycle and everybody just about splitting
their sides laughing at me.*

Chester was whispering. Their mother shook her head and
pressed her fingers against his lips.

*How long before Tommy gets back from Port Dover? Does his
uncle take him out fishing? How big is a sailboat? Are Catholics
allowed to go fishing on Sunday afternoon? Catholics can go
skating on the dam on Sunday afternoons, but Methodists
can't. . . . Why is that? What's the sense? "Remember the Sabbath
day to keep it holy". . . . "When the wind is in the west then the
fishes bite the best. When the wind is in the south it blows the bait
in the fish's mouth. When the wind is in the east then the fishes bite
the least. When the wind is in the north then the fisher goes not
forth." But not always, no sir, not by a jugful. The wind was so in
the north the day we caught the big muskie paddling across to Mr.
Dubois'. . . . A rig crossing the market square. It came out of
Market Street at the back of the church and is going kitty-corner,
one horse, trotting, rubber tires so not one of Uncle
Abel's. . . These stockings scratch me something awful under my
garters at the back of my knees. Must be the ones Grandmother
Egan knits me for Christmas. Her mitts are not scratchy but her
stockings always are. . . . Thought I was putting on my store ones.
That's me all over. "I declare Gilbert, sometimes I think you would
forget your head if it wasn't fastened on.". . . . Wish I could walk
around barefoot. The disciples did. . . . "Lest thou dash thy foot
against a stone.". . . . "Andy Moore was a short, sturdy, freckled,
little country boy, as tough as a pine knot." The reader does not
say he went barefoot but I just know he did. He did not even wear
running shoes. . . . "Blessings on thee little man, barefoot boy with
cheek of tan, with thy turned up pantaloons and thy merry whistled
tunes.". . . . Ernie can whistle through his fingers but not a
tune. . . tune, pantaloon, moon, soon. . . pants, pantries, pansies
. . . garters, garter-snakes. . . guards. . . gumption. . . galoot. . . sense
enough to pound sand. . . sense. . . shoulder braces. . . shoulder
braces. . . . He better not, he just better not. No law says I have to
go around, my chest stuck out like a pouter pigeon's. . . Pigeon,
pigeon-toed. I am not pigeon-toed. The reason I walk that way
is—*Gilbert became aware that the voice from the pulpit was no
longer the minister's preaching voice, and that people were stirring,

clearing their throats, reaching for their hymn books. ". . . the first, third and fifth verses of this grand old hymn."

For as far back as he could remember, Gilbert had looked forward to Sunday dinner at the Williamsons, yes, and everyday ones and suppers too. For some reason, perhaps because Grandma Williamson used white pepper instead of black pepper, her cooking had a different flavor than his mother's. Then there was the sort of merry-go-round thing they called a cruet in the middle of the long table—fancy bottles with vinegar, catsup, salt, pepper and so on, went in holes of its silver tray which turned so you could reach whichever bottle you wanted. Still another good thing was that Grandpa Williamson did not waste time carving. The carving was done in the kitchen ahead of time, so the minute grace was said you could start right in with your eating. At home you had to sit there and possess your soul in patience while your father carved. One more good thing about eating at the Williamsons' was that there were always two kinds of pie. If Grandpa had his way one of those would be a vinegar pie. None of the others cared for vinegar pie but it was as chewy as Mrs. Devon's homemade butterscotch. If you sat next to Grandpa he would give you a second helping of vinegar pie on the sly. Grandpa sprinkled sugar on his bread and gravy, the roast beef kind as well as the beefsteak kind. If your mother was not looking he would slide the sugar bowl your way and wink at you to help yourself.

This Sunday Aunt Boo behaved herself, not muttering and rattling her knife and fork against her plate while Grandma was speaking until Grandpa said, "Beulah stop that!" as good as telling her that if she did not mind her manners she would have to leave the table. Aunt Boo acted this way on account of what Trixie said was a case of the green-eyed monster, whatever that meant.

As soon as they rose from the table Chester's mother took him upstairs to have his rest. The aunts cleared the dishes and Grandpa stretched out on the sofa in the bay window at his end of the table. Gilbert hung around on the chance they would have a talk but his grandfather opened the *Christian Guardian*, spread it over his face to shut out the light and began his after dinner snooze. His long legs with the pointed elastic-sided shoes and only the point of his head showing made Gilbert think of soldiers stretched out on the battlefield in one of Tommy's Henty books, except that you could hear him breathing and see the watch chain across his stomach going up and down.

Gilbert wandered out to the kitchen, sat on the bottom step of the backstairs and listened to the talk. His mother came down and was helping dry the silver when a gurgling rush came from the water pipes. She made as if to go upstairs but the gurgling stopped. No sooner was she back at the sink than the gurgling came again.

"Run up and tell that brother of yours, any more of that and he's headed for trouble." Gilbert did not need to ask where Chester was or what he was up to. Except for the one in the Sunday School basement, the Williamsons' was the only water-closet he and Chester had ever used. Sure enough, there Chester was, his bloomers down around his heels, hunched down into the hole which was miles too big for him. He had a tight hold on the handle of the chain and kept pulling it, not giving the ceiling tank time to fill and causing a steady stream of water to swirl across the ledge of the w.c., within inches of his bare behind. Gilbert pulled him off the seat.

"Your bee-tee-em's splashed." He took a sheet of tissue paper from the box on the wall. "Here, dry yourself."

"I like the feel of the splashes." Chester did as he was told, dropped the crumpled paper onto the ledge and pulled the chain. Together they watched the paper being swept over the ledge and into the whirlpool below. Like going over Niagara Falls in a barrel, Gilbert thought. He helped Chester haul up his bloomers and button them to his undervest. Then they went down the front stairs to the parlor and sat side by side on the horsehair sofa taking turns looking at pictures of the Holy Land through the stereoptic viewer.

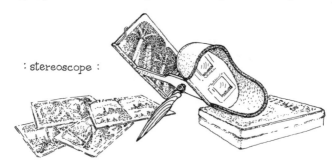

: stereoscope :

Next, for want of something better to do, Gilbert got the family album from the top of the organ and had another try at helping Chester get it through his head that when you came right down to it Aunt Trixie was their mother's half-sister, not her real sister.

But Chester still believed this was another of Gilbert's made-up stories.

"How can she be half of a sister?"

"For the simple reason they did not have the same mother, that's how. Momma and Aunt Eunice and Aunt Kate and their three brothers that played baseball and went to live in Yankeeland all had the same mother. Then she and quite a few other people died of the fever. So after a while Grandpa married their mother's sister. So that makes the one who died of the fever our real Grandma and the Grandma we have now isn't, not when you come right down to it."

"She is so my Grandma. You can have some other Grandma if you want, but Grandma Williamson is my Grandma and nobody can stop me."

"All I'm saying is, the reason Aunt Trixie has to be Momma's half-sister is—" Gilbert checked himself, closed the album with a bang, fastened its clasp and put it back on the organ. "It's awful stuffy in here, let's go outside." Now he too was mixed up. With their mother and Aunt Trixie having the same father, and with their mothers being sisters. . . . He felt as he did in school when old Burwell popped a mental arithmetic question at him and he had no idea what the answer was. Three-quarter sisters? If people heard you say that they would split their sides laughing at you.

When it came to being tony, Balaclava could not hold a candle to some streets on the other side of town, least of all to Durham Place. Quite a few houses on Durham Place had driveways right to their front doors and one of the houses had a cast-iron deer on its lawn. But after dusty old Blair Street, Balaclava was the next best thing to being in the country. The Williamson house was second to last before you went up the cemetery hill. Across the road from the cemetery there was Perry Woods. The story was, that a man belonging to a Family Compact family who went by the name of Perry died a soldier's death at Queenston Heights, helping General Brock drive the Yankees back to where they came from, with their tails between their legs. There was supposed to be a slippery elm tree in Perry Woods. The Black Bush, beyond, was all big pines which must have been growing in the days when the Indians had the run of things.

The front of the house was shaded and there was a breeze so Gilbert and Chester sat on the top step of the veranda and watched people going past. Sunday afternoon was the time for visiting the cemetery, taking flowers, tidying up the plots, or strolling around reading what was on the gravestones, "Till We Meet Again, "In Loving Memory," "Resting in the Lord," all like that. Some l ad verses none of which came up to the one on Obediah's gravestone. There were stones so old you could scarcely read what was written on them. One said, "Killed by a falling tree." There were six graves in one plot of a family, "drowned through the river ice." One was of a boy the same age as Chester. It made you think. At the far side of the cemetery a stone lay face down in the long grass. Had that person's family moved away or did none of them care any more? The cemetery had comfortable benches beside the paths and taps for watering. One Sunday when Gilbert went there with his mother and Aunt Eunice, they had a nice visit with two ladies who were trimming the grass of a plot right next to the Williamson plot.

Chester pointed. "Look at that man. What's that black thing on his arm?"

Gilbert gave Chester a dig with his elbow. "Don't point."

"What is it? What's he got it on for?"

"It shows somebody in his family just died. It's crêpe, the same as what they put on doors when somebody dies—black for grownups, white for babies, grey for in-betweens."

"If I die I would tell them to put on black."

"Like ducks you would; you wouldn't have any say about it."

"Oh yes I would. I'd make them."

"Don't talk foolish."

"I'm not a fool."

"I didn't say that, all I said was you talk like one. That's not the same." You could call your brother a muckle-headed dub or tell him he did not have sense enough to pound sand and nothing bad would happen to you. But if you called him a fool, "Raca, thou fool"—you were in danger of hell fire, the Bible said.

They watched more people pass but none of the men wore crêpe. One of the ladies had a black lace parasol but you could not go by that. Some carried flowers to put on graves but not a single solitary one of them looked out-and-out sad. Gilbert kept hoping for a funeral like the big one he sat and watched one Sunday—black horses with black plumes on their heads, men marching two by two behind the hearse with fancy little pinafores tied around their stomachs and after them a long line of carriages. But no such luck this Sunday.

After a while Chester said he felt thirsty and went inside to ask for a drink. When he did not come back, Gilbert went and lay on his stomach in the shade of the Golden Glow bushes along the side fence. The grass felt cool so he rolled down his stockings and garters to get the scratchiness out of his legs. With his chin on his hands he watched an ant climb to the top of a grass blade, down its other side then do the same thing all over agan. Ants had the name of being wise—"Go to the ant thou sluggard, consider her ways and be wise"—but this one certainly did not act wise. If you saw a person acting this way you would think he did not have much gumption. Just the same, that ant might be up to something no human being could know about. Or it might be that Holy Land ants were brighter than Canadian ones. Or it might be—A click of the front gate made Gilbert lift his head. The man was Mr. Pickering. He went up the front steps and gave the bell a twist. Aunt Trixie opened and the two of them went out the gate and down the street.

Gilbert tried to find the ant he had been watching but the one he saw down among the grass stalks must have been a different one, for instead of climbing, it tried to go deeper into the tangle of sod. Each time it came to something in its path it went under not over. Perhaps some ants were like some people, some wanted to climb, some wanted to stay with their feet on the ground. Like the time he and Ernie crossed the river on the railway bridge when Mr. Greer wasn't watching. Ernie thought it was fun to stand on the very edge and look down at the water and into the treetops on the island, while all he could do was kneel and hang on for dear life.

A rig was passing at a smart clip, not going toward the cemetery but coming into town. From what he could see of it through the pickets of the front fence, he took it to be Dr. Kirkland's buggy but when he sat up he saw it was a phaeton, probably hired from one of the livery stables for a drive in the country.

He lay down again, rolled onto his stomach and thought some more about ants. There was another way they reminded him of people. This was that they lived in big families. With some insects it was not like that. Spiders for instance. Each one made its own place and lived by itself and whatever happened to it was its own lookout. But when you were part of a family you knew about each other and what happened to each other. Not the Egans. They were scattered far and wide and did not seem to stick together, but the Williamsons and the ones they married—Obediah and his cranky wife, those who called themselves United Empire Loyalists and those who said they were no such thing, right down to his cousins in

Detroit and Cleveland and the four boy cousins in Jersey City who talked through their noses. You did not hold it against them for being Yankees and setting off fireworks in July instead of on the Queen's birthday. Yes and the ones who belonged to the family and were buried up there in the family plot were not left out—his real Grandma Williamson, Gracie and Trixie's twin, Tim who was taken by the dropsy when he was eleven and who Aunt Boo said sat up in bed and sang *Bringing In the Sheaves* just before he died. Also you could not leave out those whose pictures in the album had been taken so long ago that they were on tin, not paper—the men in stovepipe hats and the women in skirts as big around as barrel hoops and with bonnet strings tied under their chins.

After supper, before leaving for evening church, all of them including Aunt Kate and her husband would remain at table while Grandpa said evening prayer. It was always the same prayer word for word. He gave thanks for "Thy bountiful mercies beyond which we cannot ask or think," and ended by asking the Lord to take care of "all those bounded to us by the ties of nature wherever they may be." Gilbert liked to think this included the black sheep Williamson who, for all anybody knew, may never have got to the goldfields. It would not be like Grandpa, or the Lord either, to leave the black sheep out of it.

CHAPTER FIVE

Under Canvas

By the following week it was as plain to Gilbert as the nose on his face that there would be no camping at Sparrow Lake this summer. From parts of letters their mother read to them they knew that by the time their father finished marking all the papers those Toronto people had for him to mark there would not be much of July left—not much more than you could shake a stick at.

"They are not his boss," Chester said. "He can come home any day he wants. Why doesn't he?"

"For the good and sufficient reason he is being well paid for what he is doing," their mother said. "Moreover he is doing it for you, for all of us. He has plans."

"What plans? I like to know."

"And so you shall, all in good time."

Gilbert could have told Chester he might as well have saved his breath. In this house they never let out a peep until a thing had been decided. It would be dusty old Blair Street this summer, no getting around it.

But the very day after their father came home Gilbert and Chester learned the family would be going camping this summer after all.

"It won't be Sparrow Lake, so don't count on that," their father told them. "But under the circumstances it will be the next best thing."

The next best thing was to camp in a sugar bush on a farm north of town belonging to a friend of Mr. Waldy's. The farmer's name was Mr. Yarrow. Mr. Waldy had known him long before he had the hardware store, in the days when Mr. Waldy drove around selling lightning rods and Waldys Miracle Healer, Good for Man and Beast, to the farmers.

The sugar bush was only six miles out so there would be no train rides, no tickets to buy, first to Toronto then up to Sparrow Lake. One of the Abel Williamson wagons would take them and their belongings.

The morning they left, while the wagon was being loaded,

Gilbert and Chester went along to say goodbye to Mr. Wallace and Bruce. Nick was there. They got along all right. Gilbert told him about going camping and Nick said he had lots of places he could go to but he would just as soon stay home. They would have talked some more but their father let out one of his yips and waved his arm for them to get a move on. Their mother returned from the Misses Langleys' where she had taken some leftover milk for their cat. The driver reached down to give her a hand but she gathered her skirts, put one foot on the hub, the other on the rim of the wheel and was on the spring seat beside him in a jiffy. Gilbert boosted Chester over the tail-board, scrambled after him and found a comfortable place between the tent peg box and the apple barrel with the bedding and dishes. Their father got in, the driver gathered the reins, clucked to the team and they were on their way.

A few doors before they turned left at the school corner, a noo-come-oot lady stopped sweeping her porch to stare at them. I guess she takes us for some kind of gypsies, Gilbert thought, though his mother in her striped shirt-waist and what she called her boater hat certainly did not look like one. The stiff straw hat was fastened with the two long hatpins, Souvenir of Ashbury Park, which her Jersey City brother had given her. The hat had a bright blue and yellow ribbon around it.

For the first two or three miles out of town the country was all fields with stuff growing in them and pastures with cows and horses standing around or lying in the shade of tall elms. The shape of the elms made him think of giant sun parasols. The road was not wide enough for rigs to pass so one or the other had to pull over. One that pulled over was a democrat with a man and a woman. The woman was holding a baby. They were dressed all in black even the baby. Gilbert said by the look of things they must be going to a funeral but his father said not so, that those who believed as they did wore black, that they were hard workers and the best of farmers. Farther on there were more wood lots. Under a short stone bridge there was a creek with hardly any water, only bulrushes.

The Yarrow farm was a little way along a lane and by the look of its stump fences, stone and log buildings, it had been there for a good long time. Their father got down to go to the house but the door opened and a woman came to the wagon. She said for them to keep on along the lane past the cornfield, that her husband had just now gone back there to take down the bars so they could unload at the spot in the sugar bush he reckoned would suit them. "I can provide you with milk and eggs," she told their mother. "Butter too, if you are so minded." She was a short woman, only a mite taller than their mother, but a whole lot heavier.

Mr. Yarrow met them part way along the lane, so he must have been keeping his eyes peeled. He walked ahead of the horses to the spot he had picked. He limped, but if you put him down as a cripple you had another think coming—either that or he was the spriest cripple ever. The spot suited their father just fine; no overhanging branches, no underbrush only a few dry cow plats to be picked up. "There's a spring yonder, down the slope a piece," Mr. Yarrow told them. "Good sweet water." Chester might take this to mean the water had sugar in it but Gilbert knew better. It only meant the water did not have a bad taste, no wrigglers as in the rain barrels.

While the wagon was being unloaded the driver unhitched the horses and led them to the spring to water them. Mr. Yarrow helped unload. Gilbert could see him sizing up the bundles of bed slats each with their foot and head boards, the folding camp chairs, knock-down table, two packing-case cupboards, the barrel, four-hole cook stove, roll of old carpet for beside the beds, poles, ropes, bundled tents, and so on. Their father must also have noticed. "No doubt we pamper ourselves," he said. Mr. Yarrow spit on his hands, shouldered one of the bundles and said there was nothing like being comfortable. All the same, Gilbert could not help wondering if Mr. Yarrow took the collegiate teacher for some kind of sissy, even though their father had sense enough that morning not to wax his mustache.

As soon as the stove was set up Mr. Yarrow left. Their mother asked the driver to stay and have a bite of dinner but he told her he had better be getting along. After dinner there was no lying around as there usually was at Sparrow Lake. Even Chester was kept hopping, sorting tent pegs and putting things away their mother handed him. Last thing before supper Gilbert went to the barnyard with his father and helped fill the two bed ticks with straw from the stack Mr. Yarrow said they could use. Before it started to get dark they all pitched in and gathered dry branches for stovewood. Last thing before dark, their father dug the backhouse hole between two trees and nailed the seat on two poles fixed between them—only the grown-up size seat, not the two sizes as at home. In camp, the backhouse had no roof, only walls and a curtain made of potato sacks. The squares of newspaper, *Mail and Empire* mostly, were kept in a tin biscuit box so the rain could not get at them. In camp after you did your number two, you had to scrape some dirt from the pile and scatter it down the hole. You did this to keep away the germs.

Although he felt sort of tired, Gilbert took a long time getting to sleep that night. Not that this bothered him, he had nice things to think about. Yes, and there was that good old camp smell as if something of Sparrow Lake had been folded into the canvas when it was put away. There was the woodsy, deep-down smell of the ground inside the tent which made you imagine the earth was breathing. And on top of these smells there was the fresh, sunny smell of the straw on which he lay. The night seemed strangely still; no train whistles, no barking dogs, no sound of a wagon going past. When he lay awake at Sparrow Lake he might hear the far-away cry of a loon or the tinkle of tiny waves on the rocks in front of camp. Here the great surrounding maples made the tent seem a room within a room. They gave you a safe, shut-away feeling as though whatever was happening beyond them was none of your affair.

: the camp :

The first morning Gilbert and Chester went for the milk their mother came with them to talk things over with Mrs.Yarrow, but after that they went by themselves. The farmhouse was at the end of the cornfield and to get to it they took a short-cut across the orchard which had hives of bees. Not just a dozen or so as at Mr. Dubois' but rows and rows of them. Those thousands and thousands of bees made such a deep humming sound that Chester was afraid he would be stung and wanted to go the long way around. Gilbert told him that so long as he felt friendly toward the bees they would not sting him. It was like in the Daniel in the Lions' Den picture at Sunday School. There was Daniel walking around as cool as a cucumber with the biggest lion just about licking his hand and the others with looks on their faces as if they were purring. If Daniel had not trusted the lions they would have gobbled him up. But because he was friendly and trusted them he was safe. All animals, even bees, had a way of knowing how you felt about them. So the thing was to feel friendly.

Mrs. Yarrow's kitchen smelled of bread and smoked meat. If you were the least bit hungry it just about made the juices run. Some mornings before she took their covered tin pail to the spring house for the milk, she gave each of them a hunk of honeycomb to eat while they waited. Her honey had a different taste than the Dubois' honey. Clover honey she called it. Later in the summer it would be buckwheat honey. Chester wanted to know what that tasted like. "Buckwheat of course," Gilbert said. Mrs. Yarrow looked down at him over her spectacles and made him wish he had not been such a smart aleck. This was the morning she gave them a jar of apple butter. One other morning she invited them back to watch her make butter. So after they finished their camp chores they went. The churn was made like a barrel but not so wide and smaller at the top. Mrs. Yarrow stood beside it working the handle up and down, first with one hand, then with the other, then with both hands. You could see it was not easy work. She told them the churning song she learned when she was a little girl and had them sing it with her. "Come butter come," was how it went. After the butter came she took it out, salted it a little and pressed it into a wooden mould which had a four-leaf clover carved on it. This was for when it went to market so people could tell her butter from other farm butter. When she was through and everything put away she gave them cold johnny-cake with maple syrup and buttermilk to drink.

One morning when they came into the farmyard the pigs had got through the fence of their pen and Mr. Yarrow was hobbling back and forth trying to drive them back in. The pigs were half-grown and quick on their feet and no matter how Mr. Yarrow tried, they dodged him. He had lost his hat and was getting madder and madder. He kept saying things under his breath then all of a sudden he let out a yell and took the Lord's name in vain at the top of his

voice. Mrs. Yarrow must have heard him for she came from the
house with a pan of peelings and went straight into the pen. The
pigs must have known what she was carrying for they could not get
back in fast enough. While they were eating the peelings, Mrs.
Yarrow helped Mr. Yarrow close the hole in the fence. All this went
to prove what Gilbert's mother had once told him, which was that
you could lead a pig but you could not drive it. She told him the
same could be said of some people, Gilbert Egan included.

Besides chickens and a few ducks, the Yarrows kept turkeys.
When the chickens and ducks were let out, they had sense enough
to come home but the turkeys perched for the night in trees on
whatever part of the farm they happened to be in when the sun
went down. Their father said that from what he knew of turkeys
when he was a boy, wild or tame, they were with few exceptions a
brainless lot. Mr. Yarrow said that every so often one or another of
them turned up missing and that his guess was 'coons were getting
them. He said he had been meaning to build a turkey house but that
what with one thing and another he had not got around to it. Their
father offered to give a hand with the building so the two of them
sat down in the kitchen and figured how much lumber they would
need.

If there was anything their father liked more than fixing things, it
was building things. If the C.P.R. had not been finished so soon,
he would have been in his glory building bridges and railway
stations. At home when their mother wondered if it would be a
good idea to widen the back steps, put up extra shelves in the pantry,
make a larger work table for the summer kitchen, she no sooner
had the words out of her mouth before he was planning how to do
it and was getting out his tools. Gilbert was expected to help but all
this ever amounted to was standing around watching and now and
then handing a nail or a screw or whichever tool his father asked
for—"making yourself useful"—his father called it. His father
told him this was the way boys learn. But how could you be
expected to learn a thing when you were never allowed to do it?

And it would have been the same with the turkey house if Mr.
Yarrow had not given him the job of straightening nails. Mr.
Yarrow had pounds and pounds of used nails. Most of them were
the old style cut nails which he and their father agreed held better
and lasted longer than the new-fangled wire ones. Gilbert had no
way of knowing about that. But one thing sure, because the cut nails
were tapered and had square sides it was not such a hard job to

pound them straight. If you watched what you were doing you did not bang your finger, as he did now and then with the wire nails. Mr. Yarrow found him a real blacksmith's hammer and a big stone for an anvil. Every so often when he came to get a handful, Mr. Yarrow said, "you are doing fine," and once he gave Gilbert a pat on the head and said he was a steady worker. Gilbert would have given just about anything to have his father tell him that, but the only times his father had anything to say was when a nail was not straight enough to suit him and he handed it back to be done again.

When Mr. Yarrow said he was no great shakes as a carpenter it was easy to see he was not just saying it. For if he had been left to himself the turkey house would not have been much better than a shed. But Gilbert's father had other ideas. When he was what he called "framing" it, he told Gilbert to stop straightening nails, and to pay strict attention and to remember the names of the scantlings as they were sawn to length—"floor joists, studs, plates, rafters, collar ties." The doorway had a "header" and the pitched roof would have overhanging "gables." While the building was being framed, his father would pick up a scantling and tell Gilbert to give him its correct name. But some of Gilbert's guesses were wide of the mark and he would have to be corrected. He supposed all this might come in handy after he grew up and needed to build a house, but right now he was all for living in tents like the Indians. Having to stand around taking lessons made him wish his father was not so much of a teacher. Yes, and this was not the first time his father made him feel that way. But by the time the turkey house was finished he felt better about his father. Mrs. Yarrow was ever so pleased and she thanked them both for helping.

One day after dinner when their mother was in the hammock reading and their father was writing letters at the dining tent table, Gilbert asked if it would be all right for the two of them to mosey along to the farm and have a look around. His father took his time answering. First he wiped the nib on the wiper, then dipped it in the bottle, then held it over the paper. He said if the word meant what he surmised it meant, he had no objection, provided they behaved themselves and did not get in people's way.

Mr. and Mrs. Yarrow were not around but two boys Gilbert and Chester had not seen before were looking at the pigs. The older one was about Gilbert's size. He had big freckles on the backs of his hands. He was the one who did most of the talking. The other one was not much taller than Chester but sort of fat. The older one said these pigs were not growing so fast as their pigs but that there were more of them. Gilbert asked if he had seen the turkey house. He said he had but this was all he said about it. After they stood around for a while the older one said he felt hot already so they should go into the stable and cool off. The stable was part of the barn but under it. It had thick stone walls and on a day like this it felt as good as the cold cellar at home where the preserves and crocks of pickles were kept. The stalls were empty. The horsey smell was not as strong as in Uncle Abel Williamson's stable.

They were standing around fanning their faces with their straw dummies when the older boy asked Gilbert if he would like a cold drink. Gilbert said yes he would. The boy took him over to a row of kegs lying on their sides across some timbers. He pried the bung from the top side of one of the kegs, handed Gilbert a straw and told him to put it in the hole and suck. The stuff that came up had a fuzzy taste and left a kind of prickly feeling in his mouth. It was sour and Gilbert did not care for it, but because the boy kept watching him he took a few more swigs. "Suck more," the boy said. He sounded as though he was trying to stump Gilbert, so Gilbert gulped down some more before throwing away the straw. When they went out into the bright sun, Gilbert felt a little dizzy and put his hand on Chester's shoulder to steady himself.

There was a sly grin on the boy's face. "Was cider, you dummkopf."

Chester gave the boy a push. "You better not call my brother names, you just better not."

Gilbert let out a good big burp. "Aw go pull the chain," he told the boy. It was easy to see neither of them knew what Gilbert was getting at, so the laugh was on them.

Nearly every night after Gilbert got into bed he listened for the 'coon. The first night he heard it he had no idea what it was. It came from somewhere out in the cornfield. In some ways it sounded like a baby making its voice go up and down. In other ways it made him think of the trained singer in the choir when she sang solo, as for instance the one about the ninety and nine lost sheep the good shepherd was out on the mountain in the dark of night looking for. When she came to the high note she sort of took a run at it. Her voice got quavery and you wondered if she could make it. Their father must have heard the sound, for next morning he said it could only be a 'coon, or perhaps two of them calling back and forth.

This night Gilbert thought he heard the sound again but it came from farther off and he could not be sure. He fell asleep and the next thing he knew his father was standing there with the lantern in his hand and telling him to get up. "All hands on deck, there's a squall coming." His father reached across, gave Chester a shake, and told him to get dressed. The canvas was flapping and the sound of wind in the trees was like a river rushing past. Their mother came from the other side of the curtain, she had on her wrapper and her hair hung down in two long braids.

"What do you want us to do, Richard?" she asked as she helped Chester put on his clothes.

"You three stay inside and keep the sod cloth down. If the walls lift the tent will go." He handed her the lantern and made for the back end of the tent. Even there the wind had such force he had trouble retying the flaps after he went out.

Gilbert and Chester followed their mother to the front end and got down on either side of her, holding the sod cloth down with their knees and hands. The canvas over their heads bulged like in pictures of sails in a storm. The rushing sound was even stronger here. It gave Gilbert a strange, mixed up feeling as though the tent was rushing on and on into the night and the air around it was standing still. He remembered having had much the same feeling last Easter when he and Chester went out on the upper bridge on their way home from Sunday School to watch the ice going out. After he had looked down for a while at the pier it seemed for all the world like the bow of a ship with the ice cakes standing still and the pier moving upstream and crashing into them. Yes, and by partly closing his eyes he was able to imagine that the bridge, the buildings along both banks, and the dam too, were moving with the pier and that the broken ice and flood water as far away as the railway bridge were standing still.

The sod cloth to Chester's right began fluttering. Its rope loops had been shaken off its pegs but Chester got it back on in time. They heard a stake being pounded then all of a sudden Gilbert's corner of the tent began flapping and the pole took a bad lean. He heard his father shout for them to steady it but to watch for their heads if the ridge came down. Their mother told Chester to take the lantern and stand well back, then she hung onto the pole for all she was worth. Gilbert helped her but it was all they could do to keep it from getting away from them. "Oh no you don't," she told it. She would have hung onto that pole if it was the last thing she ever did.

When the stake had been driven in and the pole steadied with an extra guy rope, the three of them went on holding down the sod cloth until the worst of the squall was over.

Next morning when Gilbert and Chester came for the milk Mr. Yarrow said the storm had been a ring-tail snorter and was surprised neither of the tents had been blown down. Gilbert felt pretty certain they would have been if all of them had not pitched in, which was what you had to do when a family went camping.

CHAPTER SIX

Country Life

Gilbert was at the spring dipping water into the pail and he was taking his time about it. A person watching might jump to the conclusion he was dawdling but he was doing no such thing. And anyhow, what if he was? His mother was in no hurry for the water. Sunday dinner was over, the dishes were done, and she and his father were sitting in their camp chairs between the sleeping tent and the dining tent reading whatever the books were that they were reading. Last seen of Chester he was just lying around.

What was keeping Gilbert so long at the spring was having another good long look at the four or five water spiders or whatever their name was. Talk about your walking on water! They not only walked, they dodged back and forth like hockey players. The miracle was what held them up. If bugs half their size fell onto the water, down they would go. The answer his father gave him was something about surface tension, whatever that was. When Gilbert got right down and looked, all he could see was a tiny dimple under each foot. The dimple moved with them, the way rubber ice does with every step you take.

Gilbert poured a few more dipperfuls into the pail then squatted on his heels again to watch the spiders. He could be comfortable in this position for as long as he wanted to, his arms wrapped around his shins and his chin resting on his knees. When Chester tried it, he had to hold onto something or he would lose his balance and fall onto his behind. And if he held onto something he soon got pins and needles in his legs. Chester thought squatting was a slick trick and wanted Gilbert to teach him but their father said there was no trick to it, it was simply that Gilbert was long-bodied. He did not say there was anything the matter with being long-bodied, such as he did about toeing in or slouching and getting round shouldered. But he did not say there was anything good about it either.

Gilbert had just about seen enough of the water spiders when Chester came jogging down under the maples to tell him they had visitors, Aunt Trixie and the man from the town paper were here.

Trixie was sitting on the bench behind the dining tent with her

back to him when Gilbert came with the pail. She had taken off one
of her white, high button shoes and was wiping it with some leaves,
which was a pretty sure sign she had stepped in something coming
along the lane. He was wondering whether or not he should speak
to her when his mother came and told him to go along and say
how-do-you-do to Mr. Pickering. She had her pearl handled button
hook and handed it to Trixie.

Mr. Pickering had the camp chair across from their father and
was doing the talking so Gilbert sat down on the grass and waited.
Mr. Pickering was praising some man or other up to the skies but
after listening for a while their father came right out and said he did
not agree. He said that although he would not know the man from
Adam's off ox, if half of what the *Mail and Empire* printed about
him was true, Canada could well do without him and it was high
time he was sent packing.

One thing Gilbert could say about his father was that he was not
two-faced. This was far from the first time his father did not see eye
to eye with Mr. Pickering. "Listen to this, Frances," Gilbert had
heard his father say when the town paper came out with something
which rubbed him the wrong way. "What might have been a
serious accident was narrowly averted," . . . so on and so on. Let a
horse kick over its traces, somebody's house almost catch fire,
some workman almost fall from his ladder and this is the
balderdash we are treated to. Rarely a school board meeting but
this fellow has the trustees averring, alleging and opining all over
the place. Moreover now that I'm on the subject since he took over
the paper I see American spellings creeping in. What possesses the
man? Has he never heard of the *Oxford Dictionary?*"

When their father got onto this tack, their mother stuck up for
Mr. Pickering, though whether she did this on account of Trixie
was hard to tell. She said she found Mr. Pickering a pleasant
spoken man and that at least he was not bumptious.

If that word meant what Gilbert thought it meant, his mother
was right. Mr. Pickering was kind of plump all over, not just his
face. His hair was a little thin where he parted it down the middle.
His eye glasses were like Mr. D.V. Schiller's, the latest style with a
thin gold chain looped behind his ear.

The next thing their father and Mr. Pickering got onto that
afternoon was one there could be no argument about. This was that
month after month the Boers were giving the redcoats the worst of
it. Gilbert's father said things had come to a pretty pass when a

raggle-taggle of farmers, Dutch ones at that, were able to put Her Majesty's best soldiers on the run. Mr. Pickering said he could not understand it, there must be something wrong somewhere.

At first after his mother and Aunt Trixie came and sat down the talk did not interest Gilbert. He was thinking of moseying out to the lane where Chester was pulling grass and trying to feed it to the livery horse, but then talk got back to the Boers. His father said they must be taught a lesson for pulling the lion's tail and Mr. Pickering said some nice things about the mother country. Gilbert's mother said there were usually two sides to a story and that she would like to hear what the Boers had to say for themselves.

"The *Mail and Empire* has precious little to say about that and I do not suppose the *Globe* does any better."

Mr. Pickering agreed. "But under the circumstances, with the mother country at war—"

"Mother country my foot!"

Trixie reached and touched Mr. Pickering's sleeve. "Don't mind her. Frances has always been the rebel of the family."

"Rebel nothing. Though if it came to that I would not be the first one."

"All this is beside the point," Gilbert's father said. You could tell by his voice he was putting his foot down. "The battle has been joined and it will be a sorry day for the Empire if we do not stand together. But of course we will, 'At Britain's side whate'er betide'." He raised his hand in the direction of the Union Jack on its pole above the dining tent. "Blood will tell. Let us leave it at that."

The stump fence began at the barnyard and ended where the lane joined the main road. Their father told Gilbert and Chester to have a good look at it because stump fences were a thing of the past, at least in this part of the country, and by the time they grew up, few, if any, would be left. Wire fencing such as Mr. Waldy advertised as horse-high, bull-strong, hog-tight, was getting to be the thing.

Many of the stumps were as big around as barrels. "It took a good team and a driver who knew what he was doing to drag them into place," their father said. The stumps lay ten or so feet apart with all their tops on the lane side roots up, down and sideways making a strong, close fence on the field side. Gilbert opened his mouth to ask where so many stumps came from but he closed it in case his father got after him for asking an unnecessary question and telling him to think before he spoke, or worse still to use his eyes and not his mouth. Of course he knew where the stumps were from but it seemed a friendly thing to keep the conversation going and to show his father he was interested. The stumps came from clearing the fields which was a job his father, Mr. Dubois and Aunt Kate's husband had to help with when they were backwood boys. When one of them and his father talked about the old days, Gilbert was all ears. The hardwoods they helped cut down and burn—hickory, black walnut, butternut, white ash and oak—to plant potatoes and oats between the stumps, would be worth a small fortune today, Aunt Kate's husband said. And he should know, he went all around Ontario and Quebec selling machinery for saw-mills.

: stump fence :

There were two good reasons why no more stump fences would be built. The first was that all the fields had been cleared long ago and so there were no more stumps to build with. The second reason was one which made Mr. Wallace go in for Mr. Waldy's wire fencing the year after their father taught the Settlement school. This was that the stump fences took up too much ground between the fields. On top of that, all sorts of weeds—mullein, burdock, goldenrod, New England aster, Canadian thistles and the Scotch kind—grew among the stumps where no plough could get at them. Next thing you knew the wind took their seeds and scattered it all over the fields and you had prickles in your hay and stuff. All the same, it suited Gilbert just fine that Mr. Yarrow left his stump fence just as it was. Its wild raspberry and wild thimbleberry bushes grew so well among the stumps that you had to climb to the top of the roots to pick them. After the first few times, Chester was not much for picking berries, not even when their mother offered to make him his own little berry pie, the three-cornered, turn-over kind. But if Chester thought his brother needed him to come along, he had another think coming. When he did come he could be more bother than he was worth. Like as not he would get his pants or his blouse caught on a root and have to be helped down. If only he would stay on the lane side where the grass would not scratch his legs he would not have been such a nuisance. But when Gilbert picked on the field side where the bushes were taller, Chester came and picked on that side too. The field had been mowed so no wonder he got stubble scratches on his feet. Whenever Chester made up his mind about a thing, all the patience in the world could not get him to change it. Chester said he had as much right to pick on the field side as anybody and that he was not going to be bossed around. Each of them had a tomato can on a string around his neck and when your can was full you emptied it into the three pound lard pail. Gilbert filled his can twice as often as Chester filled his. But there was one thing you could say about Chester Egan and that was that he did not try to take all the credit and he never cheated, not even in tiddly-winks.

When Gilbert came to the stump fence by himself he had a different feeling about picking berries than when Chester came with him. When he came alone he was able to pretend he was a long-ago Indian boy out in the forest hunting with his trusty bow and arrow to feed his family at their wigwam back there in the sugar bush. Better still, he could be like the Indian boy up north in Tommy's *Boys' Own Annual,* who returned to camp with all the pemmican and stuff that he could carry and saved his family from starvation. Such a thing could easily have happened right here in this very place back in the days when the Indians had all the country to themselves. All Indians were kind, like Hiawatha, and if you believed some of the bad stories told about them you would believe just about anything. His Jersey City cousin believed Indians were in their glory when they went around scalping people, which made as much sense as what he believed about good Queen Victoria. He said she was nothing but a stuck-up old woman who went around with a crown on her head. One thing sure, when Hiawatha and his friends lived on the shores of Gitchee Gumee, they paddled wherever they felt like in their birchbark canoes and roamed the forest, they were not out to scalp people. The next time the Jersey City cousin came over and said bad things about Indians, Gilbert intended to show him the pictures in the *Hiawatha* book to prove he had been talking through his hat. Gilbert's favorite picture showed grown-up Indians, men and women, brave boy hunters and happy little children around a campfire in front of the wigwams. There were birchbark canoes pulled up on the shore and a big round moon was shining down. You only had to look at their faces to see how happy all of them were. And no wonder! Who wouldn't be happy living their kind of life?—no old Burwells, nobody all the time getting after you to toe out and square your shoulders, no Sunday School Golden Texts to learn by heart and all the rest of it. Although only one-half of Mr. Dubois was Indian he pretty near lived like that. Yes, and if you got right down to it, there still must be Indians up north living like in *Hiawatha*. Chances were that if you got on the right side of Mr. Dubois he would tell you where to find them. Say what you like, Indians had all the best of it.

Another thing you could learn from pictures in the *Hiawatha* book was that when Hiawatha roamed the forest all the animals, birds and things were not the least bit afraid of him. Even the great big deer just stood there and kept on eating. This could only be because they somehow understood he did not have it in his heart to hurt them. It was the same with Mr. Yarrow's bees. The only time Chester might have been stung was the morning a bee buzzed around his head and he took a swat at it. This made the bee buzz closer. Chester started to run but Gilbert grabbed him and told him whatever he did he must not be afraid. Chester did as he was told and sure enough the bee went away. Since that morning the two of them could come and go to the farm any time they liked and the bees took no notice. It was a good lesson for Chester to learn and Gilbert hoped he would remember it all the rest of his life. "As a man thinketh in his heart so is he" was more than just another Golden Text and Mr. Yarrow's bees were there to prove it.

Although their father would much sooner get his feet under a table than sit on the ground balancing a plate on his knee, the day he took them fishing at the old mill pond he agreed to make it a picnic. "Providing the food can be eaten out of hand," he told their mother. She made cucumber sandwiches and deviled eggs. No forks.

All four of them went. On their way there, at the far end of the stump fence, their father cut gads for fishing poles, a long whippy one for Gilbert and a shorter one for Chester. Right off Chester began swishing his around, so their father told both of them to walk behind. To get to the pond they followed a cow path across a pasture, through some farmer's wood lot and down into the hollow. Mr. Yarrow had told them the pond would be at its lowest this time of year. And he was right. Water weeds grew so thickly your line would not sink, and in case it did, all you could expect to catch were carp. Mr. Yarrow said that some evenings you could hear carp wallowing among the weeds like hogs. He said that a while ago a Pennsylvania Dutchman whose farm was farther along the road caught a twenty-five pounder. Mr. Yarrow said he would have to be almighty hungry before he ate carp but the man told him this one tasted fine. "Those Pennsylvania Dutchmen have some queer tastes, Limburger for instance." By the way Mr. Yarrow spoke about Pennsylvania Dutchmen you could tell he took them for some kind of joke. Gilbert could not see what was so funny about them. On account of Obediah's affliction sore, Gilbert supposed he and Chester must have some Pennsylvania blood in some of their veins. So had their mother and all the other Williamsons.

The place their father took them to fish was the rocky pool right below the dam. It was not much more than knee deep but trickles from between the timbers kept the water fresh. In one place a veil of water falling from the top of the dam made ripples and it was the most likely place to try their luck. But before his father rigged their lines the four of them crossed the creek bed on stepping stones to have a closer look at what was left of the old mill and its water-wheel. The building was without a roof and the blackened stone walls above where its windows had been showed that its insides had been burned out. Its upper and lower floors had fallen in and what had been its millrace was clogged by willows. Part of its water-wheel had rotted away but you could see it must have been a big one. Their father explained the difference between an overshot water-wheel and an undershot one and said this had been an overshot one. He looked inside for the millstones but if they had been left, they were covered by the jumble of charred wood of the floors.

While their father was having a look around, Gilbert asked their mother if this mill was anything like the one she and Gracie played beside when they were children on the farm back of Hamilton, the one she had the song about. The name of the song was *When You and I Were Young Maggie,* and every so often after she heard Chester say his prayers, he asked her to sing it to him. Nobody in their right mind would call Chester a softy, but at bedtime after the lamp was blown out, something got into him and he asked for a sad song, such as this one, or *The Last Rose of Summer, Darling Nellie Gray They Have Taken You Away* or the one about poor *Old Black Joe.*

"The water-wheel, or what was left of it, was at least as large as this one," their mother told Gilbert, "but the building was quite different as I remember it." She said there had been a real Maggie and that Aunt Boo knew both her and the man who wrote the song about her. The man went away to Buffalo or some such place and when he returned his Maggie was no more.

After their father finished his look around, they followed him back over the stepping stones to the flat grassy place where the picnic basket had been left. He fixed Chester's line but he had Gilbert tie on his own hook and sinker, after practising the proper knot until he had it right. "A good fisherman is never slap-dash with his tackle. Those who are must take the consequences. As with all else, there is a right way and a wrong way." The worms from Mr. Yarrow's manure pile were redder and wriggled more than those from Mr. Dubois' but if there were any fish larger than minnows under the ripples they were not interested. "Let us find bait more to their liking," their father said. He told of the big trout his father had caught with, of all things, a field mouse. Time and again he had tried every bait he could think of but that speckled beauty would not so much as look at any of them. This was a Grandfather Egan story Gilbert had not heard before.

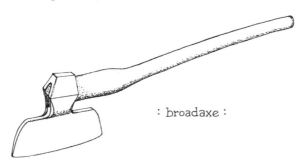

: broadaxe :

He liked the one he heard his father tell Mr. Dubois last summer, the one about his Grandfather going off fishing for a whole week every spring. In spite of his wife wanting him to get on the land, he took his fishing pole and camp things and off he went to some lake, stream or other. On his way home he stopped at farms and gave away some of his fish. Then he put away his pole and farmed and cleared land with the best of them until it was time for him to take his broadaxe and go into the woods for another winter. Mr. Dubois said there was nothing those men could not do with a broadaxe. They kept their axes so sharp they could shave with them. Gilbert's father said indeed they could and went on to tell a story which just about made Mr. Dubois split his sides laughing. The story went like this:

In those days, besides being a farmer, Grandfather Egan earned his living as a barn framer. He went into the woods when the sap was down and hewed timbers of all sizes for barns. One winter the man he hired to do the rough chopping—scoring, they called it—was gabby. A neighbor came along and nothing would do but the man sat down farther along the log Grandfather was hewing, filled his pipe and settled down for a chat. The cheek of his behind was a little bit over the line Grandfather Egan was hewing to but instead of telling the man to move—"shift his carcass," Gilbert's father called it—Grandfather Egan kept coming closer and closer with every stroke. The man went right on gabbing. Down came the broadaxe. It sliced through the bulge of his pants, took a smaller slice off his underpants and a piece of skin the size of a twenty-five cent piece from his behind. Gabby let out a yell, clapped his hand over his behind and made tracks for home, Gilbert's father said. Mr. Dubois said he could well believe it.

They looked for bait along the creek bed as far as the stepping stones but all they found were a few wrigglers and a caddis. It was nothing like the size of the dragon-fly caddis Tom the water baby talked to. Instead of the shell being made of sand, this one's was stuck together with any old thing, mostly mud. They took it to the pool and Chester tried it but no luck. Afterwards they went up to the grassy place where their mother was reading her book, sat in the shade and made short work of the cucumber sandwiches and deviled eggs. Their mother and father talked about the woman in the book—it was *Wuthering Heights,* something like that. Gilbert could not make out what the story was about and as soon as they had eaten their fill, their mother went on reading to herself and their father took out his knife and whittled. It was smaller than a jackknife, pearl handled, two-bladed and sharp as a razor. He kept

it in the lower right hand pocket of his vest along with his quill
toothpick. He called it his penknife and he was never without it,
even on Sundays. The funny thing was he never whittled except
when he was in his old clothes out camping. Then he might pick up
any piece of wood which lay handy and whittle it into something, a
canoe or a paddle, a toy spoon, depending on the size and shape of
the wood. Once he slicked a piece of wood into thin strips and
turned it into a lady's fan. This day Chester asked for a toy trout.
While his father was whittling it he told them that mills such as the
one across there at the end of the dam—he called it a grist
mill—were fairly common in pioneer days and that the larger ones,
such as Mr. Angus Dryden's, still served a useful purpose. The mill
their Grandfather Egan took his grain to was thirty miles south of
his farm in the clearing and before there was a wagon road he
carried the sack on his back. One day getting there, one day while
the grain was ground, and a long day walking home with his load.
The mill was in the small town his father took him to for Canada's
first Dominion Day. There was a platform in the market square
and speeches galore. Hot arguments too, some men saying Upper
Canada would rue the day, others saying no such thing. What their
father remembered best about the first Dominion Day was the pair
of knee-high cowhide boots his father bought for him. They had
copper toes and red cloth tops.

While their father was whittling away and telling them all this,
Gilbert wished he knew for sure what his Grandfather Egan looked
like. Did he still look as in his framed picture on the wall above the
bookcase or had his beard turned grey like Grandpa Williamson's?
The only time Grandfather Egan came to visit was the year before
Gilbert started kindergarten. What Gilbert could still remember
was his Grandfather's voice. It was a quiet, sure voice, and if ever
he heard it again he would know right off what person it came
from. The strange thing was he could not remember Grandmother
Egan's voice, yet she stayed with them for a whole month last
winter. She was a great worker. She baked so much bread that their
mother had to tell Mr. Isling, the baker, not to call. She knit every
week-day evening from supper until bedtime and unlike their
mother she did not need lamplight to knit by. She had their father
save the wood ashes from the kitchen stove. She made soap with it
and leftover fat. Her soap was a sort of jelly, but they had to wash
their hands with it until she went. Her eyes did not miss much. She
smiled but you had the feeling her smile was mostly on the outside.

What Gilbert could not make out was why their father did not tell stories about her but had story after story about his father. She never once missed church, morning or evening. She said things about their minister which anybody could see their father did not agree with but he never once told her so. She said it seemed to her Reverend Allister straddled the fence in some of his sermons and were they sure he was not a free-thinker?

One of the stories their father told about his father was one Gilbert and Chester were not supposed to hear. It happened last Thanksgiving Day at the Williamsons' right after dinner. The two of them had been excused from the table and were in the parlor sitting on the carpet playing all-fall-down with the dominoes. Their father and Aunt Kate's husband came in and sat down on the horsehair sofa across from them. Aunt Kate's husband was holding a cigar but he had not lighted it. Grandpa Williamson was not dead against smoking. Some Sundays after he took his after-dinner snooze he smoked a cigar but the rule in that house was you went outside to do it. Aunt Trixie said tobacco smoke made the house smell like a poolroom, though how she knew what a poolroom smelled like she did not say. Chester was clicking the dominoes and chattering away about nothing so Gilbert did not hear how the two men got onto the subject of tobacco but when he overheard their father say that his father was a life-long smoker, Gilbert pricked up his ears. From what Gilbert was able to make out, his Grandmother Egan was dead against her husband's use of tobacco from the very start. She said tobacco cost money and they could not afford it. He told her their sugar cost more than his tobacco so from that day on he stopped using store sugar. But he did not give up smoking and nothing she said could budge him. For years he grew his own tobacco. One of his ways of curing it was to bore auger holes in maple trees, pack the raw leaf into the holes and leave it there until it was fit to use. Aunt Kate's husband told of a man in Quebec who still did this and there were country stores which sold uncured leaf tobacco done up in bundles and mighty powerful stuff it was. Their father said he could well believe it. When he was growing up he took a few whiffs from his father's pipe and they almost bowled him over. Then and there he learned he lacked the stomach for tobacco and quite aside from the principle of the thing he could never be a smoker. After that the two began talking about other things and Gilbert got busy with the dominoes. He remembered thinking it would be fun if the two of them lit up. Or better still if he

could ever see his father and Mr. Waldy coming arm-in-arm along
Blair Street, their hats a little to one side, twirling their
walking-sticks and smoking cigars.

Their father closed his penknife and tossed the toy trout across to
Chester in a way that as good as said he did not think it was up to
much, which was a way he had with things he made but did not like
you to think he was proud of. Chester liked it and so did Gilbert.
They took it down to the pool and tried it. Except that it was white
all over and lay on its side it was a dandy. Gilbert left Chester
playing with it and moseyed on along the creek past the stepping
stones to see what he could see. After he passed the bend he came to
a fallen tree. He teetered across on it and began following an
overgrown path up the bank until he noticed a wasp nest on an
overhanging branch. The nest was no bigger than a lacrosse ball
and while he stood he saw several wasps come and go, all of them
minding their own busines. He was sure he could pass under the
nest without disturbing it. But first he stood stock still and made
himself feel friendly over every inch of his body, to make certain
the wasps knew he had a good feeling toward them. While he was
sending out this friendly feeling a wasp circled close to his head
then flew to the nest as if to tell the others they had nothing to be
afraid of. He stepped closer but before he bent down a wasp came
out of nowhere and stung him on the forehead. Another wasp
stung him through the back of the blouse. As he splashed across to
the other bank he slipped and skinned his knee.

"Dingbust you" he yelled. He picked up one stone after another
and threw them with all his strength in the direction of the nest.
When he reached the bend he sat on a boulder to catch his breath.
There was a smear of blood on his knee. He licked it off. The sand
gritted his teeth. For all he knew one of the stones had smashed their
nest but what did they expect? As he sat licking his knee, spitting out
the sand and sort of cooling off he wondered what he had been
thinking of to do a thing like that. Every living thing, even wasps,
have a right to stick up for themselves. My trouble is I'm all the time
making myself believe what I want to believe, he thought, so this is
what I get. I don't know what gets into me. All I do is fool myself. I
wish I could be more like other people. The worst of the smarting
had gone out of the stings by the time he heard his mother calling
him. His father was down at the pool taking the lines off the fishing
poles and his mother was packing the picnic basket.

"You've skinned your knee. And that bump on your forehead. Whatever happened?"

"I tripped. It's nothing much."

"Does it hurt?" Chester asked.

"No it doesn't." Gilbert turned his back on him. "Go away. I want to be by myself."

: cuspidors :

CHAPTER SEVEN

Home Again, Gone Again

There were times Gilbert wished his father would not be so lively in the morning and this was one of them. It was bad enough to have "Daylight in the swamp, show a leg, rise and shine for light is come," shouted at you up the backstairs on school mornings, but to have it come at you from the dining tent and know, even before he and Chester opened their eyes, that they would go to bed that night in their room on dusty old Blair Street was worse still.

This morning, as if to make certain there would be "none of your dawdling," their father banged the dishpan and sing-songed his "Roll up, tumble up, if you can't get up throw your money up. Come and see live lions stuffed with straw and dead dogs barking at them." He sounded for all the world like some side-show man at the fall fair. But at the table when he read from the Bible and did the Lord's Prayer while your porridge cooled, you could scarcely believe he was the same person.

There was no going to the farm that morning, no stopping in the barnyard to lean over the fence and scratch the back of their favorite pig, no visiting with Mrs. Yarrow in her good smelling kitchen. Their father had gone the afternoon before to settle up for the milk and things and the three of them had gone with him. Mr. Yarrow was not there; he was working in what she called the back forty but he certainly would be seeing them before they left for town. She told their mother she would be churning first thing next morning and would like her to have a pat or two to take along.

There had been no dew to speak of, so they did not need to wait until the sun was on the tents before they took them down. Even so, both would be spread in the attic for weeks to make certain they were dry before they were folded and put away. The canvas Gilbert's and Chester's father and mother made the tents from had "Plymouth" stamped on it. Plymouth was the place in England the boy in *Westward Ho* went to sea from. When Gilbert was reefing the walls of the dining tent and saw that name on the canvas, he liked to believe *Westward Ho* really happened and was not just another of your made-up stories.

When a family is breaking camp everyone has a job to do. Their mother's was to pack the bedding and dishes and to make sure there was pleny of food for dinner after the stove was down. Chester's job, which was not as simple a job as some people might think, was to look after the tent pegs. First he had to scrape the earth off them, then make sure the sod cloth pegs went into the box before the regular ones. This was because you do not peg the sod cloth until all the other pegs are pounded in. Gilbert was responsible for getting every last bit of straw out of the ticks and piling it for Mr. Yarrow to take back in case he needed it. On top of this job he helped his father take down the beds and bundle up the bed slats. You did not take down the potato sacks and fill in the backhouse hole until the very last in case one of you had to go. This time it was a good thing the hole was not filled in sooner, and for the reason the Williamson Cartage wagon did not show up until they finished dinner. The team was the same team that brought them and the driver was the same. The big surprise was that Uncle Abel Williamson was there on the seat beside him.

The reason they were late getting to the sugar bush was because they stopped at a farm to let Uncle Abel size up a team of Clydes the farmer had up for sale. If Mr. Waldy, Aunt Kate's husband, Mr. Wallace and any of them were not talking through their hats, Abel Williamson was the smartest horse trader around and any man who got the best of him would have to get up very early in the morning. The only time Uncle Abel Williamson came out the small end of the horn was the time Grandpa Williamson liked to tell about. It happened while all of them still lived on the Obediah farm. A band of gypsies was camped down at the lake shore and Uncle Abel was out to prove he could get the best of them in a horse trade. One evening after work he took a spavined old farm horse that had the heaves down to the gypsies and came home late that night chuckling to himself. He told the others to go have a look in the barn next morning at the fine white mare he had traded those gypsies out of. But next morning when Grandpa and the others went, there was the white mare stretched out in her stall dead as a doornail. If you listened to Aunt Boo, her brother Abel would have beaten the gypsies if he had not been tippling that night, but Grandpa said this was not the way of it.

Uncle Abel did not help much with the loading. This was on account of the sickness he had. Months and months ago when Gilbert first heard about it, he asked his father what sort of a sickness it was. His father told him it was not a sickness in the proper sense of the term, and that if he knew what was good for him he would not go around talking about it. From what Gilbert heard later, it was not caused by some germ or other but that Uncle Abel had brought it upon himself by lifting something too heavy for him onto a dray. An advert. in the *Christian Guardian* told men what happened to them when they did this. They got what the advert. called a rupture. On the very same page ladies were told of the same thing happening to them if they got "that dragged down feeling." Next thing they knew they caught falling of the womb. There were little pink pills they could take but for the men with rupture the only cure was to send away for a special kind of harness to hold their insides from popping out. Gilbert had no way of knowing if Uncle Abel wore his harness. If he did it did not show.

While their father was filling in the backhouse hole, they and their mother smoothed the ground where the guy rope stakes had been pulled out and after that they tidied up the chips where the woodpile had been. As they took a last look around to make sure nothing was being left, Gilbert thought ahead to what this spot would be like after they were gone. The pale, spindly blades of grass beneath where the beds had been would have sun and rain again, the worn path between where the tents stood would be covered with dead leaves by the time the first snow fell. For weeks this had been his family's home but from now on, the spot would be no different than any other spot in the maple woods. As at Sparrow Lake last August and the August before, this parting look around brought a sort of empty feeling, something like the feeling he had on mornings after Christmas when there were no more presents to open.

The four of them walked behind the wagon until they got to the farm house. Mr. Yarrow was waiting for them with an armful of freshly picked field corn, his first of the season. Instead of butter, Mrs. Yarrow gave them a full sized comb of red top clover honey. She said that the morning's butter was not up to standard, that the cows had got into the wild leeks or at least one of them had. She named it and Mr. Yarrow said sure as shooting this would be the one. Chester whispered could he ask her for a drink of buttermilk and his father told him none of that, there would be no stopping along the way.

Gilbert sat on the heap of tents close behind the driver. Because of his size, Uncle Abel did not take up much room on the seat. He

was not much of a talker and from where Gilbert sat it was easy to
see his side whiskers going in and out. Uncle Abel was the greatest
gum chewer ever. It must be gum, Gilbert reasoned, because if it
was chewing tobacco he would have to spit like everybody else.
Then the juice would leave a stain around his mouth and on his
chin whiskers. But those whiskers were always as white as the
driven snow. Last fall for a whole Saturday Gilbert rode around
town with his Uncle on the express wagon and never saw him spit,
not one single solitary time. His Uncle would not be chewing
slippery elm, that was only for boys, so what else could it be but
gum? Uncle Abel was not the stingy sort yet he never once offered
you a piece. Gilbert's father put his foot down against gum
chewing, he called it a disgusting American habit which came into
Canada with their game of baseball. Chances were Uncle Abel had
heard him say this and that was why he kept his gum to himself.

Except that the noo-come-oot cottage across from the school
corner had been painted, and for some new side walk planks in
front of the Misses Langleys', Blair Street had not changed much
during their weeks at camp. Because of the dry summer the lawn
had not grown much and all of it, except for the strip close to the
side fence, had turned brown. Dust on the front veranda was so
thick you could write your name in it. The first thing their mother
did was open all the doors and windows. Every room was stuffy
and those upstairs were so warm it was hard to breathe. While the
stuff was being unloaded, old Bruce came and tried to sprinkle his
trademark on a back hub of the wagon. But his legs were too short
and his pee went between the spokes. Chester took this for a joke
but it was easy to see Bruce did not like being laughed at and when
Chester tried to pat him he backed away. Or it could have been
Chester's hand smelled of pig and this was the reason Bruce would
not let Chester touch him.

After supper that evening Gilbert and Chester were taking turns
swinging in the barrel stave hammock when they heard sounds
from across the lane in the Dempster yard. Gilbert shinnied up the
back fence and walked along it to the woodshed roof. Mr.
Dempster had his hose going and was washing down his fish
wagon. Gilbert waited until he looked up then waved and called
across was Tommy home?

"Not for a couple more weeks, not till school opens."

"He must like it in Port Dover."

"Seems so." Mr. Dempster went on with his hosing. "Ask your

father to step over one of these days. No hurry, whenever he gets
around to it.''

Chester had stopped swinging and was asking to be given a hand
up but Gilbert jumped down and made for the back steps with
Chester at his heels. His father and mother were in the kitchen and
when he gave them the message he saw them look at one another.
"Not again, surely," she said.

"It's possible Frances. But let us not jump to conclusions."

Gilbert was all ears, eager to hear more but that was all the good
it did him. His mother went on with what she was doing and then
she said it had been a long day and it was high time Chester went to
bed. "You too Gilbert. Up you go, the both of you."

Gilbert knew it was no sense arguing, least of all with his father
there, but if she thought he did not see through her she had another
think coming. It was as plain as the nose on your face they wanted
him and Chester out of the way so they could talk.

Next day after their father mowed the lawn and while Gilbert was
raking it, Nick came along and they had a good talk over the front
fence. For a while last summer Nick visited his uncle at the
Junction who was a fireman on the shunting engine and let him ride
in the cab a couple of times. But this summer Nick had to stay
home. All the same, he had things to talk about which went to show
Blair Street was a pretty good place to live after all. For one thing,
Nick's name was in the paper over a four pound black bass, a small
mouth, he caught below the upper bridge. This was supposed to be
a town record. Nick said the man who wrote about it could not be
much of a fisherman because he did not ask what bait Nick used.
The truth was Nick caught it with his hands. He was walking across
the upper bridge when he saw the bass flapping among the stones
where the dye water from the knitting mill ran into the river, so he
went down and grabbed it. His mother cooked it but it had such a
queer taste they buried it in their garden under a rose bush. Nick's
mother said there was nothing like fish for roses. Nick promised to
show Gilbert the paper. Gilbert said he knew the man who must
have written it and when he described him sure enough it turned out
to be Aunt Trixie's friend Mr. Pickering.

They had a good laugh over that, but the next thing Nick told was
nothing to laugh about. This was about the skeleton some men
found while they were emptying the lime kiln across the river, the
one nearest the railway bridge. Except for its skull and one of its leg
bones, it was all broken up. At first Chief Rooney and Detective

Trotter—Archie McClintock called him Defective Trotter—
believed the skeleton belonged to one of Foxy Foster's gang who
turned up missing during the winter. But then they decided the
skeleton belonged to some tramp who crawled into the bottom of
the lime kiln to keep warm and while he slept a cartload of
limestone was dumped down on top of him. So there he lay all
bloody and smashed up until the limestone was fired. Chief Rooney
let Dr. Kirkland keep the skull in his office. Nick did not know
what the police did with the rest of the skeleton, no funeral or
anything.

There was one more thing Nick had to tell and this was that by
the looks of things he owned a dog. Ernie Yates gave it to him and
for the reason Ernie's father would not let him keep it. Before
Ernie got it, it hung around the tannery. By all the signs it had no
home of its own and did not belong to anybody. The trouble was
that Ernie's family already had a dog and Ernie's father was not for
having two of them to feed and buy tags for in case Defective
Trotter came snooping around. Nick named the dog Sport. He
said Sport was a happy dog and another good thing about him was
that we would be easy to feed, he would eat just about anything.
Nick said that until Sport got used to his new home he was keeping
him tied up. He asked Gilbert to come along and have a look.
Gilbert said he would but first he must finish raking the lawn and
stand around while his father inspected it.

As it turned out, their father was across the lane at the
smokehouse talking with Mr. Dempster and by the time he came
back and inspected the lawn supper was on the table. Next there
was the woodbox to fill and because next day was Sunday, the rule
was to carry in a few extra armfuls. After that, Gilbert had his own
and Chester's boots to shine ready for morning church. At first his
father was not for letting him go, gadding about at all hours he
called it, but then he said he could but to be quick about it, tonight
was tub night. Chester was allowed to come. Gilbert would sooner
have gone by himself, but with his father standing right there he
knew better than to raise a fuss about it.

Nick was dead right about one thing. Sport certainly was a happy
dog. All you had to do was look at him and he walloped his tail so
hard his hind end shook, not wagging it like ordinary dogs do, but
swinging it round and round. He was so glad to see you that he
wriggled. He smiled, he really did. He was half again as big as
Bruce. His hair was long, black all over and sort of tousled. The

only thing you could say against him was that he smelled, t ough
nothing like the smell he gave off when he lived at the tannery Nick
said. More and more of his smell was wearing off, Nick said, and
unless you put your nose down close and took a good deep sniff
you could scarcely notice it. Chester put his nose down close and
said he liked the smell.

Morning church was about the same as last time except that when
Mr. D.V. Schiller gave the announcements he said that God willing
Sunday School would start up again, "one week hence at two
p.m." that a teacher for a class of intermediate boys was urgently
needed and it was hoped a member of the congregation would be
guided to come forward. Another exception was that Aunt Martha,
Uncle Abel's peppery-wife, sat between Aunt Boo and Gilbert
instead of in the Abel Williamson pew across the aisle. Every time
Aunt Martha took a breath—it sounded more like a sigh—her
corsets creaked. The reason Gilbert thought of her as peppery was
partly because of her quick eyes and her snappy way of speaking,
also it was because of the story told about her when her two girls
were small. One day when the two of them were being pesky she
stopped what she was doing and said, "For two pins I would pop
the pair of you down the well, sit on the lid and have a quiet cup of
tea." The reason Uncle Abel gave for not being a regular attendant
was that he had a sick horse to look after. Aunt Trixie said it beat
the Dutch how many of Uncle Abel's horses took sick on Sunday.
She said they must have the Sunday morning sickness. When
Gilbert's father heard Trixie telling this he said he saw nothing
amusing in it. The town could do with more Abel Williamsons'
particularly on the school board. He called Uncle Abel one of the
most generous and open-handed men he knew and Aunt Kate's
husband agreed with him. The Abel Williamson stable gave away
garden manure for only the cost of hauling whereas every livery
stable in town made you pay through the nose for it.

On Monday their father returned from the post office with his
Mail and Empire and a letter from Grandfather Egan which
knocked Gilbert's plan of playing with Nick and Sport higher than
Gilroy's kite. Grandfather needed help with what he called
"cradling the oats." His oldest son had left Huron county years
ago to take up land in the new province of Manitoba, his youngest
son ran a drugstore in Ottawa, so their father, the in-between, was
the only son he could turn to. On his walk from the post office their
father must have made up his mind the four of them would go, but

when he said this to their mother she shook her head. "With Chester starting kindergarten I'll have my hands full with sewing, right up to the day school opens. Except for his Sunday best he has scarcely a decent dud to his name, and Gilbert is not much better off."

"Oh come now Frances. The change will do you good."

But as usual their mother stuck to her guns. "You and Gilbert go. Chester and I will look after things here."

Gilbert expected Chester to put up a howl over that but he kept mum. You could never tell about Chester. Sometimes he would fly off the handle over nothing, other times he was as meek as Moses.

Usually the week before school opened was when Gilbert's father bought him his boots for the year. But this year, because the weather might change or they might be away longer than expected, his father took him downtown to the Morrison and Son shoestore the very day after the letter came. Old Mr. Morrison knew all there was to know about boots and his son was not far behind him. Old Mr. Morrison was a Wee Free Presbyterian and his son was a Baptist, so this took care of those two religions. And because there was no Methodist, Catholic, Salvation Army or Holy Roller shoestore in the town, it took care of them too. Old Mr. Morrison had mutton chop whiskers on the style of Doctor Scanlon's. His son looked a little like Gilbert's and Chester's father except that he did not wax his mustache and had even less hair on his head.

The first thing Gilbert's father and old Mr. Morrison talked about was not how much the boots cost or what size but what sort of leather, oak tanned soles sewn or pegged, how the insides were made such as counter, vamp and welt. Even Gilbert knew the welt was important. If the welts wore out after the boots had been half-soled a second time they might just as well be thrown away for all the good they were. Toe caps too were parts you had to know about. The toe caps on his last year's pair were scuffed by Christmas and his father just about put a tin ear on him because of this. Steering with your toes when you were sleigh riding was what did the scuffing. But if you did as you were told and wore your moccasins you most likely banged your toes on lumps of icy snow or frozen horse buns.

The pair his father finally decided on cost a dollar and twenty-five cents. A pair just like them but with pull on straps cost ten cents more but his father did not think they were worth the difference. The first thing Gilbert did when he got home was try on the new boots to show his mother. She said they seemed a wise choice and Gilbert thought so too. They were his first ones with leather laces but they had hardly any squeak. When Mr. Mullin went up the aisle with the collection plate you could hear the squeak of his boots all over the place. There were times at school when Gilbert could hardly keep from laughing over what would happen if he came with boots like those. When old Burwell sent him to the blackboard or gave him permission to go for a drink at the water pail his boots would make so much noise she could not hear herself think. Then when she got after him for disturbing the class he would up and tell her to go talk to his father. My father makes me wear the boots, they have nothing to do with me. And when she went he could fairly hear his father taking her down a peg or two. Though come to think of it, his father probably wouldn't. Gilbert had not forgotten the time at the dinner table when he started telling something against old Burwell. No sooner were the words out of his mouth than his father laid down his knife and fork and gave him that straight, hard look. "No more of that," his father said. "A boy who behaves himself in class will have nothing to complain of." It showed how teachers stick together and that when you have one for a father you cannot be sure which side he is on.

For the train ride to Huron county, Gilbert was allowed to wear the lacrosse shoes his father brought him from Toronto—Chester's were blue with white stripes, Gilbert's were brown all over—but his father packed Gilbert's old boots just in case. The train they took was called the Flying Dutchman. Its station was back of the ice house and its track ran under that end of the railway bridge. While the family lived in the double house on that side of the river, Gilbert had walked the track for several miles with his father when they went collecting specimens, and even then weeds grew between the ties. The Flying Dutchman engine was only a two-wheeler but it had a larger cow-catcher than any three-wheeler and its smoke stack was taller, not counting the spark catcher. Its whistle sort of quavered like the yell of some big boy whose voice is changing. The Flying Dutchman had two cars, one for people to sit in and one for freight. It took the Flying Dutchman at least an hour to get to the Junction and in places along the way its engine huffed and puffed so hard that Gilbert wondered if they would ever get there.

The Junction was nothing much, no flower garden beside the station, no flagpole either. If Ruby Greer had to live in a place like this, Gilbert thought she would mighty soon stop going around with her nose in the air. The blackboard said the train they had to take was two hours late. There was a hot breeze and dust was blowing, so after they walked back and forth on the platform for a while, they went and sat in the waiting room which until nearly train time they had to themselves. The waiting room had only one spittoon and by the look of the floor around it the aim of tobacco chewers who used it was so bad they would not be able to hit the broad side of a barn. The stationmaster was nowhere in sight, his wicket was closed though his telegraph was ticking inside. While Gilbert was sitting there wishing the train would come, his father got after him for slouching. "Sit up straight and take your hands out of your pockets, otherwise I'll have your mother sew them up. If you do not mend your ways we'll have you in shoulder braces, mark my words."

The train they took had about as many cars as the westbound at home and it had the same size of engine. The car they sat in had soft seats instead of slats. Gilbert's father let him sit next the window. After the train had been going for a while a man in his shirt sleeves came along the aisle selling candies, fruit and stuff. He made jokes with people as he came along. Three or four bought things. The lady in the seat ahead bought a banana for her little girl. The girl leaned over the back of the seat and peeled the banana, then instead of eating it like a civilized person she sort of sucked on it. She had freckles all over her face and she kept staring as if he was not there. The man with the tray stopped beside their seat but their father did not so much as lower his newspaper. There were peppermints on the tray like those in Mrs. Devon's store. Gilbert tried to raise the window but could not budge it. He asked his father to do it but was told to leave well enough alone because of the cinders. From what Gilbert could see, the part of the country the train was running through was about the same as around home. He knew Huron county had the same name as a tribe of Indians and watched for some of their wigwams beside the track.

At one of the stops a family got on and took the seats across the aisle. The train had no more than started when the lady opened a cardboard box and all of them began eating. They had sandwiches, doughnuts and pieces of what looked to be chocolate cake with half a walnut stuck in the icing. Gilbert knew what his father thought of people who ate on trains. On his way home from Toronto he watched a man and a woman stuffing themselves. "Why some people feel compelled to put food into their stomachs the moment they step onto a train is beyond my power of comprehension,'' Gilbert had overheard him say to their mother. "Without the word of a lie, Frances, each of them ate enough to satisfy a hired man.''

After a while Gilbert tired of looking out the window and counting telegraph poles so he closed his eyes and pressed his forehead against the glass. This made the rumble of the train seem louder and if it had not been for the clickety-click of the rails the sound was almost the same sound as rushing water. Once when the train crossed a bridge, the rumbling became hollow and deeper, something like water tumbling over the dam in flood time. He pictured himself in a canoe being swept downstream mile after mile paddling for dear life and not knowing what was waiting for him round the next bend.

The engine whistled—three sharp toots. His father nudged him. ''Sit up and straighten your blouse. We'll soon be getting off, we're almost there.''

"Flying Dutchman".

CHAPTER EIGHT

With Music To Close

The farm they were going to was on a gravel road a mile or so from the flag station and from what Gilbert's father told him as they walked along, it could scarcely be called a farm at all. Grandfather and Grandmother Egan had left the old farm and moved onto this one after their oldest son left home to take up land in Manitoba and try to better himself. Nobody seemed to want the old farm, Gilbert's father said, and for the reason it was what people called a "hard scrabble" one. This was why Grandfather Egan never made more than a bare living from it and why every winter he took his broadaxe and went into the woods to hew timber. The new farm was only ten acres at most, some in pasture, the rest in crops of one kind or another. But what it did have besides a large carpenter shop was the most up-to-date house of any around at the time Grandfather Egan built it. "Cove siding, mullioned windows, tongue and groove flooring, every stick of it hand planed and grooved."

There was something else Gilbert was told as they walked along and it was something which knocked those other things into a cocked hat. It was that his father had a third brother whose name was Eph and who lived with Grandfather and Grandmother Egan. He was big and strong as an ox but he was what people called simple. He had the mind of a child. Eph was harmless and easy to get along with but Gilbert must be careful never to tease him or play tricks on him. If he did this Eph would fly off the handle and then there was no telling what might happen. Besides being simple, Eph was not always able to form his words properly. So for these and other reasons Gilbert's father did not name, Eph had never been to school. He could draw the letters but he was unable to either read or write. "But make no mistake, he understands what is said to him."

"What do I call him, Uncle Eph?"

His father answered no, that Eph would be enough.

The gravel road was not the easiest to walk on in lacrosse shoes and Gilbert was more than ready to turn in at the gate. Grandfather

Egan must have spotted them coming because there he was halfway down the path to meet them. He did not shake hands but as they walked along the side of the house to the back porch he put his hand on Gilbert's shoulder and kept it there until they came to the steps. Grandmother Egan was at the door. There was no hugging or kissing, nothing like that but she seemed pleased to see them. There was no sign of Eph. Grandmother said supper would soon be on the table and Gilbert's father sent him to the wash bench on the porch. He was drying his hands on the roller towel when he saw a big man with a bushy black beard crossing the yard from the stable. The man's knees sort of folded in which gave him a wobbly way of walking. Gilbert's father came out quickly and the two met at the top of the steps. The man was Eph all right.

"Richard, Richard, my bridder Richard!" His voice was high, something like a woman's. He plunked his hands on his brother's shoulders and rocked him back and forth. "Glad to see you, glad to see you."

"Glad to see you too, Eph. And see who I brought with me? He's my boy Gilbert."

"Gibbert, Gibbert, glad to see you Gibbert." Eph held out his hand and Gilbert took it. He did not feel in the least afraid. He somehow knew they would be friends.

For supper Eph sat at a side table by himself. It was easy to see he was not a tidy eater. He gulped his food so fast that bits of it fell from his lips and stuck to his beard. Also every now and then his arm gave such a jerk that the food dropped off his spoon and back onto his plate. The jerk was not as hard a jerk as Professor Vance's but all the same it was that sort of jerk. At first Gilbert thought Eph had caught the same sickness as Professor Vance caught in Paris, France. But then he decided it could not be and for the reason Eph had never gone as far from home as to school, let alone to Paris, France.

After they had their dessert—it was gooseberry pie—Grandmother Egan told Eph it was time for him to shut the hens in their coop. Gilbert would have asked to go with him but as Eph was leaving, Grandfather Egan took out his pipe, jackknife and plug of tobacco so Gilbert decided the hens could wait. Except for once at Archie McClintock's he had never been in a house when a man smoked a pipe. To sit at table right next to one who did, and on top of that who was his very own Grandfather, was too good a chance to miss.

Pretending not to watch, Gilbert took in every move. Holding the plug between the thumb and forefinger of his left hand, palm turned up, his Grandfather cut thin slices from the end of the plug, closed his knife, crumbled the slices in the palm of that hand with the heel of the other and pressed the crumbled tobacco evenly into the pipe bowl with his middle finger. Next he went to the stove, took one of the long slivers of wood from the shelf, lighted it at the damper hole, held it to the bowl and puffed. Gilbert knew the name of these slivers because in camp his father used them to save matches. They were called spills. While his Grandfather was at the stove Gilbert kept an eye on his Grandmother but she went on talking with his father which was a pretty sure sign she must have given up against tobacco long ago. The plug was the same brand Archie McClintock's father used. It had the same little tin snow-shoe pressed onto it. The other brand of tobacco had only a plain tin heart. Both brands were store tobacco. Grandfather Egan must have given up growing his own.

It was easy to see Grandfather Egan enjoyed his smoking. Gilbert had loads of things he wanted to talk about—did his Grandfather still go fishing, where did he keep his fishing pole, how big was his broadaxe—but he kept them for later. Instead he watched the puffs of smoke and sniffed in the smell of it. He liked the smell better than the smell of Aunt Kate's husband's cigars and if he decided to be a smoker when he grew up he most likely would go in for pipes. When Grandfather Egan finished his smoke, he put away his pipe, stood up and said, "Now for the chores."

The talk was not much and Grandmother Egan did most of it—what did Frances pay for eggs and butter? how were the boys off for mittens? did the church have the same minister? Right there, Gilbert thought she was in for an argument. For one thing, his father was on the church's Quarterly Official Board along with Doctor Scanlon, Mr. Mullin and Grandpa Williamson and so had a say in choosing the minister. And for another thing, when people were leaving the church Gilbert had heard them say they enjoyed the sermon. Even snippy Aunt Martha told Reverend Allister his sermon had refreshed her when he shook hands with her at the church door after morning service. So no wonder Gilbert was surprised when his father let her have her say and did not stand up to her.

Eph had taken the two water pails from the wash bench and was across the yard at the pump filling them. Gilbert trotted over and watched. Eph emptied the pails into the rain barrel at the corner of

the house and came to fill them again. Gilbert asked if he could
help pump.

Eph gave him a pat on the back. "Good boy, good boy, pump,
pump."

Eph carried those two pails into the kitchen and while he was
gone, Gilbert lifted the handle as high as it would go and listened to
water gurgling down the pipe back into the well. The sound made
him think of bubbles rising from some sunken treasure ship, pirate
gold, pieces-of-eight and all like that. He worked the handle to
repeat the sound but all that came was a coughing. He began to
feel frightened. He must have broken something, what was Eph
going to do to him? Now he was for it! He knew better than to run.
For one thing, Eph was bound to catch him and for another
running would be a sure sign he had done wrong. He put his hands
in his pockets, moseyed over to the rain barrel and was pretending
to be interested in what he saw by the time Eph returned with the
empty pails. The minute Eph finds out something is broken, he will
lose his temper and get after me, Gilbert thought. From the corner
of his eye he watched Eph work the handle. The handle came down
with a bang. But instead of losing his temper, all Eph did was bring
one of the pails to the barrel and half-fill it. "That old pump play
tricks on Eph, all the time it do," he chuckled. "But Eph fix it. He
do, yes he do."

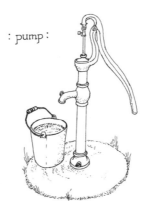

: pump :

Gilbert followed him back to the pump. Eph raised the handle as
far as it would go, poured water from the pail into the top of the
pump and worked the handle up and down so fast that you could
scarcely see the end of it. A coughing sound came from the pipe as

if some deep voiced animal down there was clearing his throat. In no time at all, water surged from the spout and splashed onto the planks.

Eph tilted back his head and laughed. When Eph laughed his mouth was a round, dark hole in the middle of his beard. Knowing he had not broken the pump was a load off Gilbert's mind and he felt like coming straight out and taking the blame. But in case Eph took it for a trick played on him while his back was turned he decided it was better to keep mum about it though one way you looked at it this was a sneaky thing to do.

That evening Gilbert was allowed to stay up until it started to get dark. Almost the first thing his father did after taking him up to their room was tell him to have a good look at the bed they were to sleep in. "Well seasoned black walnut, every inch of it. A spool bed, they call it. I well remember watching your Grandfather make it when I was no older than Chester. Your Ottawa uncle and I slept in it up to the time I left home, and I dare say it's been in use off and on since. Yet it's as perfect as the day it was made. Run your hand over the headboard—nary a flaw."

While Gilbert undressed, his father unpacked the telescope suitcase and laid their flannelette nightshirts on the foot of the bed. Gilbert's had red stripes going up and down. The one their mother made for Chester had green stripes. This was so they could tell them apart and no squabbling. the one she made for their father was white all over. The top quilt on the bed was exactly the same as the one Grandmother Egan made for them to have on their bed at home. Log cabin pattern she said it was.

Gilbert half expected his father would stand around to see that he said his prayers but he didn't. The bed on Gilbert's side was softer than their bed at home and by the feel of it his father's side was every bit as soft. There were no lumps as in a straw tick after you have slept on it for weeks. He wished his father had left the bedroom door open so he could get some idea of what was going on downstairs, what they talked about, all like that. The floor of Chester's and his bedroom had a grating where a stovepipe hole used to be before the house had the furnace put in. Their bedroom was above the livingroom and while you were waiting to get to sleep you heard the talking even though you could not catch every word. Also after the hanging lamp in the livingroom was going, enough light came through the grating to make moving shapes on the ceiling wallpaper—knights on horseback, Man Friday's footprints on the

sand, Hallowe'en false faces, wigwams, all like that. Sometimes he
gave Chester a poke and told him to look, but Chester would not
even try. This was the way he was. Often the best pictures came
when your body was ready for sleep but things kept popping into
your head, no matter what—grab bag, which-hand-is-it-
in, button-button-who's-got-the-button and that other guessing
game they played at Ernie's birthday party. Some nights when you
lie awake your mind is like a squirrel up a tree, jumping from
branch to branch and getting nowhere. *Jumping, jumping...*
pumping, pumping...spittoons, lake loons, take a jump in the lake
Miss Burwell...Andy Moore was a freckled little country boy
as tough as a pine knot...And where were your eyes when you saw
him Miss Burwell?...How many times must I tell you not to snap
your fingers, Miss Burwell? Simply raise your hand if you need to
leave the room....Tea, coffee and cocoa from which we get such
pleasant drinks are all of them some part of a plant. Read that
again, Miss Burwell. How many more times must I tell you to hold
your book properly and not to mumble, Miss Burwell? Try it again
Miss Burwell....Clickety-click, clickety-click...Two-wheelers,
three-wheelers...John Brown had a little Indian, four, five, six
little Indian boys....Well I declare here comes stuck-up Miss Ruby
Greer. Have a chaw of my tobacco Ruby Greer. Take a shot at my
spittoon, Miss Ruby Greer....When all the world is young lad and
all the trees are green....We shall come rejoicing, bringing in the
sheaves....

They must have talked late down there in the kitchen. When
Gilbert came awake there was a light in the bedroom but he lay still
and did not let on. He heard the sound of his father's watch being
wound. His father got into the long white nightshirt and knelt at his
side of the bed. His head was bowed and the bald spot showed. His
prayer was not a long one. He got into bed, reached and snuffed out
the light between his thumb and finger. Gilbert did not see him do
this but he must have because if you blow out a candle instead of
snuffing it the wick smoulders and gives off a greasy smell. Candles
are made of tallow which is the part of the sheep you do not eat.
Mutton is the part you eat.

At home when his father read out parts of the letter, Gilbert had
no more idea than the man on the moon what "cradling the oats"

meant so he upped and asked. The answer he got was that cradling is a form of scything and that surely the rest of the operation spoke for itself. As things turned out, it pretty nearly did. After he had eaten his porridge—salted just right which the porridge his father made sometimes wasn't—he helped Eph feed the pig and watched his Grandmother strain the morning's milk. Then he went to the field back of the stable where his father and Grandfather were hard at work. His Grandfather scythed the outside row and his father took the next row around the field. At first glance their scythes seemed the same as the one Mr. Yarrow used, but when he came as close as he dared without being in the way, he spotted the difference. These two scythes had a rack of light wooden spokes back of their blades. You did not need to have any imagination to speak of to understand why the racks were called cradles, and for the simple reason this was what they looked like. At every swing the cut stalks fell with a slight rustling sound onto the cradles. After the men took three or so steps—they swung with each step—they tilted their scythe handles and dumped a cradle load onto the stubble behind them. For minute after minute the two swung and stepped in time. Then one or the other would take a shorter or a longer swing and the time began again. Step, swing, step swing, step swing, dump, step step step, swing, swing step swing, on and on they went. At the far end of the field the oats stood so high that only the top half of his father showed, and not even that much of his Grandfather who was shorter but had wide, thick shoulders.

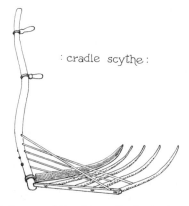

: cradle scythe :

Gilbert stood for a while then climbed the snake fence and perched where two top rails crossed and made a sort of seat. The next time they worked their way to his end of the field, Gilbert's

father told him to ask his Grandmother for a pail and dipper and
to bring them a drink. She gave him a smaller pail than those on the
wash bench and a mug for them to drink from. Eph was nowhere
around so Gilbert worked the pump himself. The water felt icy
cold and it had more of a taste than the tap water at home. He set
the pail in the shade of the fence and when the men worked their
way back to his end of the field he carried it out to them. While
they were taking a breather and resting on their scythes, Gilbert
asked if it would be all right for him to go to the stable and have a
look at the horse. The horse's name was Judy.

Gilbert's father shook his head but Grandfather Egan said,
"Why not? Just don't go into her stall and see you stand well back
from her heels. She's inclined to be skittish."

The cow had been let out to pasture that morning right after it
was milked, so except for a few wandering hens, Judy had the
stable to herself. She turned her head and looked at Gilbert as he
came in and when he spoke her name her ears lifted to show she
heard. The air in the stable was not anything as cool as the air in
Mr. Yarrow's stable under his bank barn but it was a whole lot
cooler than the air outside. The milking stool was across from the
stalls, close to the wall where harness hung. Gilbert sat on the stool
and partly unlaced his lacrosse shoes to cool his ankles. The reason
he had on his lacrosse shoes was on account of the stubble. . . . One
thing he had learned in camp that summer was that your feet have
to be tough as tough to walk barefoot on stubble. On top of that
there are always thistles. While he was fiddling with the laces one of
the hens decided to explore the straw and horse buns close to Judy's
hind feet. Gilbert expected Judy to let go with a hoof and lift the
hen higher than Gilroy's kite. But no, she never so much as let on
she knew the hen was there. The hen kept on scratching and
pecking and once she stuck her head between the hooves. But
nothing happened and after she had had her fill she moseyed out
the door.

Gilbert thought for a while then decided to find out for himself if
Judy was really a kicker. Not that his Grandfather would ever tell
an out-and-out lie, but from stories about him, such as the one
about slicing the skin off his helper's behind, he was not against
playing jokes on people. Gilbert laced his shoes, found a long
straight straw and went to the foot of the cow stall. The wall
between the two stalls was higher than his head so he was pretty
sure Judy could not see what he was up to. The post where the wall

ended was twice as big around as a stovepipe. Without showing himself he leaned against it, reached and tickled Judy's hind leg with the straw. Quick as a flash Judy let fly with a kick that jolted the post against the side of his head with such force that for a second or two he thought he was a gone goose. On top of that Judy let out a snort—it was more like a scream—which sent him out of the stable on the run. His next big mistake was going back to the field instead of keeping out of sight until he got over his scare. His father was starting another row, his Grandfather was further along it, and if Gilbert had had as much sense as God gave geese he would have vamoosed out of there even faster than he came. Instead he stood inside the gate and watched his Grandfather upend his scythe, take his whetstone from his hip pocket, spit on it and touch up the long curved blade, zing-zang, zing-zang.

His father straightened and came to the gate. One look was enough. "What happened? What have you been up to?"

"Judy—she kicked at me."

"At you? You went into her stall in spite of what you were told? Is that it?"

"No, Poppa, no. I was just standing there and she up and kicked at me."

"What's this, what's this?" Grandfather Egan called.

"He says the mare kicked at him."

Grandfather Egan put down his scythe and came. "Are you hurt, lad?"

"Nary a scratch, she gave him a scare, that's all."

"She's much too free with those heels of hers. One of these days I'll take her in hand, teach her a lesson she'll not soon forget."

Gilbert was feeling more and more of a stinker. "Maybe it wasn't me she took a kick at. Maybe it was a fly. Maybe a mosquito, more like."

"You and your maybes! The fact is you could have been badly hurt. Henceforth you are not to go into the stable by yourself. Is that clearly understood?"

"Yes Poppa."

"Then see you abide by it." He did not look as cross as he sounded. "A fine one I'd be, taking you home to your mother covered in bandages, wouldn't I?"

After the two went on with their cradling, Gilbert squatted Indian fashion with his back against the fence and gave himself a good hard talking to. How would you like it if someone played a

mean trick on you then went and told lies about you? You would
want to kick the stuffing out of them. But because Judy is only a
horse you think it does not matter. But when Grandfather
lambastes her it is going to matter a whole lot. And all because of
me. In the Ten Commandments, if you tell lies about a person you
are bearing false witness and then you are in for it. A fine one you
are, putting the blame on a poor dumb animal so you won't get into
trouble! He thought of the coal wagon driver Nick and he saw
beating his horse because it could not pull the heavily loaded wagon
up the slope from the tracks. The horse had fallen, its breath came
in gasps and the whites of its eyes showed, yet the man kept
on beating it with the butt end of his whip. He might have killed it
then and there if Police Chief Rooney had not come along, collared
him and marched him off to the lockup. If that driver had tried to
put up a fight he would have come out the small end of the horn.
Chief Rooney had been a bare-knuckle prize fighter. He grew up in
the old house next to the tannery and he went to Blair Street School.
In Chicago he knocked a man clean out of the ring, Mr. Waldy
said. Mr. Wallace took care of the horse until its owner came and
got it. Gilbert did not believe for one single, solitary minute his
Grandfather would treat a horse like that. Still if he taught Judy a
lesson she would not forget, he would punish her in some way. And
all because of a two-faced Gilbert Egan.

Gilbert looked up. His Grandmother stood in the gateway. In her
long black dress and starched sunbonnet she was at lest a head
taller than his mother, straight up and down in front and behind,
no bustle. She hitched her skirt high enough for her elastic-sided
boots to show, crossed the stubble to the nearest heap of cradled
oats and began picking up straws one at a time, keeping some,
discarding others. On account of the lies he told about Judy, Gilbert
would sooner have stayed where he was. But in case she spotted
him and got the notion he was hiding, he straightened, stood by the
fence until the pins and needles went out of his legs then went to
her. Sure enough, she needed the straws to make hats. He tried to
help but almost all his straws were not the sort she wanted; they
were either too thick or too thin, too short or too long, too soft or
too brittle, so he stood back and watched. She gathered the straws
in a fold of her apron and told him to come with her to the house,
that she had a little treat for him. On their way there Gilbert
spotted Eph bobbing up and down between the rows of the potato
patch. The treat turned out to be a slice of what she called Irish

Soda bread, fresh from the oven and well buttered. She gave him a second slice to take to Eph. He held off starting on his until he got to the patch so they could eat together. It felt good to be with Eph, not having to think of the fix he was in over Judy, nor having to make polite talk with his Grandmother on account of what she said to him—such as what a lucky boy he was to live so near a school and that his father had had to walk miles to one over a corduroy road (whatever that was), did he work hard at his lessons and remember always to obey his teacher?

The job Eph was doing was one Gilbert knew about from helping Ernie in the Yates' potato patch. The job was picking potato bugs, the hard shell ones with striped backs, their maggots and their clusters of eggs on the undersides of leaves. For the bugs and maggots you used a can with water in it and a stick or piece of shingle. You batted the bugs and maggots into the can and you squished the eggs, leaf and all, between your fingers. Eph found him a can and a stick and they worked side by side, each on his side of the row. Every so often they straightened, looked at each other and laughed, not because they had anything special to laugh about, simply because this was how they felt together. If there had been a tap, Gilbert would have shown Eph the game Ernie and he invented with potato bugs. They named it their over Niagara Falls in a barrel game. You took the biggest of the bugs, laid it on the flat of your hand, held your hand under the spout and turned the handle. Splash, over Niagara Falls in a barrel went mister potato bug! Gilbert did his best to tell Eph how the game went but Eph did not understand. He did not know men went over the Falls in barrels and he had never heard of Niagara Falls. Even so that did not bother him so everything was fine.

After supper when Grandfather Egan came from doing his chores, lo and behold he had hitched Judy to the wagon. He said they needed whey for the pig and and he invited Gilbert to come for the ride. Gilbert knew about whey because Mr. Yarrow sometimes fed it to his pigs but he did not know where it came from. Well, he soon found out. It came from cheese factories. The one Grandfather Egan drove to was straight along the gravel road, a few miles beyond the flag station. Judy took them there at a fast clip. His Grandfather let Gilbert hold the reins while he tied Judy to the hitching post. He had a tall milk can as big around as a keg roped to the box at the back of the buggy. He unroped it, swung it up to the loading platform and took it inside. Gilbert started to follow him when he saw Judy turn her head and look straight at him. When a dog looks at you, you can tell by its eyes if it is friendly or if it has it in for you. But all Judy's eyes told was that she was watching him. You can tell what a horse is thinking by watching its ears. If they are laid back, you had better watch out. Judy's ears were not laid back, they were straight up but they did not turn when he spoke to her.

Unlike Chester, Gilbert was not much for stories about humans and animals talking back and forth to each other, but then and there he would have given just about anything to have Judy tell him what was on her mind. If she had been an easy-going horse like Mr. Dempster's Nell, he would have patted her to show he was sorry for the trick he played on her and for the lie he told about her. But Judy was far from being easy-going. During the drive Grandfather Egan said she was feeling her oats and unless he kept a tight rein on her she would get the bit in her teeth. This is what horses do when they run away and smash things. Uncle Abel Williamson bought a horse who did this and got it from one of the livery stables for next to nothing because they could do nothing with it and they were afraid it would run away and people would be killed. It took Uncle Abel months to break it of the habit and even then he did not trust anyone else to drive it.

Judy was not a big horse but she was just about the prettiest one Gilbert had ever seen, not your sorrel or your chestnut but in between. During the drive home what he should do was tell his Grandfather what he had done to her. This way, he would not have to own up to it in front of his father. Just thinking about doing it made him feel better and he was sure he would feel better still after he came right out and told.

Grandfather Egan and the cheese factory man carried the can by its handles and set it at the edge of the loading platform. Grandfather Egan hopped down and, before the man could help him, he hoisted the can onto the back of the buggy, roped it, unhitched Judy, took up the reins and they were off.

Gilbert was not one of those who dive right in when they go swimming, he liked to wade in step by step, getting the feel of the water before he ducked. He was the same about owning up to something. So as they drove, he tried out different beginnings in his head...*Grandfather when you said you would teach Judy a lesson...What I forgot to say when I came from the stable...The real reason Judy kicked at me...* These were not the beginnings he needed, they had a made-up sound. He was trying to think up better ones when all of a sudden Judy snorted, lunged forward and reared.

"So that's the way of it, my girl?" Grandfather Egan wrapped the reins around his hands, leaned forward with his feet against the dashboard, clicked his tongue and told Judy, "Git!" which it was plain to see was exactly what she wanted. Gravel flew from the wheels and at every bump if Gilbert had not held on for dear life he would have been lifted clear off the seat. Pebbles from Judy's heels rattled against the dashboard and once when the buggy swerved it might have overturned, whey and all, if Grandfather Egan had not known what he was doing. By the time the station came in sight Judy was ready to slow down but Grandfather Egan showed her who was boss and did not let her. He slapped her back with the reins and made her keep going. She was all for turning in at their gate but he hawed her and took her farther along the road until her trot became a walk. When he unhitched her at the stable she went to her stall meek as Moses. Gilbert pumped her a pail of water for when she cooled off, but he did not follow his Grandfather into the stable. He did not feel like it.

Later that evening before his father came up, Gilbert lay on his side of the spool bed and imagined what he would tell Judy if she was a story-book horse and could understand what he was saying. He would give her a good hard talking to. On the drive home I was all ready to own up, he would tell her, and so I would have if you had given me half a chance. And another thing. When you kicked the post what you were trying to do was kick me so I did not tell them an out-and-out lie about you. Yes, and what if you had upset the buggy? You might have killed my Grandfather, then who would grow your oats and give it to you? Eph couldn't and my Grandmother couldn't and you would starve to death. I do not mean I will never own up but I do not see why I should take all the blame. I would have, though, if you had behaved yourself but now you will just have to wait till I am good and ready.

Two days later by mid-afternoon the last of the oats had been cradled and stooked. The way they stooked it was to stand the sheaves in short rows one propped against the other. The way they made the sheaves was to take an armful of the cradled bundles, tie them around with some of their own straws twisted

into a sort of rope and the ends tucked in. Gilbert's father allowed
him to have a try at doing this but it was not as easy as it looked and
he made a poor fist of it.

After supper while the grownups sat at table and talked, Gilbert
helped Eph fill the woodbox. Eph got down on his knees beside the
woodpile, held out both arms and Gilbert put on the wood. "More
Gibbert, more, more," Eph kept saying until it was a wonder he
could see over the load. When he started to the house, Gilbert
thought for sure some of the sticks would tumble off but none did
in spite of Eph's wobble. After that they sat together on the back
steps watching the barn swallows until it started to get dark and the
bats came out. Then they went in and sat on the bench beside the
table where Eph had his meals. Gilbert was not paying much
attention to the talk until he heard his Grandfather say that since
this was their last evening together, how about a little music? His
father said yes indeed. His Grandfather took the lamp from the
shelf, lighted it with a spill, set his chair in the centre of the floor
and got out a long parcel wrapped in cloth.

Gilbert's father beckoned him over. "How's this for a flute?
Your Grandfather made it on his lathe. Butternut wood. I
remember the tree it came from."

Grandfather Egan settled himself in the chair, parted the beard
around his mouth with the back of his hand, one side then the
other, put the flute to his lips and blew a few toots to test it—doh,
ray, me, like when Miss Burwell taught them singing Friday
afternoons first thing after recess. Some of the low notes sounded a
little bit fuzzy which most likely was on account of the beard and
not on account of how the flute was made. All the other notes came
clear. The first tune he played was a lively one and he kept time to it
by tapping his boot on the scrubbed, unpainted floor. Next came
My Bonnie Lies Over the Ocean, which Gilbert knew straight off,
words and all. When Doctor Scanlon and some other collegiate
teachers and their wives came for a social evening—krokonole, hot
chocolate, and a sing-song around the piano with Gilbert's father
playing—*My Bonnie Lies Over The Ocean* was one of their
favorites. Some of the songs they sang were in his father's *College
Song Book* and sounded silly when you are lying upstairs in your bed
and hear them coming from grownups and worst of all from
teachers.

After My Bonnie, the tune was *Pop Goes The Weasel.* Eph knew
that one and tried to sing the words, Grandfather played it for him

several times and always when the high note sounded the pop, Eph threw back his head and clapped his hands. *The Last Rose of Summer* was another tune Gilbert recognized. *The Battle of Queenston Heights,* this was the tune the town band played for Twenty-Fourth of May celebrations when the pupils of all three public schools paraded to the park carrying their little Union Jacks on sticks, then were lined up in front of the grandstand to sing it for all the people. The last thing Miss Burwell did before her class went was to make them say the words over and over to be sure they had them right. "I want this class to set an example for those of other schools," she said.

"Upon the Heights of Queenston one dark October day,
Invading foes were marshalled in battle's dread array.
Brave Brock looked up the rugged steep and planned a bold
attack;
'No foreign flag shall float,' said he, 'above the
Union Jack.'"

After playing this one, Grandfather Egan lowered his flute and while he was taking a breather, Gilbert's father asked for *O the days of the Kerry dancing, O the lilt of the piper's tune.* Grandfather Egan was not sure he remembered it but then after a few tries he got the hang of it. He had played only a few notes when Grandmother Egan rose from her straight backed chair, put away her knitting and said it was getting late. "There will be none of this in the morning." Grandfather Egan gave no sign that he had heard her. He finished the tune and ended up with *The Minstrel Boy.* Then he shook the spit from his flute, got up, returned his chair to the head of the table, wrapped his flute in its cloth and put it away in the drawer.

Gilbert started to go upstairs then remembered his father had told him not to use the jimmy-juggle under the bed except in an emergency. So he went out and did his number one into the weeds behind the woodpile. When he came back in, his Grandmother was setting the table for breakfast and his father was over by the stove whittling prayer sticks for the morning fire. Eph and his Grandfather had left the kitchen. He went straight upstairs, undressed in the dark, found his nightshirt and got into bed. He closed his eyes and pictures came, not the usual drowsy kind, but pictures as clear as those he and Chester took turns looking at with the stereoptic viewer, sitting side by side on the horsehair sofa of the Williamson parlor after a Sunday dinner—Grandfather Egan with elbows raised, his blunt fingers opening and closing holes in the flute, his heavy boot beating time on the scrubbed unpainted floor; Grandmother Egan's set face, her needles glinting; on the ceiling upside down flies in the circle of lamplight; Eph's clumsy handclaps and his happy face. Gilbert lifted his hand from the quilt and rested it on the headboard of the old spool bed. He tried to picture his father as a boy and lying here but this was a picture which would not come.

spool bed:

CHAPTER NINE

Escape

The train to the Junction was slow as molasses in January and by the time the Flying Dutchman landed Gilbert and his father at its station back of the ice house the foundries were blowing their six o'clock whistles. Crossing the upper bridge the Egans met women from the mill. Two of them must have belonged to the Methodist Church because Gilbert's father knew them and lifted his hat to them. Some foundry-men were crossing too, mostly noo-come-oots in working clothes and big tweed caps, hurrying home for super.

Gilbert had supposed all noo-come-oots lived on his side of the river because most of the other side was the tony part of town. From across the street Gilbert saw Archie McClintock's father and another man from the axe factory come out of the Royal Consort and start up the hill ahead of them.

His father changed the telescope suitcase to his other hand and they were part way up the hill when he gave Gilbert a poke in the back with his thumb. "Straighten up. Remember what I told you." Gilbert pulled in his stomach and stuck out his chest. "None of your buffonery. Unless you get over your slouching we'll put you in shoulder braces, mark my words."

Gilbert said he didn't know he was slouching.

"Exactly. That's my point. It's become a habit. Do you think I want people taking a son of mine for some poolroom loafer? I expect you to set a good example for your brother."

Setting an example! It sounded like old Burwell. This is what happens when you have a teacher for your father, Gilbert thought. He could not imagine Nick's father, or Ernie's or Archie's—least of all Archie's—telling them that. When Archie did something which went against his father, chances were he got a whaling, and that was the end of it.

After they passed the school corner Gilbert trotted ahead to open the gate and be first one home. The table was set, his mother had held off having supper, she said she was half expecting them. Chester was in the back yard so Gilbert went on out. Nick's Sport was there and he greeted Gilbert like a long lost friend, his tail

going round and grinning from ear to ear. It turned out that Sport
did not belong to Nick any more and for the reason Nick's father
would not have him on the place on account of digging holes in the
garden, worst of all digging the four pound black bass from under
the rose bush and rolling in it. Chester said their mother was not at
all sure they could keep Sport, that it would be up to their father to
decide. They agreed that first thing after supper they would ask.
Gilbert patted Sport then they went inside. Sport would have come
with them but the screen door banged shut as he bounded up the
steps.

Their mother was at the sink peeling tomatoes and arranging the
slices on a platter. The big news she had for their father was that a
couple with a baby had moved into the house across the street. It
was a large, rough-cast house with a fanlight of colored glass over
its front door. The house was empty even before the Egans moved
to Blair Street. The rough-cast plaster had peeled in spots and one
of the fanlight panes was broken. Its yard went as far along as
across from Mr. Wallace's but like its hedge, had gone wild.
Gilbert and Chester were forbidden to go there on account of an
open well but once when no one was around Gilbert had. The water
in the open well was black as ink and by leaning over, he saw toads
hunched down on a piece of board. For as long as he watched not
one of them moved. They reminded him of castaway sailors who
had given up all hope of being rescued. Just the sight of them gave
him a shuddery feeling.

"The elder Miss Langley watched them move in, she told me they
have only a few sticks of furniture," his mother said. "I was not
home at the time. They appeared to her to be respectable, the
husband was quite well dressed. I'll give them time to settle before I
call."

Gilbert wondered about that. When his mother went calling she
left her card—"first and third Wednesday"—and his father's
smaller one on the ladies' hall tables and when those ladies returned
the call they did the same. But if the people with the baby had only
a few sticks of furniture they might not own a hall table let alone a
silver tray to leave the cards on.

Their mother rinsed her hands, dried them on her apron and set
the platter on the table. "Miss Langley says Mr. Wallace went
across and cautioned them about the well so I dare say he knows
their name."

The four of them took their places, bowed their heads, grace was said. While his mother and father talked back and forth, Gilbert kept wondering about the new people where had they come from and what the man did for a living. At school every boy knew what every other boy's father did for a living and from what he could makeout, it was the same with grownups, all except the noo-come-oots. Mr. Waldy, Mr. Pickering, Mr. Dryden, Mr. Mullin, Mr. Greer, Doctor Scanlon, Aunt Kate's husband, the new chairman of the school board who ran a bank, Uncle Abel, Grandpa Williamson, D.V. Schiller and of course Dr. Kirkland, Reverend Allister and poor Professor Vance. Yes, and you did not need to be much of a snooper to know where people who did not work, such as the Misses Langley and Mr. Wallace, got their money from.

It was Gilbert's turn to clear away the plates and serving dishes and bring on the dessert and while he was doing this Chester asked about Sport. Their father said he had no real objections to them having a dog provided it was obedient but a tramp dog was another matter. "Once a tramp always a tramp, nine times out of ten but he may stay for the time being provided he behaves himself."

Sport behaved himself during the night. He did not bark and after breakfast while Gilbert and Chester were carrying in the wood he did not try to crowd past them or scratch at the screen door to be let in. He started to follow their father but when they called him back he came. They were out by the hammock trying to teach him to sit up when their mother called Gilbert into the house to try on his new school blouse before she ironed it. She held it up to show him. The collar had two rows of braid and a fancy little anchor in each corner. "Like it?"

"It's all right I guess."

She gave him that half-strict, half-amused look of hers. "It had better be. It and the other one are what you'll be wearing to school for the next year or so."

"I like the old ones better."

"You've outgrown the old ones, I'm using that pattern for Chester's. I borrowed the pattern for these and cut out one for myself. Now try it on."

He took off his old one, held up his arms and let her slip the new one over his head. He wriggled his arms into the sleeves then felt his shoulders, right and left. "Momma! It's got puffed sleeves!"

"Nonsense. They're gathered a bit, that's all. Most sleeves are."
She smoothed it with her hands. "Good. It's a perfect fit, now turn
around."

"But Momma, it's not a boy's, it's a girl's. It is, it is." He pulled
away, arched his little finger to pluck at an imaginary skirt, and
took a few mincing steps. "Have a look at my puffed sleeves, Miss
stuck-up Ruby Greer. Go on. Have a look."

She took him by the shoulders, turned him to face her and
fastened the button. "Don't be so pernickety. You're going to wear
these blouses and what's more you're going to like them. Now take
it off. Out you go."

He shrugged into the old blouse and left. Chester and Sport were
in the front yard. He plunked himself down on the hammock. If I
don't watch out first thing I know she'll have me going around like
Little Lord Fauntleroy, in a lace collar, velvet pants and long curls
down to my shoulders. The thought made him want to clap his
hand to his forehead, lean over and puke. When they had the story
read to them, they saw Lord Fauntleroy all dressed up like some
girl and with his arm around his "dear Mama," Chester tried to give
the picture a punch on the nose.

Gilbert worked the toe of his lacrosse shoe back and forth over
the dirt beside the hammock, heaping it then smoothing it. Only
one more Sunday then school. Yes, and Sunday School before that.
If they had gone to Sparrow Lake this summer this would have
been their last week in camp. If this was a good year for wild rice,
Mr. Dubois would soon be gathering his. Years and years ago when
their father was a young man up north trying to be an engineer he
watched the Indians gathering their rice. The way they did it was to
push their canoes into the rice beds, bend the stalks into the canoes
with their paddles and shake off the ripe grains. Last summer when
Mr. Dubois and their father were having another of their talks
about how things used to be, Mr. Dubois said he did the same and
if the Egans stayed at the lake a few more weeks they could have all
the rice they needed without ever going near a store.

Gilbert dug his toe into the dirt. If they only would! Instead next
Monday the school bell would ring, they would be marched in and
he would sit at the same old double-desk across the aisle from Ruby
Greer for another year. The only change would be not having Ira
on the seat beside him. He and Ira had sat next to each other even
in kindergarten. Ira always had a pig shave and there was a dandy
scar on the side of his head from falling on a broken bottle when he

was little. A week after school closed Ira's father went to work at Mr. Dryden's soap factory down river on the lower edge of town and had moved his family there. Unless a new boy showed up, Gilbert would have the double-desk and seat to himself. If one did come it would suit Gilbert to be moved in from the aisle except that if Miss Burwell did this he would have to start boring a fresh escape tunnel. The one he worked on last year was a good inch and a half into the wood of the desk and if he had engineered it right it should be close to the escape hole. The escape hole was about as big around as a slate pencil. It was not quite two inches from the front edge of the desk and was so old it must have been made by a boy who finished with school years ago. The tunnel was no bigger around than the piece of rusty bicycle spoke he bored it with but the difference in size would not matter as long as the two joined at the finish.

Sitting in the hammock watching Chester and Sport rolling together on the front lawn, Gilbert remembered the very day he started the tunnel. It was after morning recess and Miss Burwell was taking meanings. She had them read out the story in their readers about the boy who tattled on another boy and was "fairly caught." Next she had them sit in the position of attention with their hands behind their backs and whoever answered had to stand. Some girl at the back of the room stood and said that fairly caught meant fairly and squarely. Miss Burwell said this was correct which of course everybody knew without her saying so. She was starting in on some other meaning when Gilbert stood and said fairly had another meaning. Without giving him a chance to explain she told him he was contradicting and she wanted none of his impertinence. She tried to make him look like a fool right there in front of everybody. All the same she was wrong, as for instance when a person says he is fairly well, or something is fair to middling. This is like saying not too good and not too bad but only so-so. That day on his way back to school after dinner what should he spy between the planks of the sidewalk but the piece of bicycle spoke. Something which had nothing to do with him, something at the back of his head, told him to pick it up. And this was how the tunnel idea came to him. That afternoon he started boring it. Almost every day from then on while he was supposed to be working on his sums or copying letters on his slate or paying attention while Miss Burwell stood at the board pointing with her pointer, or sat at her desk hearing spellings, there he would be making her believe he was paying attention but with one hand on the edge of his desk, rolling the wire back and forth between his fingers, every day making his tunnel a little bit deeper. This was how boy heroes in stories of olden times must feel, fooling their jailers and all the time secretly tunnelling their way to freedom.

Gilbert straightened. It was high time he stopped his wool gathering. He was trying to hit on some excuse to get out of wearing the new blouses when he saw his father come in the gate, walk right past Chester rolling on the grass with Sport as if he had not seen them and go up the side steps two at a time. Gilbert wondered what was up so he moseyed in through the summer kitchen to hear what he could hear. His father was telling his mother something but when Gilbert appeared in the doorway she motioned for him to go back out. "This is not for your ears," she said.

"I'm not so sure, Frances. There is a lesson in all this. Let him stay."

The news was that first thing that morning about the time Mr. Zeigler was opening his Four Chair Barber Shop, he heard what sounded like a shot from somewhere across the street. Others heard it too. Chief Rooney was sent for. Professor Vance was found lying on the floor of his room, a pistol beside him and a bullet through his head.

"The poor man," Gilbert's mother said in a sort of whisper. "The poor, poor little man. I never dreamed it would come to this."

"Nor I. But as Zeigler put it, life in this town had become too much for him. Thank God no son of ours was in any way responsible."

"Richard, whatever do you mean? Who do you have in mind?"

"Those who made sport of his affliction, some boys among them, though they were not the worst offenders. Recently when some overdressed young whippersnapper made snide remarks concerning Vance's affliction, Zeigler ordered him out of the shop."

"Good for him!"

"But it goes deeper than that. In more or less degree we are all responsible. Had any of us on the Board ever extended the right hand of fellowship, let alone invited him to our houses?" His father drew out a chair, unbuttoned his vest and sat down. "But it's too late now, what's done is done. Like the Pharisee of old we

passed by on the other side...I talked with Trixie's friend
Pickering. He's interviewing Dr. Kirkland and Chief Rooney. The
whole sorry affair will be in this evening's paper.''

Although the paper used some words Gilbert did not have
meanings for he liked what Mr. Pickering wrote, as for instance:
''Despite a life-long handicap which would have daunted less
courageous men, the late Archibald Vance occupied a place in the
artistic life of this town which will be difficult to fill. Largely self-
taught, his appearances as violinist at concerts were gala events and
his performances as a member of the opera house orchestra were
without exception outstanding. Dr. Kirkland, opined that under
the circumstances an inquest need not be held and in this Chief
Rooney concurs. A native of upper state New York, interment will
take place in Auburn where his sole surviving sister resides.
Professor Archibald Vance will be sorely missed by music lovers
and will be long remembered by his fellow townsmen one and all.''

: toads in a well :

CHAPTER TEN

The Dog That Rose From The Dead

Monday morning before first bell, when Nick came along and yoo-hooed, Gilbert could not get out of the house fast enough on account of Chester being so wound up about starting school. Sunday night in bed he kept Gilbert awake talking about it and at breakfast he was so excited he forgot to put the brown sugar on his porridge. If he had had his way he would not have given their mother time to eat her one piece of toast before she took him. He could have got out of going to school until he turned six and if he had taken Gilbert's advice he would have. Kindergarten was all right at first but after Miss Kilgour taught you how to fold paper, weave little mats and build things by poking little sticks into soaked peas the fun had gone out of it. Gilbert had tried his hardest to make him see this but that was Chester all over, when he set his mind on a thing he would not listen.

On their way along the street, Nick said his father got it from Mr. Wallace that the name of the new people was Carter and that Mr. Carter was on the road. Nick did not know what this meant so Gilbert explained that his Aunt Kate's husband was one of those and so did not get home every night like ordinary men.

When the principal lined them up on the boys' side, Nick and Gilbert marched in together on the off chance Miss Burwell would let them sit together but no such luck. The new boy she made sit where Ira used to sit was sort of dumpy looking and he was the only boy in the whole school who wore glasses. He did not so much as open his mouth before prayers so Gilbert had no way of knowing if he would be friendly or if he just was shy. At roll call it came out that his name was Elmer Spence.

After she marked the register Miss Burwell told them what they must have when they started lessons next day. No matter which class you were in you had to have your own slate—a double one with felt binding on its frame was best—slate cloth or sponge with sprinkling bottle, at least two slate pencils, not stubs, one lead pencil with or without rubber, a pencil box, one lined exercise book and an unlined practice one which on no account was to be called a scribbler, the mere word encouraged slovenliness. Gilbert's class would be reading from the second part of the reader they used last year so their parents would be spared the expense of buying new ones. After that she dismissed them for the day.

Miss Burwell's room was first out and before they split up, Elmer Spence asked Gilbert which was the best store to buy things from. Gilbert told him The Ark and that it was around the corner from the market square. Elmer Spence nodded, pushed his glasses farther up on his nose and jogged off in the direction of the pop factory corner. Gilbert could have told him The Ark was the only place and that everybody went there no matter what church they belonged to. The Ark was owned by Mr. Oscar Upton who was a forty-second cousin of Aunt Kate's husband. He did not belong to any church but he was a believer. Besides things for school, he sold Noah's arks, dolls, jumping jacks, dummy watches that ticked, all sorts of Christmas toys, false faces and pea shooters for Hallowe'en, Twenty-Fourth of May fireworks, and colored hankies with pictures on them. His store was so full things were just about falling off the counters. On top of being a storekeeper, Mr. Oscar Upton was an artist. He painted most of the signs in town, those in store windows and big ones on cloth for what was coming for one night only to the opera house—*Uncle Tom's Cabin, East Lynn, Way Down East, The Bonny Briar Bush, Marks Brothers* and whatever minstrel show came along. He even painted signs which Doctor De Silva's travelling medicine show took around with it. On the bottom right hand corner of all his signs, Mr. Oscar Upton painted "Upton Did It" in small capital letters. Aunt Trixie said that if Oscar Upton had been a vulgar minded man those words might make you think he was hinting at something. Even Nick's father who was a hard-shell Baptist did not hold it against Oscar Upton for selling parchesi and other games played with dice.

Gilbert had no way of knowing if the Catholic school started on the same day as the public schools but if it did Tommy was a week late getting home from Port Dover and going to it. Except for now and then over the back fence it was nearly the middle of September before the two of them had another of their good long talks. Gilbert knew from his father's *Mail and Empire* that the English generals were having trouble putting the Boers in their place but until Tommy told him the truth of it he did not understand how badly things were going. Tommy's Port Dover uncle was in the Volunteers and when he came home from army camp at

Niagara-on-the-Lake, he told Tommy things which even the *Mail and Empire,* much less Grandpa Williamson's *Globe,* did not know about. For one thing the Boers were downright sneaky. Instead of standing four-square and fighting like real soldiers, they shot off their guns from behind rocks. And instead of wearing colored uniforms to show they were soldiers they wore clothes which made them hard to see. In one of Tommy's Henty books called *Cornet of Horse,* a plucky English lad not much older than Tommy went to war for the Empire and Tommy would have given just about anything to do the same but his uncle told him not a chance. While he was away, Tommy had learned some soldier songs such as *Just Before The Battle Mother, Tell Mother I'll Be There,* and one about tenting on the old camp ground the night before many soldiers would die in battle. Gilbert asked if there were songs which soldiers sang to their fathers. Tommy said not and when Gilbert asked why Tommy said this was just the way of it. Tommy had learned the tune of *Just Before The Battle Mother* and while they sat on the pile of ties watching the shunting engine he played it on his mouth organ.

As it turned out Elmer Spence knew about *Cornet of Horse* and also about another plucky young English fellow who was the hero of a book called *With Clive in India.* Elmer was born in England but he was not a noo-come-oot. Until that summer when his father came to be tinsmith for Waldy Hardware, the Spences lived beside the Ottawa River in a place by the name of Vancleek Hill where the people were all mixed up. Some spoke French, some spoke Highland Scotch, some spoke only English but in spite of that they all got along together. It may have been on account of Elmer having to wear glasses but while he lived there he never set eyes on a voyageur or a coureur-du-bois, let alone an Indian. Elmer was not much for arithmetic but he was good at meanings and when it came to drawing, nobody in the room, not even Miss Burwell, could hold a candle to him. Some mornings when they were supposed to be doing their sums he filled one side of his slate with drawings of men fighting one another with long pointed swords called rapiers. One of his favorite drawings showed a fighter falling backwards with the other man's rapier going through his stomach and sticking out his back with blood dripping from it. If Elmer sided with the falling man he printed "Pinked" under the picture and if he sided with the winner he printed "Drawing the Claret." The men were not dressed like Robin Hood and they were not in armor. They wore long cloaks and wide ruffles around their necks. In spite of being English the Spences did not go to the English church. They belonged to the Salvation Army and Elmer was learning to play the cornet. Although Elmer was different than the rest of them, it did not take Nick, Ernie and Archie long to cotton on to him and some days after school they went around together. Because of having Sport to play with, Chester did not try to tag along.

One morning while they were finishing their porridge and their mother was having her tea and slice of dry toast, right out of a blue sky their father came out with the news that he was going to move their bed to the spare room at the back end of the hall and that he wanted them on hand after school while he did it. He said that henceforth he needed their bedroom for his study. Chester practically took the words out of Gilbert's mouth by asking why when you are a teacher you need to study anymore. Their father said such was not the case. "Just you two be on hand to put away your things before I move the furniture." With that he folded his napkin, stuffed it into his napkin ring and got up from the table. "Chester have you tied your dog? No? Then do so immediately."

Gilbert waited until he heard the front door close. "Why does he have to have a room to himself."

"So he won't be disturbed, of course."

"He's a teacher. I don't understand what he has to study for."

"There are plenty of things a boy your age does not understand. Would it help any if I told you he will be studying for his degree?"

Gilbert knew the degree was not likely to be the kind which allowed Aunt Kate's husband to wear a pinny and march in funerals. "Do the other collegiate teachers have degrees?"

"Some do. Doctor Scanlon certainly has which is why he's known as doctor."

"Will Poppa study to be a doctor?"

"Gilbert, please. Whether he does or whether he doesn't is no affair of yours." She began gathering the plates. "Your hair could do with another brushing. And make sure Chester has tied the dog. We don't want any more complaints from the principal. Remember what your father said."

What their father had said was if Sport did not mend his ways, and that right soon, he was headed for the happy hunting grounds. And Sport almost got there the very next week after their father began studying for his degree. Both of them and their mother were

sorry Sport had to go but even Chester could not deny he brought it
on himself.

Sport's trouble was that when he had no one to play with him he
wandered off and came home smelling like the honey wagon.
Either that or he ate things he shouldn't eat, such as the hair and
bits of hide from the tannery which he threw up on the Misses
Langleys' front sidewalk and which Chester and Gilbert were made
to clean up. Most nights when he was shut in the shed he barked
and barked and when Chester tied him at the back steps he
scratched himself so hard that the thumping of his hind elbow
sounded all through the house. The principal's complaint was over
nothing. Sport chewed through his rope and at morning recess some
of the girls were playing ball and when he joined in he tripped one
of them and she dirtied her dress. But that was the principal all
over. Last year when the Foxy Foster big boys had the run of the
yard, he never let out a peep.

The afternoon it happened it did not take long for Gilbert to twig
what was in the wind. Chester being in kindergarten was first out
and when Gilbert got home their mother was alone in the house.
She had sent Chester on an errand to the Williamsons', he had
taken Sport with him and was not likely to be back until shortly
before supper. Next when their father got home, he changed into
his work clothes and began digging a hole close to the back fence at
the Langley side of the yard. Gilbert was all for going out to watch
and would have if his mother had not broken her rule against
piecing and let him have not one but two slices of bread and butter
with brown sugar, provided he ate them in the kitchen. Finally
when he finished eating she came out with it. She said the hole was
for Sport and that his father would explain.

His father was knee deep in the hole when Gilbert came. "You
have spoken with your mother?" Gilbert nodded. "Well and good.
When your brother gets home just you let me do the talking. We
don't want a scene. I'll use chloroform. Sport will not feel one whit
of pain. He'll be put to sleep and that will be that. What I want you
to do is remain in the house and keep your brother occupied."

Gilbert did as he was told but it was far from easy when he knew
what was going on out there. He wished his father had kept it to
himself instead of getting him in on it. If it had been me, he
thought, I would have taken Sport for a walk up the river, then told
Chester some story about him, such as a blind man needed him, or
he jumped into the river to save a person's life and got drowned, or

a friendly Indian came along and lo and behold it turned out Sport was his long-lost dog so off they went. But this way Chester will think it was partly my idea, that I even helped dig the hole. Ending a dog's life was not the same as ending a chicken's life by chopping off its head, as Mr. Yarrow and Mr. Dubois did. Dogs were more like people, even ones like Sport that smelled and were sick on people's sidewalks.

For supper it was corn on the cob, the last of the season. While their mother was draining the cobs at the sink, she sent Chester to wash his hands and told Gilbert to call his father. His father was reaching down into the hole and when Gilbert started to come, he told him to go back in, he would be along presently. Then and there Gilbert knew Sport was finished. Right after the blessing, Gilbert expected their father to come out with it. Their father was not one to beat around the bushes in order to lead up to a thing. If a thing needed saying he said it, no matter what. And so he would have if Chester had not made it harder for him by saying that on their way home from Grandpa Williamson's a man on the corner in front of the Royal Consort patted Sport and told Chester he was a lucky boy to have so fine a dog. Even Gilbert was just about hanging onto his chair but still their father did not let on. What made him come out with it was Chester asking their mother what she had for him to take to Sport for supper. Instead of answering she gave their father a look. Their father laid down his cob, wiped his mustache with a corner of his napkin and told Chester that tonight Sport would be having supper in the happy hunting grounds.

"Where's that?" Chester was not much on Hiawatha.

"It's the animals' heaven," Gilbert could not help putting in. "Isn't it Poppa?"

"Such is the belief of certain people."

"He's dead!" Chester pushed away his plate, laid his head on the table and began to cry.

"There, there," his mother placed her hand over his and patted it. "Wherever Sport has gone, he won't be hungry or cold or unwanted any more. He'll be among friends."

"I was his friend and I wanted him, I wanted him like anything," Chester sobbed. "He wasn't cold or hungry with me."

"I know, I know. But it had to come, Chester, really it did. Much as you liked him he had to go, we simply could not put up with him any longer."

A whine and the sound of scratching at the screen door made them turn. There was Sport, large as life, grinning and his tail going round and round. Chester was down off his chair and out there like a shot.

"Sport"

Their father looked flabbergasted. "Consarn it, Frances, what did I do wrong?" All the answer he got was a shrug.

Next morning the first thing Gilbert did when he got out of their bed in the back room was go to the window and look down onto the yard. The hole had been filled in and he thought, sure as shooting, Sport was at the bottom of it. But no. There Sport was scratching himself at the front of the shed where Chester had tied him. So the whole thing had a happy ending and for once their father came out second best.

CHAPTER ELEVEN

September Days

Because their father had all the say, Gilbert never let on he liked the back room, but truth to tell he liked it better than the room their father took for his study. As a lookout for what Moses called spying out the land, it was handy as a pocket in a shirt. From its back window he was able to see over the roof of the shed, past Mr. Dempster's smokehouse and watch Tommy's mother hang up her washing and come out the back door to empty the slops. At night he tried to guess which Miss Langley was which by their shadows on the blinds. The sound of trains whistling for the bridge came more clearly here than to their old room. About all he missed was hearing or seeing what went on along the street and these were things he already knew about.

But not always. The Saturday morning the tall Miss Langley came from calling on the new people across the street Gilbert and his mother had the kitchen to themselves. She had him turning the peeler while she cored and sliced the apples for pies. Astrachans they were. Sport had disturbed their father's studying by having another of his barking spells, not that he had anything to bark about, simply for the sake of hearing his own voice which was what Gilbert's father said about him when he rattled on. So Chester had taken Sport for a walk before he started old Bruce barking back. Every Saturday except at camp their mother baked six pies. "Enough and be done with it for another week," she said. "And I've yet to see any one of you turn your nose up at a second helping." Her pies were raisin, mince, ground up figs, lemon, chocolate, according to the season. But mostly apple and mostly Northern Spys, which the farmer sold them for ninety cents a barrel because they bought three barrels at a time and also because they bought their butter and eggs from his wife.

Miss Langley said she had to knock several times before Mrs. Carter came to the door with the baby in her arms. "She's a nicely spoken young thing but no sooner had I opened my mouth than I sensed my call embarrassed her, that she believed my sister and I had witnessed what took place across there the other afternoon. As indeed we had, and if the truth be known it was what prompted me to drop in on her. The visit was my attempt to assure her my sister and I as her neighbors were not allowing ourselves to be influenced by what happened."

"What did happen? This is all news to me," Gilbert's mother said.

To hear Miss Langley tell it, Mr. Carter had been driven home in a cab so tipsy that the man from the livery stable had to help him up the walk and into the house. Mr. Carter was singing at the top of his voice and trying to get the driver to join in. Miss Langley said Mr. Carter made a spectacle of himself.

Gilbert pulled a peeled apple off the prong and pushed on an unpeeled one. It was all he could do to keep from smiling. If only Ernie had seen Mr. Carter being tipsy! Recess time when Ernie Yates acted out being tipsy he had them all in stitches. He had a silly grin on his face, hiccupped, twisted his words, swayed a little but not staggering as an out-and-out drunk will do. Ernie could be a tipsy man coming out of the Royal Consort, or he could be one of the tramps he and Ira came across one time when they went fishing along the bank under the railway bridge. To do this Ernie needed an empty bottle, so he did not act out the tramp at school, only when he, Gilbert and a few others were by themselves. The tramp and two others were sitting around a little fire cooking something. Every few minutes they passed around a bottle. When it was the one tramp's turn, he held up the bottle, said "Wine is a mocker, strong drink is raging," took a swig then said "Amen brother," in a solemn voice. The second time around he stood up, made a bow, steadied himself and told them, "It is a wise son who knows his own father." Ernie supposed this was some sort of recitation and that by the way the other two laughed, it was a joke they had between them. Ernie said the easy way to act tipsy before you got the hang of it was to turn yourself around and around until you felt dizzy. Gilbert tried this and it worked. He was showing Chester how to act tipsy when their father came in the gate and saw him. He told Gilbert if he ever caught him doing such didoes again he would put a tin ear on him. "Drunkenness is not to be made light of, as I have reason to know."

Gilbert had learned that when his father got on his high horse like this it was wise to keep your trap shut and take the blame. Surely his father must know that drunk men do not act like tipsy men. Tipsy men felt happy, they joked and sang, they would not hurt a fly. You would not catch them lying in the gutter or picking fights such as the one Nick and he saw going on in the stable yard back of the Royal Consort.

The man who was doing most of the fighting was crazy drunk. One look at him told you he was a great big bully. He had the other man backed against the wall of the driving shed. The other man wore brakie overalls and had lost his brakie cap. Every time the bully hit him his head banged against the boards of the wall. One side of his face was all bloody. The men standing around should have stopped the fight but either they wanted to see it go on or else they were afraid to. The one man who tried nearly got kicked in the stomach which showed the dirty tricks a crazy drunk will do. Spit was coming from the bully's mouth and every time his fist landed he took the Lord's name in vain and said he was going to kill the brakie. And maybe he would if Chief Rooney had not come on the run. The bully turned on the Chief but he soon found out what he was up against. Chief Rooney collared him and had the handcuffs on quicker than you could say Jack Robinson.

Of course it was too early to be sure but by all the signs there would not be nearly so many recess fights this year, which was a good thing or mister punch-on-the-nose Chester would have been in the thick of it. The main reason for thinking there would be fewer fights was because all of the Foxy Foster gang except Yankee Jones had either passed their entrance or quit. Yankee Jones was never the one who egged Nick and Gilbert or any other pair to square off and take punches at one another. Not that he couldn't have. Yankee Jones could talk you into anything, which was why he was by far the slickest trader in the whole school. He could talk you into wanting what he had to trade more than you wanted to keep what he was after from you. He could make you think he was doing you a special favor. Next to Yankee Jones, Archie McClintock was the best trader in the school, at least he was the best Gilbert knew about. The first thing Archie traded was a rabbit foot he brought to kindergarten. In no time at all he had traded the rabbit foot to Ernie for a clay bubble pipe with a broken stem. By Hallowe'en he had traded the bubble pipe for a two cent peashooter, then a magnet, the kind anybody can get by sending in yellow soap wrappers. After Christmas he talked Ira into wanting the one-blader jackknife more than the IXL two-blader with a

peep-show hole in its handle, which was Ira's main Christmas
present. By Easter Archie had a Red Devil hockey stick and a
genuine rubber puck instead of the IXL and by summer he had
traded them and a home-made catapult for a good as new Joe Lally
lacrosse stick.

Although Archie McClintock was not exactly Miss Burwell's
favorite, he was one of the smartest boys in her room. But when it
came to trading he had a lot to learn and Yankee Jones was the one
who taught him, which was how Archie lost his lacrosse stick
before he hardly had time to play with it. Gilbert did not hear of
this until he came home from Sparrow Lake and Ernie told him.
Somehow or other Yankee got Archie to believe that what he
wanted more than anything was a pigeon, not an ordinary pigeon
but a genuine pure-bred tumbler. Yankee said it just so happened
that he had one and because he and Archie were such good friends
he was willing to trade it for the second-hand lacrosse stick. He
explained to Archie that when you turned the tumbler loose, it flew
up and did stunts like some sort of acrobat. Archie could hardly
wait. The first day he let the pigeon out of its coop it flew straight
up all right but instead of doing stunts, it headed off and he never
saw it again. Yankee said of all the bad luck but he did not offer to
give back the lacrosse stick. It was weeks before Archie found out
the pigeon was a homer and belonged to a fellow on the far side of
town and that Yankee had only borrowed it.

A fine one Ernie was to talk! In some ways Ernie Yates was the
most gullible boy who ever came down the pike. He just could not
get over the advertisements in the boys' magazines his cousins sent
him from Buffalo—how to become a magician, a private detective
solving big crimes, a hypnotist bending others to your will, big
money raising squabs, going from door to door selling the latest
thing in can openers, no home should be without one, make tin
look like gold with your own secret chemistry set, make pastime
your business by gathering ginseng and nature's medicines in
nearby woods. Ernie said if only he had the money to pay for any
one of these he would say goodbye to school and study at home.
What he could not get through his head was that down in
Yankeeland people talked big and that some were out-and-out
blow-hards.

With the teeter-totter gone and those big boys gone, recess time
on the boys' side was not even as exciting as recess time on the girls'
side. At least they could skip, play hop-scotch, ring-around-a-rosie

and pom-pom-pull-away. The boys could have too but they would not have wanted to be caught dead playing girls' games. Scrub and tick-and-run were out for fear of breaking windows. You were not allowed to bring your shinny stick to school so you could not play pig-in-the-market and since the boy who was it, in duck-on-the-rock got a cut on the head by trying to put back his stone you had better not be found playing that game either. So what was left but bags-on-the-mill, crack-the-whip, regular tag and squat tag and seeing who could spit the farthest? Elmer said the principal of the Vancleek school came out at recess and got them doing the hop-step-and-jump, potato races and the different ways to kick a football. He even brought his own football. But catch the Blair Street principal doing any such thing. He scarcely ever poked his head outside the door at recess.

About the only time the principal came out to the yard was the day he looked down from a window of his classroom and spotted what must have looked like a boy's head lying all by itself in the corner of the yard across from the pop factory. It so happened the head belonged to a boy by the name of Gilbert Egan. The rest of him was stuck in the hole a man had dug during the holidays, all ready for the new flagpole. The two Foxy Foster boys who grabbed Gilbert and pushed him into the hole with his arms at his sides counted on him getting loose before the bell rang at the end of recess. But why should he? Old Burwell could not blame him for not being in the line-up. When she marched them in, left right, left right, some in step and some not in step, the line made him think of a giant caterpillar humping its back as it went up the steps then going in and out of sight into its hole. With his eyes so near the ground, everything had a new and different look. Across at the pop factory two men loading boxes onto a wagon seemed to have bigger feet and sort of tapering bodies. He was able to see the underside of the wagon and part of the horse's belly. Some of the school windows were open and pretty soon he heard hand claps and squeaky little voices singing some of the kindergarten songs. Upstairs a class was reciting a times table over and over but he was not able to make out which times table it was. A while later a lady came along the sidewalk. He thought of the scare she would get if she looked his way and saw a boy's head all by itself on the playground. In case she did he stuck out his tongue as far as he

could and rolled up his eyes like a dying duck in a thunderstorm. It
was all he could do not to burst out laughing. One of his favorite
pictures in the *Water Babies* book showed Old Grimes stuck in the
top of a chimney, his plug hat covered with soot, his face
blackened, his pipe turned upside down and him saying, "My pipe
won't draw, my pipe won't draw." And all because he had been
cruel to little Tom the chimney sweep. He had been stuck in the
chimney by Mrs. Bedonebyasyoudid, and she was never going to let
him out until he said he was sorry.

But Gilbert had nothing to be sorry about, it was not his fault he
missed the line-up. If he stayed stuck in the hole until dinner time,
well, fine and dandy. He was pretty sure if he tried he could work
his arms loose and get out of the hole by himself. But nix on that,
let the boys who pushed him down the hole get him out or take the
blame. The two men finished loading boxes onto the wagon and as
it turned into the street he made it out to belong to Williamson
Hauling and Cartage.

Gilbert had half a mind to yoo-hoo them just for the fun of
it. . . .

*"Attention class, do any of you know what became of Gilbert
Egan? Yes Ruby, you may speak."*

*"Please teacher I am pretty sure if he sneaked home at recess some
of us bunch would have seen him. We were standing around at the
corner of the girls' yard and. . ."*

*"You may resume your seat Ruby. I was addressing my question
to the boys. You Archie."*

"No ma'am." (Good for you Archie, I knew you wouldn't blab.)

"Ernie? Speak up."

"Me neither, Miss Burwell."

*Why don't you look out your window, dear, sweet Miss Burwell?
Why don't you use your eyes and not your mouth? Don't bother
answering, dear sweet old Burwell, go on with your lessons and
don't mind me. What new meanings have you got for us today? In
case you are wondering, I am fairly well, thank you. I am fairly
caught in this hole but I am feeling fairly comfortable. It would not
be fair for you to keep me in over not being in the line-up. Yes, and
in case you do not know it I am fairly able to get out of here all by
myself but you have another think coming if you think I am going
to. Maybe you think I am not comfortable stuck in this hole and
you are right. But let me tell you I am not comfortable either when
you make us sit in the position of attention with our backs straight*

as a poker and our hands behind our backs. . . . The boy stood on the burning deck eating peanuts by the peck, they asked him why he did not go, because I like the peanuts so. . . . I love little pussy her coat is so warrum and if I don't hurt her she'll do me no harrum. . . The north wind doth blow and we shall have snow and what will poor robin do then poor thing? He will fly to the barun to keep himself warrum and put his head under his wing poor thing. . . . I see you up there mister principal, putting that blind up to the top. . . . Let a little sunshine in, let a little sunshine in, open wide your hearts dum-tee-dum, let a little sunshine in. . . . Let us all rise and sing the first, third and last verses of this old familiar Sunday School hymn. . . . I see you plain as anything mister principal and if you were anything like as smart as you think you are you would see me. Except that if I pulled my head in like a turtle you would never see me no matter how hard you looked.

Gilbert began imagining how it must feel to be a turtle, not a snapper but a mud one which is not vicious. He imagined the sides of the hole pressing against him to be his shell. When all of a turtle is inside its shell nothing can get at it, the shell is its fortress. But supposing—

Gilbert stopped supposing. The principal had come down the steps and was making a beeline for him. He pulled in his head and brought his eyes level with the surface of the yard. He could see the soles of the principal's boots as they lifted with every stride. To show what a fix he was in he wobbled his head to one side and looked the other way. Are you hurt, Gilbert Egan? he imagined the principal asking. Would you like a drink of water? Tell me who has done this awful thing to you and I will punish them. On top of giving them the strap I will expel them. But no, he would not tattle. For one thing he did not know the names of the two boys who grabbed him and on top of that they would have it in for him if he told on them. Besides when you got right down to it he had not tried to get away when they grabbed him. He even held his arms at his sides when they pushed him into the hole, just for the fun of it. He heard the crunch of boots on gravel, he closed his eyes and let his head fall over. A hand grabbed him by the collar and yanked him out of the hole like a cork out of a bottle.

Without giving Gilbert time to explain, the principal had him by the ear and began marching him toward the school. When the principal had a boy by the ear, that boy had better come along or it would be the worse for him. If he held back or tried to pull away he ended up with the bottom part of his ear split from the skin of his cheek. Sometimes that split took weeks to heal. Ira's did and its yellow scab was something Gilbert would sooner have not sat beside, least of all when Ira picked it. The second the principal had you by the ear he began turning his hand the other way up until he had you dancing along on tiptoe beside him, meek as Moses. If he had ever split Archie's ear, Mr. McClintock said he would come and do the same to the principal, he would take the principal by the lug and march him up and down between the lines for the whole school to see. (Lug was the name they had for ear where Mr. McClintock came from.)

The principal ordered Gilbert to wait in the hall and went in and spoke to Miss Burwell. She came out, brushed the sand from his knees and elbows and took him back into the room. His class was copying out next day's spellings from the blackboard so he got out his slate and did the same.

Ernie, Nick, Archie and most of the other boys, knew what Gilbert had been up to but they did not let on.

Going along the street at noon, Nick took a good long look at the ear. It was split, all right and as proof, when Gilbert dabbed at it with his hankie there was a smear of what seemed to be watery blood. At dinner Gilbert held off telling about it until the meat and potatoes were served. He began by making a big thing over being stuck in the hole.

"Look at me, Gilbert," his mother said. "Are you quite sure you couldn't get yourself out of that hole—a nimble boy like you?"

But his father did not catch on. His father laid down his knife and fork, and had Gilbert turn his head. "Hold still, don't pull away." He felt the place with his finger. "I tell you Frances, this will not do, it simply will not do. This is a matter which must be seen to." He picked up his knife and fork and told Gilbert to go on with his dinner. Then and there Gilbert knew the principal was in for it.

The principal's house was two blocks along the Avenue past the pop factory corner. It was a narrow, red brick one with not so much as a porch in front. Gilbert's father gave the bell a twist. The principal opened. The hall had an old smell of fried potatoes. "I have a matter to discuss with you," Gilbert's father said. He removed Gilbert's peanut scoop cap and tilted the ear toward the light. "This."

Gilbert did not expect his father to do what Archie's father said he would do but he did expect his father to give the principal a good straight talking to. Instead his father gave him back his cap, said "Off you go," and followed the principal into the front room.

Gilbert felt so let down he could have cried. I thought he was on my side but I should have known better, he told himself. When it comes to sticking up for you against another teacher you can't be sure which side he's on. Archie's father doesn't wax his mustache or carry a walking-stick or be a high man in the church. He smokes a pipe and on axe factory pay nights he goes into the Royal Consort and drinks whiskey and comes home singing, but at least Archie knows he has his father on his side. Why did I have to have a teacher for a father?

School, having to wear your stiff new boots and learn your Golden Text for Sunday were three signs summer would soon be over. The surest sign was the first time the lamp had to be lit for supper. After that pretty soon no more corn on the cob, no platter of big sliced red tomatoes, pretty soon new potatoes would not taste like new potatoes any more. It was not a time you looked forward to but neither was it a time to feel sad about. Certainly it gave you nothing like the let down feeling you had when you opened your eyes the morning after Christmas morning. It was something the same as at Thanksgiving service when the congregation rose and sang about the harvest safely gathered in and when Mr. D.V. Schiller read out the announcements he reminded people of the special missionary envelopes in aid of India's starving millions.

Another sure sign summer soon would be over was the pickle smell coming from houses as you walked along. The noo-come-oots and the lady with the tipsy husband did not seem to go in for pickles but the Lamonts, the Egans and the Misses Langley did. Balaclava was a good street for smelling pickles, even the hard up old Family Compact lady across from the Williamsons made spiced plum but of them all—chili sauce, chow-chow, green tomatoes, piccalilli, bread-and-butter, mustard, gherkin, mixed and quite a few more—the hot, sweet and sour smell of catsup being made was the one to make your mouth water. Red cabbage pickle came later around Hallowe'en, but it did not give off much of a smell. The Egans and the Williamsons did not make sauerkraut. "Leave that to the Pennsylvania Dutchmen and welcome," Aunt Trixie said.

Yes, and if you happened to think about it there was still another sign you soon would be saying goodbye to summer for another year. This was seeing all eight lamps—the two hanging lamps, the china parlor lamp with its round wick, the two wall lamps and the three ordinary table lamps—lined up on the coal-oil bench in the summer kitchen to be filled, trimmed and have their chimneys polished as soon as their mother did the breakfast dishes and made the beds. Two things their mother would not and could not abide were a wick with horns and a chimney which was not as shiny as it could be. When she trimmed wicks she did not use scissors as Gilbert had seen the aunts do. No, she pinched and plucked the charred edge of each wick between her thumb and finger, then slightly rounded both its corners so the flame would be even across the top, not shaped like a fish tail. She had the slickest way of cleaning chimney lamps. She blocked the bottom end with her cloth and blew steam into the top end. She had the steamiest breath! The few times she let Gilbert try it he huffed and puffed but made scarcely a trace of steam on the glass. She joshed him about it and said he was full of hot air. Woe betide Gilbert and Chester if they so much as laid a finger on a lamp after it was lighted. Their father warned them that many a house had been burned to the ground with all its people in it by some child who fooled with a lamp or played with matches. Sure enough, Chester's nursery rhyme book told of a boy who played with matches and the story ended, "All that was left to tell the news were ashes and his little shoes." With the story was a picture of a neat pile of ashes and a pair of curled up empty shoes.

: hanging lamp :

Their mother and their father could remember when coal-oil lamps were the latest thing. Before them it was all whale oil which most people could not afford. So they used only candles. Candles were a lot of work. They were made from tallow which is the fat of sheep. The fat had to be melted, poured into moulds with string wicks. On the farm back of Hamilton when lamps came in, which was long after Obediah got over his affliction sore, Aunt Boo and the real Grandma Williamson were so sick and tired of candle making that they collected every last candlestick, mould and snuffer, put them into a sack and dropped them down an old well. Everyone in the family was glad to see the last of candles, though nowadays Aunt Boo would use them if Grandpa Williamson let her have her way. Aunt Boo was slow to move with the times. She called trains "steam cars" and she did not seem to believe in post offices. Whenever she heard that Aunt Kate's husband was going to pass through some town where she had a relative, she gave him a letter to deliver. She never caught on that he put the one cent stamp on it and popped it into the nearest mail box.

Gilbert's new Sunday School teacher was nothing like the one they had before. The one they had before not only stuck to the lesson, he was almost as bad as Miss Burwell for memory work. He made sure you knew that week's Golden Text word for word and he drilled you on the Ten Commandments—thou shalt not kill or steal, tell lies, if you want your days to be long in the land you had better honor your father and mother; do not get after your neighbor's ox or his ass or his wife and do not commit adultery. He never explained what adultery meant but adult was a fancy word for grownups, so anybody who could put two and two together knew it must have something to do with them.

Doug did not skip the lesson but he did not keep going over and over it. The stories he told were his kind of stories. Not the kind Mr. D.V. Schiller told the intermediate boys when he gave them one of his talks, all about boys who "made their mark." In one story a poor country boy who came to the city looking for work stopped a runaway horse. Lo and behold, the rich gentleman in the carriage was a banker who needed an honest office boy. He hired the boy on the spot and started him up the ladder to success. In another story a ragged newsboy from the slums ran after a wealthy businessman who had forgotten to wait for his change. That boy ended up being a partner in the business. Then there was the boy who helped an old lady across the street. She adopted him and when she died she left him all her vast wealth. To Gilbert these Mr. D.V. Schiller stories

were his "seeth thou a man diligent in his business he shall stand
before kings" all over again.

Doug's stories were not story book stories and they were not ones
he made up out of his own head just for the fun of it. Some were
about things he had seen happen and others were of things,
outdoor things, he knew about. Doug lived by himself in a stone
cottage beside the road east of town which still was called the
tollgate. When the Family Compact ruled the roost they made
other people pay to use the road. Yes, and they might still be up to
their old tricks if William Lyon Mackenzie, Grandma Williamson's
lay preacher relative and other men had not kicked over the traces
and put them in their places for good and all. Gilbert could imagine
some stuck-up Family Compact man sitting in front of that stone
cottage all dressed up like some overgrown Little Lord Fauntleroy,
not letting poor people pass until they dug down into their pockets
and paid him. . . .

Where do you think you are going my good fellow? . . . I am
going to see a man about a pig, your lordship. . . . Nothing doing
until you fork over. . . . Where do you think you are going, you
other poor fellow, what is your name? My name is Egan and I have
come all the way from Huron county to have this sack of oats
ground for porridge. . . . Stuff and nonsense unless you pay
up. . . . My children are hungry your lordship. . . . If you do not
mind your p's and q's I will give your lordship a good hard punch
on the nose. My father came from Ireland and before that he was
Welsh. You had better look out or we will take you off that high
horse of yours. Yes, and Mr. Wallace and all the other Scotch will
come to help us.

Doug sometimes worked for farmers but he was not a hired
man. Mostly he worked for himself. In summer he would dig you a
well or build you a fence—stone, snake or picket, whichever you
wanted. In winter he cut firewood to sell, or made cedar ladders
and tamarack flagpoles right out of the woods. He knew all the
different animals by their tracks in the snow, could catch fish by
tickling them, had often watched partridges drumming and knew
about whip-poor-wills. He wore work boots on Sunday and his
clothes had the good clean smell of yellow soap. On top of all this,
he was for letting you make up your own mind about a thing, such
as when they passed around the anti-cigarette pledges for the boys
to sign. All the other boys signed and Gilbert pretty near did too,

after the scary talk the man from the anti-cigarette league gave them.

As well as stunting your growth and weakening your will power cigarettes could turn you into a fiend. The man ended his talk by telling of a boy cigarette fiend on his death bed pleading for just one more cigarette. Then Mrs. D.V. Schiller handed out the pledges and pencils. When she came to Gilbert something inside him made him put his hands behind him and shake his head.

"Take it, Gilbert, this one's yours."

He gave his head another shake. "I don't know what I'll do when I grow up. It's too early to say."

"It is never too early for good resolutions." She kept holding out the card.

"I don't think I'll ever smoke cigarettes, at least I don't want to. I might never even smoke a pipe. But suppose I sign and then go back on my word? What then?"

"Come, come Gilbert, let's not quibble."

"Don't keep prodding him, Mrs. Schiller," Doug said. He sounded blunt. "At least he's being honest!"

"There's that about it. But take the card anyway, Gilbert, and think it over."

As soon as Gilbert got home from Sunday School he showed his father the pledge and told what Doug had said to Mrs. Schiller.

His father read the pledge a second time. "He had a point there," he said, and left it at that.

CHAPTER TWELVE

Consequences

There were two reasons Gilbert and Chester were allowed to go to the Doctor De Silva Medicine Show that Friday evening. One reason was that after supper Tommy Dempster came over the back fence and offered to take them. Their mother said they could go because Tommy was reliable. Sport was the other reason. Sport was having another of his barking spells. And when Gilbert went up to the study to ask permission, their father said he had no objection providing they took Sport with them. "I find it difficult to concentrate with that fool dog's yapping dinning in my ears. But make sure you two come straight home afterward, no dawdling. Is that clearly understood?" Gilbert said it was. He promised their mother the same, then off they went.

Doctor De Silva's Medicine Show was to be in the market square for two nights only and this was to be the first night. The afternoon before when Gilbert came from the Band of Hope meeting in the church basement he saw men putting up a sort of stage in front of the town hall with Doctor De Silva's name on a banner all across the top of it. The market building was across from the town hall and took up all the lower side of the square. The side opposite the church had the Dryden House, the hotel where farmers mostly went. Next to it was Mr. Rosenberg's fur store and around the corner was The Ark. Mr. Rosenberg paid eight cents for a muskrat skin and one winter Ernie sold him three of them. Another boy at school got forty-five cents from Mr. Rosenberg for a skunk fur.

The Medicine Show stage was between the front of the lockup under the town hall and the shed where the town clerk weighed loads of hay which farmers brought to sell. Mr. Wallace was a friend of the town clerk and it was thanks to him their father knew when a good load of cordwood was on the market. The lockup door had a high window with bars across it. One Sunday as church let out the people watched Chief Rooney taking a handcuffed man inside. It turned out the man was an escaped murderer from down in the United States who had been dodging the police all over the country for months. But Chief Rooney was too smart for him.

Next evening Mr. Pickering had all about it in the town paper. Yes, and the day after that the *Mail and Empire* had a piece about it. They would have got to the market square in pleny of time before the show started if Chester had not let go of Sport's rope when they were coming down the hill. They found him chasing back and forth in the Royal Consort stable yard with two other dogs and they had a hard time cornering him. By the time they got to the square what looked like a hundred or more people were lined up in front of the stage. The stage was lighted up by two big oil flares, one on each side, and a man was up there playing on his banjo for all he was worth. The man's long tailed coat and narrow pants had wide black and yellow stripes and his bow tie was so wide it reached halfway to his shoulders. His face was blackened and as he sang he threw back his head and rolled his eyes to get the people laughing. Between verses he did a shuffling dance, jumped and clicked his heels together. At the finish he made a low, sweeping bow, extended his arm toward the curtains at the back of the stage then played something like a drum roll on his banjo. The curtains parted and out stepped Doctor De Silva.

Doctor De Silva was twice as big a man as peppery little Dr. Kirkland but he did not look much like a doctor, he looked more like a preacher except that his Prince Albert coat was fancier and he had a heavy gold chain across his flowered vest and a big sparkling ring on one finger. When he removed his hat to begin his talk to the people you saw his hair was shiny black and slicked down at the back over his collar. His voice was deep and even at the back of the crowd where Gilbert, Chester and Tommy stood, they could hear every word.

The first thing he had to sell was his specially prepared hand soap. He explained about the pores of the human skin. They were one of Mother Nature's marvels. He said this was not the time or place to quarrel with those who held the mistaken belief that men were descended from monkeys. But thanks to the lessons he learned at the knee of a God-fearing mother—so on and so on, the upshot of which was that God knew what He was doing when He put pores in people's skins. Pores helped get rid of bodily wastes. This was no easy job and until the discovery of the famous De Silva hand soap certain pores in the male and female hand had difficulty doing so. In fact some failed completely with the result that many hands which appeared to be clean were carriers of concealed dirt. They were, in fact, little better than the whitened sepulchres spoken of in

Scripture. "This I will prove, my friends, for all to see." Doctor De Silva had the banjo player bring a basin and pitcher of water, set them on the table then unsnap the Doctor's detachable starched cuffs and turn up the sleeves of the Prince Albert. The Doctor took off the big shiny ring, soaped his hands with what he said was a piece of ordinary garden variety hand soap then held them up, turning them back and front so the crowd could see. The suds were as white as the driven snow. Then in plain sight of everybody the banjo player unwrapped a cake of De Silva soap and gave it to the Doctor. The Doctor did not give his hands anything like a good hard washing but when he came to the edge of the stage and held them up you could scarcely make out where his fingers were on account of the dirty grey suds. "Seeing is believing, friends," and sure enough the proof about your bodily waste clogging your pores was as plain as the nose on your face. The banjo player also came forward. He held up a sign: "Doctor De Silva Miracle Hand Soap. It Penetrates. It Purges. It Purifies."

Next the Doctor gave his hands a good rinsing, let the banjo player dry them, put the ring back on his finger and took out his watch. "As was said of old, seek and ye shall find. For the next three minutes, and for three minutes only, my assistants will pass among you. Not withstanding the heavy demand for this miracle working cleanser, purifier, cakes of it will be offered for sale at ten cents each, ten cents only, the tenth of a dollar. Truly, my friends, a give-away price. Act quickly folks. I am a man of my word. For three minutes only." The Doctor lifted his arm and held his watch to the light. "Nine, eight, seven, six, five, four three, two, go!"

Several fellows appeared from nowhere and began moving among the crowd. Each time any of them sold a cake he held it up and shouted, "Sold Doctor, and got the money." Gilbert tried to keep track but time and again two fellows shouted "Sold" at once so he soon lost count. A noo-come-oot in a big cloth cap with a sweat cloth around his neck who was standing next to Tommy was reaching to buy a cake when the Doctor shouted, "Time." The noo-come-oot tried to get the fellow to sell him the cake anyhow but the fellow said try again the next night, that he would lose his job if he sold a cake after the Doctor called time.

Next when the fellows came in and Doctor De Silva took them with him behind the curtain, the banjo player gave the people some more of his songs. One of his songs was the one from the *College*

Song Book which the teachers liked to sing around the piano when they came for a social evening. It sounded a whole lot livelier on the banjo than on the piano the way Gilbert's and Chester's father played it. "Grasshopper sitting on the railroad track, picking his teeth with a carpet tack," and "Behind the barn down on my knees, I thought I heard a chicken sneeze," were parts of how it went. Quite a few in the crowd laughed and clapped their hands which made Sport tug at his rope and give a happy bark.

But the rest of the show gave the people nothing to laugh about. Doctor De Silva had the banjo player take away the pitcher and wash basin, bring on two glass jars as big around as stovepipes and over half as high and set them side by side on the table. One of the jars had what looked like a string of white sausages without the twist. The other held coils of what seemed to be pink garter snakes without heads or tails. Doctor De Silva stood back, extended his arm and pointed, first at one jar then at the other. He told the people that what they saw before them were specimens of tapeworms which had been expelled from a male and a female body by the Doctor De Silva Tapeworm Cure after all other medicines had failed. He said the tapeworm was one of the oldest afflictions flesh was heir to—"Like a ravening wolf it devoureth from within." He said that even the most renowned medical practitioners were often at a loss to detect its presence until too late. In some cases scrawniness and loss of weight were a sure sign. In others it was bloating, unnatural swelling of the abdomen. But always there was hunger. This made sense to Gilbert and right off he thought of the Indian famine magic lantern slides. Every last one of those starving children lined up in their little striped bathing suits had blown up bellies. What the church should send them instead of rice for their tapeworms to eat were doses of Doctor De Silva's sure-fire cure. Hardly anybody bought the tapeworm medicine and when the Doctor called time no one was reaching for it which was a pretty good sign the town tap water was safe to drink. Before he played and sang some more, the banjo player took away the specimen jars and Gilbert, for one, was glad to have seen the last of them.

The third and last thing the Doctor had for the people was his Banyan from The Holy Land and right from the first it was easy to see he took this to be the most important. He came to the front of the stage and held up a bottle turning it this way and that with his ring finger sticking out for all the people to see. The bottle was flat

with a long neck. It looked to Gilbert to be the size of the castor oil
bottle his father kept on the shelf above the sink so he could be sure
that nature called.

"Banyan from the Holy Land, my friends, Banyan from the
Holy Land." The Doctor set the bottle on the table and as he did so
the banjo player came from behind the curtain with a book so large
and heavy that he needed both hands to carry it. He set it on the
table beside the bottle. At the sight of it the Doctor took off his
fedora, bowed his head and partly closed his eyes the way some
preachers do when they are going to lead in prayer. The banjo
player stepped back, turned and went behind the curtain.

"Banyan from the Holy Land, Banyan from the Holy Land, my
friends. Let us turn as always to the Good Book and learn what
truth it has to tell us." The Doctor opened the book, moistened his
thumb and turned six or eight pages carefully, one at a time. "Ah
yes, here we have it. In chapter sixteen, verse eleven, we find these
words." The Doctor kept a finger on the place and looked up to
make sure he had everybody's attention. "I read—'The banyan
tree which groweth on the banks of the river Jordan.'" The way he
made his voice sound you would think he was in the pulpit and
starting to preach a sermon.

But no. His voice changed to the voice he used for the soap and
the tapeworm cure. "Banyan from the Holy Land is made from the
roots, the barks, the gums, the balsams and the berries of the
banyan tree." Then to help the people understand how their bodies
worked, he told them about their digestive juices, the circulation of
their blood, and what he called their various organs. Gilbert and
Chester, too, knew quite a bit about organs. One day while their
mother was going around handing out her calling cards and their
father had not come home from the collegiate, they got down the
doctor book and had fun taking turns choosing which diseases they
would have. One full-size colored picture was of a man without a
stitch of clothes on, his insides opened up and all of him showing
except his private parts—his heart, his lungs, his pipes, stomach,
womb, gizzard and all the rest of it.

Not all the sicknesses Banyan was good for were those only
grownups had. Besides la grippe, summer complaint, and night
sweat, there was inflammation of the bowels. Everybody had two
bowels, the upper one and the lower one, and when inflammation
attacked either one of them woe betide you if you did not get right
after it and use the right medicine.

Gilbert did not need Doctor De Silva to tell him inflammation of the bowels was dangerous and for the reason Vincent died from it. Gilbert and Vincent had been Sunday School friends since Infant Class. Vincent was a lot like Eph. Except that every now and then he forgot himself and peed his pants, he was as healthy as all get out. Yet the week after the Egans went camping in Mr. Yarrow's sugar bush, Vincent caught inflammation in one or other of his bowels and died in spite of everything Dr. Kirkland could do. Vincent loved to sing. He would throw back his head, open his mouth as wide as it would go, and just enjoy himself. One of his favorite songs was the one, "He's the lily of the valley, the bright and morning star, he's the fairest of ten thousand to my soul." Vincent never could get his tongue around "lily of the valley." He made it sound like "lily of gemalley."

Instead of giving the people only three minutes to buy their Banyan from the Holy Land, Doctor De Silva allowed them a full five minutes. On top of that he gave them a chance to save money by buying more than one bottle at a time. One bottle cost seventy-five cents but for every extra bottle he took off ten cents. The bottles sold like hot cakes. A man up near the stage bought three at a crack and the fellows were kept busy pushing through the crowd, holding up their arms and shouting, "Sold, Doctor, and got the money." One of the fellows—Tommy said he hung around the livery stables—was the first to sell all his bottles and had to run back of the stage for more. A woman standing next to Chester—she wore a shawl and tam-o-shanter—kept waving her dollar bill and calling, "Here! Here!" in an anxious voice. Just as the fellow was in the act of giving her a bottle and reaching for her money, up went Doctor De Silva's big white hand and he shouted, "Too late! Time!" It was like slamming a door in the poor woman's face. The fellow could see how disappointed she was and said if it was up to him he would let her buy a bottle on the sly. Gilbert wondered which disease the woman had. He could not help feeling sorry for her even though he knew the Doctor was doing the right thing in sticking to his word.

That was the end of the show. All this time Chester had remembered to keep a tight hold of the rope but when he turned around, Sport was not on the end of it. Chester's knot must have slipped. Either that or Sport had been up to his old tricks and had gnawed through it. The crowd was breaking up. A dog somewhere back of the weighing shed was having a barking spell. Gilbert was pretty sure it wasn't Sport. So was Chester. But that was him all over, nothing would do, they had to take a look. Next Chester got the notion Sport might be waiting for them in front of the church, simply because Sport once followed him to Sunday School. But then and there Tommy put his foot down. He said their father was strict, they were late as it was and if they knew what was good for them they had better start making tracks. When they came to the pop factory corner he said it was too late for him to go over the back fence so he was going home the front way.

No sooner had he passed under the light in front of Mrs. Devon's store than Chester got it into his head that Sport had been mixed up and gone back to hanging around the tannery. Down the slope he pelted bushes or no bushes, and did he ever come a cropper! One hand was scratched and he had a rip in his blouse. But at least the tumble brought him to his senses. They were passing the Misses Langley's gate when they met their father head on. He was wearing his hat and coat and carried his walking-stick. "A fine pair you are, straggling home at this hour of the night and having your father out looking for you!" He gave each of them a sharp rap on the behind with his stick. "Not a word. March straight up to your bed. I'll deal with you in the morning."

The way their father dealt with them next morning was to tell them they were not to set food outside the yard that day. "I have no wish to punish you unduly, but you gave us your word you would come straight home and you failed to keep it. Now you must take the consequences."

"But Poppa what about Sport?" Chester piped up. "I have to find him."

Their mother looked up from her dab of porridge. "Don't worry. Sport can look out for himself, he'll show up whenever it suits him. Besides I have several jobs both of you can help me with."

Staying in the yard was no great punishment for Gilbert, and if his father thought it was he had another think coming. What his father did not know was that this afternoon Nick was coming over and they were going to build a box trap for catching rats. What most people did not know was that rats hook rides in freight cars to get from one place to another. When the cars are unloaded out come the rats to make themselves at home in people's sheds and woodpiles and sometimes right inside their houses. Because the Lamont place was next to the freight yards rats came there. In the Baptist Sunday School paper for boys, it showed how to build a sure-fire rat trap. For rats you had to have a box trap with doors at both ends or they will not so much as poke their noses inside it. Nick said if this trap worked for ordinary rats they could set it down by the river under the bridge for muskrats. If it worked for muskrats they could get eight cents from the fur store any time they wanted to.

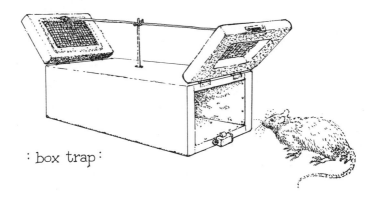

: box trap :

After the dishes were done, the beds made, the kitchen tidied and their father was up in his study, their mother set them to work. Chester got the job of turning the apple peeler. After Gilbert filled the woodbox and split his kindlings for over Sunday his mother got out the Bath brick and set him to scouring the steel knives. He was busy with this in the summer kitchen when Mr. Mullin came around to the back door to see about the coal-oil. He took the five gallon can with the tap out to his wagon and Gilbert followed with the two gallon one which had a potato stuck over its spout because the cap of the spout was lost.

While Mr. Mullin filled the cans he asked Gilbert what he thought of the show Doctor De Silva put on. It turned out Mr. Mullin was there but had not bought anything. He said he enjoyed the banjo player but that, like most medicine men, Doctor De Silva was a fake. He said that in the part of the country where he grew up medicine men were as thick as hairs on a dog's back. He said banyan trees did not grow beside the river Jordan or anywhere else in the Holy Land and the text saying they did was a made-up one. Gilbert was not sure what to make of all this. He wondered if for some strange reason Mr. Mullin had it in for Doctor De Silva.

After dinner when Nick came along he had an idea and it was one which knocked building a rat trap into a cocked hat. It was for them to put a roof and walls on his tree house so they could sleep in it some nights and use it as their club house along with Ernie and Archie, Elmer too in case he wanted to put in with them. This was not a new idea. It came to them months ago and all because of a book Nick got for Christmas by the name of *Swiss Family Robinson*. When the Robinson family got shipwrecked on a desert island they were not hard up like Robinson Crusoe who went hungry lots of times and was scared half out of his wits by Man Friday's footprints on the sand. No siree! When any of the Robinsons needed a thing, down the rope ladder and to the sea shore they went to find the very thing they needed washed up and waiting for them. But poor old Robinson Crusoe had to keep his wits about him and make his clothes out of skins the same as Indians do. All along Nick's father had put his foot down against the Swiss Family Robinson tree house. Then that morning, out of a blue sky, he said they could go ahead with it.

Nick was all for them starting the clubhouse that same afternoon and by the look on his face he felt flat as a pancake when he heard Gilbert was not allowed to leave the yard. Gilbert tried his hardest to get him to stay and work on the rat trap but Nick would not so much as step inside the gate. Instead he headed down to Ernie's house to see if he could come. If Nick had stayed, it would have been a good one on their father, Gilbert thought—him cooped up in his study doing his homework and his son Gilbert down in the yard with Nick, hammering away on the rat trap and enjoying himself in spite of not being allowed to leave the yard.

Gilbert watched Nick turn the school corner then left the gate and sat on the bottom step of the veranda, his shoulders hunched, his chin in his hands. He hoped his father would look out the window and see how miserable he felt. When his father was a boy up there in Huron county he did not have to stay inside some measly yard, he had all the woods to play in, wild turkeys to eat any time he liked, not just at Christmas and now and then some friendly Indian dropping in to see how things were going. He thought back to when they lived in the double house and his father took him up the river, into the woods and fields, the two of them together looking for specimens then sitting down side by side and eating the lunch they brought with them. He thought of the Saturday mornings after they moved to Blair Street and he was in kindergarten, when his father took him to the collegiate and let him look at things in the science room while his father was setting up experiments—things such as the long glass tube with not a speck of air in it, so that when you turned it end for end the feather inside fell like a stone, and the strips of paper which turned either red or blue depending on what you dipped them in. Most clearly of all, he remembered the surprise he got when his father showed him the skeleton in the glass case and told him it was Hoppy.

Hoppy was the rabbit Yankee Jones talked him into for his dummy watch and chain. Aunt Boo gave him the watch and chain. It was a fifteen-center, straight from The Ark. One day without asking permission Gilbert took it to kindergarten, and during the recess Yankee asked to have a look at it. Until then Gilbert had not known there was anything wrong with its click and even after Yankee told him there was he could not hear it. Yankee handed it back and said it was a good enough dummy watch, too bad the click had something the matter with it. A few days later Yankee got talking to Gilbert about rabbits, what good clean pets they were and if you gave them a box to poop in you could let them have the run of the house. It turned out Yankee had more pet rabbits then he knew what to do with.

Another day after school he invited Gilbert to come along with him and take a look at the pet rabbits, just for the fun of it. Yankee kept the rabbits in a barrel and by reaching down and lifting them by the ears he showed them to Gilbert one at a time. He asked Gilbert which of them he liked. Gilbert liked all of them. The one he liked best was white with black markings. Yankee agreed it was a dandy and would make a fine house pet but the trouble with it was it happened to be a buck. He said if Gilbert ever did decide to have a rabbit it had better be a doe. Yankee turned the rabbits on their backs, one after the other, and asked Gilbert if he could see the difference between a buck and a doe. Gilbert said he could though they all looked the same to him.

Yankee put the rabbits back in the barrel and at first Gilbert thought this was the end of it. They went outside and sat down for a talk. After a while Yankee held out his hand and said, "Let me have another look at that watch of yours." He put it to his ear, shook it, listened again and said that if he worked on it he just might be able to fix the click but then again he might not. At the

finish, long before the six o'clock whistle blew, Gilbert landed
home with a rabbit and without his dummy watch. But this was far
from being the end of it.

A grasshopper landed on the step beside him, one of the big
ones, the kind black bass mostly like. He held it by its hind legs,
looked into its monkey face and ordered it to spit tobacco juice. It
did and he released it. He thought, nowadays if I walked in and
turned a rabbit loose in the house I can just hear him getting after
me. But nothing like that happened with Hoppy. His father set
down his book and listened to all about the trade. "Yankee you say
his name is?" His father shook his head and chuckled. "Seems he's
a true son of the land of wooden clocks and wooden nutmegs."
Sure enough, as Yankee said, Hoppy was clean. She used her box
or a *Mail and Empire* spread on the floor for her, the town paper
was not thick enough. The trouble was the very first day she
nibbled every last vine hanging from their mother's window boxes
in the livingroom, and after those were gone she took to gnawing
the legs of the wicker rocker. The outcome was she had to be kept
in the unfloored part of the cellar. This worked pretty well until
their father discovered her tunneling under the stone foundations.
He talked it over with Gilbert and Gilbert agreed the best thing was
for his father to find another home for her. This explained how
Hoppy ended up in the glass case for science students to study. The
good part was that Gilbert was given all of twenty-five cents to seal
the bargain which was almost twice as much as the dummy watch
cost and which also proved Yankee was not always the slick trader
he had the name of being.

Gilbert closed his eyes, put his hand over them and pictured the
tree house, how it was and how it would be when they made it their
clubhouse. If they had a rope ladder in place of those slats nailed
across the tree trunk, nobody could get at them. . . . *Who is that
down there? What do you want? Give us the password.* . . . If all
five of them belonged they could give themselves degrees the same
as in the club Aunt Kate's husband belonged to. Or if they decided
on a different sort of club they could let in boys the age of Chester
and have them for their fags the same as English boys did in *Tom
Brown's School Days.* . . . *You down there, bring me up an apple
and be quick about it.* . . . *You other fag, straighten your shoulders,
we have had more than enough of your slouching. Here is a copper.*

Catch. Run to Mrs. Devon's and buy us five for a cent
butterscotch. No dawdling or you will get a caning on your behind.

Chester came out of the house and sat beside him on the step. "I
wish we could go looking for Sport. I asked Momma but she said
no. Why don't you ask her?"

"It wouldn't do any good." When either their father or their
mother laid down the law they backed each other up and you might
as well save your breath, you could not budge them. Their mother
was not like Ernie's mother. Every so often when Ernie's father
laid down the law, Ernie's mother would sit down and have a talk
with him and he would let Ernie out of it. But no such luck in this
house. The only time Gilbert remembered their mother going
against their father was the time she stopped him from ordering
Chester not to walk the scantling along the high back fence. Their
father told her if Chester kept that up, sooner or later he would fall
and break a leg. "Better he break a leg than have his spirit
broken," was how she answered him. Oh yes, and there was the
morning after a meeting of the Quarterly Official Board when he
told her they decided to buy all new carpet for the church and were
going to ask the congregation for pledges to pay for it. With their
mother, buying anything before you had the money saved up to pay
for it went against the grain. "Oh you men," she said, setting down
her teacup so hard she nearly spilled it. "If I ran this house the way
you men run the church we'd all be in the poor house."

Chester said why didn't they go inside and play tiddly-winks,
there was nothing else to do. Gilbert told him to play by himself,
one color against the other, that he did not feel like tiddly-winks.
What Gilbert felt like was thinking up things against his father and
as soon as he was by himself this is what he did. If Nick and Ernie
came along what he would do was go to the part of the front fence
in plain view of the study window and talk to them about the plan
for the clubhouse. He would lean half over the fence but as long as
his feet were inside the yard his father could not do a thing about it.

One of the things he thought of against his father happened the
other night at the end of supper. Gilbert had been telling his father
about tracks in the snow of the different animals as Doug explained
them. He was not talking just for the sake of talking, he believed
this was something his father would like to know. But what did his
father do? He cut him off. "Yes, yes all very interesting," his

father said, folding his napkin and pushing back his chair, "but I can't sit here all evening listening to your blather."

After a while, when Nick and Ernie did not show up, Gilbert moseyed around to the back, shinnied up the fence and stretched out on the roof of the shed. The roof sloped toward the fence but so slightly that by raising his head he was able to look along the strip of yard between their house and the fence of the empty house next door and see whoever passed along the street. If Nick and Ernie came looking for him they would yoo-hoo which was another thing his father was against. "Tell your friends, if they want you to come to the door and ask in a civilized manner, not disturb the entire neighborhood with their caterwauling."

When you are trying to go against a person and to kick over the traces you are making a mistake if you let yourself think of the good things about them. What you have to do is remember only the times they rubbed you the wrong way and acted as if they had it in for you. This is not as easy to do as a person might think. As for instance when one or another of the Foxy Foster gang tried to make him so mad at Nick that you wanted nothing more than to square off and punch him and you let yourself think of the good things about him. Very few English boys would have been able to run away to sea and have adventures if there had not been somebody at home who had it in for them. Like as not, this was the reason their father and Mr. Wallace had it out hot and heavy about the Boers. Mr. Wallace was not out-and-out on the side of the Boers but he said if the English had left them alone and had not tried to boss them the Boers would not have their backs up.

Gilbert could not see how Mr. Wallace could say anything good about people who did not act like soldiers and hid behind rocks to shoot off their guns though he did see how they must feel about being bossed around by the British. They felt the same as English boys who up and ran away because some person at home was always bossing them around. Those English boys had pluck. No wonder they had stories written about them. There were no stories about runaway Canadian boys, at least none Gilbert knew of. He rolled onto his stomach, rested his forehead on his arms and imagined he was reading:

"As our story opens, Gilbert Egan, a plucky Canadian boy tough as a pine knot, is manfully paddling his canoe up the river for all he is worth to join his friends the Indians who will welcome him with open arms. But we are getting ahead of our story. Chief

Rooney has set the town truant officer on the trail of our young hero. The truant officer is none other than Defective Trotter. But little do the police know of the underground railroad such as in Uncle Tom's Cabin, which helped negro slaves out of Yankeeland and into Canada. Once our young hero reaches Mr. Dubois at Sparrow Lake he is safe for the reason Mr. Dubois will put him on the underground railroad to his friends.

At home our young hero's mother is wringing her hands crying into her apron as well she might, and saying, 'Why oh why did I not stick up for him when I had the chance?' Little does she know she will never set eyes on her son Gilbert again until he returns as a grown man wearing costly furs and moccasins. He will give her a precious necklace made all of wampum. He will have some good present for his little brother Chester who did not grow big because he did not break the habit of sucking his thumb. For his father he will have a basswood hat which is not much of a present but if his father has any sense he will wear it and be thankful. But to get back to our story. When Defective Trotter comes back with his tail between his legs he will say, 'That Gilbert Egan is too smart for me, he has given me the slip.' Gilbert's father will say, 'Why did I all the time lay down the law to him? Why did I keep getting after him about his shoulders? If he wants to toe in that is none of my business. Why did I think because I am a collegiate teacher I know everything about animal tracks and would not listen to what he had to teach me? But now, alas it is too late. No wonder the people at church put me to scorn, curl the lip and all the rest according to the Scripture as it is written.'"

Gilbert was trying to think up an even better story when the distant sound of hammers reached him. Nick and Ernie must have come back by way of the freight yards. Were they putting on the roof or were they putting up the walls? Dingbust Doctor De Silva, dingbust Sport, dingbust their father! No work on the clubhouse tomorrow, Sunday was the Lord's Day for Baptists the same as for Methodists. Catholic boys like Tommy had all the best of it.

Chester had shinnied up the fence and was teetering along the top scantling. Gilbert reached down and helped him onto the roof. "I wish I knew where Sport got to," Chester said. "What do you think?"

"Don't ask me, I've got things of my own to think about." He had intended to keep mum about the clubhouse but now because he felt left out, he told. "They're fixing it right now. I heard them hammering. And here I am, stuck in this measly old yard. For two pins I'd up and run away."

"Where to?"

"Wherever I like. All I need to do is not report home after school. Or I could sneak away at night after they're asleep. That way you'd wake up some morning and have the bed all to yourself."

"You wouldn't Gilbert. Say you wouldn't. What would you eat?"

"Anything that came along. I'd show them I can get along without them and good riddance." Gilbert saw Chester was worried so he made the most of it.

"Don't go, please. I don't want to be up in the room all by myself."

"Too bad for you."

Chester screwed up his face. "Don't go. Please! I'm going in and tell her."

"Go ahead, see if I care." He watched Chester walk the fence, jump and streak it for the back door. He did not believe for one minute his mother would wring her hands and cry into her apron like in the story. But one thing sure, she was in for a good hard scare.

He shifted to the edge of the roof and kept his eyes on the back door expecting her to come and try to talk him out of it. Or she might get his father to come and ask what this was about.

But only Chester came and he took his time climbing back to the roof.

"What did she say? What did she say? Don't be so long about it. Is she scared?"

"She said to wait and have your supper first, you'll be a long time hungry." Chester fished in his blouse pocket and held out a cookie. "She said to give you this."

"She can keep her rotten old cookie for all I care." Gilbert turned away. "I wouldn't eat it if she paid me." But she better watch out, she just better had. One of these days. . . .

CHAPTER THIRTEEN

By Any Other Name

The strip of yard next to the empty house was what the Egans had to use for their lane, as for instance when their coal and wood was delivered, the winter's ashes carted away, and the night every year or so when the honey wagon came.

The second Saturday morning after the clubhouse idea started, Gilbert had to help his father tidy up this strip. Ernie was coming for the afternoon, he and Gilbert would straighten nails then carry some lids of old fish boxes Mr. Dempster said they could have and use them to finish the roof.

To make himself useful, Gilbert as usual had to stand around and hand things, such as the sickle and the pruners his father used to trim back branches of the lilac and snowball bushes which overhung the fence. Gilbert kept track of which tool his father would need next and everything went along fine until it was time for him to go to the station and get his father's *Mail and Empire* from Mr. Greer.

Until that fall Gilbert's father walked down town after school to get his *Mail and Empire.* Then he would read it in the evening. But by having it at noon he could get up to date on what was happening in South Africa where the Boers were running rings around the British. The British general's name was French but he was not a Frenchman. Like Tommy, their father was sure things would go better for the British if only they would let another general by the name of Buller have the run of things. From what Gilbert could make out General French was an old stick-in-the-mud.

Some noons their father read out things for their mother while she cleared the table, but mostly he read to himself. And for the reason their mother, like all the Williamsons, went by what was in the *Globe*. She said the *Mail and Empire* was such a hidebound Tory paper she took what was in it with a grain of salt. Some noons when their father had to answer nature's call he took the paper out back with him so he would know what was happening before he started back to the collegiate.

This Saturday instead of going for the paper by way of the

freight yards, Gilbert went by the Avenue on the off chance Mrs. Devon had anything new in her store window. Going by .he Avenue would take a few minutes longer but if he jogged right along his father would not know the difference and could not say he had dawdled along the way. Mr. Greer was behind the wicket and had the paper ready for him, so he did not lose any time. He was part way between the school corner and the Misses Langley's gate when he heard a couple of loud bangs, one right behind the other. One of the Miss Langleys, the tubby one, who was sweeping her front steps, came to the gate and looked around to see what was up. Just then there was another loud bang. The young Mrs. Carter ran from her house carrying the baby. Gilbert's father had come from the lane and headed across to the old house with Mr. Wallace close behind.

Their mother and Chester were in the kitchen and had not heard the shooting which was no wonder with the apple peeler rattling away. When Gilbert told them they dropped everything and came out. All was quiet for the next few minutes. Then Mr. Wallace came and asked their mother to make a pot of good strong coffee. But because of the deadly drug caffeine she had no coffee. She said for Mr. Wallace to ask the Misses Langley and as Gilbert started to follow she called him back. He wanted like anything to know what was happening and calling him back was a pretty sure sign it was something she did not want him to know about—as when she and the aunts were talking and he tried to listen. "This is not for young ears," was how she put it. But no. What she called him back for was to hand him a shin-plaster and tell him if the Misses Langleys were out of coffee he was to scoot for Mrs. Devon's and buy some. The Misses Langley did have coffee and Gilbert got to the kitchen just in time to hear Mr. Wallace give them the rights of it.

"So in he went and me behind him," Mr. Wallace was saying. "T'was a sorry sight met out eyes, yon Carter on the floor with his revolver, taking shots at empty whiskey bottles and things which weren't there. The man had the snakes, ladies, if so you ken my meaning. Had it been left to me we'd have sent for Chief Rooney but this lad's father wouldna' hear of it. In he walks and says to Carter, 'What nonsense is this? Give me that gun.' And I'm teltin' ye ladies, without the word of a lie, Carter did."

If Nick had heard Mr. Wallace tell about it he might have got it through his head that just because their father waxed his mustache, wore a collar and tie to work and carried a walking-stick, this did not mean he was a dude. But Nick had been down at Ernie's most of the morning and had missed the shooting. So that afternoon while the three of them worked on the clubhouse, Gilbert told them about it.

"Give me that gun"

Gilbert said there was nothing to it. "He just walked over and said, 'I have had quite enough of your nonsense. My certes Carter you had better take your finger off the trigger and stop pointing your gun at me or it will be the worse for you. Hand it over and be quick about it. I will not put up with any of your dawdling.'"

Ernie and Nick looked at one another. "Your Paw said all that?" Ernie asked.

"Well...just about. But that's a teacher for you."

That night and for most of Sunday Mr. Wallace and their father took turns looking after Mr. Carter. On Monday the Carters left for what Mrs. Carter said would be a short trip. Chief Rooney took the revolver.

Something Nick decided when they had the fish box roof nailed on was that the clubhouse would not hold more than the three of them. Gilbert did not mind leaving Archie out of the club, though mostly he and Archie hit it off. What he did mind was leaving Elmer out of it, because it was getting to be that next to Ernie and Nick, Elmer was his closest friend.

This was not simply on account of sitting next to Elmer in school. Elmer was one of those who would go out of his way to help a person when that person was in trouble. He was not like the Pharisee of old who walked by on the other side when a person he did not know was in some kind of fix. As for instance, Elmer did not know Chester from a hole in the ground. But when he heard Chester had lost his dog, Elmer asked around downtown on Saturdays when he went to make himself useful in the tinsmith shop and run messages for Mr. Waldy.

One day early in October Gilbert got permission to hear Elmer play Salvation Army tunes on his cornet. He let Gilbert have a try at it after shaking out the spit. Elmer's grown-up sister who worked in the mill played the tambourine and marched with the Salvation Army band on Sundays. Another day after school they marched in Elmer's yard to the tune of *Shall We Gather At The River,* Elmer playing his cornet and Gilbert keeping time with the tambourine. Band of Hope marching was going around and around in the Sunday School basement behind the lanky girl with wrinkles in her stockings who tried to boss things. She was always the one who carried the banner. The rest of them clapped their hands to the tune of some Band of Hope song played on the Infant Class piano by the choir's trained soloist.

Some Saturday afternoons that fall there was nothing doing at the clubhouse when, for instance, Nick's mother kept him raking leaves or Ernie had to stay home waiting for his father to cut his hair. On those afternoons Gilbert was allowed to go downtown with Elmer so they could run Mr. Waldy's messages together and make themselves useful in the tinsmith shop.

One of their first errands together was to the house on Durham Place which had the iron deer on its lawn. Elmer and Gilbert were behind the counter with the clerk helping him sort different sizes of wood scrws into separate boxes when the telephone bell rang. The clerk turned to the wall and answered, "It's for you, Mr. Waldy," he called. And when Mr. Waldy came, "Mrs. Albert on the line." Albert was the name of the bank manager who got to be head of the school board after Mr. Dryden had his fill of it.

Mr. Waldy set his unlighted cigar on the ledge of the telephone box, pushed back his hat and held the receiver to his ear. "Yes Mrs. All-bear, what can we do for you?" All-bear? He's got the name wrong, Gilbert thought. "Yes we stock that very brand, none better...Yes ma'am...Certainly ma'am. We have it in three sizes, small, medium and large. Which size do you prefer?...Very good, Mrs. All-bear...Yes, yes, immediately....By all means. Thank you....Not at all. Thanks again." Mr. Waldy hung up the receiver, winked at the clerk, shrugged and put the cigar in his mouth. He went to a shelf behind the other counter, brought a small tin of silver polish, wrapped it, told them where to take it, and gave each of them a copper.

They jog-trotted all the way and got to the Albert house in jig time. Instead of a bell, the Alberts' front door had a shiny brass knocker. Gilbert gave it a couple of bangs and a tall thin woman opened. She was all in black except for a starched white apron and a frilly white cap on her head. She took the parcel but not before she gave them a penny lecture for coming to the front door instead of going around to the back, to what she called the tradesmen's entrance. The way she looked down her nose at them it was easy to see she thought she was the whole cheese. If Gilbert had said what he felt like saying he would have told her to go pull the chain. One good thing, with Mr. Albert out to turn the school board against Doctor Scanlon, it served him right to have a wife like that. But when they got back to the store, the clerk said it must have been the maid who gave them the talking-to. He said Mrs. Albert was a short woman with a front like a roll-top desk. To show them what he meant by that he made an in-and-out motion with his hands.

When Gilbert first found out that Mr. Albert was out to turn the other men on the board against Doctor Scanlon you could have knocked him over with a feather. Doctor Scanlon was one of those teachers who are as scarce as hens' teeth. Everybody liked him and looked up to him—town people, church people, his students, everybody. Long ago when Doctor Scanlon came from Huron county high school to be principal of the collegiate, one of his Huron county students liked him so much he followed him to the collegiate. On top of that when the young man was trying to make ends meet teaching at the Settlement, what did Doctor Scanlon do but make him the collegiate's science teacher. And for anybody who does not know it, that man was Richard Egan.

The first Gilbert knew what was in the wind was after school a few days before Sport wandered off. Gilbert was filling the woodbox and their father was in the livingroom talking to their mother. Chester was out in the yard whooping it up with Sport and the fire in the kitchen stove was crackling so Gilbert missed most of what was being said. But it was plain their father was laying down the law, not to her but over something which had happened. Gilbert stopped piling the sticks of wood and listened for all he was worth. "I tell you Frances, that upstart must not be allowed to ride roughshod over others. . . . When Dryden gave up the reins, it was agreed by all, Albert included, the Doctor should remain as principal until he retires a few years hence. . . . Now this! For my part, any man whose word is not as good as his bond is beyond contempt.''

Saturday was market day and on market days most of the people who came to Waldy Hardware were farmers. Like Mr. Yarrow they were not the sort to hurry. After they bought what they came for, they stood around and talked. This suited Mr. Waldy down to the ground because he was a talker with the best of them. He could talk them into buying things they thought they had no use for, such as the combined knife and fork for one-armed men or a can of the new style ready-mixed paint, which according to Ernie's father, was not much better than whitewash compared to what you mixed yourself. Neither of the other two hardware stores went in for ready-mixed paint, which went to show that Mr. Waldy was ahead of his time. Because of having gone around selling lightning rods and his Magic Healer, he knew all the farmers by their first names, and what they were up against on their farms. Like Grandpa Williamson he was on the side of Laurier even though he had not shaken hands with him, which Grandpa Williamson had. All the same, when he talked with farmers who were on the other side, Mr. Waldy put in with them against playing second fiddle to the Yankees. No matter which side of the fence a farmer was on, he and Mr. Waldy did not have it hot and heavy as when Mr. Wallace and Gilbert's father argued on how the country should be run.

Mr. Waldy was not the only one kept busy on market days. Elmer's father also had his hands full. One Saturday he had two tin milk pails, a dipper, a clothes boiler, a barnyard lantern and a four gallon cream can to mend while the farmers who brought them stood around and talked. The tinsmith shop was on the second floor at the front of the building and to get to it, Elmer and Gilbert had to go past the horse blankets and sweat pad table to the back of the store, up some stairs and between two long rows of second-hand stoves. One of the coal heaters was higher than Gilbert's head. It had fancy doors with mica windows of different shapes and sizes, a nickel-plated rail to warm your feet and on top it had a knight in armor riding a galloping horse. Each time Gilbert passed that wonderful heater he had to stop and take a look. Across from it was a smaller heater with a statue. This was the top part of a lady who had lost most of her arms and whose nightdress had slipped so far down that her bulges showed though not anything like the roll-top desk the clerk said Mrs. Albert had.

coal heater:

Elmer's father did not look like Gilbert thought he would. He was the size of Mr. Dempster, bald and he wore thick glasses. One of his feet clinked when he walked because he had a metal thing fastened to the sole of his boot. While he was soldering or figuring out something he whistled through his teeth but so softly you could not make out the tune. He had two soldering irons and used one while the other was heating in the little charcoal stove on his workbench. When the hot solder and iron touched the milk pails and the cream can, they gave off the smell of burned cheese. With the clothes boiler the smell was of yellow soap, the same as when the one at home boiled over. That Saturday while he was not mending things for the farmers he kept busy making stovepipes. He said with cold weather coming on, Mr. Waldy would need stacks of stovepipes. He put the sheets of metal through a machine with three rollers which bent them into shape. Next he riveted the seams then did what he called the crimping. He let Gilbert and Elmer have a try at the machine but it was all they could do to turn the handle.

By the time they started home there wasn't much left of the afternoon. Elmer was for going by way of the market square but

Gilbert offered to show him the inside of the telephone office, Aunt
Trixie and the other woman on their high stools with metal things
over their ears. As it turned out Gilbert decided they had better not
go in. Grandpa Williamson was at the counter talking with a man
and another man was waiting. The axe factory did not work on
Saturday afternoons so there was nothing to see there either. After
they passed the Royal Consort, Gilbert decided to mosey along and
give Ernie a yoo-hoo so Elmer went on up the hill by himself.

Gilbert yoo-hooed and Ernie came from whatever he was doing
in the backyard. His haircut was the next thing to a pig shave and
the skin above his ears and on the back of his neck was white as
paper which made what hair was left look like a sort of reddish
skullcap. They talked about the clubhouse and made up what nails
to bring Monday after school. Gilbert told about the store and the
tinsmith shop and about Mrs. Albert wanting to be called Mrs.
All-bear. Quick as a wink Ernie went Mr. Waldy one better and
called her Mrs. All-bare-behind. They had a good laugh over that.
Ernie said that while he was sitting on the chopping block in the
woodshed having his hair cut, they heard a shot. It turned out that
a man who lived across the road from the tannery had shot a dog
that was chasing his chickens. Right off, Gilbert thought Sport was
a goner. But Ernie said not. By the time he got there, the man had
stuffed the dog into a potato sack with some rocks and was getting
ready to dump it in the river. Ernie said he had yet to see the potato
sack which would hold old Sport even with his legs doubled up.

Gilbert went on up the short-cut path to the Avenue. A little way
along, across from Mrs. Devon's, two big boys were taking turns
shooting at sparrows pecking horse buns in the road. Gilbert was
all eyes. He had never seen what they told him was a Daisy airgun.
They did not hit any of the sparrows but some of their shots came
close. You could see the spurts of dust where the shots landed. The
only gun Gilbert had ever laid hands on was the cap pistol Aunt
Kate's husband gave him one Christmas and he did not have that
long and for the reason his father took it away from him for
pointing it at people. After the sparrows flew away, the boys let
Gilbert take a shot at the horse buns. He hit one though he could
not be sure it was the one he aimed at. They let him hold the gun for
a minute. He ran his hand along its shiny barrel and over the
wooden part which you hold against your shoulder. Then they
winked at one another and took the gun away.

"Don't you wish you had a gun like this?" one of them asked.

That was about the most foolish question he could have asked because then and there Gilbert would have given just about anything to own one. "I think I will buy one just like this," Gilbert said, just to show them. He knew they didn't believe it. Neither did he, but he had to say something.

"Do you know what this gun costs? It cost a dollar and twenty-five cents. Where would you get a dollar and twenty-five cents?"

"Easy. All I would need to do is ask my father." This was another thing he didn't believe but he had to say something. He could see the two boys did not know what to make of him. So before they cornered him he kept on going. Besides he was in a hurry to do his number one. He got there in the nick of time. Chester was using the small hole so Gilbert used the large one which they were not supposed to use. Because of being in a hurry and because of listening to Chester's gab, he sprinkled a few drops on the seat, nothing much, nothing to speak of.

Their father was in the summer kitchen shining his and their mother's shoes for Sunday. Gilbert sat on the end of the coal-oil bench to have a talk. He told about the tinsmith shop, the farmers and Mr. Waldy, all like that and about Mrs. Albert calling herself All-bear. He started to tell the joke Ernie made of the name but his father said none of that, he had better be respectful. Next he made a big thing over shooting with the airgun. He said in case they ever owned one they would be able to shoot their own meat, such as partridges where Doug lived, instead of having to pay Mr. Schiller or Mr. Smith the butcher for chickens and all like that.

"If it's buying you an airgun you're leading up to, you'd best get any such notion out of your head. Your father is a poor man and the sooner you realize it and act accordingly, the better for all concerned."

This was the very first time Gilbert heard their father call himself poor. Saying money does not grow on bushes was one thing, it was something anybody might say. But to come right out and call yourself poor! There were two sorts of poor—the poor in spirit Jesus told about and there were the poor galoots and poor misguided Reformers such as Mr. Wallace, that their father talked about. Right then, he sounded like both these kinds.

Gilbert went out and sat on the back steps. When it came to buying things their father was either sky high or at the bottom of the ladder. As for instance with the apple peeling machine which cost a lot of money and which their mother liked but said she could have done without. Before that, the carpet sweeper, and which she told him right out they simply could not afford. Before long you heard him saying, "I tell you Frances, I am at my wits' end, I scarcely know where to turn." Then there was the row he raised over Aunt Trixie using a few of his one cent stamps the time she came to help out when their mother was not up to scratch. "I have no objection to your sister helping herself to my stamps but I do wish she would leave a note. Otherwise how can I balance my accounts?"

Their father finished shining the shoes, came down the steps and went into the backhouse. He came out buttoning up and mad as a wet hen. "A fine one you are wanting a gun when you can't shoot straight with the one you've got! You know the rule. How many times do I have to tell you?"

"I would have, only Chester was on our seat."

"Leave Chester out of this. You're the one responsible. You're much too prone to making excuses."

"I wasn't blaming him Poppa. All I said was. . . ." But his father did not stop to listen. He took the shoes inside and Gilbert heard him send Chester upstairs with them. Then he came out and got busy sawing wood on the sawhorse and splitting it for Sunday.

Gilbert went in, partly to keep out of sight but mostly because of the way his father had got after him. Their mother had the table set and the hanging lamp pulled down. She struck a match on the underside of the table, waited for the sulphur to burn off then touched it to the wick.

"It's not fair, Momma," he came out with. "You should have heard him."

"I did. And I heard you too." She put the lamp chimney back on, turned up the flame and popped the burnt match into the stove.

"Well I don't care. All the time getting after me."

She turned sharply. "That's enough of that, young man."

"I didn't mean anything Momma."

"I don't know what you meant but I do know what you said, and I want no more of it, not another word. Just you trot up to your room and think things over until I call you to supper."

Chester was in their mother's and father's room, probably snooping, which suited Gilbert just fine because after what happened downstairs, first one of them and then the other getting after him, he did not want to talk to Chester or to anybody else. He went quietly along the hall to the back room, closed the door and knelt at the window. Mr. Dempster had his smokehouse going and the thin blue-grey smoke sort of mixed with the dusk. Mr. Dempster used oak for smoking. Mr. Dubois did the same and oak chips were what Michael Williamson gathered when he was an old man and they let him go to the wood lot with a shawl over his shoulders and a basket on his arm. Gilbert pushed up the lower part of the window and leaned out. The smell of good old woodsmoke could take him a long way from here and the trouble he was in. It would take him to summer camps at Sparrow Lake, to those collecting trips up the river when he was little, when his father was different and did not get after him, the two of them sitting together and eating lunch beside a fire of twigs; to Obediah not much older than Tommy leading his packhorses through the forest on his way to Upper Canada; to night fires with friendly Indians and happy-go-lucky voyageurs.

But no smell of woodsmoke came to him. He closed the window, rested his forehead on the sill and knelt there in the twilight. If only I could have one of them on my side, he thought. But no, they all the time stick together. Gilbert Egan if you had sense enough to pound sand you would stop talking balderdash and show some gumption. Gilbert what a name!

Filbert, gimlet, giblets. No boy in any story, not a single solitary one in the whole school had to go around with the name Gilbert. Why didn't they name me Fauntleroy and be done with it?. . . Hello there Fauntleroy. In case you do not know it, your lace collar makes me laugh. Where did you get those velvet pants? Is that your dear mama you are leaning against? Why do you not sit on her knee and be done with it? Bill or Tom or Jim Egan would have been more like it. Better still, after Gracie died why didn't Mr. Waldy marry Frances Williamson instead of letting Richard Egan get ahead of him? Bill Waldy or Tom Waldy or Jim Waldy, how would one of those sound? Jake? Jake Waldy whose father smokes big cigars, who would never get after me about toeing in and squaring my shoulders, who would not be caught dead waxing his mustache and going around with a walking-stick, and who takes his boy Jake driving behind a high-stepping horse, selling Magic Healer and

lightning rods. . . . Farmer Brown this is my boy Jake. He is as
tough as a pine knot. He runs messages with the best of them. We
get along just fine.

The door opened and Chester came in. "What are you doing?"
"Use your eyes. Can't you see what I'm doing?"
"Did they send you up over something?"
"None of your business."
"They could have."
"I got something to tell you. A dog down at the tannery got shot
for killing chickens. It might have been Sport."
"How do you know?"
"Ernie said. He couldn't be sure. The man had him in a sack.
But it probably was. Sport hung around the tannery. You know
that as well as anybody."
Chester screwed up his face to keep from crying. Gilbert felt like
a stinker. But with those two getting after him, he had to take it out
on somebody.

CHAPTER FOURTEEN

Interlude

Gilbert Egan was one of those who should remember to take a good hard look before they jump. If he had known what his mother had up her sleeve for him he would not have got the notion she had it in for him, which is what he did the day she sent him to his room. But it was not until the week before Hallowe'en he was told about it.

The surprise could not have come at a better time. The clubhouse was finished and it had room enough for the three of them. But on school days it was hardly worth climbing up there because it was dark inside by five o'clock. And on Saturdays his father seemed to go out of his way to think up chores for him. "I'm not at all sure we should allow him to go traipsing over there," Gilbert heard him say to their mother. "How do we know what he's up to in that tree house of theirs?"

: tree house :

"Would you sooner he went downtown and hung around the poolroom?" Gilbert could imagine the look in her eyes when she asked.

"There you go, Frances. Be logical. The poolroom has nothing whatever to do with it." You could tell by his voice he was stumped.

Gilbert was not sure he knew the meaning of that word but one other time his father used it, their mother came out on top.

It was over a Toronto man who rented a house in the tony part of town, opened an office and came to both morning and evening service. Their father was all for having him on the Quarterly Official Board. Their mother said she did not trust him and when their father asked why, what reasons did she have, she said none at all, it was simply that she did not trust him. This their father called not logical. But sure enough, by spring the man was gone leaving D.V. Schiller and quite a few other storekeepers whistling for their money. Even so, their father said she had to admit the man was kind to his wife and children.

The surprise was that his mother was going on a train trip and that she was going to take him with her. She called it an airing, getting away from the house. Aunt Trixie called it kicking over the traces but that came later. Their mother was not much for going around to afternoon teas or trotting from door to door with her calling cards. Although she belonged to the Ladies' Aid she was not much for church suppers either. She called church suppers stewing and brewing for a lot of men who would be better off if they did not stuff themselves. At morning service when Mr. D.V. Schiller read the announcements and told the ladies what food to bring, she let what he said go in one ear and out the other. She said the ladies would save themselves a lot of fuss and hullabaloo and be further ahead if they gave the money directly instead of adding the cost of the food to their grocery bills.

The trip they were going on was to a relative Gilbert had not set eyes on since the evening he came to supper while they lived in the double house across the river. He was her Uncle Ben and he so seldom visited any of them that Trixie called him an old stick-in-the-mud. He was a country doctor at some small place halfway between town and the Junction. He came from their mother's side of the house. By all accounts his grandfather was doctor to the kilties who shinnied up the cliffs just in time to get into the battle on the Plains of Abraham. After both sides cooled down the grandfather married a lady who spoke only French. He did not know French but this did not stop them from having a lot of children and hitting it off quite well.

Uncle Ben was all for the United Empire Loyalists even though he was not one of them. He did not get riled up over how the Family Compact ruled the roost in the old days though he probably would not have touched any of them with a ten-foot pole. The aunts said he was peppery and that Frankie was by far his favorite.

Friday was the day their mother picked for the visit. This suited Gilbert down to the ground. Not only for the reason Miss Burwell was going to make his class choose sides for another of her spelling matches and Ruby Greer was sure to be one of the two who did the picking. If she picked him he would want to tell her to go chase herself. On top of this, being away on Friday would get him out of going to Band of Hope which had not turned out to be anything like what he thought it would be when the lady who ran it talked him and two others of his Sunday School class into joining it.

The morning they left was so cold and blustery their mother had to wear her old winter coat which all of them would be glad to see the last of. The edges of its cuffs were worn and its sleeves had too much puff. The new one she was saving up for and would buy in time for Christmas would be the same as Aunt Kate's with a collar from an animal by the name of Alaska sable. Alaska sables were probably some relation to skunks. For when you pressed your nose into their fur it had a teeny bit of skunk smell though nothing like the one those boys got forty-five cents for.

Chester had been excused from kindergarten and as a treat he was to spend Friday and most of Saturday with the Williamsons. The wind down by the river had sleet in it and was so strong that as they crossed the upper bridge they walked with their backs to it. They took Chester up the hill and most of the way along Balaclava then made a beeline for the station. The coal heater in the passenger car was going full blast and in no time at all Gilbert took off his reefer.

Gilbert's Uncle Ben was not at the station to meet them and his mother said she had not expected him to be. His house was across the road from the small stone-walled station. It too was of stone, larger and with two front doors. The nearest door was to what she said was the waiting room. The door they went to was opened by a tall, grey-haired lady. She said they were expected, hung up their coats and took them into a large front room. She said the Doctor should soon be back from his morning rounds. Gilbert expected her to sit down and visit the way ladies do. But not a bit of it.

As soon as she closed the door behind her, Gilbert got up from the sofa and took a look around the room. The first picture to

catch his eye was the very same one Tommy had, only this one was
a whole lot larger and it had a frame around it. *All That Was Left of
Them* was the name, and it showed the stuff British soldiers were
made of in the days of the Light Brigade, Tommy said. It showed
all who were left after the charge of the Light Brigade lined up,
some still on their horses and some whose horses had been killed as
they rode into the Valley of Death. The nearest soldier in the
line-up was a boy not much older than Tommy. He had a bandage
on his head with blood on it and he looked as if he was having a
hard time to keep from falling off his horse. The point of his spear
was bent from sticking it into some enemy or other. Tommy
thought he was a Cornet of Horse, which was the name of the boy
hero in one of Tommy's Henty books. The man on the horse next
to the boy looked something like Mr. Waldy. You could see he
was ready to put his arm around the boy in case he toppled from his
horse on account of being wounded. Tommy said if only we had
soldiers with as good stuff as those they would never have let the
Boers bottle them up in the Siege of Ladysmith like ours were.

The picture on the wall across from *All That Was Left of Them*
was a lady with her hair down and in her nightdress sitting on a
stump in a swamp. She had her head cocked and one hand to her
ear to show she was listening. Sure enough she was, the picture
had *Listening for the Fairies* printed on it. An owl as big as a turkey
gobbler was flying past her knee and if she had her wits about her
she would have been scared stiff. The person who made the picture
must have stuck in the owl to show it was night time which is no
time to be sitting in a swamp in only your nightdress. The lady's
bare feet and arms should have been covered with mosquito bites.
It was easy to see that *Listening for the Fairies* was all in the
person's imagination, nothing like *All That Was Left of Them*
which showed the real thing.

His mother was looking at something on a stand beside the bay
windows so he went over. It was a bunch of imitation flowers under
a glass bell. Aunt Boo had one just like it in her room. Different
colored hairs were looped or twisted into the shapes of leaves and
petals. All the hair came from her friends and relatives who were
dead. Aunt Boo could tell you which was which—the hair of her
cousin Hester's little girl who got drowned by falling down a well,
straw colored hair like Chester's and who it belonged to, her dear
friend who was taken by inflammation of the bowel. She did not
have any of Gracie's hair and for the reason hair flowers went out

of style while Gracie was still alive. She said having the hair flowers in her room made her feel close to the dear ones who had gone before. But seeing the hair of people molting in their graves long before he was born gave Gilbert a spooky feeling when he stopped to think about it. His Uncle Ben's hair flowers did not give him that feeling, they probably came from people he did not know from a hole in the ground.

A rig turned into the driveway and his mother said it could only be Uncle Ben's because of the two spotted dogs trotting abreast close behind it. She said they were coach dogs and that as far back as she could remember they were the kind he went in for. The rig was a phaeton with a gig lamp at each end of its dashboard. Because of the weather, its side curtains were on. The horse was not one of your high-steppers. Its tail was not docked and it did not have a check rein pulling up its head, which was a pretty sure sign Uncle Ben was kind to his horses. It did not even have a buggy whip standing in its whip socket. A man came from back of the house and held the horse's bridle while Uncle Ben got out with his satchel. Then the man led the horse away with the two dogs still close to the back wheels.

: phaeton :

Uncle Ben wore one of those caps made of twirly black fur along the lines of the one Mr. Waldy wore for curling. His overcoat came well below his knees and had a short cape attached to it. From what Gilbert was able to see of him from the bay window he was no taller than Uncle Abel Williamson but his movements were quicker. He went up the steps to the door of his waiting room two at a time.

Gilbert was still at the bay window when Uncle Ben came into the room. Right from the first it was easy to see Uncle Ben thought a lot of their mother and that she did of him. When they shook hands he took both of hers in his and he called her Frankie. Gilbert was all ready to shake hands but all he got was a friendly nod, none of this—what reader was he in? did he like his teacher? and all the rest of it. The Toronto business man took the cake for that. He even asked Gilbert what he and his brother wanted to make of themselves when they grew up. It had taken Gilbert a minute to know what he was getting at and before he had, their mother answered for them. She said she did not greatly care what they were when they grew up so long as they were honest men. As it turned out, this was a pretty snippy thing to say to a man who up and left Mr. D.V. Schiller and those other storekeepers whistling for their money.

Until that day at his Uncle Ben's, Gilbert believed that everybody, including people in Yankeeland and all other foreign lands, had dinner at noon, except perhaps the people in India when they had another of their famines going on. At home when the Ladies' Aid put on a bang-up dinner they called it supper. Lunch was what you took with you when you went fishing or collecting specimens or for eating on trains in case your father was not against it.

All the same, lunch at Uncle Ben's was not to be sneezed at. The lady who served it did not sit at table, she brought in the food, one thing after another. As it turned out she was Uncle Ben's housekeeper and the man who looked after the horse was her husband. First there was pea soup, then two kinds of cold meat, mutton and some other kind, red cabbage and green tomato pickle, pumpkin pie. And doughnuts in case you had room for one. The table was made of some dark polished wood and instead of one big cloth, there were little ones in front of where you sat. Uncle Ben sat in a high-backed chair at the head of the table, their mother sat on his right and Gilbert sat across from her. Uncle Ben did not ask the blessing but you could not take that to mean he was an unbeliever. The big thing was that after the three of them sat down, in came the two dogs like trained soldiers and sat bolt upright on either side of Uncle Ben's chair. When he held bits of meat in front of their noses they would not so much as sniff until he told them they could have it.

After the meal the dogs marched out and the three of them went to a smaller sitting room which had a side door between it and the waiting room. The door was kept open in case somebody came for medicine or to have their sickness attended to. Uncle Ben must have seen Gilbert was curious because without being asked he told Gilbert he could go in and have a look around but not to so much as lay a finger on anything. Uncle Ben had quick eyes and a choppy way of speaking. He was one of those who do not go beating under bushes, one you had better not try fibbing to.

The waiting room had a large cupboard with glass doors and different kinds of doctoring tools on its shelves—scissors and knives and saws for opening up people to find out what was wrong with their insides. These showed that Uncle Ben was miles ahead of Doctor De Silva's kind of doctor, tapeworms or no tapeworms. Gilbert sat down on one of the chairs, pressed his hands over his stomach to pretend he was a sick person waiting to find out what could be done for him—could he be excused from school, would he get better or in spite of everything would he be taken? But try as he would be could not think up anything so he went back into the livingroom.

Uncle Ben must have fixed up most of his sick people. Only a few of them came that afternoon so there was plenty of time for him and their mother to sit and talk. Gilbert stayed over by the window, pretending he was on the lookout for whoever came. His mother's back was to him so he missed some of what she said. Once when she came out with something Uncle Ben chuckled. "Still the same Frankie with a mind of her own."

That afternoon for the first time ever, Gilbert saw his mother as a separate person, not as part of the family, not belonging to any of them but as a person all by herself. The feeling he had was as if he came into a room and there in front of him was a person who was not a stranger but was one he knew very little about. The thought was not easy to get used to but it stayed with him for the rest of the afternoon, while the housekeeper lady served them tea and while Uncle Ben walked with them to the station. On the train it began to blur, until by the time they were home, his father there and everything the same, she became only his mother again.

CHAPTER FIFTEEN

Some Two-Sided People

There are some days so much the same they are like so many peas in so many pods—school days and even days at camp when nothing much happens. There are those days which stick out like sore thumbs which you would just as soon forget about. And there are days which stay in your mind like special days marked on the calendar. A calendar day is the first day you are allowed to go barefoot, or the day the first corn on the cob is on the table or the first evening the lamp is lit for supper. The day the storm windows are put back on is not quite as much a calendar day but it is one which tells you good old winter is just around the corner.

The morning after Gilbert and his mother got home, his father was up and had the porridge made earlier than on school days. Mr. Wallace was coming to steady the ladder and after their storm windows were on, their father would help Mr. Wallace put on his. Mr. Wallace was not much for climbing ladders.

It was all right for his father to wear old clothes, the ones he wore at camp, when he helped Mr. Wallace and did outside chores for the Misses Langley. Nobody said anything when he walked halfway around the block morning, noon and night to keep the smokehouse going when Mr. Dempster had la grippe, or whatever it was that he had. But when his father walked across town in his old clothes and carrying his tools to mend the Williamsons' front steps he got himself talked about. Aunt Trixie was the one who told. Two ladies living on Balaclava talked about him over the telephone. Trixie would not give their names, she said this was against the rules, but like as not one of them was the gone-to-seed Family Compact lady who lived across the street from the Williamson house. By all accounts both ladies were hot under the collar. One said things had come to a pretty pass when a collegiate teacher paraded through the better part of town dressed like a common laborer. The other lady put in with her on that. She said a collegiate teacher had a position to keep up and that on a salary of eight hundred dollars a year there was no excuse. Trixie said there was the same sort of talk when the Baptist minister painted his own house, that none of the three

Presbyterian ministers would do such a thing, let alone the Church of England one who was so much the born gentleman he did not shovel the snow from his own walk.

The storm windows had been cleaned and lined up in the shed days before. First thing that morning before Mr. Wallace came to steady the ladder, their father put on the downstairs windows with Gilbert as usual standing around and handing him things. By the middle of the morning all the windows were on. They left the storm doors until later and got to work on Mr. Wallace's windows in case the wind got up. When you are teetering at the top of a ladder hanging onto a storm window with both your hands is no time to have the wind give you a push and make you lose your balance. As it turned out, the wind that morning never amounted to more than a breeze. Even so it had little Sandy sawing wood so fast you would think he had been sent for. Sandy was the name Mr. Wallace gave to the little whittled-out hired man Mr. Wallace had on his weather vane. When the windmill part of it went around, it turned a sort of crank which made the top half of Sandy's body move back and forth. Sandy's hands held a tiny, make-believe bucksaw and one of his feet held the stick of wood on the sawhorse. Sandy looked so real that people on the street sometimes stopped to watch him working. He wore a whittled straw dummy and had a red bandana hanging from his hip pocket. On windy days he sawed so fast he made you tired just to look at him. On stormy nights when the wind was howling and Gilbert was snug in bed he felt sorry for little Sandy sawing away hour after hour out there in the dark and the cold. In the book of *Uncle Tom's Cabin* that stinker Simon Legree made the slaves work like that and when they stopped he up and whipped them. Yes, and those Egyptians were every bit as mean to the children of Israel until Moses came along and took them down a peg or two. Only for him, The Chosen People might never have made it to the River Jordan, banyan or no banyan. Moses got them manna and water from the rock. The sad part was Moses never got there himself. Chester said the Lord did not play fair with Moses.

When Mr. Wallace and Gilbert's father worked together they called each other by their last names. This would not sound polite to some people but it was a whole lot more polite than when they got started on Laurier and Mr. Gladstone and the rest of it. When all the windows were on, Mr. Wallace invited them into the kitchen to sit a bit and warm their hands. Old Bruce was dozing behind the stove and did not bother to look up. Mr. Wallace had a dandy big turnip for them. A friend out at the Settlement had brought him a sack of them and to Gilbert's way of thinking, a slice of crisp juicy turnip with salt on it was as good as a cookie any day. Mr. Wallace said his Settlement friend was Dan Goudy and surely Gilbert's father remembered him. Gilbert's father said indeed he did, but that was water over the dam long since, and to thank Goudy for the turnip. Gilbert got the feeling there was more behind this but had sense enough not to ask. He knew if he did he would be wasting his breath.

Grandma Williamson, Chester and Aunt Boo had the house to themselves when Gilbert got there that afternoon. He had looked forward to coming but he had no more than stepped inside the door and taken off his reefer before he knew this was another of those times when Aunt Boo let the green-eyed monster get the better of her. When Grandma Williamson spoke to her all she did was mutter, and the minute Grandma Williamson's back was turned she made as if to spit at her. It was hard to believe she was the same Aunt Boo he sat next to in church and stood beside for the singing, helping hold her hymn book. No wonder the Ladies' Aid called her sweet little Miss Williamson. They would not have believed she was the same person if they saw her while the green-eyed monster had hold of her.

Well, maybe she was not the same person. Gilbert had to admit he had two sides to him, the side that fitted in at home and the side who was all for running away when things did not suit him. Certainly their father had two sides to him, the school teacher side and the camping side. Their mother was more like one person, no matter what. Elmer and Ernie seemed always the same. So was Eph unless you teased him. You could not always count on Archie but with Nick you always knew. Probably everybody had different sides to them only did not let it show. But when the green-eyed monster had Aunt Boo in its grip she did not care who knew, she made no bones about it. That Saturday afternoon she was so downright mean and spiteful to Grandma Williamson, Gilbert pictured her riding on a broom with a witch's hat on her head, her bustle sticking out behind and her elastic-sided shoes showing below her skirt.

Yet at other times when he and Chester had her to themselves upstairs in her room, she was as nice as pie. She told them stories of family happenings even before Obediah came along. Better still she sang them a song nobody else in the family knew. It told about General Brock or some other general sending the Yankee soldiers home with their tails between their legs and of what happened when the cannons went off and "smoke rose up as high as our church steeple." When Aunt Boo sang "steeple," her wavery voice rose higher and higher and seemed to come to a point like the top of the steeple on the town's biggest Presbyterian church.

But nothing like that this afternoon. Instead of helping Grandma in the kitchen, Aunt Boo did just the opposite. When Grandma laid down the knife to put more wood in the stove, Aunt Boo snatched the knife and hid it. No sooner had Grandma gone into the pantry than Aunt Boo dipped more water into the kettle to keep it from boiling. The minute there was talking, she began humming "In the sweet bye and bye, we shall meet on that beautiful shore." If Grandma Williamson had been Grandmother Egan she would have put her foot down but Grandma Williamson had the patience of Job. Grandpa Williamson would have done the same, except that as soon as he came in the front door and was hanging up his overcoat away went the green-eyed monster and butter would not melt in Aunt Boo's mouth.

What with Saturday bath night and their boots to shine for Sunday, Gilbert's orders were to have Chester home by dark. If their father could have been persuaded to let in the telephone, as the aunts wanted him to do, they just might have been allowed to stay for supper at the Williamsons'. Their father was not against the telephone, all he said was forking out three dollars a month for it was out of all proportion. Their mother was not against it either though having been a hello girl, the telephone was no new thing to her. She did say that having a telephone put you at everyone's beck and call.

Except in hot weather, Saturday nights were the ones when more than any other nights of the week, Gilbert went right off to sleep instead of lying awake imagining things. There he would be in bed after his bath in the warm kitchen, wearing a fresh smelling nightshirt, back to back with Chester, the flannelette sheet and covers tucked under his chin. But that Saturday night was another of Chester's worry nights. When Chester put his mind to it he could worry over anything that came along, such as where had Sport got to? was the Carter baby all right? where had he left his Infant Class Golden Text card? the mess he made of folding paper hats in kindergarten, the lock-jaw you died from if you cut the skin between your thumb and finger. This night he was worrying his head over Aunt Boo, and was the green-eyed monster who got into her one of those devils who got into a herd of swines in the Bible and made them jump down a steep bank and kill themselves?

Gilbert told him that in the first place swine was only a fancy name the Bible had for pigs, and that in the second place what Aunt Trixie called the green-eyed monster was only one side of Aunt Boo which showed how she was feeling. He could have made a point of it by asking Chester how would he behave if the body part of him stopped growing when he was twelve. But asking this would only have given Chester one more thing to worry about so Gilbert kept his trap shut on that. Instead he said they should remember all the nice things Aunt Boo did, the stories she told them. Also there were the dummy watches and picture hankies she gave one or other of them at Christmas. They kept on remembering nice things to say about Aunt Boo until their father called from his study for them to settle down.

At church next morning Aunt Boo lived up to the nice things Gilbert and Chester had said about her. When the lady in the pew in front of them had trouble finding a hymn book Aunt Boo offered hers. She gave Doctor Scanlon her sweetest smile when he passed the collection plate and at the end she extended the right hand of fellowship to just about everybody who came along. It turned out this was Missionary Sunday so Reverend Allister whittled down his sermon to make room for the special speaker. The Methodist Church had two sorts of missions, the Home and the Foreign. This Sunday it was Foreign. The Home missionaries told about the needs of the Canadian Indians and the Foreign missionaries told mostly about India where there was another famine going on. In Canada, when Indians needed rice they got into their canoes and gathered it the way Mr. Dubois did. You would not catch a Canadian Indian standing around like bumps on a log waiting for the missionary to give them rice. Not on your tin-type! But it seemed to Gilbert that in India this was what the hungry people were up to. The people who gave Foreign missionaries the most trouble were the rice Christians. Rice Christians stayed away from church until they needed rice then they showed up to sing and pray with the best of them. Nick said some Baptist boys acted like this until the Sunday School picnic came along. China too had famines though nothing like as many as India had. In China girl babies were partly to blame for famines. So what did the Chinese do but throw the girl babies in the river. This way they got rid of famines until another crop of girl babies came along.

While the missionary up there behind the pulpit was talking away, Gilbert sized up the coat of the lady in front of him and wondered if it was anything like the winter coat their mother would have in time for Christmas. The fur of the Alaska sable on Aunt Kate's collar was longer and darker than the fur on the lady's collar but either kind would look all right on their mother. After the missionary had said his say about famine, he told of other things the poor people of India were up against. The very worst was the way they were treated by the stuck-up people. The stuck-up people thought so much of themselves that if the shadow of a poor person fell on what they were eating they would throw the food away for fear it would poison them. The stuck-up people lived in the toniest part of town, their houses were like palaces and except for the servants poor people were not allowed to set foot inside them. Living in India would have suited Mrs. All-bear and her bossy school board husband down to the ground....*Here is your silver polish, Mrs. All-bear. My friend and I got it here as fast as we could....If you do not mind me saying so, the iron deer on your lawn must have cost a lot of money.... Watch out my shadow does not fall on your Christmas dinner. If it did you would have to throw away the turkey or it would make you puke.*

The Sunday School lesson that afternoon was about the sheep that got lost. Doug said sheep had not changed much since Jesus' day and this was why they needed shepherds to look after them. He said cats were far from being the only animals that could find their way home, dogs usually could, providing they had a home to go to. This made Gilbert tell about Sport and ask Doug to be on the lookout for him. Horses and cows sometimes got lost. But when it came to brains, Doug said give him a run-of-the-mill pig any time. Doug had all kinds of interesting stories about animals and every boy in the class listened for all he was worth. The first thing they knew, lesson time was over and the Infant Class in the other room was singing the same collection song Gilbert sang when he was in Infant Class—"hear the pennies dropping, count them as they fall, every one for Jesus, He will get them all." Doug let Gilbert go around the class and collect the copper from each of them, then hand out the Sunday School paper. After the Intermediate School superintendent gave them his little talk, the trained soloist lady went to the piano and the girls' and boys' classes rose and joined in the closing hymn. The trained soloist lady was a friend of the Band of Hope lady who talked Gilbert and the other two boys into joining. Usually when Sunday School was let out she came to remind them to come straight from school Friday afternoon. But the three of them were thinking of quitting so they ducked out before she nailed them.

Instead of going straight home, Gilbert took Chester to hear Elmer play his cornet. But Elmer was not there. Nobody was, most likely they were away marching with other Salvation Army people. The partly built house next door had got its roof on so Gilbert and Chester went into the yard to have a look around. There was a deep ditch leading in from the street and the part of it next the sidewalk was covered with planks to keep people from falling in. The part under the planks made Gilbert think of Robinson Crusoe's cave and if he had not been wearing his Sunday clothes he would have jumped down and taken a look inside. If he and Nick and Ernie had any gumption they would have made a cave instead of a tree house for their club. With winter just around the corner, the tree house was no place to sit around in, wind and snow coming in between the boards.

When Gilbert and Chester got home, Aunt Trixie and Mr. Pickering were in the front hall getting ready to leave. Aunt Trixie had on her coat and gloves and was fussing with her veil and their father was helping Mr. Pickering get into his overcoat. By the sounds of things their father was laying down the law over something. "I tell you anyone with half an eye can see what the fellow's leading up to. Your readers should be informed. Why shillyshally?"

Gilbert could not make out what Mr. Pickering had to say to that but it could not have been much because their father kept on arguing until Mr. Pickering and Aunt Trixie went to the door.

From what Gilbert could make out, there were different kinds of Sundays—Catholic Sundays, Church of England Sundays, and Methodist, Baptist and Presbyterian ones. Catholic Sundays were over by noon, after that Catholics were free to go swimming, skate on the dam and in bad weather stay inside and have games with dice, such as snakes-and-ladders, parchesi and other forms of gambling. You could say for Church of Englanders they turned out full strength for morning service, then if all of them were like the ones on Balaclava they were not so particular about the rest of the day, tennis and afternoon tea on the lawn. It was hard to tell about the Presbyterians, they looked strict enough and their churches had the loudest bells in town. But this did not stop Dr. Kirkland from exercising his trotting horse on Sunday when he went to answer a sick call. From what Gilbert knew of Salvation Army people they did not mind enjoying themselves on Sundays, marching and playing music and all the rest of it. One thing sure, when it came to not doing everyday things on Sunday the Methodists took the cake. Though if you listened to Nick, Baptists would scarcely lift a finger on their Sundays.

: wash day :

Gilbert had no way of knowing about other Methodists but the Richard Egans and the Williamsons were not against starting the Monday wash last thing on Sunday, or at least getting ready to start it. What they did before they went up to bed was set up the wooden tubs and fill the wash boiler with cold water. While their father did this, their mother cut slices from a cake of yellow soap. The name of the soap was Surprise. Each cake had a coupon on its wrapper. By cutting out enough coupons and sending them in you could get an IXL two-blader. IXL's were about the best. Gilbert had been saving coupons for two years to get one. Only the white clothes went into the boiler. They were put in layer by layer with a good sprinkling of soap slices between and a few spoonfuls of coal-oil. Very early next morning, in winter hours before daylight, down came their father to heat the boiler and the pots of extra water on the back of the stove. He kept the fire going full blast. The tubs were on two chairs close together, one tub for the washboard, one for the wringer. When he had the clothes bubbling he called up the backstairs for their mother. He carried the clothes to the tub on a stick made from a broomhandle with one end flattened, added water and they set to work, one at the washboard, one turning the wringer. The kitchen windows clouded with steam and the wash day smell went up the stairs. By the time the porridge was made, and Gilbert and Chester called, the washing was in the basket ready for the line, the tubs and things returned to the summer kitchen and the floor wiped. Doing the washing was women's work so neither Grandpa Williamson nor their father hung the clothes on the line. Nick said his father didn't either. Though on account of Grandpa Williamson's habit of singing and whistling while he helped, his next door neighbor had a pretty good idea of what he was up to so early in the morning, at least in summer with the windows open.

More than ever since their father began studying for his degree, Gilbert and Chester knew Mondays were days they had better mind their p's and q's. This may have been because he got out of the wrong side of the bed to help do the wash. Or it may have been because he had another week with the same old thing at school ahead of him which was how Gilbert felt. It was hard to tell about their father. All Chester had to do at the breakfast table was to put his hand to his head to be told to stop twisting his hair. With Gilbert it was the same old thing about shoulders. Every so often right after breakfast he was made to stand against the wall, "head erect, chin in, shoulders back, heels together, toes at an angle of forty-five degrees." Yes, and like as not if he was in the house when his father came home from the collegiate, Gilbert had to walk around with a book balanced on top of his head. This had something to do with what his father called carriage. It made Gilbert feel like some animal out of a circus.

That Monday when Gilbert reported after school he asked if he could mosey on down to Ernie's. His mother had no objection providing he was home by dark. And so he would have been except that by the time he was at the pop factory corner something made him change his mind and go along to Elmer's instead. As it turned out, Elmer's mother had sent him to the tinsmith shop with a message. So for want of something better to do, Gilbert went and had a look at the tunnel under the sidewalk. Nothing had changed except that the wind had blown a lot more dead leaves into the hole. Nobody was around so Gilbert jumped down and went inside.

At first he could scarcely believe how warm it was down there.

Robinson Crusoe must have had his thinking cap on when he decided on a cave instead of a tree house though perhaps the Swiss Family knew what they were doing, in case there were rattlesnakes and cobras in their South Sea Island. And if their house was in a coconut tree they could reach out and help themselves. But Ontario was different, snow any day now. Gilbert got up off his hunkers and carried in armful after armful of leaves then snuggled down in them. Leaves would do for covers instead of goat skins. What you would need was a fire. A charcoal burner like those Mr. Spence used for soldering would be just the ticket. By hanging some canvas over the door of your cave and using a candle you could be as snug as a bug in a rug.

He wriggled deeper into the leaves. How would it be living all by yourself? Doug did fine living by himself and so did Mr. Wallace. When you lived by yourself you would have the say about which kind of porridge, white or brown sugar, and when it was your bedtime. A slight rumbling came from above, a rig passing or somebody clumping along the sidewalk. If you lived in a cave you would have to keep it a secret. Or would you? Just because your father rubbed you the wrong way and your mother sometimes did too was no reason for you to go off by yourself. Just because your parents lived in glass houses and could not see themselves as others saw them was no reason for you to throw stones at them. If you had a place of your own, such as a cave, you and your parents could be the friendliest of neighbors. Whenever you felt like it you could go across and split their kindling for them and on Saturdays you could take turns with Chester at the apple peeler. You could walk home from church together and they could invite you in for Sunday dinner. It would be like the college song the collegiate teachers sometimes sang when they came for a social evening—"Love your neighbor as yourself as the world you go traveling through. Never sit down with a tear or a frown but paddle your own canoe." That last always made him think of Mr. Dubois and good old Sparrow Lake. Nick and Ernie could visit you, Chester too providing he behaved himself.

Gilbert wriggled deeper into the covering of leaves. He thought back to the afternoon at his Great-Uncle Ben's when he first saw his mother not as his mother but as a person all by herself. The only time he came near to seeing his father that way was the day his father marched straight up to Mr. Carter and made him hand over his gun, the way Mr. Wallace told the Misses Langley about it.

Supposing there was a man you wanted to be friends with and it turned out he was your father, would this make any difference between you? Or supposing the man was as old as Mr. Waldy or even Mr. Wallace? Would this make any difference when he called you his son?

Gilbert got to his feet, shook off the leaves, felt his way along the ditch and climbed out. The street light at the pop factory corner was on and houses along the street had their lamps lit. The six o'clock whistles must have gone! After the cave, the wind chilled him and he made for home in a jog trot. In case he decided to make a cave for himself it need not have so high a roof or be as long as the one in the ditch. But it should be wider with room for his sleeping place, the charcoal stove and a box or two to sit on. Instead of a ditch, it should have a hole with a ladder. In bad weather you could cover the hole with boards to keep out the rain and snow. Robinson Crusoe's cave had a storeroom at the back but this could come later in case he had a lot of stuff. He could almost feel how cozy he would be, the charcoal fire going and everything just right. It would not be the same as if he up and ran away! They would know where he was. If he explained things they would have nothing to get after him about.

He remembered to close the gate behind him and was up the steps when the side door opened and there was his father blocking the doorway, larger than life with the light of the room behind him. "Well, well. What boy is this? Are you sure you haven't come to the wrong house? Speak up. What have you to say for yourself?"

Gilbert was stuck for an answer. "Nothing, I guess." This was like at the end of a visit when you have nothing more to say except goodbye then start for your own place. He backed down the steps, went along the walk, not hurrying, again remembering to close the gate behind him, and started toward the school corner. He was passing the far end of the Misses Langleys' front fence when he heard the gate click and his father's quick steps. Gilbert did not stop or so much as turn his head, just kept on walking until his father caught up with him.

His father turned him and put an arm around his shoulders. "Come, come. Supper's waiting."

His father did not take away his arm until they were inside their gate. The last time Gilbert remembered the feel of his father's arm around him was the night he cried and cried from earache, and that was while they lived in the double house across the river.

CHAPTER SIXTEEN

Decisions

By taking off its wheels and putting on runners you could turn your delivery wagon into a delivery sleigh in two shakes of a dead lamb's tail. When the snow came to stay this is what Mr. Mullin did with his coal-oil wagon, though of course you would not make your buggy, phaeton or surrey into a cutter by doing this. With Mr. Dempster it was a horse of a different color. In summer the women went out when they heard him toot his horn, to choose the fish they wanted, but no woman would stand in the snow at the back of a fish sleigh pointing out which whitefish, Great Lake herring, cisco or pickerel she wanted and be frozen half to death while Mr. Dempster weighed it and handed out her change. Yes, and what fish man in his right senses would drive along street after street, up there on the driver's seat tooting his horn to let the women know he was coming? His long white apron would look mighty queer tied on top of his overcoat. Mr. Dempster had other jobs than peddling fish. In winter he was caretaker of the curling rink and he looked after the ice house, getting the sawdust and all that. Tommy was right when he said you would not catch his father hanging around the Royal Consort waiting for something to turn up. Tommy was proud of his father and made no bones about it. He said when you have a father who was in good Queen Victoria's navy you have something to be proud about.

Since the snow came Gilbert missed his talks with Tommy. But one day after school both of them came to Mrs. Devon's on errands for their mothers. Tommy said there was a good chance he would be going to Volunteer camp with his Port Dover uncle next summer, to be a drummer boy or perhaps a bugler. He said by all the signs his voice was changing, that when he got excited it sort of wobbled which is what happens when you start growing up. Gilbert knew about this because Yankee Jones' voice was going the same way. Tommy said if the Boers kept the British soldiers bottled up inside Ladysmith much longer there would be nothing for it but to send Canadian Volunteers to get them out and put the Boers on the run. It was too early to say but his uncle's regiment might be the one to be sent.

The evening after his talk with Tommy, their mother tucked them in and took away the lamp, and after Chester stopped squirming and got to sleep, Gilbert tried to imagine Tommy marching into battle blowing his bugle or beating on his drum. In case they gave him a horse to ride Tommy would know how to look after it on account of sometimes looking after Nell. When all that were left of the Volunteers lined up after the battle, would Tommy have a handkerchief with blood on it tied around his head? Tommy Dempster was good stuff so he would have been in the thick of it and was bound to have been wounded. In pictures after a battle bandages were as thick as hairs on a dog's back—head bandages, arm bandages, leg bandages. There was never one soldier shown with a wound in his stomach or with his insides hanging out, which would have made some people sick to look at.

But suppose Tommy was not among those who lined up? Suppose he lay far from home in a soldier's grave? Who would be the one to tell his mother? like in the song Tommy sang while the two of them sat on the pile of ties watching the shunting engine and waiting for the through freight to go past. "Just break the news to mother and say there is no other...." something, something, "kiss her dear sweet face for me, for I'm not coming home." Gilbert was not sure of the words but he was sure he did not want to be the one to tell Tommy's mother. Somebody has to tell her, you are Tommy's best friend so it is up to you to tell her.... *May I step inside a minute, Mrs. Dempster? My that is a nice dress you have on. By the smell of things you are baking more of your good cookies, the kind you used to give Tommy and me after school. Not right now Mrs. Dempster, I do not feel like having a cookie. Well, Mrs. Dempster, I will not keep beating around the bushes. I have bad news for you. You had better sit down. Here, take this rocking chair, and get out your hankie. Your son Tommy is not ever coming home. You will never set eyes on him again and for the reason he lies in a soldier's grave. He said for me to kiss your dear sweet face for him. But in case you are like my mother and do not go in for kissing I will leave that up to you.*

Gilbert and Chester's father and mother did not often take an evening out, even before he began doing his degree homework after supper. But when they did, such as for a mid-week prayer meeting or for krokonole and a sing-song at some other collegiate teacher's home, they had one or the other Miss Langley come and look after things, sticking to the rule about bedtime and making sure there was no danger of the lamp being upset. Leaving children to look after themselves in the evening is one sure way for parents to lose them. Every little while the *Mail and Empire* and Grandpa Williamson's *Globe* told of this happening. Yes, and one time a family down river near the soap factory had all five of their children go up in flames because no one stayed to look after them.

The tubby Miss Langley was the one Gilbert and Chester liked to come. The tall one was all right, but she was strict about bedtime and she would not let you so much as lay a finger on the living-room leaf table if a lamp happened to be on it. She was more like a man, she did all the digging in their garden and looked after the snow shovelling, she even tried her hand at carpentering. She could saw straight, split wood and hammer nails. When she hammered a nail she went at it lickety-split, you would think she was mad at it. The tubby one was not strict about bedtime and even after she sent them up they could talk for as long as they felt like it. On top of this she was good at tiddly-winks.

The Wednesday evening after the first real snow their father and mother said they would stay at the church later then usual, there was to be an after-meeting at which the missionary from India would give a talk and show lantern slides. Chester was a pretty slick tiddly-winks player but that evening he lost game after game and got so mad at himself that he stamped upstairs and went to bed. Gilbert put the tiddly-winks away, checked the furnace dampers as his father had told him to do, then lay on the carpet beside the hot air register. Miss Langley got out some knitting she had brought along, a tiny jacket for the Carter baby, she said it was. It and a pair of what she called bootees were going to Mrs. Carter in time for Christmas. She said that ever since Mrs. Carter stayed with them at the time of the shooting, they had kept in touch. Miss Langley said she shrank from thinking what might have happened if Gilbert's father had not stood up the drink-crazed Mr. Carter and taken the gun away from him. "Mr. Wallace tells us your father hails from Huron county. My sister and I grew up in Bruce." Gilbert got her to tell about Bruce county when she and her sister lived there, did they have Indians and were any of them her friends? She said she knew some of them by sight but they pretty much kept to themselves which was not a bad idea all things considered. Gilbert told her about Sparrow Lake, Mr. Dubois, how

Indians gather rice and all the rest of it. The two of them were still
at it when his father and mother came.

As soon as Miss Langley was out of the house, Gilbert's father lit
into him. "Why in heaven's name don't you keep your wits about
you? This house is like an oven! Come here. How often must I
show you how to adjust these dampers? But not you! You never
pay attention. See what you've done! You've kept the furnace
going full blast all this time. Coal costs money, I'd have you
understand."

Gilbert said he thought he did what he was told.

"You thought! You thought! That's you all over. Off to bed
with you. Out of my sight. Git!"

Gilbert scooted for the backstairs but halfway across the kitchen,
something in his mother's voice stopped him in his tracks.
"Richard! At prayer meeting tonight we heard a good deal from
you about the Grace of God. I'd like to see more of it in this
house."

His father was slow to answer and when he did his voice was
troubled. "Frances. If it wasn't for the Grace of God you would
not be able to live with me."

Although Gilbert was mad at his father, mad clean through, all
of a sudden he was sorry for him too. It gave a queer feeling to be
right there and hear his father being taken down a peg or two.

A person might easily run away with the idea that if you are
cooped up in school snow or no snow does not make any difference
to you. But that person would have another think coming. If for
instance the snow is coming down fast and thick she lets you out
early in the afternoon for the reason the room has no lamp and
soon gets dark. Of course on the girls' side next the windows there
is still light enough for them to see what they are doing without
squinting up their eyes. But on the boys' side not so. Tidy your
desk, sit at attention, class stand, dismiss, no shoving or pushing in
the hall. Another difference snow makes is at recess time. If the
snow is coming down fast and thick, and if you are not in
kindergarten or one of those teacher's pets the same as Ruby Greer,
who is allowed to remain in the room, out you go, the whole kit and
caboodle of you and into the play-shed. What the girls did in their
play-shed was hard to say except that they did a lot of silly
screaming and laughing. In the boys' play-shed it is bags-on-the-

mill and other rough and tumble games. Morning recess after a snow, fresh tracks and snow angels all over the yard. Before you line-up, take turns with the broom, stamp the snow off your boots or there will be a wet place on the floor under your seat as if good old Vincent sat there.

In other ways too, the first big snow before Christmas was along the lines of starting a fresh chapter in a book. Instead of the sound of wagon wheels and horses' feet, all you heard were sleigh bells of different sorts. Mr. Mullin had a string of little bells which tinkled. Mr. Quigley the milkman had one fair-sized bell on each shaft and you could hear him coming from the time he turned the school corner. Downtown delivery sleighs had bells of their own. The same with cutters and sleighs of farmers driving along Balaclava coming to or from market on Saturday. On clear cold nights the sound of the town clock seemed to come from high in the sky, not from the town hall tower. For morning and evening services, the big Presbyterian bells sounded louder than ever. Next thing you knew, Mr. Pickering, Aunt Trixie and their friends would start up their snowshoe club for another winter and you would see them parading around like voyageurs in their long-tailed toques and with colored sashes around their middles. After they tramped around for a while with their feet wide apart they piled into one or another of their houses for hot chocolate and games. If the house was a Methodist house they played parlor games along the lines of blind-man's-buff, button-button-who's-got-the-button and pinning-the-tail-on-the-donkey. If the house was a Church of England or Catholic house they might play a game called euchre which is done with the sort of cards gamblers use in their dens. The story was that the winter before, in one of the Church of England houses, they had a moccasin dance. The Ten Commandments are not against dancing but even so you would not catch a Methodist doing it any more than you would catch them doing work on Sunday.

If Gilbert and Chester had known what was happening down at the church that evening while they were playing tiddly-winks with the tubby Miss Langley, they would have felt flat as pancakes. Which was how they did feel when their mother told them next morning while they were getting ready for school. What had happened was that she up and pledged the new coat money to help feed the starving people of India. Chester blamed the missionary for talking her into it and was all for giving him a good hard punch on the nose. But this was no way to talk and she told him so. The thing about their mother was she had a mind of her own and you could not talk her into doing a thing unless she wanted to. She could see through people and know what they were up to as for instance the Toronto business man their father thought was the whole cheese but who turned out to be a snake in sheep's clothing, and the visiting preacher who went on and on about temperance. "A fine one he is to talk temperance," Gilbert heard her say, "up there in the pulpit with a great roll of fat over the back of his collar. When he sits at table he should practice what he preaches."

Their mother said that some of the starving came to the missionary's church and he could not bear to turn them away hungry. Gilbert said they could be rice Christians and would give the church the go-by once they got over being hungry. She said Christian or no Christian they were God's children, which made Chester say that then it was up to God to feed them and not expect her to. Gilbert said not only that, she could have borrowed the money from the Lord's Tenth box there on the sideboard and paid it back later, it was her and their father's money to begin with. She told the two of them to stop worrying their heads about the coat, the old one would do her well enough for another winter. She said it was a case of casting your bread upon the water. Gilbert knew the rest of that one, he had it for a Golden Text. It said if you cast your bread upon the water it would return to you after many days. But when you got right down to it if it returned at all it would be mush, which was what happened when he fed crumbs to the minnows at Sparrow Lake.

Another thing happened the same day which took the wind out of Gilbert's sails. If he had had his say he would not show his face again at Band of Hope no matter what the other two boys did, but he was not allowed to have the final say. A couple of times since the last meeting he had sort of hinted to his mother he wanted to drop out but this time he decided to come right out and ask. Instead of going straight to the study his father was in the livingroom sitting in his Morris chair reading the latest *Christian Guardian* and Chester was in there too doing whatever he was doing, so Gilbert and his mother had the kitchen to themselves.

His mother heard what he had to say then shook her head.

"Joining was entirely your idea, no one put you up to it. It's not fair to the others to come and go just as it suits you."

Gilbert started to explain that the two boys were thinking of quitting but his father interrupted him. "What's this? What's this?" He came to the doorway, his paper in his hand.

That was like him all over. Gilbert, Chester and their mother would be talking back and forth having a good time but instead of joining in, his father would get up and leave, as good as telling them he was not the least bit interested in their chatter. Then he would hear a bit of what they were saying or maybe them laughing over something and back he would come, all ears, expecting them to repeat it. He made you wish you had kept your trap shut. More than once their mother got after him about it, but she could have saved her breath for all the good it did.

This time no explaining was needed and for the reason their father must have been listening and had not missed a word. "There is to be no dropping out for trumped up reasons. Your mother has said all that needs saying on that score. You have put your hand to the plough...." and so on and so on.

Gilbert gave up. There was no denying that the one about putting your hand to the plough made more sense than the one about casting your bread upon the water. But even so, why rub it in?

Sure enough the two boys did not show up that Friday afternoon. Except for Gilbert the whole shebang of them were girls. The one Gilbert had to march beside while they sang about being the army of temperance, drinking only cold water and being healthy and strong, had the sniffles and did not have sense enough to put her hand over her mouth when she sneezed. At the finish Gilbert would have been the first out if he had not needed to rummage around to find his mitts among the coats and things piled on the benches back of the piano. Just as he found them, he heard the Band of Hope lady tell the piano playing lady she had just the song for him to sing at the Christmas concert. "Gilbert is such a manly little fellow and he has such a clear sweet voice," she said. And the lanky girl standing right there! Gilbert could have puked.

CHAPTER SEVENTEEN

Surprises

That winter after a fresh fall of snow during the night, Gilbert's father depended on him to help, and it was a different sort of helping than just standing around handing things. While his father shovelled the sidewalk, Gilbert looked after the steps and the path to the backhouse. It was like being one of the Thoroughgood Family, each pitching in and doing his part. Better still when his father called up the backstairs for him to rise and shine it was like being an English boy sailing around the Horn in a storm and having the first mate shout, "all hands on deck." Another way of looking at it was pretending he was a boy by the name of Richard Egan jumping out of the spool bed and getting into his knee-high cowhide boots with the copper toes to help his father in the depth of winter and maybe with the wolves howling in the Huron county forest.

Other winters before his father called the family for breakfast Gilbert lay in bed and heard his father shake down the furnace, fold back the sloping cellar doors and go out to sift the ashes and save the pieces of unburned coal. The next sound was the scrape of the snow shovel on the cement walk to the gate. After that no sound from the plank sidewalk. But this winter being out in the cold and the wind working with his father while his mother and his brother lay warm in their beds gave a good feeling. It made him think he amounted to something.

Weeks before Gilbert began helping with the snow shovelling his father depended on him in another way which was to go downtown for the mail each Saturday and to get the *Mail and Empire*. This allowed their father to have all of his Saturdays for studying. Their father had got such a bee in his bonnet over studying that except for the mid-week prayer meeting he spent his evenings at it too. One supper time when Chester asked why he stopped going curling with Mr. Waldy on Friday evenings, the answer was in their father's no-more-of-that-from-you tone of voice. "To put food in our mouths and clothes on our backs, that's why," his father told him. After he went upstairs they asked their mother. She explained that a

collegiate teacher with a degree was better paid and that studying
for his degree had been in their father's mind for years. It would
not be easy but Doctor Scanlon was helping him.

The news that Doctor Scanlon was helping their father with his
lessons gave Gilbert things to think about. Doctor Scanlon must
always have been a top-notch teacher for their father and those
other Huron county fellows to pull up stakes and follow him to the
collegiate. And they weren't boys like collegiate boys nowadays.
Nowadays, ones the size of Tommy went. Two of the Huron
county fellows had mustaches according to the picture. Aunt Trixie
was the only one of Grandpa Williamson's children who got to the
collegiate and she said even in her time none of the boys wore short
pants. Grandpa Williamson's sons lit out for the United States
soon after they finished public school. They got jobs there on
account of being crack baseball players. Cricket was the game at
the collegiate then and they made fun of it, the Jersey City cousins
still did. But let them stand behind the wicket when Mr. Pickering
was bowling and they would mighty soon change their tune.

One of the Huron county fellows came on account of going to be
a minister and on account of Doctor Scanlon knowing the Greek
language and being able to talk it as well as write it. Gilbert and
Chester's father never went after Greek but he knew some words in
the Latin language, such as when the family was packed up to go
camping and he would call the baggage *impedimenta*. Aunt Trixie
said that nobody could touch Doctor Scanlon as a teacher and on
top of that you respected him. If you fibbed about coming late or
not doing your homework he listened to you but all the time he
knew what you were up to—none of this hauling you on the carpet
and reading you a penny lecture. He left it up to you to tell the
truth.

Gilbert wondered if Doctor Scanlon was older than Grandpa
Williamson or if it was the other way around. Grandpa Williamson
scarcely lifted his feet when he walked and when he hurried he
broke into a funny little jog trot. When Doctor Scanlon passed the
collection plate his hand trembled a little but except for that he
looked pretty spry. The story was that when he and Mrs. Scanlon
were at Grimsby for the summer, he went in swimming no matter
how rough Lake Ontario got and he dived right through the biggest
waves. So why was there talk of his being too old to keep on as
principal? If you went by what Aunt Trixie and the other hello girl
picked up on the telephone there was quite a bit of that going

around. Trixie said Mr. Albert was at the bottom of it. She said all you needed to do was take one look at the cut of his jib to know he was one of those who walk roughshod over people who did not have the starch to stick up for themselves. It was all very well for their mother to say Trixie was a bit of a flibbertigibbet and some things she said should be taken with a grain of salt. Aunt Trixie kept her eyes open and she could put two and two together. On top of this she had Mr. Pickering to tell her what was in the wind.

The Saturday Grandfather Egan's parcel came was the coldest day yet. It was so cold that the packed snow on the plank sidewalk at the school corner squeaked with every step Gilbert took, and from the top of the hill he saw steam rising where the waste water from the woollen mill ran back into the river. There was no one on the sidewalk clear down to the Royal Consort. This gave Gilbert a chance to practice his voice wobbling. If he practised it in the house, sure as shooting out would come the goose grease. Goose grease under a piece of flannel pinned around the neck was their mother's cure for a sore throat. The grease was from the New Year's goose of the winter before and after a summer on the pantry shelf it had a smell. Aunt Boo said slices of fat pork under the flannel were an even surer cure and that best of all were fried onion poultices to the feet. Their father snorted at such beliefs. He said they were as unscientific as the wizened potato Mr. Wallace kept in his hip pocket for the rheumatism. Aunt Boo had a sure cure for whooping cough in babies, which was a spider in a walnut shell on a string around the baby's neck. Aunt Boo was a great believer in old medicines but she said if you had inflammation of the bowel or the galloping consumption it was sure sign you were sent for.

In case he could not hit on a better way to get out of the Band of Hope, Gilbert had decided to try voice wobbling when he showed up at the church next Friday after school. He would march, sing the army of temperance song and all the rest of it, never letting on until the lady took him with her to the piano. There he would be standing beside her meek as Moses. . . .

And how is our manly little Gilbert Egan feeling this afternoon may I ask? Here is the song we have picked out for you. These are the opening notes. Plunk, plink plunk-plunk. Try them in your sweet clear voice. . . . I would like nothing better than to sing for you and to be in your Christmas concert. The trouble is my voice is changing. . . . What's this? What's this? . . . . Oh yes it is. You could

*not notice it while we were marching. I do not blame you. The
lanky girl was hollering at the top of her voice as usual. . . . Gilbert
Egan I am so sorry to hear this. You are so young. Is there nothing
the doctor can do?. . . . Do not fret your head about me. I will think
of you when I am far away in South Africa blowing my bugle or
beating my drum, or for instance if I am living up north with some
of my Indian friends. Would you like to shake my hand? Goodbye
now.*

The parcel was about three inches thick and twice the size of the
family Bible. Along with the parcel, the man at the wicket handed
out a postcard which had the one cent stamp printed right on it.
The rule against reading other people's mail was only for letters, so
while Gilbert stood at the post office radiator to warm himself he
took a look to see what the card had to say, which wasn't much,
only, "Letter with contents received. I was hard put to it. Parcel
with this. Winter early here. Henry B. Egan." The writing was easy
to read, not like Grandpa Williamson's when he made notes on the
backs of envelopes. When Grandfather Egan had something to say
he did not waste words so the postcard was the next best thing to
hearing him speak. Henry B. Egan. . . Gilbert wondered what the
B. stood for. Yes, and the Henry was news to him. When Grandma
Williamson spoke to Grandpa she often called him John, the same
as at home when their mother said Richard. But there on the farm
cradling the oats he never once heard Grandmother Egan use
Grandfather's first name. Or him use hers, come to think of it. But
this was nothing to go by, it was probably a way they had between
them.

If the parcel had been a soft one Gilbert would not have been in
any hurry to get home with it to find out what was inside. He would
have gone home by way of the railway station. And for the reason
that if it had been soft it was sure to be more mittens and scratchy
knitted stockings. But the parcel was anything but soft. It felt like a
box and things inside rattled when he shook it. Last Christmas
Grandfather Egan sent their mother a bird's-eye maple
potato-masher he made, a mustache-cup for their father and the
whittled jumping jack for Chester saying it was for both of them.
But Christmas was almost three weeks away, so the parcel was not
likely to be presents. If the parcel was for their mother she probably

would have opened it right off. She was no flibbertigibbet, she could possess her soul in patience but she did like surprises, real life ones and in the books she read.

But with their father it was a different kettle of fish. Surprise or no surprise, he made a big thing about keeping on an even keel, or keeping his feet on the ground as he sometimes called it. One of the things he got after Gilbert about was over letting himself be carried away. His idea seemed to be never to look forward to a surprise in case it did not pan out. Even on Christmas morning he was not for opening presents until after the Bethlehem story and the porridge. Ernie and his sister were allowed to come downstairs and open their presents hours before daylight, but none of that in the Egan house.

His mother was mashing the potatoes when he came in. She told him to leave the parcel on the sideboard and to take the postcard upstairs to his father. His father read it then looked at him. "You've taken the liberty of reading this, I suppose. Well, no matter. Tell your mother I'll be down directly."

All through the meal their father did not so much as glance at the parcel. He drank his tea, helped himself to a second piece of pie, took his quill toothpick from his vest pocket and asked what had become of his *Mail and Empire*. It was only after Gilbert explained that he came straight home with the parcel that his father pushed back his chair and went to the sideboard. Even before he cut the string, he said he knew what was in it. "I happened to come across it on his work bench while we were up there, Gilbert and I," he told their mother. "Even then it was in the making." What it turned out to be was the slickest checkerboard Gilbert had ever set eyes upon. The squares were of light and dark wood—white ash and black walnut their father said—and were so neatly fitted together no cracks showed and even when you felt it with the flat of your hand you could not tell where one ended and the other began. "No slipshod workmanship there, or ever will be so long as he has breath in his body." The board was hinged to make a box and inside it were the men, light and dark to match the squares. The rest of the box was filled with unshelled butternuts. A piece of paper said "To Gilbert from Eph" and below were some squiggly lines where Eph had tried to write his name. Their mother brought a dish to hold the butternuts, their father put the men in a drawer, opened the board full size and set it up on the plate rail. He said it was not to be treated as a toy, that later when they were old enough to value it they could use it.

Although their father was not for getting surprises he was not against handing them out, as for instance the two he gave Gilbert the following week. The first was that Gilbert did not have to keep on with the Band of Hope after all. His mother probably had something to do with this. One bedtime when he was kicking over the traces about being the only boy among all those girls, she asked what was so terrible about girls? and he told her they made him feel like a fish out of water. She was taking away the lamp when she asked so he could not see her face but by the sound of her voice she was having fun with him. She said she did not like having a fish out of water for a son and that she might speak to his father and see if anything could be done about it. Sure enough, next day his father told him he did not have to go. His father said let this be a lesson to him not to let himself be carried away and rush headlong into doing what he would be sorry for later.

The other surprise was that if Gilbert would take on the job of telephone messenger boy and promise to stick to it, his father would have a telephone put in before Christmas. From stories and talks the Sunday School superintendent gave, Gilbert knew about telegraph messenger boys. But telephone messenger boys were new to him. Telegraph messenger boys wore uniforms and caps like railway conductor caps. They were smart as whips and when it came to getting a foot on the ladder of success, ragged but honest newsboys and boys who helped rich old ladies across streets were not a patch on them. As his father explained it, the job of a telephone messenger boy was to deliver what were called long distance appointment slips to people who did not have telephones. As for instance when some out-of-town person phoned Grandpa Williamson's office and asked Aunt Trixie to have a town person they wanted to talk with come to the office at such and such a time. Gilbert had been in the office when a town person came for an appointment. The town person went into a booth, Aunt Trixie turned the crank below the switchboard, said, "I have your party on the line, go ahead please," and there the two of them would be, miles apart and talking back and forth. Grandpa Williamson had other telephone messenger boys in different parts of town and needed one on or near Blair Street. Only boys with telephones in their houses could be messengers. This was so that when Aunt Trixie had an appointment she could get hold of them in a hurry. The boys were paid ten cents for most messages and as much as twenty-five cents for a message to the edge of town. If the message had to be taken at night they were paid even more. The story went that an older boy had earned enough to buy himself hockey skates, real ones with puck stops.

Right from the drop of the hat, Gilbert was all for being a telephone messenger boy and he said so. His father said fine but to bear in mind there was to be no dropping out this time, no taking messages only when the spirit moved him. People would be relying on him and a big company like the telephone company would not stand for on-again-off-again people working for it. Gilbert said he would never be like that, no matter what. He imagined himself being like Dr. Kirkland, fighting his way along drifted roads to save the life of a sick person, he would deliver the messages in spite of everything.

"Moreover it will teach you how to handle money," his father was saying, "whether or not you decide on a business career. I'll show you how to keep accounts, but more on that later." Gilbert turned to leave the study. "One thing more. No word of this to your mother. She will be able to phone for her groceries and what not, no bundling up, no slippery sidewalks."

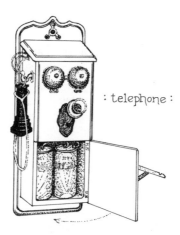

: telephone :

Two afternoons later when Gilbert and Chester came from school the first thing they spied when they came in the side door was the telephone on the livingroom wall. The box at its top end was for the crank and the bells. The middle part for speaking into was away higher than Chester's head. Even Gilbert would have to stand on a chair to use it, supposing he was ever allowed to. "The telephone is not a toy, I want that clearly understood at the outset," their father had said. The box at the bottom held the electric batteries. These were not strong enough to shock a person. The box had a sloping top and a ledge to make a sort of desk. The telephone's number was two-three-six. Chester had to know if it worked, which was him all over. To show him it did, their mother turned the crank and held the listening part to Chester's ear. "Aunt Trixie!" he shouted. You would think it was the end of the world. He wanted to talk but their mother took away the listening thing and put it back on its hook.

The man who put in the telephone left a pad of appointment slips. This was so Gilbert would not have to streak it down to the office when there was a message for him to deliver. Instead, Aunt Trixie would tell their mother what to write on the slip and away he would go with it.

The very first time Gilbert ever spoke on a telephone in his whole life was the evening after theirs was put in. Their father was upstairs studying away. Gilbert and Chester were stretched out on the carpet on either side of the livingroom hot air register while their mother read them some more of *Evangeline*. The telephone bells rang. She laid the open book on the arm of her chair and went to answer it. She beckoned. "It's for you, Gilbert."

"Me? Who is it?" he whispered. She shrugged and held the listening thing to his ear.

"Hello," a voice said polite as pie. "Is this one-eight-nine-nine?"

"Nope." Right off, he could not remember what their number was but he knew it wasn't that.

"Look at the calendar please." The voice broke into a titter. He heard a click and that was that.

His mother put the listening thing back on its hook. "Well, she didn't have much to say for herself, did she?"

"Snoopy know-it-all."

"Who was it? Who was it?" Chester asked.

"You deaf or something? Some snoopy, know-it-all smart-aleck." The voice was a put-on voice but if she thought she could fool him she had another think coming, Miss snoopy, know-it-all, smart-aleck, stuck-up, teacher's pet, pug-nosed Ruby Greer.

CHAPTER EIGHTEEN

Standing At The Portal

Gilbert Egan was not one of those who get the Christmas spirit by thinking about it or by going around singing *Jingle Bells* and hollering Merry Christmas to every Tom, Dick and Harry they came across. The Christmas feeling was something that came over you the way the camping feeling did before they packed up and went. This year it came over him not while he was lying awake counting the days, not by hoping for certain things in his stocking, not by looking in store windows, not even by *O Little Town of Bethlehem* for Intermediate Sunday School's closing hymn. This year the Christmas spirit came during the sleigh ride Miss Burwell took the whole shebang of them on the last afternoon before holidays started.

Miss Burwell could not have picked a finer day for the sleigh ride if she had the say of it. No getting around it though, it was the coldest day yet, and Probs, in the *Mail and Empire* the day before, said there was likely to be more cold in store. But there was no wind and the sun shone full tilt. Before she dismissed them at noon, Miss Burwell went over everything step by step—she was a great one for going over things step by step. The sleigh was the largest in town and would easily hold all of them, boys on one side, girls on the other. It would have plenty of clean hay and buffalo robes. All should wear their warmest clothing, this went without saying. Bring foot warmers, those whose parents have them, if not a brick heated in the oven and well wrapped. Five cents to help pay the cost of the sleigh and a second five cents for hot chocolate at the ice-cream parlor. They just might be treated to music during the ride. Gilbert knew what that would be. She had asked Elmer to bring his cornet. "Keep your seats until I give the word. Boys are to remember no jostling in the hall, the other classrooms must not be disturbed."

The only foot warmer Gilbert's parents had was the pig his mother took to bed with her on cold nights, and even if he had been allowed to, he would not have shown up with it for the sleigh ride for fear of being called a sissy. It was made of the same sort of pottery as the pickle crocks. It had the shape of a loaf of bread with a screw cork on top. After it was filled with hot water it kept warm for hours. Instead of his boots, he put on his last winter's worn-out moccasins. When Gilbert wore moccasins he practiced walking Indian fashion and looking behind him at the snow to see if he was doing it right. This was the reason his moccasins wore out sooner than Chester's, their father said. Chester made a point of toeing out. Not only because their father did but because he wanted to be different from Gilbert.

Their mother was all for protecting the chest, and from doctor book pictures Gilbert, and Chester too, saw the sense of this. Lungs were like sponges and could freeze in very cold weather. The brother of their mother's friend had his lungs frozen while helping build the C.P.R. over the Rocky Mountains. No matter how strong your lungs were you had better look after them or next thing you knew you had the galloping consumption. Aunt Boo said Gracie might not have been taken if she had kept to flannel and high necked dresses. Newspaper back and front made good chest protectors. Pages from the *Christian Guardian* folded in half were Gilbert's size. The only thing he had against the *Christian Guardian* under his blouse was that it crackled every so often when he took a deep breath. The town paper was softer but it was the one which got cut into squares for out back. The *Mail and Empires* were kept for under carpets at spring cleaning.

Two of Miss Burwell's plans for the sleigh ride had to be changed. Elmer was not allowed to bring his cornet. He had a chapped lip and if he blew on his cornet the spit inside might freeze. The other change was the sleigh was not an Abel Williamson's, it was from one of the livery stables. One good thing, it came earlier than expected. None of the boys brought a foot warmer. Some of the girls had bricks. As they all piled in, Gilbert spotted a soapstone warmer like the one Waldy Hardware had in its window. He did not need three guesses to know which girl brought it. Sure as shooting she was the stuck-up, smart-aleck daughter of a station agent by the name of Mr. Greer.

Before Miss Burwell got in she made sure there were enough buffalo robes and that everyone was settled. While she was doing this, Gilbert saw the driver let go a gob of tobacco juice onto the snow and get rid of his quid. His ear flaps were loose and the collar of his sheepskin coat was turned up but from what Gilbert could see of his face he was the livery stable fellow who dared not sell the poor sick woman the bottle of Banyan from the Holy Land after Doctor DeSilva called "too late."

When Miss Burwell had everything seen to, the driver gave her a hand up to the seat beside him and they were off. The horses were sorrels and had more get-up-and-go to them than any of Williamson Cartage draught horses. Gilbert was wedged between Elmer and Nick. Archie and Ernie were near the back where they could hop over the tail board and run behind to warm their feet. Elmer's face looked different without his glasses. The nose part got broken at morning recess and Elmer's father would have to solder it. Bags-on-the-mill was no game for people who have to wear glasses.

The off horse wore the bells and they jingled in time with every step it took, like in the song. At the far end of Archie's street the driver shook up the team and they went along at a fast clip. Just before the tollgate corner a farmer coming to town with a load of cordwood drew over to let them pass. Some of the girls called Merry Christmas and waved to him and he waved back. He had his collie dog on the load beside him which made Gilbert think of Sport and the Christmas he might be having—provided he had not gone to the happy hunting grounds.

Gilbert hoped they would turn left onto the tollgate road so he could get some idea where Doug lived. But the driver turned right, past a low stone farmhouse with blue smoke rising from its chimney. Cows in the barnyard standing broadside to the sun to warm themselves, every fence post with its rounded hat of snow, Miss Burwell riding with them not getting after him any more, all of them happy and friendly as all get out. It was soon after they passed the farmhouse that the Christmas feeling came. Gilbert did not think the sleigh bells and the singing had anything to do with it any more than the hymns and the organ had anything to do with the time he saw God. It happened one Sunday morning when they lived in the double house across the river when Chester was not much more than a baby and only Gilbert and his father went. The service was over, people were moving along the aisles saying how-do-you-do to each other and extending the right hand of fellowship back and forth. Gilbert was standing around waiting to go home and wondering if she would give them mince pie for dinner. The end wall of the church back of the organ was in the shape of a high pointed cave. The organ pipes made shadows there and it was in those shadows Gilbert saw God. God was nothing like a person but he was as real as a person. He was looking down on all the people and giving them his blessing. Knowing this gave Gilbert a safe feeling, the Lord is my shepherd and all the rest of it.

A couple of miles after the stone farmhouse it was the driver's turn to pull over on account of a loaded hayrack coming down the hill and the horses holding back against their breeching straps and not being sharp shod, a team of Clydes, they looked like. The farmer hollered down from the top of the load and thanked the driver for pulling over. Everybody wished him a Merry Christmas and Happy New Year and on they went. Soon after that the three noo-come-oot girls started up a song of their own. They must have brought it from England because only Elmer knew it. The words were about a partridge in a pear tree and so on and so on one thing after another. Elmer said it told about the twelfth night which was something they had in England, something the same as Burns' night which Archie's father, Mr. Wallace and Aunt Kate's husband had songs about. Ruby Greer and the girl who sat next to her in school were the only two who got the hang of it.

By the time the team took them to the Durham Place turn-off, tree shadows were stretching out and hollows in the snow began to have the bluish look which can be a sign of another cold night. The iron deer in front of the Albert house was belly deep in snow and had more of it on its back. Ernie made quite a thing of it. "Everybody look at the deer with snow on its back all bare behind," he shouted. Only Gilbert and Nick twigged. When the driver pulled up in front of the ice-cream parlor they all could not get out fast enough. Miss Burwell shooed them inside and waited for the driver to put blankets on the horses before inviting him inside, a sure sign she was standing treat.

Ernie's father was related to the people who ran the ice-cream parlour. They lived above the ice-cream parlor and had a balcony. Sometimes Ernie got invited there to watch the Twenty-Fourth of May parade or the circus one. Ernie's cousin, sort of a forty-second one, was nowhere in sight that afternoon. Ever since things got too much for Professor Vance, Gilbert would just as soon not be in that boy's shoes when the roll was called up yonder on judgement day. Though of course the boy had no idea what tagging after the professor to get a swish of his cane would lead to.

The ice-cream parlor's hot chocolate could not hold a candle to the hot chocolate Gilbert's mother sometimes made after church on

winter evenings before he and Chester went to bed and their father
and mother tackled the wash. She also made it when the collegiate
teachers came for a social evening. She made it with grated
chocolate, not on the nutmeg grater but on a special one she kept
just for that. She served it in fancy cups and a skin formed on it
almost as soon as it was poured. In case you were greedy and sipped
yours too soon you ended up with a burned mouth. Aunt Boo was
against hot chocolate. She said it clogged the system. She was
pernickety about what she drank. Green tea was best and senna tea
helped in some sicknesses.

By the time the driver got them back to the school, the foundry
moulding shops were going full blast and sending flames from their
stacks. The pointed flames reminded Gilbert of huge Christmas
candles against the dark sky. Miss Burwell reminded them to go
straight home then said to give three hearty cheers for our driver.
Which they did. Somebody said—it was Nick of all people—three
cheers for our teacher. Somebody else said three cheers for the
horses then home they went. For supper the Egans had fluffy baked
potatoes, with chopped Spanish onions and a jug of hot milk and
butter. Gilbert ate all of his potato skins and talked Chester into
giving him some of his. The potatoes were fluffy as popcorn, the
onions just right and the skins chewy with the flavor of nuts.

By the look of things, the telephone company was short of
messages for Gilbert to deliver. All through the week since his
business talk with his father, only two had come and neither was a
twenty-five-center. There was no denying that if he multiplied
twenty cents a week by the number of weeks in the year it would
add up to a lot of money. But this was a case of counting chickens
before they crossed the bridge. Here it was with Christmas just
around the corner and with only forty-seven cents in his bank to
pay for presents. Chester was even worse off. So even if they did
not give each other so much as a candy cane their presents to their
mother and their father would have to be pretty measly ones.

Even if lots of messages had come through, Gilbert would still
have been in a fix. And for the reason the telephone company
would not pay up until after the end of the month. It was all very
well for Mr. Scrooge's nephew to make a big thing of having the
Christmas spirit when he was as poor as a church mouse, Gilbert

thought, but it was not the nephew who paid for the Crachits' turkey, it was rich old Mr. Scrooge.

The Ark was the place for presents no matter how hard up you were. Everybody went there. The morning Gilbert and Chester went, the store was half-full of people buying things or just looking—dolls, rag ones, ones with real china heads, all sizes, more sorts of games than you could shake a stick at, rocking horses, jack-in-the-boxes, Noah's arks, ladies' perfume to make them smell nice, dust caps, bibs with pictures on them for babies to slobber on, tin whistles, kazoos, mouth organs, sweet potatoes, little brushes for brushing crumbs off tables, pen-wipers all colors and shapes, nine pins, carpet balls, dumb-bells and Indian clubs for building up the muscles, Santa Claus false faces, jackknives with peep-show holes in their handles, glass paper weights with Niagara Falls inside them, china doorstops in the shape of pussycats, frogs, mud turtles, skate straps but no skates, spittoons for spitting in, bubble pipes and on a table at the back, tobacco pipes made of cherry wood with the bark left on, corncob pipes, clay pipes and packages of cards gamblers use in their dens for playing with.

Picking the right present for their father did not take long. It was a pen-wiper twice the size of the old one he kept on his desk. It had a knob on top to hold it by so he would not get ink on his fingers. The lady behind the counter said she was sure he would like it. Picking a present for their mother was a different kettle of fish. If they had enough money they would have bought her the pincushion shaped like an overgrown strawberry which was filled with a special kind of dust to keep needles from rusting. Aunt Trixie had one just like it and she said it was as handy as a pocket in a shirt. Next, the lady tried to sell them a tiny satin pillow—"sashay" she called it—which by the smell their mother already had in her upper right hand bureau drawer along with her gloves, hankies and things. While they were trying to make up their minds, the lady went to wait on some people and while she was gone Chester hit on the very thing. Gilbert could almost hear their mother saying it was just what she needed. It was a long handled toasting fork made of twisted wire which she could use at home and which would come in mighty handy when they went camping. The price of it was twenty-five cents and by each putting in twelve cents and Gilbert chipping in the extra copper they could buy it and each have something left over.

The lady wrapped the pen-wiper and toasting fork in one parcel and Gilbert took charge of it. "You stay here or go home, whichever you like. I want to take a walk around and I don't want you following me."

"Me either. I already know what to get for you."

"Something in here?"

"Not all of it. I hope you'll like them."

"It's more than one?"

"No use fishing. You've talked about them. It's nothing to wear."

Gilbert's walk took him past all of the store windows on one side of Main Street and most of them on the other. Picking a present for a six-year-old like Chester was not going to be easy. Six-year-olds were neither one thing nor the other. Mr. Wallace had a saying which went they were neither flesh, fowl or good red herring. In some ways this saying fitted Chester to a tee. There he would be, tickled pink over weaving strips of colored paper into a mat, or over pushing little sticks into water-soaked peas, and at the same time looking down his nose at boys in Infant Class not old enough for kindergarten. When he felt tired or cross you would catch him sucking his thumb and twisting a piece of his hair. Next thing he tried to tag along to Nick's or Ernie's. On top of this he was pernickety. Some days butter would not melt in his mouth then he would get mad at you over nothing and stay mad so long you heard him gritting his teeth in his sleep, though Aunt Boo said it was worms.

Main Street with Christmas just around the corner was something a person would not want to miss—cutters and delivery rigs with their bells, the road two feet deep with packed snow and higher than the sidewalks and with winter just beginning, flocks of English sparrows making short work of steaming horse buns. So many people coming and going with parcels in their arms they now and then bumped into one another, said Merry Christmas or excused themselves. Squire's drugstore—Mr. Squire was not a believer but he had a clubfoot and everybody went to him—had strong lights behind his two huge bottles of colored water hanging from the ceiling of his window. The shoestore showed just about every kind of shoe including moccasins with beaded toes which made Gilbert wonder what sort of Christmas those Indians were having, Hurons or whatever they were. Both dry goods stores had their windows chock-a-block with stuff. One of them, the one

Aunt Eunice worked in, even had a lady's corset, garters and all, over to the side of its window. Gent's Furnishings had men's and boys' coats, boxes of the new celluloid collars and paper collars at a bargain. Schiller's Grocery had turkeys galore and under them Merry Christmas spelled out with oranges and cranberries. After Mr. Albert's bank, the other drugstore had its music-box playing chimes. The Atelier showed its latest photographs, babies and weddings mostly. Lamont's Jewelry—no relation to Nick—had its window decorated, sparkling rings and watch chains scattered around on velvet. Waldy Hardware had a sign, "What is Home Without a Hammer?" and all around it different sizes and shapes of them. The Catholic grocery had a barrel chuck-full of oysters in its doorway, and with it, boxes of finnan haddie and smoked herring which made your mouth water, just the smell of them. The ice-cream parlor was going great guns. It showed trays of Christmas candies and one with their special peanut brittle. Aunt Trixie said it was their peanut brittle which made their name and that drummers from all over laid in a supply of it when they came to town. The hay and feed store had a big cage of canaries and you could hear them singing even through the glass. Next the empty store where Bon Ton Upholstery used to be. After it the Wee Free Hardware. Gilbert was going on past—Waldy Hardware was good enough for him—when he saw a sign in the window which made him wonder if he was seeing things. "Snowshoes twenty-five cents," was what he read! What a present! If only the telephone company would pay up ahead of time! He read the sign again and it made him feel flat as a pancake. It did not say snowshoes, it said snow shovels. It was for such mistakes Miss Burwell got after him. He went back to The Ark, made sure Chester had left, and bought one of their little tin pocket compasses. The price was twenty-five cents but the lady said on account of him being a good customer she would let him have it for the eighteen cents he had left.

That year because Christmas day came on a Monday, the big Christmas service was the morning before. It was the same in all the other churches from what Gilbert could make out. One thing you could say about Methodists, they stuck together through thick and thin, which was what Grandpa said the Williamsons always did. Maybe the Presbyterians did too though why did they have those two big churches on opposite sides of the opera house square and why did the Wee Free Presbyterians have theirs on the other side of the river?

More Methodists than you could shake a stick at came to that Sunday morning service—so many of them that they filled every last pew and there were not enough hymn books to go around. Grandpa Williamson, Mr. Mullin and Doctor Scanlon, the three of them, had all they could do extending the right hand of fellowship to people as they came in. Uncle Abel Williamson was lucky not to have a sick horse that Sunday so there he was squeezed between his wife and some other short fat lady. The little old honey man and his frizzy-haired wife came, the two Chinese laundrymen came and Doctor Scanlon had them in his pew. The choir had more men singers and instead of the trained lady soloist singing all by herself, she, the Band of Hope lady and the two mill girls got together and gave *It Came Upon A Midnight Clear* after Mr. D.V. Schiller read the announcements. Every last hymn was a Christmas hymn and the people sang up so well you could scarcely hear the organ. The sermon was more like a story and Chester listened instead of squirming.

From what Gilbert's and Chester's father had been saying, old Santa was poor that year. But the presents in the Egan livingroom that morning told a different story. Moosehide moccasins for both of them which by their smoky smell only Indians could have made, three books for the two of them—*Beautiful Joe*, a faithful mongrel that stayed with his mistress in spite of his being a tramp like Sport, *Rab and His Friends*, about a collie belonging to a Scotch shepherd which took such good care of the shepherd's sick wife that it lay under the table while she was being operated on, another book of fables, the boy who cried wolf once too often, and so on, this one with pictures—a singing top for Chester and a mouth organ for Gilbert. This year Aunt Boo gave Chester the dummy watch and Gilbert the picture hankie. Chester said the compass would come in handy when he needed to know which way was north. His present to Gilbert was the very same wire puzzle Gilbert played with in the Ark. With it were two of the only sort of fish hooks a trout would look at. Each hook was on a card and had its catgut leader. The hooks were called snells. In *Water Babies*, trout were the most high-toned fish next to salmon so they had to have special hooks. Their mother said the toasting fork was just what she needed and their father made no bones about liking his new pen-wiper.

The big surprise, the biggest in years, was the Royal Scroll. The card said it was from Santa but the writing was their father's writing. The Royal Scroll was for the whole family. It was a narrow

box about the size of a page of the *Mail and Empire*. It had a prop
on the back and when you stood it on its edge the front folded
down and made a sort of desk. A crank came with it. It had two
holes at one end. If you put the crank in the top hole and turned,
you saw New Testament pictures one after the other. If you put the
crank in the bottom hole and turned, up came Old Testament
pictures three in a row. These were about twice the size of
postcards. Each New Testament picture was the size of the *Windsor
Magazine* or of *Scribner's* in case you were one of those who went
in for Yankee magazines. Even if a person was some kind of
heathen and did not know any of the Bible stories, the pictures were
better than any magic lantern show. The Old Testament pictures
took you from the snake in the Garden of Eden. You saw Abraham
ready to sacrifice his son to show his trust in the Lord, you saw
Joseph's coat of many colors which were even brighter than the
colors of Mr. Pickering's cricket blazer, Daniel in the lions' den,
the three men in the fiery furnace walking on the red hot coals,
Moses in the bulrushes, slave drivers cracking their whips over the
Chosen People, those two sinful cities going up in flames and Lot's
wife looking back at them before she was turned to salt. The
saddest one was poor old Moses up on the mountain all by himself
looking across at the Promised Land. The colors were
beautiful—better by far than the colors of the Golden Text cards.

The Royal Scroll was not the only surprise their father had up his
sleeve for them that morning, though this one was mostly for the
house. He had it in the spare bedroom and they all went up to see it.
It turned out to be a pillow sham holder. Gilbert and Chester were
not old enough to have shams for their pillows and if Gilbert had
the say of it they never would. From all he could make out pillow
shams were a bother. If they were not starched enough they
slumped over the pillows and looked untidy, if they had too much
starch they stood up stiff as boards. The pillow sham holder was to
keep them looking just right. It was a wire frame as wide as the bed
to hold both shams. It fastened to the headboard and was hinged
there so it could be swung up out of the way at night and swung
down in daytime to hide the pillows and make them look as if they
had not been slept on. This one was the first Mr. Waldy had got in
and he told their father they would soon be all the rage. Their
father said, be that as it may, sham holders were quite a wrinkle
and the man who invented them had his head screwed on straight.
After showing how it worked he had their mother bring shams and

helped her fasten them into the frame. He asked did she think he should buy a second one for their room but she said not for the time being, this one looked nice just where it was. Gilbert got the feeling that what she thought of pillow sham holders was more like what she thought of three-wheel egg beaters than it was like what she thought of the apple peeling machine their father bought her.

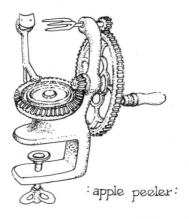

: apple peeler :

As always, the Williamson house was the place for the big Christmas dinner. Before their mother got them dressed up to go, each was allowed to eat his orange. No nuts though, it was too early in the day for nuts. Besides, the butternuts Eph had sent had such hard shells they had to be cracked with a hammer and the woodshed was the place for that. Gilbert got permission to wear his new moccasins. As they crossed the upper bridge they saw the ice above the dam as far as the railway bridge, and beyond to the turn of the river was dotted with people, some shovelling rinks, others skating on rinks already cleared. No horse racing allowed on Christmas Day.

Grandpa Williamson had a saying his table was like the Methodist Church, it always had room for one more. To prove he was right all you needed to do was show up there for Christmas dinner. Aunt Eunice, the quiet one, had invited the store dressmaker who lived by herself. Aunt Kate and her husband brought some Bruce county friend who could not get home for Christmas, and of course Mr. Pickering was there large as life. Grandpa had brought along two old ladies from church who always made a fuss over Aunt Boo. There was even a telephone lineman. Gilbert would not have been surprised if the Yankee cousins had come flocking over the border to find out what a good Canadian turkey tasted like. The table had so many extra boards put into it that Grandpa's chair was backed against the sofa in the bay window and at the other end it was a narrow squeeze between Grandma's chair and the sideboard.

Grandpa never had liked to carve and he made such a poor fist of it that for ordinary meals it was done in the kitchen. But for Christmas dinner it had to be done at the table. Gilbert's and Chester's father was the one who did it and if there was anything he had a swelled head about, it was his carving. While Grandma and a couple of the aunts were working, all the others were sitting around in the parlor talking. But not Richard Egan, he was out in the kitchen sharpening the knife, testing it with his thumb, rubbing it back and forth on the steel, testing, rubbing, until he had it sharp as a razor. One Christmas when Aunt Eunice laid a spill cloth over the table cloth where the platter would be, Gilbert heard his father tell her in so many words to remove it, that it would not be needed.

This time when everything was ready and the turkey brought in, Grandma and the two aunts took off their aprons, called the people to the table and showed visitors where to sit. When all were settled, Grandpa asked his usual blessing and added the part from his after supper prayer about "all those bounded to us by the ties of nature wherever they may be."

Although Richard Egan waxed his mustache and went around with a walking-stick, he was not one of your show-offs. But when it came to carving a turkey you could put him down as one. Instead of starting in right after the Amen, he sort of sat back and studied the turkey, letting on that a turkey was something new to him and he did not know how to begin. After sizing it up, he pressed the point of the knife to the joint of the drumstick and lo and behold the drumstick came off. He laid it on the platter with his fork, went through the same performance with the thigh and then without so much as raising his elbows took off the other drumstick and thigh. Next he tried his luck with the breast meat which sliced so easily you would think the knife did it all by itself and that all he did was keep his fingers on the handle. When he spooned out the stuffing not so much as a crumb fell on the table.

Aunt Kate asked each person "which meat", then took around the plates. When it came to Mr. Pickering's turn he said just a leg and a wing and a piece of the breast would do for him. The Bruce county man said he was twelve years old before he found out

turkeys had anything but necks which made people laugh though
you could tell most of them had heard that one before. Aunt
Eunice served the mashed turnips and Aunt Trixie looked after the
potatoes. Besides the cranberries there was spiced plum and red
cabbage pickle. Gilbert sat next to Aunt Boo. She never once
rattled her plate or muttered. Or if she did, no one heard her above
the talk. Plum pudding as usual, mince pie too if you had room for
it. Nuts and Christmas candies to taper off. From start to finish,
the day was a fine beginning for the holiday week.

That year for the first time in his life Gilbert was taken to Watch
Night service. Only he and his father went. Chester was too young
to stay up until midnight and their mother would not have come
anyway on account of the cold and slippery sidewalks on the hill.
Scotch people such as Mr. Wallace, Aunt Kate's husband and
Archie McClintock's father celebrated New Year's Eve but with
your dyed-in-wool Methodists it was a different story, especially
this year when a whole long century would end.

Nothing like as many people showed up for the Watch Night
service as for the Christmas service. There were so many empty
pews the minister had the people come forward and fill the front
pews between the two main aisles. There was no choir, only the
organist. After the *Praise God From Whom All Blessings Flow* and
the first hymn, the minister came down from his pulpit and stood
inside the altar rail. He gave thanks for the Christian witness of
those who had gone before and spoke of the better day which was
coming when men would hammer their swords into ploughs. This
made Gilbert think of the soldiers cooped up in Ladysmith with
nothing to eat but the meat of their horses.

Having a minister so near instead of high up in the pulpit made
all he talked about seem real to Gilbert. At the end, the minister
took out his watch, held it in his hand and had them rise and stand
in silent prayer. Gilbert closed his eyes. He could really feel the
seconds ticking away. It was like holding his breath as he waited for
the town hall clock to strike. At any second the nineteen hundredth
century would end and there would never, ever, be another one. On
top of this nobody in the church, probably nobody in the whole
town unless they lived as long as Noah or that other man in the
Bible, would see the end of this new century which was just around
the corner. The old century was slipping away faster and faster. Or

was it standing still and were the people slipping past it? He thought of that time on the train to Huron county. There he was at the window counting telegraph poles as the train rushed past them. Suddenly, without so much as a blink of his eye, the train seemed to be standing still and the poles were rushing backwards. Backward, turn backward, O time, in your flight.... The town hall bell boomed twelve, the organ played *Standing At The Portal of the Opening Year,* and everybody sang. They all wished each other a Happy New Year and because he was the youngest person there, the minister, Mr. Mullin, Mr. D.V. Schiller and quite a few others came and shook hands with him. The year one thousand nine hundred had arrived and if Miss smart-aleck Ruby Greer tried any more of her tricks he would know how to get the best of her.

CHAPTER NINETEEN

Elmer And Others

Gilbert's father had a saying that a penny saved was a penny earned. Penny is a Yankee word for a copper. Another of his sayings was that a fool and his money are soon parted. He also said if you looked after the coppers, the dollars would look after themselves. When things settled down after New Years, and about the time of the January thaw which came late that year, Gilbert's father got him a bookkeeping book and gave him lessons in how to use it in his telephone messenger business. The book was about the size of the one Mr. Mullin carried in his pocket for keeping track of what people paid him for coal-oil. It had a black oilcloth cover. Gilbert's father's account book was not much larger but it had a red leather cover. Gilbert's father had divided each page of Gilbert's book into three parts. At the top of one part he had Gilbert write EARNED, at the top of the middle part SPENT, and at the top of the third part ON HAND, which was for what you had left at the end of each month. Everything should be kept track of, no matter if it was only a few cents for stamps or ten dollars for another ton of coal. Only spendthrifts did not keep track of where they stood. As for instance if Gilbert got paid for a twenty-five-center, spent two cents for candy at Mrs. Devon's on his way home, lost four cents playing in the snow, how much of his twenty-five cents would he have on hand? First you made a sum of what you spent then did a take-away from what you were paid. But for example if you spent another two cents for a new slate pencil, gave Chester a birthday present which cost eight cents and you let another two cents burn a hole in your pocket at Mrs. Devon's, where would you end up?

With January almost gone, Gilbert still had so little bookkeeping he could do it in his head. That month's three ten cent messages added to the two he was paid for at the end of December was less than Elmer got from Mr. Waldy during the same time. Then after school on the first day of the thaw along came a twenty-five-center. The party's name was Mrs. Finnerty. She lived across the tracks almost a mile past the end of Blair Street. She made him take five cents for having come so far. Even after he told her the telephone company paid him she said she wanted him to have it. At supper when Gilbert said Mrs. Finnerty was a nice lady, his mother said she was pleased he thought so. "I didn't tell you before you went, I didn't want you jumping to conclusions, but it so happens Mrs. Finnerty is Foxy Foster's auntie. She just about raised him."

"But how did he get to be a hold-up man?"

"Like many another, by taking a wrong turning," their father said.

"How did he get his gang?" Chester asked.

"They're not his gang, they only call themselves that," Gilbert said. "He wouldn't know them from a hole in the ground."

Chester asked where Foxy was and their father said this was no doubt something Chief Rooney would like to know. "But that's beside the point. The point is, as with Mrs. Finnerty, we must take people as we find them, Foxy or no Foxy."

That evening after the story, Chester was sent up to bed by himself and Gilbert was given a good, straight, friendly talking to. His father said he was sick and tired of reminding Gilbert about his shoulders—his posture, he called it—and that no doubt Gilbert was too. The time had come to stop nagging, to take steps. They had asked Dr. Kirkland's advice and were told there just might be a weakness there. Even if there was not, having to wear shoulder braces for a few weeks might bring results. The long and the short of it was that Gilbert was told to peel off his blouse and undershirt right there in the living room, to stand straight and hold still for what his mother said was a fitting. She had straps made from folded strips of cloth and pins galore. Two of the straps went under his armpits and over his shoulders. These were joined by a wider strap across his back on top of his shoulder blades. Gilbert did not so much mind the straps under his arms, but when she tightened the back strap he made a fuss. "You've got it so tight I feel I'm falling over backwards. You make me look like some girl, two bumps in front." His mother told him to stop squirming and said something else he could not quite hear because of the pins in her mouth.

When she had the back strap the way she wanted it, his father told him to stand back. "Better, much better, a vast improvement. And remember it's for your own good we're doing this." He had Gilbert take a walk around the room then showed him how to get out of the braces without having them undone. "Your mother will have them ready for you. If you have trouble getting into them, call me. Now off to bed with you."

As it turned out, getting into the braces was not much of a trick and Gilbert started wearing them the next day. They made him sit up straighter in school more like in the position of attention and they sort of pinched when he took too deep a breath. But at least they did not creak like Aunt Martha's corsets did. Elmer might have noticed the difference but he was not there. He had felt sick the afternoon before and Miss Burwell let him go home at recess time. She said there were la grippe germs going around.

By Saturday cold weather was back and whole stretches of the river were covered with new hard ice. Gilbert took his spring skates and went down for the afternoon. In case a message came through he would pay Chester five cents for coming to get him. Another reason Chester did not go was that he was too young for spring skates but felt ashamed to be seen with his bob skates which only small children wore in case they fell and cracked their heads or their ankles were not strong enough for real skates. The soles of Chester's boots were not strong enough to hold spring skates, even supposing he had a pair.

: skates :

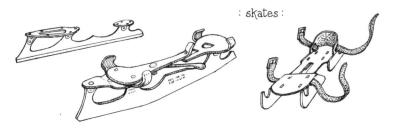

Gilbert got out of the house with his red devil hockey stick without his father seeing it. His father was against boys skating around with hockey sticks—"bent double and charging ahead as if their lives depended on it," he said. Hockey was a fine game, he had nothing against it. Many a rough and tumble game of shinny he'd played and devil take the hindmost. But proper skating was quite a different matter. His father admired Mr. Pickering's style of skating around with his hands clasped behind his back like some dude. Either that or kicking up his heels showing Trixie how to do the figure eight.

On his way down the slope to Ernie's, Gilbert met Nick coming up. Nick had forgotten to bring his skate wrench and was going home for it but Gilbert had his so they went on down together. Nick had the strongest ankles, he did not need skate straps. Archie and Ernie were already on the ice but instead of making up a game of scrub hockey, the bunch of them decided to do some sailing. A good stiff wind was blowing down river so the four skated against it At the word go they unbuttoned their reefers and held them wide. On the clear, hard ice only a puff would have sent them along, so with the strong wind they scooted faster than they could have skated. They ran four races between the bridge and the patch of frozen-in bulrushes below the gas-works and Ernie won all four of them. But no wonder, with a reefer which came almost to his knees. Ernie said that the night before some fellows did a torchlight procession. They broke off bulrushes, dipped them into coal-oil and lighted them. He said they seemed like big fireflies moving in the dark.

At Sunday School next afternoon, boys from one of the other public schools told of a horse falling through the ice down river near the soap factory. The horse came near to drowning, and would have but for a man who came with a rope and helped it out. The lesson that Sunday was the ninety and nine and Doug told them the man who saved the horse was in the same boat as the shepherd who saved the lost sheep. The Royal Scroll had a picture of the good shepherd doing this and when Gilbert came home he set up the Scroll on the livingroom floor and he and Chester sat on the carpet and looked at all the New Testament pictures.

Elmer did not show up at school on Monday or on Tuesday either. Wednesday morning Gilbert almost missed the line-up. He had dawdled over his porridge and for the reason his father had not put enough salt in it. The rule was you ate up your porridge no matter what. If you didn't, there it would be in front of you at dinner and there was no getting around it. Gilbert was the last to take his seat. Miss Burwell waited for him to get settled then instead of having the Lord's Prayer she came to the front of her desk and stood sort of looking over their heads. You could tell by her face something was up. The room was so quiet you could hear a pin drop. She told them she had sad news, that Elmer was dead. She had them bow their heads. Then instead of the prayer she went through *The Lord Is My Shepherd*, all by herself. Then, no talking, get out your slates for arithmetic.

At recess the story went around that it was inflammation of the bowel, not la grippe. Every so often that day, when the very last thing he wanted to think about was Elmer dead, Gilbert's mind went back to Elmer sitting next to him, the inflammation inside him nibbling away to finish him off. Some people got spared and some got taken and there was no telling ahead of time which was which. No more marching, no more playing on the cornet for good old Elmer Spence.

On his way back from dinner Archie came by way of the Spence house. He said no doubt about it, there was a grey crêpe on the Spences' door and most of the blinds were down. Miss Burwell had Gilbert stay after four to sort out Elmer's things from their desk, his reader, exercise and copybooks, slate, pencils, sprinkling bottle and so on. Gilbert half expected her to have him deliver them but she said she would look after that herself. In one way Gilbert wanted to go but in another way he didn't, so it was just as well that was how it worked out. On the back of Elmer's slate there was Elmer's drawing of the two men in capes fighting with rapiers. Gilbert thought of leaving the picture for Miss Burwell to see but rubbed it out. Leaving it would be like tattling on Elmer.

The day before the funeral when they came in from afternoon recess Miss Burwell had them put away their books and said she was taking them to have a last look at their classmate Elmer Spence. When they had all bundled up and put on their toques and mitts, she marched them past the pop factory and along the Avenue to the house. The lady who opened the door had them stand in the hall and took them into the parlor a few at a time, girls first. The funeral-flower smell—the first smell Gilbert remembered—was in the hall. One of the girls, not Ruby Greer, came from the parlour with tears in her eyes but the others, girls and boys too, came out looking straight in front of them and with a fixed expression on their faces. Gilbert was not at all sure how he would be seeing a dead person for the first time, but he did all right, even when he stood beside the coffin. Elmer's eyes were closed so he did not seem strange without his glasses. Only the top part showed. He wore a soft white shirt and a little bow tie and his hands were crossed on his chest. The lady touched Gilbert's shoulder, pointed at one of the wreaths and whispered it was from the class. Miss Burwell had not asked any of them to bring money so she must have paid for it herself.

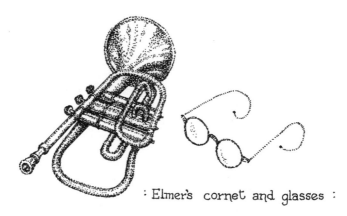

: Elmer's cornet and glasses :

Miss Burwell marched them back to the school before dismissing them. Ernie and Gilbert marched together. Ernie said there was a plate under the clothes on Elmer's stomach but how could he know that? He said something Elmer ate must have started the inflammation, something the stomach could not handle. Gilbert did not believe that either. If eating wrong things was what brought on inflammation of the bowel, Grandpa Williamson should have died long ago after years and years of vinegar pie. Yes and Uncle Abel too who should have turned up his toes ages ago from swallowing tobacco juice by the gallon, letting on he was chewing gum and with never so much as a stain on his white beard. Aunt Boo said he was a slave to the habit long before he left the farm.

The shoulder braces were hard enough to get used to at any time but Sundays were the worst. If he had been allowed to wear them next his skin it might not have been so bad but his mother said not to because if he did they would soon be soiled and perhaps shrink with washing. She said to wear them on top of his undershirt and his father backed her up as usual. His mother made their underwear and he had nothing against it except it felt scratchy for a while after it was washed. It was all very well for her to tell him this was all in his imagination but Nick and Ernie said the same about the underwear their mothers made. Every so often the mill sold off scads and scads of woollen cloth which had nothing wrong with it except a few pulled threads. The cloth was snapped up in no time by mothers from all over town—"pure wool, none of your strength-giving cotton," his mother said. What made it scratchy for a while after she washed it was that she hung it over the hot air register Saturday nights after he and Chester had their baths. This way it was all ready for Sunday. The scratchiness wore off except where the braces pressed the cloth against his skin. It felt like mosquito bites under his arms and across his back. No wonder his father got after him for squirming during the sermon.

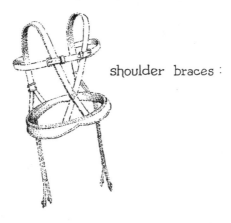

shoulder braces :

Sitting still in school was no picnic either. Even though he had all of the seat and desk to himself, Elmer's side was still Elmer's side. If Miss Burwell had moved some boy from the back of the room to sit there it would be like not taking off your cap at the Williamsons' when a funeral went past. It used to be when Elmer held up his hand and was allowed to leave the room, Gilbert would watch his chance and when Miss Burwell was writing on the board he would slide over. But not any more. No nudging either or taking a squint at the picture on Elmer's slate. So to take his mind off things, he fished the piece of bicycle spoke out of his desk and did some more boring in the escape tunnel. He had scarcely worked on it after Elmer came along.

The morning of February twenty-eight, the day news came Ladysmith had been relieved and the Boers sent packing, was a sparkler. A foot or more of fluffy snow had sifted down during the night. Gilbert was out helping his father shovel the walks when the town hall bell began ringing—not as quickly as when there was a fire but a whole lot quicker than when it struck the hour. Next, church bells all over town began ringing. The air was so clear you could even hear the Baptist one. Their father got on the telephone and Gilbert followed him in to find out what was up. The night hello girl gave them the news.

Blair Street School and all other schools let out for the day. Tommy Dempster shot off firecrackers, a sleigh load of collegiate fellows and girls drove around town, blowing horns and cheering. Union Jacks on every flagpole. Gilbert's and Chester's father stayed at the station to get his *Mail and Empire* off the westbound from Toronto. He read out parts to their mother. He said General Buller was a man after his own heart and that henceforth there would be no more twisting of the lion's tail. No skating that day because of the fresh snow. So Nick, Archie and some Catholic school boys whose father worked at the Royal Consort tramped the snow in the Yates' old chicken yard and Ernie got his father's permission for them to flood it and have it for hockey next day. That afternoon Archie brought his toboggan and they had some dandy slides down the slope to the tannery. They kept at it until the foundry whistles blew, not so many of them though because the two biggest foundries had shut down after Christmas as Aunt Kate's husband and the Bruce county man were afraid they might.

Aunt Trixie came for supper and to use the sewing machine for a dress she was making, and Mr. Pickering called for her when he came from reporting the school board meeting. After Gilbert went to bed he could hear the talk going back and forth between his father and Mr. Pickering. By the sound of things their father was laying down the law and he was still at it when Gilbert fell asleep.

Earlier that same evening before their father came from his study to join in the talk, Mr. Pickering came out with some news which surprised everybody and which hit Gilbert smack between the eyes. This was that some doctor or other down in the United States had found a way of saving the lives of people who had inflammation of their bowels. What this doctor did was open you up and take out a thing which every person had and which went by the name of the appendix. In case you swallowed grape seeds or toothbrush bristles they were likely to get stuck in your appendix. Next thing you knew your bowels caught the inflammation and like as not you were a

gone goose. Mr. Pickering said if Dr. Kirkland had known about
the operation the Spence boy might not have died. Then and there
Gilbert made up his mind that when the next grape season rolled
around he would spit out every single, solitary seed and would
make sure Chester did the same. Neither of them was old enough to
be given a toothbrush so they had nothing to worry about on that
score.

Two weeks after Gilbert began wearing the braces his mother had
to back water about the scratchiness being all in his imagination.
While she was scrubbing his back she saw for herself where the
strap rubbed his shoulder blades and said she would do something
about it. And so she did. But next morning when he saw what he
was in for, he just about raised the roof. What she had done was
sew two long elastics with a corset garter on the end of each onto
the back strap. When she tried to fasten the garters to his stockings
he pulled away and said nobody could make a sissy out of him. He
made such a row about it that his father came up the backstairs on
the hop and lit into him. It was easy to see the two of them were in
this together. "You have brought this on yourself. The remedy is
entirely in your hands. Sissy or no sissy you are to wear those
garters for a week. At the end of that time if you show us you do
not need shoulder braces, well and good. The braces will have
served their purpose. I will say no more. Let us see what happens."

At morning recess two days later, a bunch of the big boys had
bags-on-the-mill going in the play-shed, so Gilbert, Nick, Ernie and
a few others went over and got in the game. It was pretty rough and
tumble. Gilbert was wriggling free feet first from under the heap
when somebody yelled, "Hey look. Girl's garters!" One of the big
boys grabbed Gilbert, yanked up his pant leg and took a look. The
pants Gilbert's mother made for him were looser and wider than
those of the pants Nick's mother made for him. "Well I do declare,
see what we got here, little old Girl Garters Gilbert!" Everybody
laughed, even Nick and Ernie had smiles on their faces. They made
Gilbert feel knee-high to a grasshopper. He was so ashamed and so
mad he could have cried, all of them standing around and laughing
at him.

"Don't blame me. You think I want to? It's doctor's orders on
account of a disease I got."

"Like ducks! What disease?"

"I don't know the name of it." Gilbert felt cornered. "The one

Professor Vance had, for all I know. The one he caught in Paris, France."

Did that take the grin off their faces! "You never told us," Ernie said.

"No sense worrying you. That's why I kept it to myself. In case I get over it I can stop wearing the garters." Gilbert could see they only half-believed him so he straightened his pants and walked away letting on he didn't much care about what they thought.

Right after dinner that noon Gilbert ducked up to his room, got rid of the braces, stuffed them under the mattress, then squared his shoulders against the wall, pressing them back as hard as he could. He took a walk around the room and had a look at himself in the glass. He fished his round garters out of the drawer and put them on. He flattened his shoulders against the wall harder than before and took a last look in the mirror. Goodbye and good riddance, Girl Garters Gilbert Egan.

But not quite. Or was it all in his imagination? The girl who sat next to Ruby Greer had a brother in the principal's room and several times that afternoon Gilbert was pretty sure the two of them were making fun of him. First one and then the other glanced across the aisle then the two of them put their hands over their mouths to keep from laughing, rolling their eyes like dying ducks in a thunderstorm and making them so big they just about popped out of their heads. Gilbert kept on boring the escape tunnel and never once let on he knew they so much as existed.

CHAPTER TWENTY

Spring Fever

Gilbert Egan did not set himself up as one of your know-it-alls. But because he had a father and a grandfather on the Quarterly Official Board, an aunt in Ladies' Aid, another in Young People's and a mother who had her own ideas about how the head men of the church spent people's money, he was able to put two and two together on the way his church was run. The way he saw it, the head men of the Methodist Church ran things from Toronto. They sent out special preachers to strengthen the feeble knees and win back-sliders into the fold, to tell about India's starving millions and they asked for special collections every chance they got. They had a big say at Conferences and on the Stationing Committee. The Stationing Committee was the one which told some ministers to keep the same churches whether they wanted to or not and moved others to different churches. That spring at Conference time, the minister the Egans took in came from Muskoka. He was lanky and had a sort of anxious face. He looked about as old as Mr. Pickering. At table his Adam's apple went up and down with every swallow. When Gilbert's father had him ask the blessing he did not hurry through it as Grandpa Williamson did. He had Indians in his congregation but he did not have much to say about them, except that when he visited their camps he went in his canoe. At Christmas they snowshoed in for the presents church people sent in the missionary barrel. He said he looked forward to leaving the Home Mission field and to being called to a charge in some settled part of Western Ontario where his wife's relatives were and where life would be easier for her.

But too bad for her it did not turn out that way. The last day of the Conference when he came to supper any such hope had gone up the spout. He said the Stationing Committee was sending him back to Muskoka for another four years. His voice sort of trembled when he said it. He said it was the Lord's will and they must obey.

"The Lord's will my foot!" Gilbert heard their mother say under her breath. She did not have much use for the chairman of the Stationing Committee. When he was just an ordinary minister and she was still a hello girl he stayed with the Williamsons at Conference time and gave her a little talking-to for reading novels which were books your Simon-pure Methodists were against. So what did she do but sauce him. The novel he caught her reading was called *The Return of the Native*. She still had it with her other books. Gilbert had taken a look through it but it had nothing to do with Indians that he could see.

Gilbert was not on the side of the Stationing Committee but all the same if he had been in that minister's shoes he would have thanked them for sending him back to Muskoka for another four years. Home Missionaries had all the best of it—no starving millions, no rice Christians banging on their doors. Instead, Indians for friends, visiting them in their wigwams, watching them sew moccasins and make birchbark canoes. Like as not it was the minister's wife who put the bee in his bonnet about leaving Muskoka. She might be what Aunt Trixie called a complainer, such as the woman Mr. Pickering's hard up brother was married to. If the minister's wife had her way and the Stationing Committee moved him to a regular church there he would be with two sermons every Sunday rain or shine, having to keep an eye on the Ladies' Aid and the Young People's, extending the right hand of fellowship to every Tom, Dick and Harry who came along. He would have to be all dressed up like a collegiate teacher if he so much as poked his nose outside his yard.

No getting around it, Home Mission missionaries were the lucky ones. As for instance the two Doug told about. William Evans who fished and hunted with Indians for years and who showed them how to do their A-B-C's in their own language. Or John Macdougal who hunted buffalo and could make pemmican with the best of them and who sent the Yankee whiskey traders of Fort Whoopup back over the border with their tails between their legs. Talk about adventure! None of your run-away English boys, not any boy in any story Tommy told about, could hold a candle to Home Mission missionaries. At least to the ones the Methodist Church sent out.

Soon after the minister left, their mother began coming down to breakfast in her wrapper which was something she had not done as far back as Gilbert could remember. If this was because she had spring fever, Gilbert could honestly say he felt the same. Nothing much at school interested him except the tunnel. Any day now he should have it joined up with the escape hole. The yard was muddy and had puddles from melted snow. This made the play-shed so crowded at recess you could scarcely get in edgeways. So unless you were a marble player what was there to do but stand around waiting for the line-up bell to ring. Gilbert liked playing marbles, so did Chester. But on account of their religion they were not allowed to play for keeps and nobody would play with them just for the fun of it. Playing for keeps was a form of gambling. Nick's church was as much against gambling as the Methodist Church but Nick played for keeps and never let on at home. He had the widest span of any boy in their room so he almost always won. On top of this his mother had him on sulphur and molasses.

On account of their mother not feeling so spry, Aunt Trixie came two or three evenings a week and helped out with the ironing, spring cleaning such as fresh paper on the shelves and running up and down the stairs for things. Aunt Trixie was lively and she came out with whatever was in her head so it was fun to have her around. One evening when she came she said she was mad enough to spit pink ink. Ever since the two biggest foundries closed down, Methodist ladies and ladies of the other churches had been knitting and sending food baskets to noo-come-oot families whose men were out of work. That very afternoon while she waited at the bank corner for a dray to pass she heard two noo-come-oot men talking. One of them said, "These colonials are kind to us." The other man said, "Why shouldn't they be? We own them." As she told this, Trixie tried to mimic their way of talking but it came out like the Jersey City cousins talked. Gilbert could imagine those two noo-come-oots in their tweed caps, tight coats and pants, with mufflers around their necks instead of collars looking down their noses at Trixie. "Talk about biting the hand that's feeding you," she said to their mother.

When something rubbed Aunt Trixie the wrong way she was not one to hide her light under the bushes. "Richard should understand that Mr. Pickering does not have the final say on what goes on in the paper," Gilbert overheard her tell his mother one evening. "If he had, Mr. Albert and his toadies would be having their knuckles rapped. What goes on at school board meetings is only the half of it. When I'm at the switchboard I'm not exactly deaf you know."

That Saturday morning on his way to the station for the *Mail and Empire*, Gilbert would have taken a look inside their tree house to see how it had stood the winter. But Nick was not home so he kept on going. A couple of tramps squatted in the sun behind a pile of ties. The tramps did not speak and he kept on going. Tommy knew a lot about tramps, how they lived out of doors and would not work at steady jobs. They went south at the first sign of frost and rode the freights north in spring. They were as sure a sign that spring had come as when frogs began croaking in the bulrushes after the ice went out, or when somebody heard wild geese flying north high up in the moonlight. Next to Indians and maybe those French-Canadian voyageurs, tramps had all the best of it.

Some Saturday mornings when he came for the paper, Ruby Greer was in the waiting room acting as if she was the whole cheese but this Saturday she must have had sense enough to stay upstairs where she belonged. On his way out he took a look into the horse trough to see if it had any water skaters but of course it hadn't.

This was the Saturday for him to have his boots half-soled so after he took the paper upstairs to his father he went straight downtown to Mr. Swanson's, whose cobbler shop was at the top end of Main Street across from the town's second largest livery stable. Mr. Swanson did not talk Canadian but he was easier to understand than some noo-come-oots. Nobody knew for sure he was not a believer but he did not go to any church. The stuff he chewed was not tobacco, its spit was darker than tobacco juice and there was not so much of it. The reason he had to chew it was to keep from getting the galloping consumption from germs on people's boots. The glass in his spectacles was not as thick as the glass of the spectacles Elmer used to wear.

What you did when you went to have your boots half-soled was take out the laces so Mr. Swanson could have a good close look at them before deciding what to do. He was certainly no slouch but on the other hand he did not rush things. Like the copybook said, "What is worth doing is worth doing well." If you were one of those who had a second pair of boots, you wore them and left the others to be mended. But when the ones you came in were the only ones you had you sat in your stocking feet and waited while he worked on them. Mr. Swanson's work bench was the same low bench he sat in the middle of. His part was a little lower than the end parts on which he kept his tools, leather and all sorts of things. He had all different sizes and shapes of iron feet so that whichever one fitted the shoe he was working on could be shoved inside while he sewed or nailed. Gilbert and Chester's father said Mr. Swanson knew more about boots than the two shoestore men which was saying a lot. Their father had a saying that only a poor workman blamed his tools and that as a cobbler Mr. Swanson was one in a thousand. Their father also called Mr. Swanson the town's Socrates, whatever that meant.

Farm boys, in the country Mr. Swanson came from, learned to make their own boots, beginning with the hide fresh off the cow. An old bootmaker went from farm to farm each winter to teach the boys the whole of it. The farm where Mr. Swanson grew up was beside the ocean so he learned to make sea boots as well. But ever since he came to live smack in the middle of Canada there was no more of that. He still missed the sea, he told his father.

While Mr. Swanson was sewing on the new soles, Gilbert became so interested he got down from the stool and came to have a closer look. Mr. Swanson used one long single thread with a needle at each end. Only they weren't needles, they were pig bristles, Mr. Swanson said. He rubbed the thread back and forth over a lump of beeswax until the bristles became part of the thread. He used his awl to make the holes, a few at a time. One needle went in from one end of the hole and one from the other. Next he crossed the needles so that when the thread was pulled tight each hole had a knot of thread inside it. This was to make sure the stitches would hold. Gilbert decided that if it worked out for him to go north and live with the Indians this is how he would sew his moccasins.

During the winter the idea of living with the Indians came to Gilbert only now and then. But with the leaves coming out, the grass green, the robins back and all the rest of it, he thought about it more and more. In school while he worked on the tunnel it kept popping up and in bed at nights it was the same. Maybe it was the spring fever or more likely it was something in his blood. If his father had been an Indian or a voyageur, Gilbert would have believed there was something the matter with him if he did not want to clear out for good and all. This was probably how the tramps felt.

In bed one night, just for the fun of it, Gilbert made himself believe his father was not what he thought he was. Like in the story, his father was an Earl's son who had put tarnish on the family's shield and had to leave old England and never set foot on it again. Or it could be that some servant in the castle had mixed up the babies. Or this could just as easily have happened on the sailing ship when Great-grandfather Egan was bringing his wife and baby from Ireland. There had been a terrible storm and only for a brave midshipman all hands would have been lost. The babies were so mixed up that even their mothers could not tell whose was whose. *Poppa sit here beside me. I have something to say to you but in case you do not know, it is a wise son who knows his own father. You are not what you think you are. You do not need to go around all dressed up and you can throw away your walking-stick. Truth to tell, you are the son of a poor Irish farmer and I have the lost will right here in my pocket to prove it. . . . Thank you Gilbert. I have been mixed up all my life and did not know it. I will shave off my mustache and make a fresh start. As your copybook says, it is never too late to mend.* But this was the wrong tack so Gilbert tried again. . . . *Is this the wigwam of the Chief? May I come in and smoke the pipe of peace beside you? Thank you. . . . You will be glad to know that the baby boy you lost on the shores of Gitchee Gumee when he slipped out of his birchbark papoose did not die after all. It turns out that a Huron county broadaxe man by the name of Henry B. Egan found him and raised him as his son. Your long-lost little boy goes by the name of Richard Egan. He is a collegiate teacher and he is my father. But it will be all right with me if you want him back. From now on I will call you my grandfather for this is what you are. If you have room in your wigwam I want to come and stay with you. I can make your moccasins, I am pretty good at paddling a canoe and I toe in so you can always tell my tracks. . . .*

By keeping his eyes shut tight, Gilbert saw the smile on the noble old face. Next he tried the voyageur but he did not know enough about voyageurs to make the picture come.

By all the signs, Gilbert's father and mother had put their heads together to make it hard for him to run away. Not by getting after him but by being nice as pie to him. As for instance when he forgot himself and slouched or did not use his handkerchief or put his elbows on the table, all they did was remind him. But if you are going to run away you must have something to run away from, or what is the use of leaving in the first place? Anybody with sense enough to pound sand would know that. What he needed was to have his father tell him to stop making so much of himself or putting a tin ear on him over something he forgot to do. Yes, and his mother was not much better. As for instance the morning he did not finish up his porridge yet at dinner he ate the same as the rest of them. What they should have done was make him keep on wearing the shoulder braces, garters and all. Either that or make him show his face at Band of Hope no matter what. But the way things were going they would have to part as friends.

I have nothing against you Poppa and Momma. You did not know any better. You did the best you could. . . . Poppa, I hope you pass your exams and get your degree in flying colors. Momma go around in your wrapper as long as you please, it will be all right with me. . . . Do not look so down in the mouth. When I am big I will come back and see you. I might even bring my best Indian friend. Poppa if you are at the end of your tether because money does not grow on trees I will not let you and Momma starve. I will send you down a birchbark canoe full of pemmican, roots and all. Take care of my little brother Chester and do not let him suck his thumb or punch people on the nose. We are bounded by the ties of nature wherever we may be. Here is my right hand of fellowship. Goodbye.

CHAPTER TWENTY-ONE

Comings and Goings

One morning before their mother came down to breakfast their father told them that a friend of their mother's by the name of Mrs. Lehman would be coming that afternoon for a visit. Gilbert asked if the lady had visited them before and was told that indeed she had but that it was years ago and it was highly unlikely he would remember her. That day after four when Gilbert and Chester came from school Mrs. Lehman was there and was making herself at home.

Right off Gilbert knew he had never set eyes on her before. She was a black-haired broad-shouldered woman about the size of Mrs. Yarrow which was as good as saying she was a pretty big woman. Truth to tell, she was so big that when she went up and down the backstairs one of the boards creaked which it did only when their father stepped on it. Right from when she shook hands with them, Mrs. Lehman got their names straight which was more than some ladies did and which showed she had her head screwed on straight. One thing though, she had the makings of a busy-body. When it was time to start getting supper, down she came in a starched white apron and took charge of things, which if you got right down to it left their mother twiddling her thumbs. At table she and their father did most of the talking—how the war was going, what made Schiller's Grocery boost the price of sugar when other stores didn't, and weren't people living beside the river lucky there was no flooding when the ice went out. By her talk and by the cut of her jib it was plain she knew her p's and q's. Because of having spring fever their mother did not read to them and they said goodnight downstairs. Mrs. Lehman was all for seeing them to bed but their mother told her they could manage.

Next morning Gilbert and Chester had no more than opened their eyes when their father poked his head in the doorway and told them their mother had given them a baby brother. As if they had asked for one! It took a minute for that to sink in and by the time it had their father was halfway down the backstairs.

"Where did she get it?" Chester asked.

"Don't ask me. She had it, that's all I know. That's how they get to be mothers. How else do you suppose?"

When they were dressed Mrs. Lehman marched them in to have a look. Their mother lay with the covers up to her chin, her two long braids on the counterpane on either side of her and with a sleepy half-smile on her face. All they could see of the baby was its head and this was enough for them. It had a wrinkled red face and instead of a nose like a human being, all it had were two nose-holes

"Well now, do you like him? Shall we ask your mother to keep him?"

"It's up to her," Chester said.

Gilbert felt the same. Of course if it had been a girl baby and they were living in China with a famine going on she could have thrown it in the river and be done with it. But whatever she did with it had nothing to do with them.

All the same you would think it had, the questions people asked—the Misses Langley, the aunts, Nick's mother, Mrs. Devon. "Who do you think he takes after?" With that red tomato face! "Aren't you just dying to hold him?" "Have you picked a name?" That last was something Gilbert wished he knew about. It would be just like their mother to go in for another fancy name. Chester was bad enough but at least he could call himself Ches which was the name of the town's best lacrosse player. But what could you make of a name like Gilbert? She must have picked those names out of books, novels most likely. He would not be all that surprised if she picked Fauntleroy when it came to naming It.

But it turned out It was going to be called Henry B. after their Grandfather, Henry B. Egan, the best broadaxeman in Huron county, who danced Irish jigs on the ridges of barns, who could cradle oats until the cows came home, who could make just about anything out of wood, who went fishing for a whole week and told his wife to go chase herself when she got after him to get on the land! Henry B. Egan, Gilbert said the name to himself over and over until he almost tasted it. Henry B. Egan, Hank for short, the toughest boy in Blair Street School. He can spit the farthest, pee the highest without missing the trough and if it's a good loud fart you're looking for he takes the cake.

But no Henry B. for Girl Garters Gilbert.... *Say what you like, Poppa and Momma, but you put your heads together and gave It the name which should belong to me. What you have done is up and cheat me out of my birthright, like in the Bible....No use*

shaking your heads, this is what you did. . . . No, I am not mad. I
have not turned against you. But I must stick up for myself, Once I
shake the dust of this town off my feet you can write the name of
Gilbert on a piece of paper and throw it in the river for all I care.
The Indians are not like you, they will let me pick my own name.
When I pick Hank there is not a thing you can do about it. I am
sorry you did this to me. After I am far away up north, you will be
sorry too. But what earthly good will this do you? By then it will be
too late.

The last day of school before Easter holidays, Gilbert, Chester,
their father and Mrs. Lehman were at supper when the telephone
rang. Their father went to answer. Gilbert hoped it would be a
message for him to deliver—only two had come all that
month—but no such luck. When his father returned to the table he
sat staring at his plate, not eating. Then he looked up and told them
the call was from Mr. Greer. A telegram had come that
Grandfather Egan was dead.

"I'll run up and tell Momma," Chester said, but his father made
a sit-down motion with his finger. Chester had not so much as set
eyes on his Grandfather Egan, so what could it mean to him? But
Grandfather Egan meant just about everything to Gilbert, and if
the tears had tried to come he would have let them. After a minute
or two they went on eating, not talking, even Mrs. Lehman had
nothing to say for herself. Gilbert kept from looking at his father,
even when his father asked him to pass the butter he did not look
up. If he had he would have felt he was snooping. For that little
while they were not a boy on one side and his father on the other,
but more like in the spool bed, the two of them together.

The telegram said for their father to come at once so he took the
train the next morning. The first night he was away the baby
squalled like a cat with its tail in the gate. Their mother would have
had visitors galore if Mrs. Lehman had not put some of the ladies
off. Yes, and Mr. Wallace came to the door to ask about the baby.
Only he called it a bairn. Gilbert and Chester got used to the nose-
holes. Once they thought the baby smiled at them but Mrs. Lehman
said it was wind. Sunday afternoon the three aunts took turns
holding the baby. As they passed it around Mrs. Lehman said to

mind the little back. The chubby Miss Langley brought a bonnet. She said she was sorry it was pink but all along something told her the baby would be a girl. There was stove wood and kindling split ahead so in one way and another everything went off without much trouble.

Their father got home Tuesday in time for supper. He said the farm would have to be sold lock, stock, and barrel. Grandmother Egan would live with friends in St. Mary's but Eph would have to be looked after. Gilbert said Eph could live with them but was told this was out of the question. Their father said if Mrs. Lehman would help out for another week or ten days he would make a quick trip to Ottawa to talk things over with his brother and see what could be done. Mrs. Lehman said she would be pleased to stay, that so far as she knew she would not be needed elsewhere for at least a fortnight—whatever that meant. Their father told her he would take Gilbert with him which would leave her with one less to look after.

The train ride was mostly at night. The car was stuffy, Gilbert's throat felt dry and every little while he went to the end of the car and took a drink, on account of which he had to do a number one pretty often. Each time he went he turned up the seat. The sign said not to let go while the train was standing in stations which you did not have to be smart to know was a sensible idea. Gilbert held onto himself and went only when the train was moving. Then a rush of air came up. When there was light enough to see down, the ties were not much more than a blur. They went so fast you could not begin to count them. Looking down the hole while the train was going lickety-split was what Miss Burwell would have called a new experience.

Uncle Will's drugstore was not one of your pokey hole-in-the-corner stores. The bottles of colored water in its window were twice the size of those in Mr. Squires' window. Uncle Will and Aunt Maud lived above the store. They had no balcony except a small one on the floor above which was mostly bedrooms. Gilbert and his father slept in the same room but in separate beds which was a good thing on account of his father staying up so late to talk things over with Uncle Will. Aunt Maud had a hired girl who came right after breakfast and stayed until late. She pretty near had to on account of them having dinner at night after the store was closed. They had two telephones, one in the store, one in what Uncle Will called his den. At dinner, Aunt Maud rang a little bell for the hired girl to come and change the plates. The hired girl wore a white pinny and a frilly cap. She was a whole lot younger than the woman who came to the door when Gilbert and Elmer delivered the silver polish for Mrs. All-bare-behind. That one was sour-faced.

By all the signs Aunt Maud was one of your society women. She put herself out to please Gilbert's father though Gilbert could tell the two were not in the same boat over lots of things.

The store had more kinds of medicines than you could shake a stick at. In the back where Uncle Will mixed things and filled bottles, he had a glass jar with blood suckers in it. These were not your common garden variety of suckers, they were the ones doctors used to suck the bad blood out of people.

The second morning while Uncle Will was busy in the store, Gilbert and his father took a walk around town. They had a look at the waterfall and across the river at the factory where the sulphur matches are made. Ottawa went in for statues and Gilbert's father read out what was on them. Next they went inside the big building and a man came to show them around. He took them into a room far bigger than the church at home and with more than just the one gallery. This was where the laws were made. No laws were being made that day so all the desks were empty. After showing them around some more, the man said a class of boys were waiting to shake hands with the Prime Minister and there would be no objection to Gilbert joining the line-up. At that you could have knocked Gilbert over with a feather. Even his father seemed to think it was a big thing in spite of being on the other side of the fence. The man led them to a sort of waiting room and sure enough, there the boys were with their teacher. Gilbert took his place at the end of the line.

For a while nothing happened. Then a side door opened and in came Mr. Laurier. He went along the line and shook hands with each and every one of them. "Give me your hand, little man," he said to Gilbert. He did not stick his arm straight out as some men do in church when they extend the right hand of fellowship. He bent his elbow and sort of leaned forward. His hand was long with straight fingers and they had a firm grip. Not like some handshakes which make you feel you are shaking hands with the tail of some flabby old fish. He wore a high stand-up collar and a tie which was different than the ties of ordinary men. His hair was long at the back and his eyes were kind. He did not have mutton chops or any other sort of whiskers. He made Gilbert think of Doctor Scanlon except that Doctor Scanlon was ever so much older.

After the handshaking, Mr. Laurier gave the boys a little talk. He told them Canada had need of boys like them, that its future would soon be in their hands. Some of them might be called upon to make its laws. One or another of them might stand where he stood. He probably would have talked some more, but the door behind him opened, he said goodbye and had to leave.

At dinner that evening, Gilbert waited his chance to tell about shaking hands with Mr. Laurier but Aunt Maud was so full of herself he could not get a word in edgeways. To hear her tell it you would think she and Mr. Laurier were old friends, that they sat across the aisle from each other in school. She did not actually call him by his first name but if she had, Gilbert would not have been surprised. She said he charmed people wherever he went. Even Grandpa Williamson would not have gone that far.

After dinner Aunt Maud went off with two other ladies to something with a fancy name which turned out to be a concert. Gilbert was allowed to stay up for an hour or so while his father and Uncle Will decided what should be done and got it down on paper. Uncle Will wanted the spool bed. Gilbert's father would take some of the carpenter tools, ones he did not have or which were better than his. Eph would get the flute, though of course their mother would have the final say on all this. The place where Eph would stay was called the county farm which by the sound of it was where Eph would like to be. After everything was written down, Gilbert's father told him it was time for bed. The way he said this gave Gilbert the feeling the two of them were going to get onto things they did not want him to hear.

Except that it did not have pillow shams, the bedroom Aunt Maud gave Gilbert and his father knocked the spare bedroom at home into a cocked hat. It had such a big mirror that when you stood in front of it you saw yourself from your head down to your toes. The first night after his father went downstairs and Gilbert got undressed he looked at himself, with not a stitch on, his pee thing and all. It was the first time in his life that he saw the whole of his body at one time. The Royal Scroll picture showed Adam being so ashamed of himself on account of his pee thing that he covered it with a leaf. But until Adam saw himself, like in some mirror, he had no need to be ashamed. When Gilbert saw himself from head to toe with his pee thing showing he sort of knew how Adam must have felt.

The room had an electric light instead of a lamp but you did not need a light to go to bed by on account of the street light. The only thing Gilbert had against the room was the sound of rigs. On Blair Street there was either mud or dust to dull the sound. Here the street was cobblestones and these made quite a clatter. Ottawa had a lot more bells than at home and they rang at all hours of the night. Both beds had lace counterpanes which you fold and put away before getting in.

After Gilbert got in he did some more thinking about Mr. Laurier and the talk he gave them. It was hard to imagine Mr. Laurier would not always be there to make the laws and keep the country on the right track. And that handshake! Just the feel of it! I am the only boy in our whole town to shake his hand, Gilbert thought. Like as not the only person outside Grandpa. Wait till he hears. When Mr. Pickering hears he probably will put me in the paper.... *"Fame came recently to a boy of our town in the person of Gilbert Egan, son of Richard Egan, science master at the collegiate and grandson of Mr. Williamson, for long local and district telephone manager and acquaintance of none other than Alexander Graham Bell, when on the occasion of his visit to Ottawa he shook hands with the Prime Minister of Canada in the person of Mr. Wilfrid Laurier. Modest though he is, Gilbert opines and points with pride..."* and so on and so on.

Gilbert turned to the wall and closed his eyes. He saw himself in the huge room along with all the other law makers. It is his turn to speak. As he stands at his desk, all the others stop writing and assume the position of attention.... *If it is all right with the bunch of you, here are some more laws I think we should make.... Go right ahead, Mr. Gilbert Egan.... Thank you, I will. First off how about a law to stop people wanting to put tin ears on other people or calling them blatherskites? What do you say about Stationing Committees who tell people where to go whether they want to go or not?...Do I hear you say to pull the chain on them? Fine. How about a law against school board chairmen who want to be the whole cheese and who have stuck-up wives?...Fine then, let us go ahead with it.... How about this one? On account of this is a free country people should not have to toe out unless they feel like it. Another one...people who come along and give you a jab in the*

*back with their thumbs because you happen to be slouching should
be made to mind their own business. My certes, yes. And people
who put check reins on their horses should be locked in jail. Next
time the Boers twist the lion's tail we should rub their nose in it. Oh
yes, it is all right for ordinary Yankees to come for the summer but
the blow-hard ones should not be allowed to set foot across the
border. I do not know how you feel about collegiate teachers who
study for exams instead of going camping but I think we should put
our foot down and be against it. This is all I have to say until I
think up a fresh batch. Now start writing. Three cheers for Mr.
Wilfrid Laurier.*

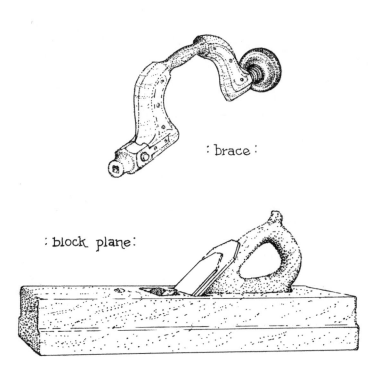

: brace :

: block plane :

CHAPTER TWENTY-TWO

Standing Idly By

Most of Gilbert Egan's big ideas, such as helping Mr. Laurier keep Canada on the right track, were all in his imagination. They were like water skaters skittering back and forth on the surface of his mind. Yes, and except for when his father got after him or things did not go to suit him, you could say the same about his idea of running away. Until on in May this too was pretty much a made-up story. But when he or Chester so much as mentioned going camping for the summer, the subject got changed so fast you would think it was a hot potato.

At first Gilbert thought Henry B. was the trouble. But that was not the whole of it, not by a long chalk. Staying so their father could have all summer to study for his degree seemed to be at the bottom of it. The worst of it was you could not get them to come right out and say, one way or the other. All you got when you fished around was, "all in due course," . . . "we'll see when the time comes." It was talk like this which decided Gilbert to clinch things and take the bit between his very own teeth. One night in bed when he and Chester talked about Sparrow Lake and the fun they used to have there, Chester got so worked up over not going that he pounded his fist into his pillow and said some mean things about their father. Gilbert told him not to fuss, that their father was doing the best he could to put food in their mouths and clothes on their backs. So no matter what he did they should not hold it against him, or against their mother either for siding with him. Gilbert surprised himself by saying this but when you will soon be going away and may never set eyes on the person again, you cannot help sticking up for him. Then and there, if Chester had not gone and blabbed that other time, Gilbert might have told him what was in the wind. But no, he would not tell any of them he was clearing out, not Nick, or Ernie or Tommy. Least of all Tommy who said English boys who ran away to sea instead of facing the music were short on pluck. A day or so after holidays began, providing it wasn't raining or even if it was, Gilbert would get permission to mosey over to the Williamsons. But instead of landing there he would duck behind the ice house and follow the Flying Dutchman track under the railway bridge, past the lime kiln until he was clear out of town. Next he would cut across the fields to the road leading past Mr. Yarrow's farm. Before dark he would duck into the woods, over by the old mill if he got that far the first day, and make an Indian size fire. Only greenhorn campers went in for big fires, his father once told him. He would have supper with some of the food he had brought. After a good night's sleep he would put on his mocassins and leave his boots behind forever. In case Defective Trotter, who was truant officer, was on his trail, toed in moccasin tracks would put him off the trail. Another thing he must remember to do before he left the woods was stain his face and hands Indian color with the juice of bark. But even then, his mouse-colored hair might give him away. To be on the safe side he should hide in daytime and travel by night. This is what slaves did to escape from Simon Legree and all those other cruel slave drivers who cracked the whip over them every bit as hard as the Egyptian ones did to the Chosen People to make them build the pyramids. Yes, and the picture was right there in the Royal Scroll to prove it. The slaves used the big dipper to guide them, "following the gourd", they called it. He thought he knew which stars made the big dipper—he had his father to thank for that—but he must remember to make certain sure before he cleared out.

Lying there in the back bedroom making plans night after night, he wondered how Chester would feel having the bed all to himself for ever and ever. Would the feeling be like the feeling he had after Elmer died—that though Elmer's place was empty it still sort of belonged to him? Would they keep on thinking of his place at table as Gilbert's place after they took away his chair? Would his mother forget he was no longer there and say not to put his elbow on the table and his father ask him to pass the butter? When Henry B. was big enough to sit at table what would they tell him about his first-born brother? Michael was Grandpa Williamson's first-born brother and all you ever heard of him, except from Aunt Boo, was that he was the black sheep of the family who went to the California goldfields and was never heard from again.

Is that you Henry B.? Well this is your first-born brother Gilbert speaking to you on the telephone. I have an Indian name now but go ahead and call me Gilbert for the sake of old times. O time, in your flight and all that. Get our mother to recite it to you. Can you hear me?. . .then stand up on the chair and hold the receiver closer to your ear. . .Now can you hear me? This is a long distance call, far more than a twenty-five-center but do not worry, I am paying for it with some beaver skins and a pair of moccasins I made. . .Oh no trouble, I make scads of them with my special stitch. . .Is that so?. . .My certes, Henry B., how your voice has changed. You used to squawk and your eating habits just about turned me sick. When our mother fed you at one or other of her bumps—all that guzzling and lip smacking. . .Oh, how is our in-between brother Chester getting along?. . .Oh has he? That is good to hear. I thought he might be locked up for punching people on the nose. . .Is our Momma all right?. . .Fine, fine. Does Poppa sometimes get after you for talking balderdash? Or for being too full of yourself? Well, never mind. You must forgive him, he does the best he can. You must do like I did at the last and turn the other cheek. . . .How is the telephone messenger business? Are you making scads of money?. . .Good for you. I am glad you are not at the end of your tether. You are earning a whole lot more than I ever did. . . .Well all I can say is you must attend strictly to business. If you do not watch out, first thing you know they will have you standing before some king or other. . . .Well be a good boy and eat up your porridge, salt or no salt. Remember not to be too full of yourself. . . .See you keep to it. . . .I better hang up now. Here come my Indian friends in their birchbark canoe. . . .Remember we will always be bounded together by the ties of nature let the chips fall where they may. Oh, one last thing. How are all of you enjoying the load of pemmican I sent down?. . .Roots and all?. . .Don't eat too much of it. Leave some for good old Chester. Goodbye. . . .And the same to you, Henry B.

When General Buller, Baden-Powell and the rest of them put their heads together and won the relief of Mafeking, they gave Queen Victoria a dandy present one week before another of her birthdays rolled around. On May seventeenth while Gilbert and Chester were still in bed they twigged something was up—the town hall bell and the church bells were ringing like all get-out, Tommy tooting his father's fish horn, and downstairs the telephone ringing to give their father the news. The schools did not let out that day as they had for the relief of Ladysmith, but all the same it was a big day for the town. That day's *Mail and Empire* was full of it—the flying column, Baden-Powell making the Boers look silly on account of his scouting tricks. Down at the Royal Consort, somebody let go with the bagpipes every so often. And groups of out of work noo-come-oots on the street corners with little Union Jacks in their buttonholes and acting as if they owned the earth. At school Miss Burwell said some nice things about the victory and how good a queen Queen Victoria was. When Gilbert passed this on to Chester all he got was a look. Chester had nothing against Queen Victoria any more than their mother had. All the same they put in with Mr. Wallace and did not think Queen Victoria was the whole cheese. They did not believe everybody should bow down to her. The way Chester saw it, why should Queen Victoria make such a big thing over going without sugar on her porridge? And why should Aunt Boo and nearly everyone else give her a pat on the back for eating up her breadcrusts? If the palace bread was anything like the bread Mr. Isling's bakery delivered, or half as good as the bread Grandma Williamson sometimes baked, any queen with sense enough to pound sand would know the crusts are the best part.

A few days before the Twenty-Fourth, while Chester was having an easy time of it swinging in the barrel hammock, Gilbert's after-school job was helping their father put on the screen doors. He was standing around at the side door handing things when the telephone rang. Their mother answered and called that it was Mr. Pickering. Their father went in and Gilbert followed. Their mother had Henry B. on the sofa and was changing his napkin. It seemed that every time you turned around, Henry B. wet himself. If he didn't stop he would end up like Vincent and no one would want to sit beside him. Their mother handed Gilbert the wet napkin and told him to take it to the summer kitchen and put it in the pail. Gilbert made a face and held the sopping wet napkin between his thumb and finger as if he could not bear to touch it. His mother told him he need not be so finicky, that when he was a baby he did not always smell like a rose either. Gilbert got back from the summer kitchen as fast as he could. Mr. Pickering was doing most of the talking. Gilbert could tell by the look on his father's face that something was up. Gilbert's father said he had his principles and that he would not stand idly by. He thanked Mr. Pickering for letting him know what was in the wind. After he hung up he stayed at the telephone sort of chewing at his mustache. "They've done it,

Frances, just as I feared. Pickering was at the board meeting."
Suddenly he gave the table such a bang with his fist that Henry B.
jumped. "By George, Frances, I'll do it. I have no alternative. I
will dig ditches first." He gave the crank a twist and asked Trixie to
connect him to Mr. Albert. "If he's not at the bank, try his
house...It's urgent."

Although Richard Egan was a steward of the Methodist Church
he was not one for turning the other cheek when he had his Irish
up. Or for going in for the Grace of God either. Gilbert could
hardly wait for what came next but when his father caught sight of
him he told him to gather up the tools and take them back to the
shed and be quick about it. "This is not for your ears so close the
door behind you."

If Chester had so much as twigged what was said in the livingroom that afternoon he would have piled on the questions. So in
bed that night Gilbert decided to keep mum about it, at least until
he was sure which way the wind was blowing. By all the signs, his
father had his back up over Mr. All-bare-behind twisting the other
school trustees around his finger to get in some up-and-coming
principal to take Doctor Scanlon's job. Gilbert was all for Doctor
Scanlon but he did not let himself get worked up about it. And for
the reason that when the collegiate opened after summer holidays,
Gilbert Egan would be living in a wigwam and have a different
name. One thing though, if his father stopped being the science
master and dug ditches for a living, Gilbert wished he could be
there to see—his father going to work like Nick's father and Ernie's
father, no walking-stick, no mustache wax, never dressed up except
on Sundays. In bed that night, Chester grinding his teeth on
account of worms, Gilbert imagined Archie McClintock's father
and his father going into the Royal Consort on pay nights, then
coming out arm-in-arm, happy as all-get-out and singing one of
those wild Scottish songs at the top of their voices....*Mr.
McClintock, if your boy Archie takes it into his head to go up north
and live with the Indians do not put your foot down to stop him.
My first-born son Gilbert took the bit in his teeth and went north to
live with the Indians and I am ever so proud of him. What this
country needs are more boys like him. My certes, yes. Trust them to
keep the country on the right track and stop those blow-hard
Yankees from getting the run of things....Aye, aye, Richard
Egan. We are such good friends may I call you Dick?...My certes,
yes and I would like to call you Donald..... You do that, Dick my*

friend....Donald, before we go home, let us take a walk along Durham Place and throw some rocks at Mr. All-bare-behind's iron deer just for the fun of it....Aye, aye Dick. We will do that....Who is this I see coming, smoking a big cigar. By George if it isn't our old friend Mr. Waldy. Waldy, Donald and I are going to throw some rocks at Mr. All-bare-behind's iron deer. Will you join us?....Thank you, I would like nothing better but I must get back to my store and sell some more hardware, stovepipes, pillow sham holders and things. That Mrs. All-bare-behind is a stuck-up woman so throw a few rocks for me....We will do that. We will throw some big ones. Come along, Donald. Let us sing another song. What will it be? Do you know the one, My Bonnie Lies Over the Ocean?...Aye, aye....Then let us sing.

When it came to fireworks displays none of Richard Egan's were to be sneezed at. Then, something came over him or got into him and he sort of let himself go. Other times he was likely to get after you for wasting string or not picking up a bent nail or not using your slate pencil down to the last inch. But with the Queen's birthday just around the corner it was a case of expense be hanged. He was probably The Ark's best fireworks customer—pin wheels, Roman candles, fiery fountains, grasshoppers, sky rockets and anything else the fireworks factory down in Hamilton could think up. That May with the relief of Mafeking and the Queen's birthday rolled into one he gave Blair Street people a display they would not soon forget. The noo-come-oots across from the school corner said as much for Mr. Egan, colonial or no colonial.

All the aunts except Aunt Boo came. The Misses Langley and Mr. Wallace were invited and sat on the veranda, and of course Mr. Pickering was there. At the finish up went the sky rockets two at a time. One of the burned out sticks landed on the roof of Mr. Dempster's smokehouse though nobody knew this until Chester spotted it next morning from the back bedroom window.

After the show while the rest of them sat on the veranda and talked, Gilbert moseyed out to the kitchen where his mother and Aunt Kate were getting the sandwiches and lemonade ready to serve. The way the wind was blowing was that in a few weeks their father would leave the collegiate and the board would have to find a science master. Aunt Trixie must have been the one who told, which is something your true-blue hello girl would not do. Gilbert remembered hearing their mother get after Trixie about telling what she heard over the telephone. Their mother said that when Gracie and Frankie Williamson sat at the switchboard they kept things to themselves and that if they hadn't some ears in town would have been burning.

Their mother was running the tap to get the coldest water for the lemonade when Aunt Kate brought up the subject. "It's no affair of mine, Frankie, but let's hope Richard knows what he is doing. These are not the best of times. And supposing he does find a suitable position elsewhere, there'll be your moving expenses to think of." Their mother said they had gone over that, which left Gilbert wondering. "Oh, I've no doubt you'll manage. But to leave town after all these years?"

Gilbert wondered still more when their mother said she wouldn't mind that. "A change is as good as a rest, they say."

Just then Trixie came bouncing into the kitchen with Mr. Pickering at her heels to carry out the trays, so the talk had to end right there.

But by then Gilbert had heard enough to know the digging ditches part was only so much talk and would never come to anything. Not that he was going to cry his eyes out. Whatever job his father took was up to him. When they parted it would be as friends except that he would not be like the Prodigal Son and ask his father to divvy up. The Prodigal Son was one of Gilbert and Chester's favorite Bible stories. It had an exciting beginning, had trouble in the middle and everything coming out right at the end. Instead of keeping track of his money, the Prodigal Son spent it on riots and became so hard up he took a job feeding the corncobs and peelings to pigs the same as at Mr. Yarrow's. Sure enough this gave him pains in his belly, so he came to his right senses and made tracks for home. His father spotted him coming over the hill, ran to meet him, fell on his neck, got right up and kissed him. In that country there was nothing wrong with kissing. Back the two of them went to the house and got ready for a big dinner when along came the other son and tried to put a stop to it. In every good story there has to be a person you cannot like. The other brother was such a person. Not only did he have the green-eyed monster but on top of that he was as bad a whiner as Adam who blamed all his trouble on the woman.

In stories some English boys who run away to sea leave home in such a hurry they do not have time to take a last long look around. This is not the case with boys who leave to seek their fortunes in lands far across the sea. These boys take a good look around them before they say goodbye forever to their native soil. Which is exactly what a boy by the name of Gilbert Egan was doing in that Ontario town during the month of June in the year nineteen hundred. Many things Gilbert looked at while the June days slipped away—the curve of boughs shading the barrel stave hammock, the drift of smoke from Mr. Dempster's smokehouse, Grandfather Egan's wonderful checkerboard, the figures on the gingersnap jar on the sideboard—became clear as stereoptic photographs in his mind, nothing blurred, every last thing clear and easy to remember. Sounds too. At night the rustle of a moth's wings against the screen of the back bedroom window, train whistles from beyond the bridge as clear as notes from Elmer's cornet. Even the perfume of the Ed Pinaud Mustache wax had a fresh smell as they sat at the breakfast table.

In school the smell of lilacs was stronger than ever he remembered it. No wonder, with the girls lugging in lilacs by the armful for Miss Burwell to stick in fruit jars, pickle bottles and canned tomato tins on every window sill. The lilacs Ruby Greer brought were white, just to be different. The lilac smell was so strong it shut out the chalky blackboard smell and even the sour smell of his slate rag. The only thing he had against the flower smell was that it made him think of Elmer's funeral.

When you know for sure you are soon going away and will never come back, you cannot help having a kind feeling toward the people you will leave behind. As for instance not getting riled any more with his father and Chester no matter how much they rubbed him the wrong way. He would do just about anything for Nick and Ernie. In school when he did his spellings he put his mind to it, and forgot the tunnel, not to be a teacher's pet but to show Miss Burwell that for once he could do them right. It was like this all along the line. For instance when Ruby Greer dropped her pencil and it rolled under his desk, he pushed it far enough across the aisle with his boot for her to reach it. One day after school while he and Nick and Ernie were fixing up the tree house, he came close to telling them that soon they would have it to themselves. But at the last minute something stopped him. When he left he would do it like the Arabs in the song the collegiate teachers sang when they

came for another of their social evenings. He would fold his tent
and silently steal away. Except that he would not have a tent but
would sleep out of doors until the time came when he had a
wigwam of his own. He imagined Nick's face when he came to the
door the morning after.... *Mrs. Egan can Gilbert come out to
play?...Dearie me, no, Nick. Your friend Gilbert has gone from
us. Defective Trotter followed his tracks for miles but then he lost
them.... Too bad for Gilbert, Mrs. Egan. Too bad for me too, he
was my best friend.... Cheer up, Nick. That boy will be all right,
he is good stuff. He is a chip off the old block. He must have some
drops of Indian blood in his veins although we did not know
it.... He must have, Mrs. Egan, else he would not toe in.... Nick,
here is twenty-five cents of Gilbert's telephone money. He left it for
you and Ernie with a note for you to spend it any way you
like.... That is just like him all over. Thank you Mrs.
Egan.... Now run along Nick. I heard my baby squalling like a cat
with its tail in the gate.... Goodbye Mrs. Egan. Now you have
nobody to fill your woodbox and carry in your kindlings....
Chester will do that. He is a willing worker and he does the best he
can. Now I simply must go. That baby by the name of Henry B. is
the loudest squaller.*

: shinplaster :

The afternoon Gilbert went with his father to buy Eph's birthday
present, Mr. Waldy was standing in the open doorway of his store,
keeping an eye on things.

One of the things he was watching for was to put the scoot on
any dog which started to lift its leg against what Waldy Hardware
had on the sidewalk in front of its windows such as both sorts of

wheelbarrows, lawnmowers, coils of garden hose, the latest thing in butter churns and so on and so on. Mr. Waldy's other reason was that with people out of work he had to keep his eyes peeled for passers-by he might be able to turn into customers, such as the one-armed man he talked into buying the all-in-one table knife and fork make especially for one-armed people.

Gilbert was all for sending Eph a birthday present. He was pleased his father brought him along and on the way downtown they decided a jackknife would be just the thing. After the Ottawa trip when Gilbert told Nick Eph would go to live at the county farm, Nick said county farm was a fancy name for the poorhouse. Gilbert thought Nick was talking through his hat but after he asked his father he was not so sure. His father said "in a sense," and that "it all depends," which was no answer one way or the other.

Mr. Waldy took them to the counter and said he had the very article they had in mind. "Genuine staghorn handle, the best of steel, large blade, medium blade, castrating blade, complete with full-length, snap-on, nickle-plated safety chain at no extra charge. Take a feel of how she fits the hand. . . . Let the lad here take a heft. She'll cost you money Egan but she's full value. You can't do better."

After Mr. Waldy wrapped the knife the two of them stood talking, so Gilbert moseyed across to the other counter and had a look at some hatchets. One of them was the nearest thing to a tomahawk. He wished he knew the price but if he asked now his father might twig. He would wait and come in by himself a day or two before he left.

From what he could hear, the two of them were talking about the school board and his father was getting his Irish up all over again—his principles and not standing idly by. Mr. Waldy kept nodding but said something about looking before you leap.

"I dare say I was too hasty but it's done now," Gilbert's father said.

Mr. Waldy gave another nod and said there were more ways to kill a cat than choking it with butter.

CHAPTER TWENTY-THREE

Hold-ups

July the first fireworks were not a patch on May the Twenty-Fourth ones. Down in Yankeeland they let off theirs four days late, which went to prove they were not as up-and-coming as some of them made out to be. The last day of school was only in the morning, no lessons to speak of, clear out your desks, pack up your slates, books and pencils. Gilbert passed, along with everybody else. But even if she had kept him back he would never again sit at this desk. Or at any desk in all of Blair Street School or any other school. While he was tidying up he ran the bicycle spoke into the escape tunnel, measured that distance on the top of the desk and proved that all his work was for nothing. The tunnel was farther in than the escape hole, so if he had kept on boring until the cows came home he would never have got out.

After Grandpa Williamson paid him his June messenger money the black oilcloth bookkeeping book showed he had saved up the price of a five dollar birchbark canoe with enough left over for beads in case he ran into Indians who were not friendly. This left only a few coppers for the tomahawk so he decided to start without it. His Indian friends would let him have the loan of theirs until he skinned enough beavers and sold enough wild rice to buy one. From here on, his main job was to get hold of a knapsack. Either that or find a hankie big enough to hold his belongings. In a pinch one of Henry B.'s napkins would do. Sling it on a stick over your shoulder and away you go—Dick Whittington, the ragged but honest English boy who ended up the mayor of London.

Only in the case of the Canadian boy by the name of Gilbert Egan, the bells could ring until they were black in the face before he would turn back once he was headed north. But before he left he should know what lay ahead for the rest of his family. Would his father come down off his high horse and start digging ditches, or would he get the science teacher job in some other town and they would live there?

As the days went by it seemed to Gilbert his father and mother had put their heads together to make it hard for him to leave. As for

instance his father offering him the extra piece of pie, almost forcing
him to take it, when always before he kept it for himself. Yes, and his
mother scarcely getting after him about slamming doors and running
up the stairs two steps at a time. His father was never much for seeing
around corners but his mother was and for all he knew she might
have twigged. Even Chester and Henry B. seemed in on it. Chester
kept from flying off the handle and most nights Henry B. did not let
a peep out of him.

Stealing away like the Arabs was one thing, all they had to do was
fold up their tents, collect the tent pegs and go. But leaving your
home and family to live in the north with the Indians was a horse of
a different color. Another thing which kept holding Gilbert back
was the weather. It was all very well to lie in bed and see yourself
sleeping under trees. But when you stopped imagining and thought
of people and cows that were killed by lightning when they took
shelter under trees it was high time you put on your thinking cap.
After most bad thunderstorms the *Mail and Empire* told of some
farmer or hired man who got killed when the tree he was standing
under was struck. Grandpa's Toronto *Globe* told the same. And in
the town paper when just the tree was hit Mr. Pickering made a big
thing about it. "What might have been a serious accident was
narrowly averted," and all the rest of it. On top of everything when
you have a mother who puts on her rubbers and her bathing cap at
the first crack of thunder and makes you stay on the bed beside her
until the worst is over you are all for lightning rods. So far that July
there had been no bad thunderstorms but sooner or later one was
bound to come along. Some nights there was heat lightning and the
far-off rumble of thunder. Each night the air felt hotter with not
even the sheet over you. Every day when Gilbert went to the station
for his father's *Mail and Empire,* he read the Probs as he walked
home. So far each day's Probs said for settled weather. But even
so, you never knew. Sooner or later there would be a ring-tail-
snorter of a thunderstorm, trees being struck right and left, blue
flames running along the wires. Much as he wanted to start, a
person had to be careful.

If the thunderstorm had come and got it over with, and if his
father had not quit the collegiate and still not found another job,
Gilbert might have been as far north as Muskoka by the middle of
July. Not that he blamed his father for getting after Mr.
All-bare-behind. Far from it. He was as proud of his father, or
nearly as proud, as when his father walked up to Mr. Carter and

made him stop taking shots at snakes which were not there and hand over the revolver. His father walking straight into that old house and doing what he did made Nick change his tune about a man who went around all dressed up and who waxed his mustache. From that day on, any boy who said Mr. Richard Egan was a stuck-up dude had better keep his trap shut in front of Nick Lamont if he knew what was good for him.

The afternoon Gilbert told Nick and Ernie what his father said to Mr. All-bare-behind over the telephone, Ernie laughed so hard he pretty nearly fell out of the tree house. "You should have heard him," Gilbert told them. "Just you listen to me, you old blather-skite. Not another peep out of you. You are nothing but a johnny-come-lately who is too big for his britches. When it comes to my old friend and teacher Doctor Scanlon you are knee-high to a grass-hopper. You are not fit to undo his bootlaces let alone lick them. Now you keep your trap shut. Not another word or I will be over there so fast it will make your head swim and I will rub your nose in it. I did not come from Huron county for nothing. Keep your iron deer. Your stuck-up wife too, for all I care."

"Go on. He never went after him like that!" Ernie said.

"No, but he could have. You should hear him when he gets his Irish up."

Nick said he knew about that. "Like in the driving shed." Nick's father got the story from Mr. Wallace and Nick was there. This was the first time Gilbert had heard anything like the whole of it. The reason Richard Egan got the job of teacher for the Settlement school was because none of the teachers before him would stay on account of two big fellows—grown men, one of them worked for Mr. Goudy, Mr. Wallace's neighbor—who came to the school house on opening day to make trouble. They pushed their way in and made believe they were there to learn their A.B.C.'s, such as holding up their hands to answer questions then making stupid answers. They mighty soon learned the young fellow from Huron county was one teacher who would not put up with any of their didoes. He took off his coat, rolled up his sleeves and invited them to come with him to the driving shed, where he took them on one at a time. When they saw he was too much for them, they both pitched in and tried to put the boots to him. Even so, he gave them such a lambasting that the one wore a beefsteak over his eye for a week and the other one left the township on account of being laughed at.

Ernie said it must have been a dilly of a fight, better than any you would see back of the Royal Consort. One thing sure, it proved that when some men get their Irish up they do not have to turn the other cheek just because they are believers.

Except for Sunday morning church, Gilbert and Chester were allowed to go barefoot every day since school let out. It took a while for their feet to toughen up but as soon as Gilbert's did, he used the short-cut to the station to get his father's *Mail and Empire*. The track past the freight shed was mostly cinders which are hard on the feet. So most mornings when he got to the station he cooled them in the horse trough. One morning while he was cooling off and fanning his face with his straw dummy he noticed Ruby Greer at an open upstairs window looking down at him as though she owned the place, horse trough and all. He half expected she would tattle, but if putting your feet in the trough was against the rules, Mr. Greer did not speak to him about it.

By the end of July anyone who kept his eyes and ears open and who had a hello girl by the name of Trixie for his aunt would have known that Richard Egan was in a pickle. Which was why the first thing he turned to in his *Mail and Empire* each morning was the Teachers Wanted. It is one thing to get your Irish up but keeping it up is a horse of a different color. His trouble was that in everything he was either hills or hollows. As for instance spending money on three-wheel eggbeaters and pillow sham holders and setting off more fireworks than Blair Street had ever seen, then turning around and making a big thing about saving bits of string.

: three-wheel egg beater :

Frances Egan was not like that, or if she had her ups and downs she kept them to herself. This is not to say she was one of your happy-go-luckies, easy come, easy go. She could see around a corner before she came to it and she knew on which side her bread was buttered.

Aunt Kate was another who could see around a corner. Which was why she kept a sharp eye on Teachers Wanted in the *Globe*. Both papers said the same and what it amounted to was that jobs for science teachers were as scarce as hens' teeth, most of all for those without degrees. Since the end of school, the only science teacher wanted was one for the town of Berlin. And of course for one at the collegiate. Both jobs had been snapped up faster than you could say Jack Robinson.

So there you were. To make things worse Trixie listened in on the talk about Mr. Richard Egan which she said made her mad enough to spit pink ink. One woman said this would teach Mr. Richard Egan not to be so hoity-toity. The other woman said indeed it would and that with a wife and three children she could not imagine what the man was thinking of. Jumping from the frying pan into the fire, she called it. The women were trustees' wives but Trixie said she would not name them.

If you want to live long in the land, you should honor your father and mother no matter how much they hold you back. This does not mean you should knuckle under. All it means is you had better think twice before you hoe your own row, paddle your own canoe and leave them in the lurch. On the other hand a boy with pluck will let the chips fall where they may. Either way it is far from being an easy choice to make. If the thunderstorm had come sooner and if it had not brought so much rain that the ground was too wet to sleep on, Gilbert would have stuck to his plan and cleared out before his father was at the end of his tether and scarcely knew which way to turn.

Still another thing which kept Gilbert from leaving was the news that Foxy Foster was on the loose again and had done another of his hold-ups. The person he held up this time was Mr. D.V. Schiller who was alone counting his money after his store was closed on Saturday night. Trixie phoned the news. She said the town was full of it. After church next morning people stood around to hear Mr. D.V. Schiller tell about it. After he locked up he was at his desk counting the money before putting it in his safe when he happened to look up. There was Foxy, the same sly grin on his face—impish, Mr. Schiller called it—as when he was a boy and ran errands for the store when Mr. Schiller clerked there before he owned it. Foxy must have been hiding inside when the store closed. "Sorry to trouble you, Mr. Schiller," says Foxy nice as pie. With that he scooped up the money, stuffed it in his pockets and was out and away before Mr. Schiller got his wits about him and telephoned Chief Rooney.

Three nights after the hold-up, the word was the police had Foxy cornered on the railway bridge, Chief Rooney at one end and Defective Trotter across the river at the other. But by morning when they closed in—no Foxy. Some said he must have jumped and swum ashore but a fellow who knew Foxy before Foxy took the wrong turning said he could not swim for sour apples and that in the dark he gave Defective Trotter the slip. Talk about your Artful Dodgers!

So there were three more days wasted. On top of that, while Gilbert was waiting around to see what happened to Foxy, he had let Ernie and Nick talk him into doing a bones-and-bottles, together with Archie and two friends of his. So unless he went back on his word, Gilbert saw no way of getting out of that. Ernie brought his express wagon and Archie brought his. At half-a-cent a pound they did pretty good on the bones—sixteen cents—but practically all the medicine bottles they collected were the kind Mr. Squire had no use for. It was Mrs. Devon's copper clothes boiler which did the trick. The rags-bones-bottles man paid them two cents a pound for it, no arguing back and forth and Archie keeping a sharp eye on the scales. If it had been up to Gilbert they would have divvied the money. He could have used his share toward the tomahawk if Mr. Waldy did not ask too much for it. But the others were for spending the whole of it then and there. So off they went to Mrs. Devon's.

Archie was better at mental arithmetic than any of them so they agreed for him to do the buying. Mrs. Devon did not come from her kitchen right off so Ernie opened and closed the door harder to give the bell a louder tinkle. That brought her. She must have been baking, she had flour on her arms. One look and she knew what they came for. She went straight to the candy counter. Everybody's first choice was an all-day sucker. Since there were six of them and the suckers were six for five, that round was easy except that one of Archie's friends changed his mind and said he would take a Long Tom popcorn instead. Archie asked who would take the extra sucker, the one they had already paid for. Mrs. Devon changed and Ernie agreed to take the extra only he wanted his second one to be lemon flavor. Mrs. Devon fished around on the tray, found him a lemon and made the change. The next round was a licorice whip for everybody—one cent each, which came out even. The real mix-up came with the butterscotch, gum drops, peppermints, different numbers of them for one cent. What with the whispering and pointing, and head shaking, Archie got rattled. He told Mrs. Devon they would have to start over. He took them to the other side of the store while they chewed the rag over what to buy. Mrs. Devon said to call when they made up their minds, and went to her kitchen. She came back before they were ready and spent the time sorting what she had put into the bag and returning the different candies to their trays. She may have felt cross but after all they were good customers. To make things easier for her they chose mostly one-centers. The last round was chew-chew, a gum which had a peppermint flavor but which was mostly candlewax. Gilbert took a third licorice whip instead. Mrs. Devon handed over the bag, Archie handed over the bones-and-bottles money and out they went.

The three licorice whips may not have been the reason but that night Gilbert had a dream so real it showed him which way the wind was blowing and knocked the props clean from under him. In the dream he was walking along a cement sidewalk with no end in sight. On either side all was grey and flat. His boots felt heavy as lead and their soles stuck to the cement with every step, the kind of sticking a magnet has. He came to a crack in the sidewalk but try as he might he could not step across it. He was stuck there like a fly on sticky paper. The dream was so real that when he came awake he felt all tired out. In one of the Royal Scroll pictures, the king of Egypt's dreams were signs from heaven and he needed Joseph to tell him what they meant. Gilbert would never have gone so far as to call his dream a sign from heaven but he did not need a Joseph to come along and tell him what it meant. It meant his plan of living up north with the Indians was not-to-be, which was the name the tubby Miss Langley had for her plans that did not work out, such as missing the Niagara Falls moonlight excursion because of her hay fever, not having the young Mrs. Carter and the baby to do things for, and when Sport dug up her pansy bed.

Lying awake in the dark Gilbert's not-to-be was as plain as Miss Burwell's writing on the blackboard. What with thunderstorms, wet ground, Foxy's hold-up, the bones-and-bottles day, a baby brother coming along, his parents going out of their way to be kind to him, his father out of a job and with no ditches to dig, no money growing on bushes, he would be a stinker if he ran away and left them flat. Nobody could say he lacked the pluck to go, they could not put him down as Girl Garters Gilbert. But when you are bounded together into a family by the ties of nature.... *Momma do not use any more Lord's Tenth money buy coal-oil. Here is some of my telephone messenger money for you to pay Mr. Mullin week after week....Poppa it is high time you had your boots half-soled. Take this, keep the change and spend it for more Ed Pinaud mustache wax....Hello, hello, is that you Mrs. Albert?...Yes it is. Who is calling?...The wife of a school trustee is calling. Have you heard what the Egan boy is doing to put food in the mouths of his family and to put clothes on their backs?...Indeed I have...Our husbands should be ashamed of themselves for what they did to Doctor Scanlon...Oh, do you think so?...Yes I do. So there....Mr. Pickering are you going to put it in the paper about Gilbert Egan saving his family from going to the poorhouse?...I would like nothing better but Gilbert does not want me to. He is too modest.... Will the boy in the second to last pew from the back please stand up....Who, me Reverend Allister?...Yes you, Gilbert Egan. I want the congregation to have a look at you. You are a shining example. You may not stand before kings but you will live long in the land. You gave up your dearly beloved plan for the sake of others....Oh, it was nothing. I was glad to help them all I could....Thank you, Gilbert. Sit down. A special offering to help the Egan family will now be taken.*

Chester stirred and Gilbert moved farther to his side of the bed. Now he knew more than ever before how Moses must have felt, up there on that lonely mountain, in sight of the Promised Land and knowing he would never get to it. Dusty old Blair Street or some other old street in some other old town, forever and ever, no wigwams, no birchbark canoes, no Indian friends.

CHAPTER TWENTY-FOUR

Promised Lands

"This week our town is losing one of its most highly respected citizens in the person of Mr. Richard Egan, for years a valued member of the collegiate's teaching staff and of the Methodist Church's Quarterly Official Board who with his wife and three young sons has accepted a lucrative teaching position in the city of Vancouver, British Columbia. At a gala affair last evening the entire collegiate staff expressed their regrets at the imminent departure of so valued a confrere and presented him with a solid brass desk set as a token of their lasting esteem. Earlier in the week Mr. Egan's contribution, both in an official capacity and otherwise, to his church's welfare was eloquently expressed in a suitably framed illuminated address, presented to him on behalf of the entire congregation by Mr. D.V. Schiller of Schiller's Grocery. The presentation was made at a church function at which Reverend Allister presided. Refreshments were served by the Ladies' Aid of which Mrs. Egan was an erstwhile member. The Ladies' Aid presented Mr. Egan's spouse with a well-chosen sewing basket of Oriental design. It is worthy to note that Mrs. Egan, known to her many friends as Frankie and daughter of Mr. Williamson local and district telephone manager, was one of Canada's pioneer 'hello girls,' a position now filled by her youngest sister, the able and popular Trixie. In passing it should be mentioned that Mr. Williamson was personally acquainted with Mr. Alexander Graham Bell, famed inventor of the telephone, during the latter's sojourn in Brantford.

"Mr. Egan was an ardent curler, his skill with the 'rocks' contributing in no mean degree to the successes of the Waldy Hardware Rink at local bonspiels.

"The Egans' host of friends join in wishing them safe journey and all success in their new abode. Our town's loss is Vancouver's gain."

"Vancouver papers please copy."

Even before Mr. Pickering put it in the paper, the news got around that the Egans were moving out to British Columbia, lock, stock and barrel. Everybody knew British Columbia was part of Canada on the far side of the Rocky Mountains but hardly a soul had ever been there. The only one Gilbert heard about who had was a man who worked for Mr. Wallace at the Settlement, then pulled up stakes and went there almost as soon as the railway was finished. One afternoon going through the Rockies the engineer let him ride on the cowcatcher to enjoy the scenery. If the railway had not been finished so soon, if Gilbert's father had married somebody else and if Gilbert had been born out there among the mountains, what an exciting life he would have had! But as things stood, all Gilbert knew was that after the Rockies, British Columbia went downhill clear to the ocean. From what Gilbert could make out, British Columbia was mostly noo-come-oots and Indians. A Home Missions missionary who gave a talk at church showed pictures of those Indians. Instead of wigwams they lived in houses, some as big and bigger than the freight shed. Their canoes were hollowed out logs. Until they became believers, they had idol poles with graven images in front of their houses. After they became believers they chopped down their idol poles and came to church instead. If Tommy Dempster knew what he was talking about, the rivers of British Columbia were so chock full of salmon you could walk across them on their backs. What with the good fishing and all those Indians, Gilbert could hardly wait. Talk about your Promised Land!

The last three days before the Egans left they lived at the Williamsons. Seeing the last of Blair Street gave a Gilbert a mixed up feeling. Mr. Wallace gave Gilbert and Chester a small bag of Scotch peppermints to have on the train, and the tubby Miss Langley brought Henry B. a blue bonnet. Their father said to take the barrel hammock along to Nick and this was when they said goodbye. Only they did not come right out and say it. Nick gave Gilbert a friendly punch on the chest and Gilbert gave him one back just for old times' sake and then they stood and grinned at one another. Ernie got the spring skates on account of no ice out there and the grass staying green all winter. Ernie said he just might mosey out to British Columbia one of these days and catch a few salmon, just for the fun of it.

At the Williamsons', Gilbert and Chester had the attic room where both sides of the ceiling sloped down. The room had what was called a dormer window and from it you could see up Balaclava to the cemetery and the woods across. Aunt Eunice said a whip-poor-will lived in the woods and that some nights not long after dark you might hear it singing. Gilbert had never heard a whip-poor-will but Doug had talked about them after lesson. Doug said the whip-poor-will sang those very words and that the singing always made him think of clear cold water being poured into a stone jug on a hot and dusty day like, say, at haying time.

Gilbert and Chester slept on separate cots. Other years when the Jersey City cousins came, two of them used the attic room. In daytime because of the roof, the room was hot but it cooled off at night because it was high up and because the window opened wide and caught whatever breeze there was. The last night before they left, Gilbert and Chester talked and kept on talking until Chester fell asleep. Gilbert sometimes wished he could do like Chester, turn over, close his eyes and go right off to sleep. But on that last night if he had, he would not have heard the whip-poor-will, and for all he knew the chance would never come again. The song was exactly as Doug had said—clear cold water filling up a jug, the last of its three notes the highest. Gilbert went quickly to the open window but the song did not come again. He imagined it drifting over the cemetery and the graves of people who had gone before, people he knew, like Elmer, people he never knew—the real Grandma Williamson, Gracie, Trixie's little boy twin, the Williamson baby that died in Yankeeland but was brought to lie beside others of the family. Their family had come from such far-away places—Wales, Ireland, England, Scotland, the persecuted little country beside the river Rhine. He thought of the Kiltie doctor and the French lady who married after the battle of Quebec, and of young Obediah and the Pennsylvania Dutchman leaving home to find their promised lands. The thing was, you never knew if the next place would be your promised land until you got there. Until you did, your promised land was all inside your head. Would British Columbia turn out to be his promised land? And would a whip-poor-will be singing there?

Hubert Evans, Canada's oldest working novelist, was born in Vankleek Hill, Ontario, in 1892, and moved in 1926 to Roberts Creek, British Columbia, where he raised his family and built the sea-front home he still occupies. An honorary life member of the Canadian Authors' Association, he published his first book in 1926 and has since that time added over 200 stories, 60 serials, a dozen stage plays and seven further works of fiction including the west coast classic *Mist on the River*. In 1976 he launched a fresh career as a poet with a successful collection of verse, *Whitlings*, and followed this with another, *Endings*, in 1978. *O Time In Your Flight*, a major new novel in which Evans relives one crucial year from his small town childhood in 19th century Ontario, was completed in his 87th year.

―――――――――

"I am not surprised that this author's work has appeared in over a dozen anthologies and three foreign languages. It has simplicity, strength, and heart."—CHRISTIAN SCIENCE MONITOR

―――――――――